THE
OMEN
MACHINE

BY TERRY GOODKIND

TERRY GOODKIND

THE OMEN MACHINE

HARPER
Voyager

HarperVoyager
An imprint of HarperCollins *Publishers*
77–85 Fulham Palace Road,
Hammersmith, London W6 8JB

www.harpercollins.co.uk

This paperback edition 2012
1

First published in Great Britain by
Harper *Voyager* 2011

Copyright © Terry Goodkind 2011

Terry Goodkind asserts the moral right to
be identified as the author of this work

A catalogue record for this book
is available from the British Library

ISBN: 978 0 00 730373 1

This novel is entirely a work of fiction.
The names, characters and incidents portrayed in it are
the work of the author's imagination. Any resemblance to
actual persons, living or dead, events or localities is
entirely coincidental.

Printed and bound in Great Britain by
Clays Ltd, St Ives plc

MIX
**Paper from
responsible sources**
FSC C007454
www.fsc.org

FSC™ is a non-profit international organisation established to promote
the responsible management of the world's forests. Products carrying the
FSC label are independently certified to assure consumers that they come
from forests that are managed to meet the social, economic and
ecological needs of present and future generations,
and other controlled sources.

Find out more about HarperCollins and the environment at
www.harpercollins.co.uk/green

THE
OMEN
MACHINE

T here is darkness," the boy said.

Richard frowned, not sure that he had understood the whispered words. He glanced back over his shoulder at the concern on Kahlan's face. She didn't look to have understood the meaning any more than he had.

The boy lay on a tattered carpet placed on the bare ground just outside a tent covered with strings of colorful beads. The tightly packed market outside the palace had become a small city made up of thousands of tents, wagons, and stands. Throngs of people who had come from near and far for the grand wedding the day before flocked to the marketplace, buying everything from souvenirs and jewelry to fresh bread and cooked meats, to exotic drinks and potions, to colorful beads.

The boy's chest rose a little with each shallow breath, but his eyes remained closed. Richard leaned down closer to the frail child. "Darkness?"

The boy nodded weakly. "There is darkness all around."

There was, of course, no darkness. Streamers of morning sunlight played over the crowds of people coursing by the thousands through the haphazard streets between the tents and wagons. Richard didn't think that the boy saw anything of the festive atmosphere all around.

The child's words, on the surface so soft, carried some other meaning, something more, something grim, about another place entirely.

From the corner of his eye, Richard saw people slow as they passed, watching the Lord Rahl and the Mother Confessor stopped to see an ill boy and his mother. The market out beyond was filled with lilting music, conversation, laughter, and animated bargaining. For most of the people passing nearby, seeing the Lord Rahl and the Mother Confessor was a once-in-a-lifetime event, one of many over the last few days, that would be recounted back in their homelands for years to come.

Guards of the First File stood not far away, also watching attentively, but they mostly watched the nearby crowds shuffling through the market. The soldiers wanted to make sure that those crowds didn't close in too tightly, even though there was no real reason to expect any sort of trouble.

Everyone was, after all, in a good mood. The years of war had ended. There was peace and growing prosperity. The wedding the day before seemed to mark a new beginning, a celebration of a world of possibilities never before imagined.

Set amid that sunlit exuberance, the boy's words felt to Richard like a shadow that didn't belong.

Kahlan squatted down beside him. Her satiny white dress, the iconic symbol of her standing as the Mother Confessor, seemed to glow under the early-spring sky, as if she were a good spirit come among them. Richard slipped his hand under the boy's bony shoulders and sat him up a little as Kahlan lifted a waterskin up to the boy's lips.

"Can you take just a sip?"

The boy didn't seem to hear her. He ignored her offer and the waterskin. "I'm alone," he said in a frail voice. "So alone."

The words sounded so forlorn that they moved Kahlan to reach out in silent compassion and touch the boy's knobby shoulder.

"You're not alone," Richard assured the boy in a voice meant to dispel the gloom of such words. "There are people here with you. Your mother is here."

Behind closed eyelids, the boy's eyes rolled and darted, as if looking for something in the darkness.

"Why have they all left me?"

Kahlan laid a hand gently on the boy's heaving chest. "Left you?"

The boy, lost in some inner vision, moaned and whined. His head tossed from side to side. "Why have they left me alone in the cold and dark?"

"Who left you?" Richard asked, concentrating in an effort to be sure he could hear the boy's soft words. "Where did they leave you?"

"I have had dreams," the boy said, his voice a little brighter.

Richard frowned at the odd change of subject. "What kind of dreams?"

Disoriented confusion returned to haunt the boy's words. "Why have I had dreams?"

The question sounded to Richard like it was directed inward and didn't call for an answer. Kahlan tried anyway.

"We don't—"

"Is the sky still blue?"

Kahlan shared a look with Richard. "Quite blue," she assured the boy. He didn't appear to hear that answer, either.

Richard didn't think that there was any point in continuing to pester the boy for answers. He was obviously sick and didn't know what he was saying. It was pointless to try to question the product of delirium.

The boy's small hand suddenly grabbed Richard's forearm.

Richard heard the sound of steel being drawn from scabbards. Without turning, he lifted his other hand in a silent command to the soldiers behind him to stand down.

"Why have they all left me?" the boy asked again.

Richard leaned in a little closer, hoping to calm him at least. "Where did they leave you?"

The boy's eyes opened so abruptly that it startled both Richard and Kahlan. His gaze was fixed on Richard, as if trying to see into his soul. The grip of the thin fingers on Richard's forearm was powerful beyond what Richard would have believed the boy capable of.

"There is darkness in the palace."

A chill, fed by a cold breath of breeze, shivered across Richard's flesh.

The boy's eyelids slid closed as he sagged back.

Despite his intent to be gentle with the boy, Richard's voice took on an edge.

"What are you talking about? What darkness in the palace?"

"Darkness . . . is seeking darkness," he whispered as he drifted down into incoherent mumbling.

Richard's brow drew tight as he tried to make some kind of sense of it. "What do you mean, darkness is seeking darkness?"

"He will find me, I know he will."

The boy's hand, as if too heavy to hold up, slipped off Richard's arm. It was replaced by Kahlan's as the two of them waited a moment to see if the boy would say any more. He seemed to finally have fallen silent for good.

They needed to get back to the palace. People would be waiting for them.

Besides, Richard didn't think, even if the boy did say more, that it would be any more meaningful. He looked up at the boy's mother, standing above him, dry-washing her hands.

The woman swallowed. "He scares me, he does, when he gets like this. I'm sorry, Lord Rahl, I didn't mean to distract you from your business." She looked to be a woman aged prematurely by worries.

"This is my business," Richard said. "I came down here today to be among people who couldn't make it up to the palace yesterday for the ceremony. Many of you have traveled a great distance. The Mother Confessor and I wanted to have a chance to show our appreciation to everyone who came for our friends' wedding.

"I don't like to see anyone in such obvious distress as you and your boy. We'll see if we can get a healer to find out what's wrong. Maybe they can give him something to help him."

The woman was shaking her head. "I've tried healers. Healers can't help him."

"Are you sure?" Kahlan asked. "There are very talented people here who might be able to help."

"I already took him to a woman of great powers, a Hedge Maid, all the way to Kharga Trace."

Kahlan's brow creased. "A Hedge Maid? What kind of healer is that?"

The woman hesitated, her gaze darting away. "Well, she's a woman of remarkable abilities as I hear told. Hedge Maids . . . have talents, so I thought she might be able to help. But Jit—that's her name, Jit—said that Henrik was special, not sick."

"Does this happen with your son often, then?" Kahlan asked.

The woman worked some of the cloth of her simple dress into her fist. "Not often. But it happens. He sees things. Sees things through the eyes of others, I think."

Kahlan pressed her hand to the boy's forehead a moment and then ran her fingers back through his hair. "I think maybe it's fevered dreams, that's all," she said. "He's burning up."

The woman was nodding knowingly. "He gets like that, all fevered and such, when he sees things through the eyes of others." She met Richard's gaze. "Some kind of telling, I think. I think that's what he does when he gets like this. Some kind of foretelling."

Richard, like Kahlan, didn't think the boy saw anything more than fevered visions, but he didn't say so. The woman already looked distressed enough.

Richard also didn't hold much favor with prophecy. He liked prophecy even less than he liked riddles and he didn't like riddles at all. He thought people made far more of prophecy than was justified.

"Doesn't sound at all specific," Richard said. "I don't think it's anything more than a childhood fever."

The woman didn't look to believe one word of it, but she also didn't look inclined to contradict the Lord Rahl. It wasn't all that long ago that the Lord Rahl was a greatly feared figure in the land of D'Hara, and with good reason.

Old fears, like old grudges, lived long lives.

"Maybe he ate something that was bad," Kahlan suggested.

"No, nothing bad," the woman insisted. "He eats the same things I eat." She studied their faces for a moment before adding, "But the hounds have come around bothering him."

Richard frowned up at the woman. "What do you mean, the hounds have come around bothering him?"

Her tongue darted out to wet her lips. "Well, hounds—wild hounds I think—came sniffing around here last night. I had just run out to get us a loaf of bread. Henrik was watching our bead wares. He was scared when the hounds showed up so he hid inside. When I got back they were sniffing and growling around the doorway of our tent, the hair on their backs standing up all stiff and such. I grabbed a stick and chased them off. This morning he was like this."

Richard was about to say something when the boy abruptly twisted wildly. He lashed out with clawed fingers at both Richard and Kahlan as if he were a cornered animal.

Richard jumped up, pulling Kahlan back out of the boy's reach as soldiers brought swords out.

Quick as a rabbit, the boy darted away toward the confusion of tents and crowds. Two soldiers immediately raced after him. The boy dove under a low wagon and popped up on the other side. The men were too big to follow and had to go around the wagon, giving the boy a head start of a dozen strides. Richard didn't think his lead would last long.

In an instant the boy, with the soldiers hot on his heels, vanished among the wagons, tents, and people. It was a mistake to run from men of the First File.

Richard saw that the scratch on the back of Kahlan's hand had drawn blood.

"It's just a little scratch, Richard," she assured him when she saw the look in his eyes. "I'm fine. It just startled me."

Richard glanced down at the lines oozing blood on the back of his own hand and let out a sigh of frustration. "Me too."

The captain of the guards, sword in hand, stepped forward. "We'll find him, Lord Rahl. Out here on the Azrith

Plain there's no real place to hide. He won't get far. We'll find him." The man didn't look at all pleased that someone, even a boy, had drawn the Lord Rahl's blood.

"Like the Mother Confessor said, it's just a scratch. But I'd like you to find the boy."

A dozen men of the guard detail clapped fists to their hearts.

"We'll find him, Lord Rahl," the captain said, "you can count on that."

Richard nodded. "Good. When you do, see to it that he gets safely back here to his mother. There are healers among the people selling their wares and services. Bring one here when you find the boy and see if they can help him."

As the captain detailed additional guards to search for the boy, Kahlan leaned closer to Richard. "We had better get back up to the palace. We have a lot of guests."

Richard nodded. "I hope your boy is well soon," he said to the woman before starting out toward the immense plateau atop which sat the People's Palace, the place he had inherited when he had inherited the rule of D'Hara, a land that he had never even known existed as he'd grown up. In many ways D'Hara, the empire he ruled, was still a complete mystery to him.

A penny for your future, sir?"

Richard paused to look down at the old woman sitting cross-legged out of the way at the side of one of the many grand halls of the People's Palace. She leaned back against the wall beside the base of a marble arch that soared several stories overhead as she waited to see if she had won herself a new customer. A brown cloth bag with her belongings along with a thin cane lay close up against her hip. She was dressed in a simple but neat long gray woolen dress. A cream-colored shawl lay draped over her shoulders as protection against the occasional bite of departing winter. Spring had arrived, but so far it had proven to be more promise than substance.

The woman smoothed back stray strands of brown and gray hair at her temple, apparently wanting to look presentable for potential customers. By the milky film over her eyes, the way her head tilted up without facing anyone accurately, and her searching movements, Richard knew that the woman couldn't see him or Kahlan. Only her hearing would be of any help in taking in the grandeur all around her.

Out beyond where the woman sat, one of the many bridges

in the palace crossed the hall at a second-floor level. Clutches of people engaged in conversation strolled across the bridge while others stood at the marble balusters, gazing down on the vast passageway below, some watching Richard and Kahlan and their accompanying contingent of guards. Many in the thick crowds of people strolling the expansive corridors of the palace were visitors who had come for the festivities of the day before.

Though the People's Palace was more or less under one roof, it was really a city tightly clustered atop a lone, immense plateau rising up out of the Azrith Plain. Since the palace was the ancestral home of the Lord Rahl, parts of it were off-limits to the public, but most of the expansive complex was home to thousands of others. There were living quarters for people of every sort, from officials to merchants, to craftsmen, to workers, with other areas set aside for visitors. The sprawling public corridors linked the city palace together and provided access to it all.

Not far from the woman sitting against the wall, a shop window displayed bolts of cloth. Throughout the palace there were shops of every sort. Down inside the plateau hundreds more rooms provided everything from quarters for soldiers to yet more shops for residents and visitors alike.

The narrow road rising along the side of the plateau that Richard and Kahlan had ridden up after visiting the market was the fastest way up to the People's Palace, but it was narrow and in places treacherous, so the public was not allowed to use it. The main route for visitors, merchants, and workers of every sort was through the great inner doors and up the passageways inside the plateau. Many people never ventured all the way up to the palace at the top, but came to shop at the market that in peaceful times sprang up down on the plain, or to visit some of the hundreds of shops along the way up inside the plateau.

The sheer inaccessibility of the city palace, if the drawbridge on the road was raised and the great inner doors were closed, made assaults futile. Throughout history sieges of the palace withered out on the inhospitable Azrith Plain long before the strength of those in the palace began to wane. Many had tried, but there was no practical way to attack the People's Palace.

The old woman would have had a hard time making the climb all the way up the inner passageways to the palace proper. Because she was blind, it must have been especially difficult for her. Although there were always people wanting to know what the future held, Richard supposed that she probably found more customers up top willing to pay for her simple fortunes, and that made the climb worth the effort.

Richard gazed out at the seemingly endless corridor filled with people and the ever-present whisper of footsteps and conversation. He supposed that the woman, being blind, would be attuned to all the sounds of the people in the corridors and by that judge the enormity of the place.

He felt a pang of sorrow for her, as he had when he had first spotted her sitting alone at the side of the hallway, but now because she could not see the splendor all around her, the soaring marble columns, stone benches, and elaborately patterned granite floors that glowed wherever they were touched by the streamers of sunlight coming in from the skylights high overhead. Other than his homeland of the Hartland woods where he had grown up, Richard thought that the palace was just about the most beautiful place he had ever seen. He never failed to be awed by the sheer overwhelming intellect and effort it must have taken to envision and construct such a place.

Many times throughout history, as when Richard had first been brought in as a prisoner, the palace had been the seat of power for evil men. Other times, as now, it was the center of peaceful prosperity, a beacon of strength that anchored the D'Haran Empire.

"A penny for my future?" Richard asked.

"And a worthy bargain it is," the woman said without hesitation.

"I hope you aren't saying that my future is worth no more than a penny."

The old woman smiled a slow smile. Her clouded eyes stared without seeing. "It is if you don't heed the omen tendered."

She blindly held out her hand, a question waiting for his answer. Richard placed a penny on her upturned palm. He imagined that she had no other way to feed herself except by offering to tell people their future. Being blind, though, in a way gave her a certain marketable credibility. People probably expected that, being blind, she had access to some kind of inner vision, and that belief probably helped bring her business.

"Ah," she said, nodding knowingly as she tested the weight of the coin he had given her, "silver, not copper. Clearly a man who values his future."

"And what would lie in that future, then?" Richard asked. He didn't really care what a fortune-teller might have to say, but he expected something in return for the penny.

She turned her face up toward his, even though she could not see his face. The smile ghosted away. She hesitated for just a moment before speaking.

"The roof is going to fall in." She looked as if the words had come out differently than she had intended, as if they surprised her. She looked abruptly speechless.

Issued

Kahlan and some of the soldiers waiting not far away glanced up at the ceiling that had covered the palace for thousands of years. It hardly looked in danger of falling in.

A strange fortune, Richard thought, but the fortune had not been his real purpose. "And I predict that you will have a full belly when you sleep tonight. The shop not far back, to your left, sells warm meals. That penny will buy you one. Take good care of yourself, my lady, and enjoy your visit to the palace."

The woman's smile returned, but this time it reflected gratitude. "Thank you, sir."

Rikka, one of the Mord-Sith, rushed up and came to a halt. She flicked her single, long blond braid back over her shoulder. He was so used to the Mord-Sith wearing their red leather outfits that he found it somewhat strange to see them now wearing brown leather, another sign that the long war was over. Notwithstanding the less intimidating outfit, there was suspicious displeasure in her blue eyes. That, coming from a Mord-Sith, he was more than used to.

A dark look had settled into Rikka's flawless features. "I see that the word I received is true. You're bleeding. What happened?"

Rikka's tone reflected not simple concern, but a Mord-Sith's rising anger that the Lord Rahl she was sworn on her life to protect appeared to have run into trouble. She was not simply curious, she was demanding answers.

"It's nothing. And it's not bleeding any longer. It's just a scratch."

Rikka cast a dissatisfied look at Kahlan's hand. "Do you two have to do everything together? I knew we shouldn't have let you go out without one of us to watch over you. Cara will be furious, and with good reason."

Kahlan smiled, apparently to dispel Rikka's concern. "Like Richard said, it's just a scratch. And I don't think that Cara has reason to be anything other than contented and happy today."

Rikka let the claim go without objection and turned to other business. "Zedd wants to see you, Lord Rahl. He sent me to find you."

"Lord Rahl!" The woman at his feet clutched at his pant leg. "Dear spirits, I didn't realize . . . I'm sorry, Lord Rahl. Forgive me. I didn't know who you were or I would not have—"

Richard touched his fingers to the woman's shoulder to cut off her apology and let her know that it wasn't necessary.

He turned to the Mord-Sith. "Did my grandfather say what he wants?"

"No, but by his tone it was clear to me that it was important to him. You know Zedd and how he gets."

Kahlan smiled a bit. Richard knew all too well what Rikka meant. While Cara had for years been close to Richard and Kahlan, ever watchful and protective of them, Rikka had spent a great deal of time with Zedd at the Wizard's Keep. She had become familiar with how Zedd frequently thought the simplest things were urgent. Richard thought that Rikka, in her own way, had taken a liking to Zedd and felt protective of him. He was, after all, still First Wizard as well as the grandfather to the Lord Rahl. Even more important, she knew how much Richard cared about him.

"All right, Rikka. Let's go see what Zedd is all wound up about."

He started to take a step, but the old woman sitting on the floor tugged his pant leg to stop him.

"Lord Rahl," she said, trying to pull him closer, "I would

not ask for payment from you, especially since I am but a humble guest in your home. Please, take your silver back with my appreciation for the gesture."

"It was a bargain struck," Richard said in a tone meant to reassure her. "You held up your part. I owe you payment for your words about the future."

She let her hand slip from its grip of his pants. "Then heed the omen, Lord Rahl, for it is true."

CHAPTER

3

Following Rikka deep into the private, warmly paneled corridors of the palace, Kahlan spotted Zedd standing with Cara and Benjamin at a window overlooking a small courtyard at the bottom of a deep pocket formed by the stone walls of the palace that rose up out of sight. A simple, unadorned door not far beyond the window provided access to an atrium where a small plum tree grew beside a wooden bench sitting on a stone pad surrounded by lush green ivy. As small as the room was, it still brought a welcome bit of the outdoors and daylight into the deep interior of the palace.

Kahlan was relieved to be away from the public corridors, away from the constant gazes that were always on them. She felt a profound sense of calm as Richard slipped his arm around her waist, pulling her close for a moment. He laid his head atop hers as she leaned in toward him. It was a moment of closeness that they didn't generally feel comfortable allowing themselves when in public view.

Cara, wearing her white leather outfit, stood gazing out the window into the courtyard. Her single blond braid was perfectly done. Her red Agiel, the weapon carried by Mord-Sith that always hung at the ready by a fine chain on their wrists, stood out against the white leather like a bloodstain on a snow white tablecloth. An Agiel, looking like nothing more than a short leather rod, was just as lethal as the women who carried them.

Benjamin had on a crisp general's uniform and wore a gleaming silver sword at his hip. The sword was no ceremonial accessory. Countless times Kahlan had seen how commanding he was in combat, seen his heart. She had been the one who had appointed him a general.

Kahlan had expected that Cara and Benjamin might be dressed casually. They were not. They both looked ready for the war that was over. She supposed that as far as both of them were concerned, there was never an excuse to relax their guard. Both their lives were devoted to the protection of Richard, the Lord Rahl.

Of course, the man they guarded was far more lethal than either of them. Dressed in his black and gold war-wizard outfit, Richard looked every bit the part of the Lord Rahl. But he was more than that. At his hip he wore the Sword of Truth, a singular weapon meant for a singular individual. Yet despite the weapon's power, it was the individual behind it that was the true weapon. That was what really made him the Seeker, and what made the Seeker so formidable.

"Were they watching all night?" Zedd was asking as Kahlan and Richard came to a halt beside Richard's grandfather.

Cara's face turned nearly as red as her Agiel.

"I don't know," she growled, still glaring out the window. "It was my wedding night and I was otherwise occupied."

Zedd smiled politely. "Of course."

He glanced over at Richard and Kahlan to greet them with a brief smile. Kahlan thought that the smile looked a bit briefer than she would have expected.

Before his grandfather could say anything else, Richard interrupted. "Cara, what's going on?"

She turned to him with a heated look. "Someone was watching us in our room."

"Watching you," he repeated in a flat tone. "You're sure?"

Richard's face didn't reveal what he might be thinking about such a strange claim. Kahlan noted that he did not dismiss Cara's assertion out of hand. Kahlan also noted that Cara hadn't said that it *felt* like they were being watched. She said that they *were* being watched. Cara was hardly a woman given to skittish delusions.

"It was an eventful day yesterday, with a lot of people gathered for your wedding, with a lot of people all watching you and Benjamin." Richard gestured toward Kahlan. "Even now, as much as I've gotten used to people watching Kahlan and me all the time, when we're finally alone I sometimes can't shake the feeling people are still staring at me."

"People watch Mord-Sith all the time," Cara said, clearly not liking the implication that she was only imagining it.

"Yes, but they watch out of the corner of their eye. People rarely look directly at a Mord-Sith."

"So?"

"Yesterday it was different. You aren't used to people looking directly at you. Yesterday everyone was looking at you and Benjamin—looking directly at you. Every eye was on you. It wasn't what you're used to. Could it simply be a feeling left over from being the center of so much focus and attention?"

Cara considered the question as if she hadn't thought of it that way. Her brow finally drew tight with conviction. "No. Someone was watching me."

"All right. When did you first have this feeling that someone was watching you?"

"Just before dawn," she said without hesitation. "It was still dark. At first I thought there was someone in the room, but there wasn't anyone in there other than the two of us."

"Are you sure that it was you they were watching?" Zedd asked, the question sounding innocent enough. Kahlan knew better.

Silent up until then, Benjamin looked puzzled. "You mean you think they may have been watching me?"

Zedd directed a meaningful look at the tall, blond-headed D'Haran general. "What I mean, is that I'm wondering if they were actually watching the both of you."

"We were the only ones in there," Cara said, her growl back.

Zedd tilted his head toward her. "You were in one of the Lord Rahl's bedchambers."

Understanding suddenly flashed in Cara's intense blue eyes. With the realization, her voice turned from annoyed to icy as she took on the demeanor of the interrogator, a role that fit Mord-Sith as well as their leather outfits. She narrowed her eyes at the wizard.

"Are you suggesting that someone was looking into that room to see if it was Lord Rahl in there?"

She had clearly caught Zedd's meaning.

Zedd shrugged his bony shoulders. "Were there mirrors in the room?"

"Mirrors? Well, I guess . . ."

"There are two mirrors in that room," Kahlan said. "There is a tall one off to the side, on a stand beside the bookcase, and a smaller one over the dressing table."

The room was one of Richard and Kahlan's gifts to Cara and Benjamin. The Lord Rahl, while in his palace, had the choice of a number of bedchambers—probably an ancient defensive ploy to thwart assassins. There were probably more private rooms belonging to Richard in the palace than he had visited or was even aware of. Richard and Kahlan had wanted Cara to have one of the lovely rooms as hers and Benjamin's whenever they were at the People's Palace. It only seemed right, seeing as how Benjamin was the head of the First File, the Lord Rahl's guards when he was in the palace, and Cara was Richard and Kahlan's closest bodyguard.

Richard, having grown up as a woods guide, had thought that one bedroom was more than adequate. Kahlan thought so as well. They also had rooms at the Confessors' Palace, in Aydindril, as well as yet other quarters set aside for them in various other places.

Kahlan didn't really care what rooms they had, or where, as long as she and Richard were together. In fact, some of her happiest memories were of living one summer in the small house Richard had built for them in the wilderness of Westland.

Cara had willingly accepted the room in the palace. No doubt in large part because it was close to Richard and Kahlan's room.

"Why do you want to know if there were mirrors in the room?" Benjamin asked. His voice, too, had changed. He was now the general in charge of the Lord Rahl's safety at the People's Palace.

Zedd lifted an eyebrow and fixed the man in the meaningful gaze. "There are those, I hear tell, who have the ability to use dark forms of magic to gaze through mirrors into another place."

"Are you certain of that," Richard asked, "or is it just idle gossip?"

"Gossip," Zedd admitted with a sigh. "But sometimes gossip turns out to be reliable."

"And who can accomplish such a thing?" Richard's voice, it seemed to Kahlan, was sounding very much like the Lord Rahl demanding answers. Whatever was happening, it was making each of them edgy.

Zedd turned his palms up. "I don't know, Richard. It's not something I can do. I'm not familiar with the skill, or if it is even true. Like I said, it's gossip I've heard, not personal experience."

"Why would they be looking for Lord Rahl and the Mother Confessor?" Cara asked. She was clearly now more upset over that than she had been when she had thought someone was looking in on her and Benjamin.

"Good question," Zedd said. "Did you hear anything?"

Cara considered for only an instant. "No. I heard nothing and I saw nothing. But I could feel someone looking."

Zedd twisted his mouth as he considered. "Well, I'll put a shield on the room for you to keep prying eyes out."

"And will a shield of magic be able to stop the product of gossip?" Richard asked.

Zedd's smile finally returned. "Can't say for sure. I don't know if such an ability is real or not, and I don't know if there really was someone looking in on that room."

"There was," Cara insisted.

Kahlan spread her hands. "Seems that the simplest thing to do would be to cover the mirrors."

"No," Richard said in a thoughtful tone as he gazed into the atrium, "I don't think they should cover the mirrors, or put a shield on the room."

Zedd planted his fists on his hips. "And why not?"

"If someone, somehow, was looking in on that room and we cover the mirrors or shield the place, then they can't look in there again."

"That's the point," Kahlan said.

"And then they would know that we were aware of them and we won't know why they were looking in there."

Zedd stuck one long bony finger into his disorderly thatch of wavy white hair and scratched his scalp. "You lost me, my boy."

"Well, if whoever was looking in there was really looking for Kahlan and me, then they've already learned that it wasn't us in that room. So, if we leave the room unshielded and the mirrors the way they are, and Cara doesn't feel like she is being watched again tonight, then that would confirm that they weren't actually interested in Cara and Benjamin. If they're really looking for Kahlan and me, then they will have moved on to look elsewhere."

Kahlan knew Richard well enough to know that there was some inner calculation going on in his head.

Cara fingered the chain holding her Agiel as she thought it over. "That makes sense. If they don't come looking in again tonight then that means they're probably looking for you and the Mother Confessor."

Zedd gestured offhandedly. "Or it could mean that it wasn't real and that you were only imagining it."

"How do we find out who could be doing such a thing? Looking into a room like that?" Benjamin asked, before Cara had a chance to argue.

Zedd shrugged. "I'm not saying that such a thing is even possible. I've never heard of any specific magic that could do such a thing, only rumors of it. I think we're all letting our imaginations get away from us. Tonight, let's try to be a little more objective, shall we?"

After a moment of silent consideration, Cara nodded. "I'll pay more attention tonight. But I wasn't imagining it."

Kahlan could tell by the way Richard was staring blankly into the atrium that he was already thinking about something else. The others sensed the same thing and waited in silence to see what was on his mind.

"Have any of you heard of Kharga Trace?" he finally asked into the quiet.

Kharga Trace?" Benjamin asked.

He hooked a thumb behind his weapons belt and frowned down at the floor, trying to recall if he'd ever heard the name before. Zedd shook his head. Kahlan could see in Rikka's eyes that she knew the name, but instead of answering herself, she glanced at Cara, deferring, as all the Mord-Sith did, to Cara's implicit authority.

"Kharga Trace is in the Dark Lands," Cara said.

Richard picked up on the subtle, but chilling, change in her voice. His gray eyes turned from the atrium to focus on her.

"Where?"

"The Dark Lands—an outlying region of D'Hara." She aimed a thumb over her shoulder. "To the north and east of here."

"Why is it called the Dark Lands?"

"Most of it is beyond the reach of civilization. It's a place something like the Wilds—isolated, insular, inhospitable— but instead of being flat and open like the Wilds, it's mostly a vast, trackless land of mountains and dark forests. That makes it too hard to reach the isolated tribes in the farther reaches, or to even find them. But if you go into those remote places they inhabit, you run the risk that they will find you."

Cara's words were all business, as formal as they would be for any report the Lord Rahl might have asked for, but her tone had an icy edge to it. "The weather there is overcast and gloomy most of the time. In the Dark Lands one rarely sees the sun. That might have been the origin of the name."

By the way Cara had carefully framed the suggestion, Kahlan suspected that the name might have had other origins.

"But civilized people live there, call the place home," Richard said. "After all, it's part of D'Hara."

Cara nodded. "In Fajin Province, besides the ruling city of Saavedra, there are small towns in valleys here and there, a scattering of mountain villages, that sort of thing, but beyond those outposts of civilization lies a dark and forbidding land. People don't wander far from the towns and when they do they stay to the few roads. Not a lot is known about the region because there isn't much trade there, in part because there isn't much there worth trading for."

"What's the other part?" Richard asked.

Cara paused only momentarily before answering. "Many of those who go into the Dark Lands are never seen again. Most people avoid straying from settled parts. From time to time, even some of those who live there, and do stay to the roads and shut themselves in at night, are never seen again, either."

Richard folded his arms. "What would be the cause of these people vanishing?"

Cara shrugged. "I can't say for sure, Lord Rahl. It's a place of superstition, black arts, and tight lips. People don't speak of things they fear lest those things come looking for them."

Richard didn't let it go at that. "Superstition doesn't cause people to vanish."

Cara, in turn, didn't shy from his intent gaze. "Whispers say that scavengers of the underworld hunt the Dark Lands."

Everyone collectively took a breath as they considered such a grim warning.

"There are places like that in the Midlands," Zedd finally offered. "Some of it is superstition, as you say, but there are also places where talk of dangerous things is well founded."

Kahlan certainly knew the truth of that. She was from the Midlands.

"I think that may be the case with the Dark Lands as well," Cara agreed. "But the uncivilized regions are more vast, more remote, than such places in the Midlands. If something goes wrong in the Dark Lands there is not going to be anyone to come help you."

"Why would anyone live there?" Kahlan asked.

Cara shrugged. "Despite how savage, or harsh, or destitute a place might be, it's still home to those who were born there. Most people rarely stray far from home, from what they know, for fear of what they don't know about other places."

"Cara is right," Richard said. "We also have to remember that it's still a land with people who fought alongside us for our freedom, who stood with us. They also lost a great many people to the war."

Cara conceded with a sigh. "True enough. I knew a few soldiers from Fajin Province, and they fought fiercely. None of them were from Kharga Trace, though. From what I've heard of it, Kharga Trace is even more inhospitable than the rest of the Dark Lands. Few people, if any, actually live in the Trace. Few would ever have reason to venture in there."

"How do you know so much about these Dark Lands?" Kahlan asked.

"I don't know a lot, actually. Darken Rahl used to have dealings in the Dark Lands so that's the only reason I know anything at all. I remember him mentioning Kharga Trace once or twice." Cara shook her head at the memory. "The Dark Lands rather fit his nature, as well as that of his father before him. They both used brutality and fear to maintain rule over the people who live there. He often said that it was the only way to keep the Dark Lands in line.

"Like his father before him, Darken Rahl also sometimes sent Mord-Sith to the Dark Lands to remind the people there of their loyalty to D'Hara."

Richard frowned. "So you've been there, then?"

"No, he never sent me. As far as I know, none of the Mord-Sith who are still alive have been there."

She gazed off at nothing in particular for a moment. "Many of those he sent never came back."

Cara's blue eyes finally turned back to Richard. "Darken Rahl used to send Constance."

Richard met Cara's meaningful gaze but he said nothing. He had known Constance when he had been a captive of Darken Rahl.

He had been the one who had killed her.

Since the war had ended Richard and Kahlan had learned a little more about D'Hara, though much of it was still a mystery to them. It was a vast land, with cities they had never known about before, much less visited. There were also districts in far-flung places like these Dark Lands that were so remote that they were more or less self-governing.

"Most of the city and district leaders are here now," Benjamin said. "As far as I know, despite how distant and primitive some of those outlying lands might be, none dared to ignore an official invitation to our wedding from the Lord Rahl himself. With them all here we can inquire more about Kharga Trace, if you like."

Richard nodded absently, his mind apparently already on to the next part of his inner equation.

"Richard," Zedd said when the conversation stalled while they all watched Richard staring off into the distance, "I heard that you're doing something with all the books in the palace."

"We're organizing them all," Kahlan said when Richard failed to hear the question.

"Organizing them?"

"Yes," Richard finally said, having heard the question after all. "With all the thousands of books here in the palace it's virtually impossible to find information when we need it. I don't even have a way of knowing if information I might need even exists in one of the libraries. There is no one who knows where everything is located or what's there.

"So, I'm having the information organized. Since Berdine can read High D'Haran, and already knows a lot about the different libraries, I put her in charge. Nathan is helping as well."

Zedd looked skeptical. "That's an incredibly complex task, Richard. I'm not even sure that such a thing is possible, even with the prophet helping Berdine. I think I ought to see what you're doing and how you're doing it."

Richard nodded. "Sure. Come on, I'll take you down to one of the larger libraries where Berdine is working. I was going there anyway. There's something I want to look into."

Kahlan wondered what.

As they started out, Kahlan hung back, snagging Cara's arm to hold her back as well. They both slowed, letting the others think that maybe they wanted to talk about the wedding and Cara now being married—something that as far as Kahlan knew had never happened before. Until Richard came along, who would ever have had the unthinkable thought of a Mord-Sith marrying?

"What is it?" Cara asked in a low voice.

Kahlan glanced toward Richard, Zedd, Benjamin, and Rikka out ahead, engaged in conversation. The rich carpets muted their words as well as their footsteps.

"Something is going on. I don't know what, but I know Richard well enough to know when he has the bit in his teeth."

"What would you like me to do?"

"I want a Mord-Sith to stick close to him at all times."

"Mother Confessor, I had already made that decision when Zedd told us that whoever was looking in the room might have been looking because it was Lord Rahl's room."

Kahlan smiled and put a hand on Cara's shoulder. "Glad to see that marriage hasn't dulled your senses."

"Yours either. What do you think is going on?"

Kahlan drew her lower lip through her teeth.

"Earlier today a boy with a fever told Richard that there is darkness in the palace. I think it was just the fever talking, but I know Richard and I know that those words stuck in his head.

"Just before we came down here, an old woman, a fortune-teller, stopped Richard and told him that 'The roof is going to fall in.' Then, when we come down to see you, we find out about this business with someone looking into your room."

"What do you suppose Lord Rahl is thinking?"

Kahlan looked over to meet Cara's intent blue-eyed gaze. "If I know Richard—and I do—he's thinking that he has just met the third child of trouble."

"I knew I should have put on my red leather this morning."

"No need to get ahead of ourselves. I'm only being cautious. Just because Richard is thinking it, that doesn't mean it's true."

"Mother Confessor, when Lord Rahl gets like this trouble usually follows."

"There is that," Kahlan agreed.

Kahlan watched Zedd pace across the gold and blue carpet and back again toward the heavy mahogany table, his long robes swishing around his legs when he turned, as if they were having trouble keeping up. Windows up on the balcony level lit the long library with cold, flat light. Through those windows she could see that since they had been down in the market earlier in the day, iron gray clouds had moved in, bringing the threat of a spring storm.

Though there were windows along that far wall of the balcony, the lower floor of the library near ground level had none. Kahlan thought that the library must be somewhere near to being under the Garden of Life, located in massive parts of the palace above them. Because of the complex construction of the palace it was hard for her to tell for sure.

Off in a far corner, Nathan leaned against a fluted wood column broader than his broad shoulders. With a ruffled shirt, high boots, and green cape hooked to one shoulder, to say nothing of the sword he wore, he looked more like an adventurer than a prophet. But a prophet he was. Under the warm yellow light of a reflector lamp mounted on the column in the shadowy niche he looked totally engrossed in the study of a book.

Before Kahlan, books lay in orderly stacks and disorderly piles at random intervals all along the length of the table. Papers sat in batches among the books, along with lamps, ink bottles, pens, and empty mugs. Reflector lamps on the columns at either end of rows of shelves helped illuminate the more secluded areas of the library. With the overcast, and despite the lamps, gloom had settled over the still room.

Berdine, wearing a brown leather outfit, folded her arms and leaned against the table as she, along with the rest of them, watched Zedd pace. While her eyes were as blue as Cara's, her wavy hair was brown rather than blond. She was shorter and curvier than most of the other Mord-Sith.

Unlike most of the other Mord-Sith, Berdine was fascinated by books and had many times proven to be a tremendous help to Richard in ferreting out useful information among the thousands of volumes. While Berdine usually went about her book work with bubbly enthusiasm, she was no less deadly than Cara or any of the other Mord-Sith.

Zedd finally came to an impatient halt. "I'm not convinced that it can work, Richard—or at least, work effectively. For one thing, there are many ways to classify books, as well as books that contain more than one subject. If a book is about a city located beside a river, and you place it in a section on cities, then later when you need information about rivers you won't be aware that this book on cities might have something important to say about a river."

He sighed as he glanced around the library. "I've been reading and studying these kinds of books my whole life and I can tell you from long experience that you can't always pigeonhole a book in a category."

"We've taken that into account," Richard said with quiet patience.

Exasperated, Zedd turned to a disorderly pile of books on the table, and after taking a quick look at a book that lay open on the top, he picked it up. He waggled it before Richard. "And then there are books like this. How do you find a classification for things that don't even make any sense?"

Berdine scratched the hollow of her cheek. "Which book is it? What's it about?"

Zedd closed it briefly to read the title. "*Regula*," he announced in annoyance. He scanned a few pages, then shook his head in surrender. "I don't know what the title means and after looking at it I have even less of an idea what it's about."

As he handed the book to Berdine, Kahlan could see that after the title *Regula* on the spine, there was a strange circular symbol with a triangle in it embossed into the leather. Inside that circle with a triangle lay a curving, hooked symbol that she'd never seen before. It looked something like the number nine, but it was backward.

"Oh, this one," Berdine said as she flipped over a few pages. "Some of it is in High D'Haran, but a lot of it isn't. I suspect that it's a wordbook."

Zedd puzzled at her a moment. "What does that mean?"

"Well, I can understand bits of it, the parts that are in High D'Haran, but I'm not sure what all these weird squiggly lines and symbols mean."

"If you're not sure what it is," Zedd fumed, "then how can you even classify it?"

Richard laid a hand on Zedd's shoulder. "We'll put it on the list with all the other books that make no sense to us. That is its classification for now: unknown."

Zedd stared at him for a moment. "Well, I guess that makes some sense."

"Oh, it's not unknown, Lord Rahl," Berdine said. "Like I was explaining, I think it's a wordbook."

"A wordbook?" Zedd waggled a finger over the open book Berdine was holding. "It's full of all those peculiar symbols, not words."

"Yes, I know." Berdine brushed a stray lock of wavy brown hair back off her face. "I haven't been able to study it much, but I suspect that the symbols are an ancient form of writing. I saw a place that referred to it as the language of Creation."

Zedd harrumphed. "Sounds like you could classify it as 'useless.' I think this is going to be such a common problem that I'm not sure I see the point of all this work."

"Look," Richard said, "there have been times when we've gotten into a lot of trouble, or couldn't prevent trouble, because we couldn't find answers when we needed them.

"In the past there were scribes who kept track of the vast amount of information in each library. From what I know of it, they were responsible for particular books, or specific sections of a specific library. If there was need for books that might contain information on a particular subject, the scribes could be consulted and they could narrow the search to books where answers were most likely to lie.

"Without all those knowledgeable scribes who knew about and cared for the books, the vast information in the libraries is, for all practical purposes, inaccessible. We need a way to find books on any given subject in order to find answers.

"Since the last time you were here we've begun cataloging everything. We're trying to create a system to include all the books in all the libraries so that if we need answers we have a way to find information on specific topics."

Zedd gestured to the table. "That's these stacks of papers?"

Richard nodded. "I don't want to move the books around too much because I don't know why they're in a particular library, or for that matter why they're on particular shelves. Other than dangerous books on magic that are placed in restricted libraries, I haven't been able to figure out any logic to where books are kept, but it's possible that there is a reason for them being where they are. Without knowing the reason, I don't want to move them around and chance inadvertently creating a new problem.

"So, we're making up a sheet for each book with its title, location, and some kind of description of what's in the book. That way we can sort the pages into categories instead of having to sort the books themselves.

"In the example you mentioned, we would have a sheet for the book in with the cities category and we'd make a copy of that sheet to put in the rivers category. That way, we're less likely to miss important secondary information."

Zedd looked around at the row upon row of shelves. There were thousands of books in this library, and it was only one of many in the palace.

"That's going to be a lot of work, my boy."

Richard shrugged. "We have a wealth of information in the tens of thousands of books in various libraries throughout the palace, but no effective means to find specific information when we need it. Instead of fixating on that problem, I came up with a solution. If you have a better one, then I'd like to hear it."

Zedd's thin lips pressed tight for a moment as he considered the problem. "I guess not. I have to admit, what you say makes sense. I used to do something similar, but on a much, much smaller scale."

"The First Wizard's enclave, at the Wizard's Keep," Richard said as he nodded. "I remember the way books were stacked in piles all over the place."

Zedd stared off into memories. "I put books about specific things I wanted to have at hand together in stacks. I had once meant to organize them on shelves. Never got around to it, though, and there were relatively few books there in that one place. Maybe now, with the war ended, when I get back to the Keep I can finally return to that long-forgotten work."

"Lord Rahl had us start here, in this library, because for the most part it doesn't seem to contain especially valuable or rare books," Berdine said, drawing Zedd's attention away from his memories. "Back when Darken Rahl was the Lord Rahl, he didn't use this library that I saw. I think that means the books here are less important."

"That you know of," Zedd admonished. "You can't depend on that to say that at least some of the books in here might not be rare . . . or dangerous."

"True," Berdine said. "But some of the other libraries have books that we know for a fact are filled with dangerous things."

"We thought this would be a good place to start," Richard said, "before we move on to the larger or more restricted libraries. And if there are important books in here we'll now know they're here because we will eventually merge all the sheets on all the books. That way we'll know where any of the books on any given subject are located, no matter which library they're in, no matter if they are scattered all over the palace."

Zedd seemed to have calmed down. "That makes sense."

"So," Richard said as he gestured to the book on the table that Zedd and Berdine had looked at before, "when we do have a book like that one, we mark it unknown, or I guess maybe 'wordbook,' as Berdine suggested."

"Well actually, Lord Rahl, that one happens to be unlike anything else I've run into. I was going to talk to you about how we should handle it. It's not unknown, exactly, but it's not exactly a wordbook, either."

Richard folded his arms. "You said it was a wordbook."

"Possibly, but I can't classify it that way," she said.

Richard frowned at her. "Why not?"

"Well, what I meant was that it was starting to look that way, but I can't tell for sure."

Richard scratched an eyebrow. "Berdine, you're confusing me."

Berdine leaned over and pulled the book back. She flipped it open on the table, looking up at Richard as if she were about to pass on some bit of juicy gossip.

"Look here. This book was rebound. This isn't its original cover."

Zedd, Kahlan, and even Cara leaned in a little to see the book.

Richard focused on it with renewed interest. "How do you know?"

Berdine ran her finger along the inside of the spine where it attached to the back cover. "You can see here where it was mended together, but it doesn't match. The book itself isn't complete. Most of it is missing. This binding was made specially to hold only what was left."

Richard cocked his head to try to see the book better. "Are you sure that most of the book is missing?"

"I am." Berdine turned the last page back over and tapped the words in High D'Haran at the end of the book. "Look here. Except for some of the book's beginning, most of the pages were removed. They inserted this note as a last page to explain what they'd done."

Richard took the book off the table and read to himself. As he silently worked out the translation, a little of the color left his face.

"What does it say?" Kahlan asked.

Richard's troubled gaze rose to meet hers. "It says that the rest of the book was removed and taken to '*Berglendursch ost Kymermosst*' for safekeeping. This remaining part, here, was left as a marker."

Kahlan remembered that name. *Berglendursch ost Kymermosst* was High D'Haran for Mount Kymermosst. Mount Kymermosst was where the Temple of the Winds had originally been built.

Three thousand years ago the Temple of the Winds, because it contained so many dangerous things, had somehow been cast out of the world of life to where no one could get to it.

It had been hidden away, out of reach, in the underworld.

On occasion over the intervening thousands of years, there had been those who had traveled to the world of the dead to try to get into the Temple of the Winds. None had survived the attempt.

Until Richard.

He had gone alone to the underworld and had been the first in thousands of years to set foot in the temple.

When he had unlocked the power of the boxes of Orden to end the war, he had righted a number of wrongs, eliminating dangers and traps that had killed a great many innocent people.

He had also returned the Temple of the Winds to the world of life, to its rightful place atop Mount Kymermosst.

CHAPTER

6

"Well," Zedd finally said into the hush, "at least you know where the rest of this book is located." His bushy brows drew down over his intent hazel eyes. "When you told me that you had returned the temple to this world, you said that no one but you can get into it. That is the case, isn't it, Richard?"

It sounded to Kahlan more like a command than a question.

Despite the intensity in Zedd's voice, the tension finally eased out of Richard's posture. "Right. Whatever the rest of the book contains, it's safely locked away."

Richard let out a sigh as he closed the strange book and placed it back on the table. "Well, Berdine, I guess that you should mark the sheet for *Regula* as unknown and put down its location as both here and in the Temple of the Winds."

Zedd turned back to Berdine, as if wanting to save the topic of the Temple of the Winds for later, for a private conversation with Richard. "So, you are making up a page for each of the books in here?"

Berdine nodded as she scooped up a fat stack of papers. "Each of these pages is a book. In this case, all the books in this stack are books of prophecy. We put down the title and include some of what the book is about if we can."

"That way," Richard said, "by having a sheet of paper on each book, we'll eventually have a virtual library of all the books in the palace. I don't think prophecy can be of much help to us, but at least we'll know where all those books are located and what subjects they revolve around."

Kahlan thought that was a slim chance. Most books of prophecy contained random predictions, not subjects about which prophecy was written. Prophets, gifted people who were once not so extremely rare as they became over the centuries, wrote down any prophecy that came to them, whenever it came to them, about whatever came to them. As a result, many books of prophecy had no chronology much less common subject, making them notoriously difficult to categorize.

More than that, though, they were only really meant to be read by other prophets. A person without the gift could not properly interpret a prophecy's meaning by the words alone. Prophecy, written or spoken, rarely turned out to mean anything like what you thought it meant. Rather, the vision it invoked in prophets contained the true meaning.

Everyone turned when Nathan walked up along the opposite side of the table. "And I'm here to look over all the books of prophecy to help with categories, if they apply. I've spent my life reading prophecy so I'm usually already familiar with each volume. Just listing them as prophecy is usually the most that can be done, but at least we'll then have an inventory of all of them and know where each is to be found."

"Nathan's help is invaluable," Berdine said. "I don't even try to categorize books of prophecy."

Richard folded his arms as he leaned a hip against the table. "Speaking of prophecy, Nathan, in the halls today I ran into an older woman who tells fortunes."

Kahlan had been wondering how long it would take Richard to get around to the second child of trouble.

"Was she blind?"

"Yes."

Nathan nodded. "Sabella. I've met her. She's the real deal."

"You mean that you think she really can tell people their fortunes?"

Nathan held his thumb and finger barely apart. "Little ones. She has only a very small amount of genuine ability. Most of what she says is pure embellishment, telling people what they want to hear so she can earn her way in life. A lot of what she does is to make the most likely future sound as if she had seen it in a vision. For instance, she might tell a young woman that she sees marriage in her future. Hardly divination, as most young women will marry.

"But she does have a smidgen of actual ability. If she didn't, I would have brought her to your attention. I don't think you would want a charlatan in the palace cheating people about prophecy any more than I would."

Kahlan was well aware that Nathan, the only living prophet that she knew of, was rather protective of the reputation of prophecy. Richard didn't place much belief or reliance in prophecy, but Nathan did. He viewed Richard's avoidance of prophecy, his free will, as the balance that prophecy, like all magic, needed to exist.

"Is there anyone else here who, while obviously not gifted like you, at least has some genuine ability with prophecy?" Richard asked.

"There are several people in the palace who have a small amount of talent at predictions. Everyone has a spark of the gift. That's how they interact with magic, including prophecy."

Nathan gestured vaguely. "Everyone, from time to time, has had a sudden thought about a friend or loved one they haven't seen for ages. They may be overcome with a need to see that person. When they do, they discover the person is sick or maybe just passed away. Most people have experienced a feeling that someone they haven't thought about for ages is about to visit, and suddenly they knock on the door.

"Most people have had such little foreknowledge from time to time. These are all manifestations of prophecy. Because we all carry at least a small spark of the gift, this ability, even though very weak, will sometimes produce an omen.

"In some it's a little stronger, and they regularly experience these minor prophetic events. While not true prophecy such as I have, this does give them the ability to see a shadow of the future. Some people are self-aware enough to pay attention to these little inner whispers."

"And you know of people like that here at the palace?"

Nathan shrugged. "Certainly. One woman works on the official kitchen staff. She is visited by small premonitions. There is another, Lauretta, who works at a butcher shop in the palace. She, too, has a hint of ability. In fact, she has been pestering me to convince you to come see her. She claims to have something for you, some omen."

"So why haven't you?"

"Richard, there must be ten people a day who want me to use my influence with you to gain them some favor, to have you buy their wares, to get them an audience with you, even to invite you for tea so they might give you their advice about issues that are important to them. I don't bother you with matters you don't have time for. Lauretta is a good enough woman, but she is especially strange, so I haven't brought her to your attention."

Richard sighed. "I know what you mean. I've run into a number of those people on my own. . . ."

Kahlan thought that Richard was often a little too patient with people. She thought that he let them take up too much of his time, divert him from more important matters, but that was just the way Richard was. He was simply, innocently, interested in everything, including people's lives and concerns. In that, she could see some of Zedd in him. It was also part of what she loved about him, even if from time to time it tried her patience.

"So, what did Sabella, the blind woman, tell you?"

Richard gazed off into a distant corner of the library for a moment before looking back at the prophet. "That the roof is going to fall in."

Nathan stared, unblinking, for an even longer moment. "That kind of foretelling is too specific. It's beyond her ability."

"Well, that's what she said." Richard appraised the ashen look on Nathan's face. "Are you sure it's beyond her ability?"

"Afraid so."

"Do you know what the prophecy means?"

Kahlan thought that Nathan might not answer, but finally he did. "No, can't say that I do."

"If you don't know what it means, then why do you have that look on your face and how do you know that it's beyond Sabella's ability? How do you even know that it's a real omen and not simply an empty warning she made up in exchange for a coin?"

Nathan took the stack of papers from Berdine. "Most of the books in this library are rather common," he said as he thumbed through the pages. "I've been reading books of prophecy my whole life. I'd venture to say I know just about every one that exists. Most of these books here, including the books of prophecy, are copies that can be found in libraries in any number of other places."

Nathan finally found the sheet he was looking for and pulled it out. "Except this one. This one is a rather curious volume."

"What's so unusual about it?" Richard asked.

The tall prophet handed the sheet to Richard. "Not a lot until today. That's why I haven't studied it much."

Richard scanned the page. "*End Notes*. Strange title. What does it mean?"

"No one is really sure. This is a particularly ancient work. Some think it's merely a compilation of random bits of longer prophecies that have been lost over the ages. Others have believed that it means exactly what it implies, that it contains notes about the end."

Richard frowned up at Nathan. "The end? The end of what?"

Nathan arched an eyebrow. "The end of time."

"The end of time," Richard repeated. "And what do you think?"

"That's the odd thing about it," the prophet said. "I don't know what to think. Having the gift, as I read prophecy I often have visions of their true meaning. But this book is different. I've looked at it a number of times throughout my life. When I read it I have no visions.

"What's more, I'm not the only one. Part of the reason that no one is sure of the meaning of the title is that other prophets have had the same difficulty with this book that I have. They, too, had no visions from the prophecies in it."

"Doesn't seem so hard to figure out why," Cara said. "It sounds to me like that simply shows that what's written in the book aren't real prophecies. You're a prophet. If they were real prophecies you would know it. You would have the visions."

A sly smile overcame Nathan's face. "For someone who knows nothing about magic, you have managed to arrive at the heart of the issue. That has been the contention of many who say they are random snippets and therefore too incomplete to be viable, or that the book is a fraud." The smile ghosted away. "There is only one problem with that theory."

"And what would that be?" Richard asked before Cara could.

"Let me show you."

Nathan marched off down the center aisle with Richard, Kahlan, Zedd, Cara, Benjamin, and Berdine in tow. Rikka stayed back by the door to the library where she had been standing guard to make sure they weren't disturbed. At the very end of the room Nathan started scanning the titles in the tall, ornately decorated bookcase against the wall. He finally bent and pulled a book from a lower shelf.

"Here it is," he announced as he showed them the spine with the title *End Notes*. After searching for a moment, he handed the open book to Richard and tapped a place on the right-hand page.

Richard stared at the words as if he was having trouble believing what he was seeing.

"What does it say?" Kahlan finally had to ask.

Richard's gray eyes turned up to her. "It says, 'The roof is going to fall in.'"

"You mean just like that old woman said today?" Kahlan frowned. "What does the rest of it say?"

"Nothing. That's the only thing on the whole page."

Nathan glanced around at the small group surrounding him. "It's a fragment prophecy."

Richard stared at the writing in the book. Benjamin seemed puzzled. Zedd wore a stony expression that deepened the wrinkles on his angular face. Berdine looked decidedly worried.

Cara scrunched up her nose. "A fragment prophecy?"

Nathan nodded. "A prophecy so concise that it can appear to be nothing more than a fragment, a snippet. Prophecy is usually at least a little more complex than this and usually a great deal more involved."

Richard glanced down again at the book. "Or it's simply empty boasting."

Nathan straightened. "Boasting?"

"Sure. Someone wanted to make themselves sound impressive so they came up with something that sounds specific but isn't."

As Nathan cocked his head, his long white hair brushed his shoulder. "I don't follow."

"Well, how long ago do you think this was written?"

"I can't be sure, but the prophecy itself has to be several thousand years old, at least. Possibly much older than that."

"And in all that time since then don't you suppose that a roof or two has collapsed? It's an impressive-sounding prophecy, saying a roof is going to fall in, but it's really nothing more than like announcing on a sunny day that you predict that it will rain. Sooner or later it's going to rain, so such a prediction is pretty safe to make. In the same way, over the years, sooner or later, a roof is going to fall in. When it does, that event makes the person who said it sound prophetic."

"That makes sense to me," Cara said, happy to have the magic of prophecy defanged.

"There's only one problem with that," Nathan said.

Richard handed back the book. "Like what?"

"Empty predictions are usually open-ended. Like you say, sooner or later it's going to rain. But with real prophecy they repeat themselves. You might say that the omen resurfaces to remind people of it."

Richard looked up at Nathan from under his lowered brow. "You mean to say that you think that because this woman today repeated this fragment prophecy that means it's real? That the time for it has arrived?"

Nathan smiled the slightest bit. "That's the way it works, Richard."

Kahlan noticed someone arrive at the doorway. By the robes with gold trim she recognized the man as a palace official. Rikka spoke briefly with him, then hurried down the aisle.

"Lord Rahl, the reception is beginning. The new husband and wife should be there to greet people."

Richard smiled as he put his arms around Benjamin's and Cara's shoulders and started them toward the door. "Let's not keep people waiting for the guests of honor."

As he made his way into the grand hall, Richard scanned the crowd, looking for the man Cara had told him about. Kahlan slipped her arm through his and leaned closer as they followed Cara and her new husband.

"I know that you have a lot of things running through your head, Richard," Kahlan whispered to him, "but let's try to remember that this party is for Cara and Benjamin and we want it to be remembered fondly."

Richard smiled. He knew what she meant. Beginning with the first party he had taken her to on the day he'd met her, they never seemed to do well at parties for one reason or another. On more than one occasion they had turned out to be disastrous. But that had always been during the long struggle to survive the war.

"Yes, we do." He gave Kahlan a little nudge as he leaned close to her. "They do make a great couple, don't they?"

"That's the Richard I love," she whispered with a smile.

The vast room was filled with the drone of people enjoying the banquet. Tables spread with food of every sort drew throngs while palace staff in sky-blue robes circulated through the gathering with platters of smaller finger foods.

The blue color of their robes had been Cara's choice. Richard hadn't asked the reason for her choice, but he suspected that it had been because it was not a color that Mord-Sith wore. He was just happy that she had picked something pretty.

"Go on," he said to Cara. With a slight shove at the small of her back he urged her to go out among the people who had turned out for her and Benjamin's reception. As Cara waded into the sea of people he was heartened to see her smile back over her shoulder at him. Would wonders never cease.

As he watched Cara and Benjamin graciously accept the warm wishes of all the people from lands near and far who started to flock in around them, he was only half listening to Kahlan and Zedd talking. Zedd was telling her about all the things that were new in Aydindril, about the repairs that had been completed at the Confessors' Palace, where she had grown up, and about all the businesses that had returned.

"It's so good to hear how vibrant Aydindril is once again," Kahlan said. "Richard and I can't wait to return for a visit."

Although there were hundreds of women all dressed in their finest dresses, Richard didn't think that any of them looked anywhere near as stunning as Kahlan. Her white Mother Confessor dress, cut square at the neck and elegant in its simplicity, caressed her perfect form. It made her long brown hair look all the more luxurious, and her green eyes even more bewitching.

While he thought that she was the most beautiful woman he had ever seen, it was the intelligence Richard could see in those eyes that had captivated him from the first moment he had come face-to-face with her. In the years since he had come to know her, to love her, she had never once given him reason to doubt his first impression of what he had seen in her eyes. Waking every morning to look into those green eyes made him feel like he must be living a dream.

"It is wonderful to see the place so alive and thriving," Zedd was saying, "but I tell you, Kahlan, the trade in prophecy is becoming exasperating."

Richard abruptly looked over at his grandfather. "The trade in prophecy? What are you talking about?"

Zedd ran a finger along his angular jaw as he considered his answer. "Well, ever since the war ended and people moved back into Aydindril, prophets of every sort and stripe have also moved in. People are as eager to listen to prophecy as they are to gossip.

"Some people want to know if they will find love. Some want to know if they will be successful in their trade or business. Some believe that the future holds doom and gloom and they want to hear the forewarnings of terrible things to come. Some even want to hear the predictions about the end of the world, and so they listen with rapt attention to how all the signs are coming to pass."

Richard was dumbfounded. "Signs? What signs?"

"Oh, you know, like the full moon came up and was triple-ringed one night. Or that spring is late this year. Or that it didn't freeze on the last full moon. Silly things like that."

"Oh," Richard said, relieved to hear that it was only the typical end-times warnings that always cropped up around some event like an eclipse, or a change of season. Often it was merely ordinary events linked together into sure signs of the impending extinction of the world of life.

There seemed to be some inner need in many people to believe that the world would end in some cataclysmic event. Usually in the very near future.

Zedd clasped his hands behind himself. "Seems like everyone wants to know what fate holds for them. Prophecy, and the passing along of prophecy—or even the trade in it—seems to be a preoccupation of just about everyone of late."

Kahlan's green eyes flashed with concern. "I don't recall such a prophecy trade in Aydindril. I've seen it on a small scale in any number of places, but I don't recall it being as noteworthy in Aydindril as you say."

"Well it is now. Seems like on every corner someone is offering prophecy, fortunes, and predictions. For everyone who wants to know the future, there seem to be any number of people who claim to be able to tell them what it will be."

Richard eased closer to Kahlan. "Isn't that the way it's always been? People have always wanted to know the future."

"Not like this. There is a growing business in prophecy, and a growing number of people who are willing to pay for it and then are eager to pass on any warnings they hear. The city has become a cauldron of prediction and foretelling, with it all becoming the grist for gossip. I have to tell you, Richard, it's starting to have me concerned."

When a server in blue robes approached and bowed, holding out a tray, Kahlan took a glass. She took a sip before turning her attention once more to Zedd's story.

"With the war over, people don't have that constant fear on their minds. They're used to living in dread, so they're probably turning to dire predictions of the future to fill that nagging ghost of worry now that the real worry is dead."

Richard rested the palm of his left hand on the pommel of his sword, declining a drink when offered. He had not drawn the sword since the first day of the winter past. He would be happy if he never needed to draw it again.

"Kahlan is right. For years people lived in constant terror that they wouldn't live to see another day. With the war finally ended they wake every day to realize that they do have a future—a real future. They want to know what that future holds. I'd rather they created their own future, built lives from their own dreams, but I suppose that many believe that fate holds secrets for them, and prophecy can reveal it."

Zedd waved off the server before going on. "Could be." He watched the crowd churning through the great hall for a time. "But it feels like more to me," he added under his breath.

Kahlan smiled. "See? The war is over and even you can't give up worrying. You're doing the same thing that they're doing. You should relax a little. The world is at peace."

"Peace," Zedd huffed. He turned to them both with a chilling look. "There is nothing as dangerous as peacetime."

Richard hoped Zedd was wrong, that, as Kahlan said, he was simply so used to worrying that he was falling into old habits. He supposed that he knew how Zedd felt. Even though there was peace, he couldn't help worrying, either.

Richard was worried about what Cara had said, that someone had been watching them. He was also concerned about the fact that the prophecy from the old woman, Sabella, had turned out to be the exact same prophecy that had been in the book *End Notes*. Prophecy had caused Kahlan and him no end of trouble.

Most of all, though, Richard was concerned about what the boy down in the marketplace had said, that there was darkness in the palace, and that darkness was seeking darkness. He had no tangible reason to worry about words that seemed to have been born of fever. Indeed, Zedd and Nathan hadn't been worried about the boy's words when he told them what had happened. They both thought Kahlan had it right, that it was nothing more than fevered illusions.

But Richard was worried about those words. Something

about them seemed more than a simple fever. They touched something deep within him. Especially now, since people from all over were gathered at the palace.

Richard noticed Rikka watching the crowd. She looked like a hawk searching for a mouse. Cara, off a ways across the room, kept an eye on Richard and Kahlan even as she smiled and greeted people. He saw other Mord-Sith standing off to the sides, watching people. Several of them, closer to Richard and Kahlan, were wearing red leather. For some reason, he wasn't altogether unhappy to see that. Even if it was peacetime, he was glad to see that they were remaining vigilant.

Richard leaned a bit toward his grandfather. "Zedd, do you think that what Nathan said was right?"

Zedd frowned. "About what?"

Richard smiled at passing guests before answering. "That real prophecies repeat themselves. That they resurface to reinforce the validity of the prophecy. That they repeat themselves to remind people of the prophecy, so to speak."

Zedd gazed out at the crowd for a time before answering.

"I'm not a prophet. My gift does not manifest itself in that way. But I am still a wizard and as such I've studied prophecy, among other things, my whole life, so I know about prophecy. There is some truth in what Nathan told you."

"I see," Richard said as he noticed the captain of the guard that had escorted them down to the market that morning making his way across the room. For some reason the man's jaw was set with grim urgency.

People saw the captain's purposeful stride and made way for him, yet the celebration, the lilt of laughter, the drone of conversation throughout the room went on unabated. Benjamin saw the man as well and straightened, looking suddenly more like General Meiffert than husband Benjamin. Several

Mord-Sith started to close in, apparently thinking, because of how serious the man looked, that they might need to keep him away from the Lord Rahl and the Mother Confessor, who were there to enjoy themselves and didn't need to be bothered with business. Cara gave them a slight gesture, though, and they let the man pass without intervening.

The captain came to a smart halt and clapped a fist to his heart. "I apologize for interrupting you, Lord Rahl."

Richard bowed his head slightly in recognition of the salute. "It's all right. Did you find the boy, Captain?"

"No, Lord Rahl. We've looked everywhere. The boy is gone."

Richard thought that sounded a little too definite. "He has to be somewhere down there. He's sick, he couldn't have gone too far. Keep looking. I'm sure your men will find him."

The captain cleared his throat. "Lord Rahl, two of my men, two of the men who went after the boy, were found dead just a short while ago."

Richard's heart sank at the thought that these brave men who had fought so long and suffered so much had died now that peace had finally arrived.

"Dead? How did they die?"

The man shifted his weight. "I don't know, Lord Rahl. There were no wounds or anything like that. They had not drawn their weapons. Their faces showed no last indication of trouble. They were simply lying peacefully in a narrow passage behind rows of tents. They was no sign of any kind of struggle."

Richard's fingers tightened around the hilt of his sword. "And they had no wounds?"

"No, Lord Rahl. They were just plain dead."

8

Not long after Richard had sent the captain to collect a larger force of men to help find the boy, the delegations from various lands who had come for the grand wedding saw their opening and began gathering in around Richard and Kahlan. While many of them expressed their gratitude to the two of them for all they had done to end the threat of tyranny, some wanted to ask questions. Everyone was eager to hear what the Lord Rahl and Mother Confessor had to say in answer to those questions.

Richard had met some of the representatives, ambassadors, and emissaries over the past few days as they had arrived at the palace, but many of the gathered people he didn't know. The smiles and the gratitude, as well as the questions, seemed genuine.

After dispensing with the formality of expressing their delight with being invited, with the warmth of their reception, and with the beauty of the palace, they all quickly fell into asking questions about trade policy and the establishment of uniform laws. They wanted assurances that what they had heard, that they would all have the chance to be involved in such things, was true.

With urgent matters of war and the need for supplies and men now a thing of the past, everyone was turning to considerations of how to use their resources and goods to the best advantage of their own homeland and people. It was clear that the unity they had all felt during the war had softened and each of them was concerned that their land might now somehow be placed at a disadvantage when it came to trade and matters of law.

Richard let Kahlan assure them that there would be no restrictions on trade, and that they needn't fear special favors to some that would put others at a disadvantage. Many of the people were from the Midlands. She reminded them of her policies when she had ruled the Midlands as the Mother Confessor and assured them that now being part of the D'Haran Empire would not change those matters of fairness. Her calm manner and authoritative demeanor made them confident in the truth of what she said.

A number of the officials reminded her that in the Midlands most of the lands were formally represented in Aydindril, sometimes with rulers of the lands spending extended periods of time there, sometimes with emissaries and representatives, but there were always officials of some sort at hand so the different lands could always be involved in the decisions of the council or in matters of setting laws. Kahlan assured them that the People's Palace was now the formal seat of power in the D'Haran Empire, so there would be similar arrangements made for them and their representatives to have permanent quarters from where they could participate in the shaping of their common future. Everyone seemed not merely relieved to hear this, but genuinely pleased.

Kahlan was used to being in command and carried her power with an easy grace. She had grown up mostly alone because, as a Confessor, she had grown up being feared. When Richard had first met her he saw people tremble in her presence. In the past people saw only the terrifying power she wielded, not the nature of the woman behind that power, but in the time she and Richard had fought on behalf of these people, she had come to be admired and respected. People had come to look up to her.

At the most inopportune moment, in the midst of Kahlan's answers to questions, Nathan marched up behind Richard, took hold of his arm, and pulled him back a little. "I need to speak with you."

Kahlan paused in her answer about an ancient boundary dispute. She had been telling people that there was nothing to dispute; they were all now part of the D'Haran Empire and it didn't really matter where a meaningless line was drawn on a map. As she fell silent, every eye went to the tall prophet. They all knew who he was.

Richard noticed that Nathan had the book *End Notes* in hand, with one finger acting as a placeholder in the book.

"What is it?" Richard asked in a low voice as he took several steps back from the suddenly silent crowd watching him. Prophecy was apparently of more concern to them than matters of trade or arbitrary boundaries.

Nathan leaned in and spoke confidentially. "You told me that the boy you encountered down in the market today told you something about darkness in the palace."

Richard straightened and turned back to look around at all the people watching him. "I'm sorry for the interruption. If you will excuse me it will only be a moment."

He took Nathan by the arm and moved him back a few more steps toward the double doors all along the wall at the back of the room. Zedd came along, as did Kahlan. Cara and

Benjamin, not far away, took the hint in the look Richard gave them and drew the attention of the delegates by asking about how the rebuilding was going in their homelands.

Once sure that no one was within earshot, Richard turned back to Nathan. "The boy said that there is darkness in the palace. He said that darkness is seeking darkness."

Without a word, Nathan opened the book and handed it to Richard.

Richard immediately spotted the line all by itself: *Darkness is seeking darkness.*

"That's the boy's exact words," Kahlan said, a tone of concern clearly evident in a low voice.

Richard almost said that it had to be coincidence, but he knew better. Instead he asked, "Anything else about this, this fragment prophecy anywhere else in the book?"

"I don't know," Nathan said with obvious frustration. "I have no way of knowing if anything in the book is connected to anything else. For all I know, everything else might be tied to this darkness prophecy, or none of it is. I don't even know if the other one, the one about the ceiling falling in, is connected to this line about darkness seeking darkness."

Richard knew it was.

He was more than skeptical that it could be a coincidence that the boy spoke a line from a book that contained another line in it that the old woman had spoken. He knew it couldn't all be connected by chance. He remembered the surprised look on the woman's face when she had told him his fortune, that the roof was going to fall in, as if that hadn't been what she had meant to say.

Richard had learned that his gift often manifested itself in unique ways. Some texts called him the pebble in the pond, because he was at the center of ripples of events. Incidents that at first seemed like chance events were in fact often elements that were somehow drawn to him, or drew his attention, by his gift, by the ripples he created around him. Such events could appear to be coincidence until he dug deeper.

Or until the sky fell in on him.

He knew now for certain that he couldn't let this lie and let events get out ahead of him. He needed to dig deeper.

He let out a deep breath. "All right. There's nothing we can do about it at the moment. Let's not get all these people worked up by letting them know that something is wrong."

"We don't know that there really is something wrong," Zedd reminded him.

Richard didn't want to argue that there was. "I hope you're right."

"The way prophecy works," Nathan reminded Zedd, "it's likely that this is all connected somehow."

Zedd's face twisted with a sour expression, but he didn't challenge the point.

Richard tapped his thumb against the hilt of his sword as he ran all the events through his mind for a moment. He couldn't see any connection between the three events. He couldn't even imagine any.

That wasn't true, he realized. Darkness seeking something could be connected to Cara's feeling that someone was looking into her room in the night—in the dark.

He turned to Nathan. "You said that there's a woman who works for the palace and that she is visited by small premonitions."

"That's right. She's general kitchen help, usually doing preparation work like cutting up things for the palace cooks, but she helps out with other things when extra people are needed. As a matter of fact, I believe she's one of the people in the blue robes helping serve tonight." He glanced around without trying not to look obvious. "I don't see her at the moment, though."

"And you said that there was another woman, Lauretta, I think you said her name was, who has a hint of ability. You said that she wanted to see me because she has something for me, some kind of omen."

Nathan nodded. "That's right."

"As soon as we can break away from here I want you to take me to see her."

"Richard, I'd be happy to take you there, but it's likely nothing. These kinds of things usually turn out to be a whole lot less than one thinks they are. People often believe that the most mundane and innocent things somehow have sinister implications. It's likely nothing meaningful."

"That would please me just fine," Richard said as he checked on the people waiting for him. "Then I won't have to worry about it."

"I suppose so." Nathan gestured toward the wall of doors behind them. "We're near the kitchens. Lauretta works for a butcher who helps supply the palace for affairs like the wedding and this gathering here today. Her quarters aren't far. When you feel like taking a stroll we can go see her."

Richard nodded. "For now, let's get back to our guests."

CHAPTER

9

Richard stepped back to the waiting group of officials, mayors, regents, representatives and even a few kings and queens of some of the lands in what used to be the Midlands before they were all joined into the D'Haran Empire. When Zedd and Kahlan went with him, Nathan tucked the book under his arm, put on his widest smile, and came along.

Nathan, being the only living prophet as well as a Rahl, was well known to just about everyone at the palace. That, and his flamboyant nature, made him a celebrity of sorts. He dressed the part, with a ruffled shirt and a fashionable green cape. Elaborate engraving covered the gold scabbard and sword at his hip.

Richard thought that a wizard of Nathan's abilities wearing a sword made about as much sense as a porcupine carrying a toothpick to defend himself. Nathan claimed that the sword made him look "dashing." He enjoyed the looks he got, usually acknowledging them with a broad grin and, if the looks came from a woman, a deep bow. The more attractive the woman, the wider his smile tended to be. The women often blushed, but they almost always returned a smile.

Despite being somewhere near to a thousand years old,

Nathan often approached life with the glee and wonder of a child. It was an infectious nature that attracted some people to him. Others, no matter Nathan's often pleasant nature, considered him to be just about the most dangerous man alive.

A prophet could tell the future and in the future pain, suffering, and death often lay in wait. People believed that, if he chose to, he could reveal what fate awaited them. Nathan dealt with prophecy; he could neither invent it or make it happen. But some still believed he could. That was why many considered him dangerous.

Others considered him profoundly dangerous for an entirely different reason. They feared him because there had been times when prophecies he revealed had started wars.

There were those women who were drawn to that aura of danger about him.

When asked why he would bother to carry a sword, Nathan had reminded Richard that he was a wizard as well, and he carried a sword. Richard protested that he was also the Seeker, and the Sword of Truth was bonded to him. It was part of him, part of who he was. Nathan's sword was more ornamental. Nathan didn't need a sword to reduce someone to ash.

Nathan had reminded Richard that, Seeker or not, and no matter how he framed it, Richard was far more deadly than the sword he carried.

"Lord Rahl," a stocky man in a red tunic asked as everyone gathered close, "may we know if there is some prophetic event lying ahead for us?"

Many in the crowd nodded, relieved that the question had finally been asked, and moved in a little closer. Richard was beginning to suspect that the answers to such questions were the only things they were really interested in hearing from him.

He looked around at all the eager faces watching him. "Prophetic event? What do you mean?"

"Well," the man said, sweeping an arm expansively, "with so many gifted right here, First Wizard Zorander, the prophet himself, Nathan Rahl"—the man bowed his head toward Richard—"and not least of all you, Lord Rahl, who has more than proven to everyone what a remarkable gift you possess, surely you would have to be privy to the deepest secrets of prophecy. We are all hoping, since we are all gathered here, that you would be willing to share with us what such prophecy has revealed to you, what it holds in store for us."

People in the gathered crowd voiced their agreement or nodded as they smiled hopefully.

"You want to hear prophecy?"

Heads bobbed and everyone inched in closer, as if they were about to be privy to a palace secret.

"Then heed what I say." Richard gestured to the gloomy gray light coming from the windows at the far end of the room behind the crowd. Everyone glanced briefly over their shoulder, then turned back, lest they miss what Richard would say.

"There will be a spring storm the likes of which has not been seen for many years. Those of you who wish to return home sooner rather than later should plan to leave at once. Those who delay too long will shortly be stranded here for a number of days."

A few people whispered among themselves as if Richard had just revealed the secrets of the dead. But most of those waiting for his word on the future seemed to be a great deal less impressed.

The heavyset man in a red tunic held a hand aloft. "Lord Rahl, while that is fascinating, and I am sure quite prophetic, and no doubt useful to some of us here, we were hoping to hear of things more . . . significant."

"Like what?" Nathan said in a deep voice that rattled some in the crowd.

A woman in the front dressed with layered golds and greens forced a smile. "Well," she said, "we were hoping to hear some true words of prophecy. Some of fate's dark secrets."

Richard was feeling more uneasy by the moment. "Why the sudden interest in prophecy?"

The woman seemed to shrink a little at his tone. She was trying to find words when a tall man farther back wove his way between people as he stepped forward. He wore a simple black coat with a turned-up, straight collar that went all the way around. The coat was buttoned to his neck so that it pulled the collar nearly closed at his throat. He wore a rimless four-sided hat of the same color.

It was the abbot Benjamin had told Richard about.

"Lord Rahl," the abbot said as he bowed, "we have all heard warnings from people who have been endowed with an element of insight into the flow of events forward in time. Their dark warnings trouble us all greatly."

Richard folded his arms. "What are you talking about? Who is coming up with these warnings?"

The abbot glanced about at his fellow guests. "Why, people back in all of our homelands. Since arriving at the palace, as we have talked among ourselves, we have discovered that we are all hearing dark warnings from soothsayers of every sort—"

"Soothsayers?"

"Yes, Lord Rahl. Diviners of the future. Though they live in different places, different lands, they are all speaking of dark visions of the future."

Richard's brow drew lower. "What do you mean by diviners of the future? They can't be true prophets." He gestured to his side. "Nathan here is the only living prophet. Who are these people you're listening to?"

The abbot shrugged. "They may not be prophets, as such, but that does not mean they are bereft of abilities. Capnomancers have seen dire warnings in their readings of sacred smoke. Haruspices have found disturbing omens in animal entrails." The man spread his hands innocently. "Those sorts of people, Lord Rahl. Like I say, diviners of the future."

Richard hadn't moved. "If these people are so talented and know the future and all, then why are you asking me about it?"

The man smiled apologetically. "They have talents, but not to compare with yours, Lord Rahl, or with those remarkably gifted people with whom you surround yourself. We would value hearing what you know of ominous warnings in prophecy so that we might take your word back to people in our homelands. From what they have been hearing, they are uneasy and hoping that we will return with word from those at the palace. A spring storm, while noteworthy, is not what concerns us most. It is the whispers and warnings we have all heard that worry us."

Richard could not disguise his glare as stood before the silent crowd watching him. "Your people want to know what the Lord Rahl has to say on the subject?"

There were nods all around. Some people dared to inch forward again.

Richard let his arms down and stood taller. "I say that the future is what you make of it, not what someone says it will be. Your lives are not controlled by fate, or set down in some book, or revealed in smoke, or laid out in a twisted pile of pig intestine. You should tell people to stop worrying about prophecy and to put their minds to making their own future."

Nathan cleared his throat as he took a quick step forward. "What Lord Rahl means to say is that prophecy is meant for prophets, for those with the gift. Only the gifted can understand the complexities tangled up in a genuine prophecy. Rest assured, we will worry about such things so that you don't need to."

Some in the crowd reluctantly seemed to think that made some sense. Others were not satisfied. A thin woman, a queen from one of the lands in the Midlands, spoke up.

"But prophecy is meant to help people. It is set down so that those words elicited by the gift will come forward through the dark tunnel of time to be of use to those of us who will be touched by those prophecies. What good is prophecy if the people aren't informed of what it has to say about their fate? What use is the gift for prophecy if not to help people? What value is prophecy if it is kept secret?"

Nathan smiled. "Since you are not a prophet, Your Majesty, how can you know that there is a prophecy that is relevant, one that you would need to know about?"

She fingered a long jeweled necklace, the unseen end of which was located somewhere down in her cleavage. "Well, I suppose . . ."

Richard rested the palm of his left hand on his sword. "Prophecy causes more trouble than it ever helps."

"We have encountered prophecy," Kahlan said as she stepped up beside Richard, drawing everyone's attention, "profoundly frightening core prophecy speaking specifically of Richard and of me. Had we followed the grim warnings in those prophecies, done what they said must be done to avert disaster, it would have actually ended up being not only our destruction but the destruction of all life.

"Had we done as you now wish to do, and heeded the words of those terrible prophecies, you would now all be dead at best, or worse, slaves in the hands of savage masters. In the end those prophecies turned out to be true, but not in the way that they sounded. Prophecy is profoundly dangerous in the wrong hands and not intended to be heeded in the way it sounds."

"So, you are saying that we can't be trusted with knowing our own future?" There was an edge to the queen's voice.

Richard saw the flash of anger Kahlan's green eyes and answered before she could. "We're saying that the future is not fixed. You make your own future. If you believe you know the future, then that changes the way you behave, changes the decisions you make, changes how you live and how you plan for your future. Such unthinking choices could be ruinous. You need to act in your own rational best interest, not upon what you think prophecy says is in store for you.

"The future, at least for the most part, is not fixed in prophecy. Where prophecy may be valid it is not something that can be comprehended by just anyone."

While that didn't entirely satisfy people, it did take some of the wind out of their excitement to hear some juicy omens.

"Prophecy has meaning," Nathan said, "but the true meaning can only be unraveled by those gifted in such things, and I can tell you that those things are not revealed in a pile of pig guts."

When she saw the hesitancy in the crowd, Cara, in her white leather outfit, moved in to Richard's left. "D'Harans have a saying: the Lord Rahl is the magic against magic; we are the steel against steel. He has more than proven himself to all of us. Leave the magic to him."

Coming from a Mord-Sith, those words had a chilling finality.

The crowd seemed to realize that they were not merely pushing into areas where they didn't belong, but overstepping bounds. Somewhat shamed, they spoke quietly among themselves, agreeing with one another that it made sense that maybe they should leave such matters to those who were best able to deal with them. Everyone seemed to relax a bit, as if having just pulled back from the brink.

Out of the corner of his eye to the right, Richard saw the blue robes of one of the serving women coming up on the far side of Kahlan.

The woman gently laid her left hand on Kahlan's forearm as if wanting to speak to her confidentially.

That, more than anything, was what got Richard's attention. People didn't just come up and casually lay a hand on the Mother Confessor.

As she came around and turned in toward Kahlan, Richard saw the haunted look in the woman's eyes and the blood down the front of her robes.

He was already moving when he saw the knife in her other hand sweeping around toward Kahlan's chest.

CHAPTER

10

Time itself seemed to stop.

Richard recognized all too well the eternal emptiness between the heartbeats of time, that expectant void before the lightning ignition of power.

He was a step too far away to stop the woman in time, yet he also knew that he was too close for what was about to happen.

It was already out of his hands and there was nothing he could do about it.

Life and death hung in that instant of time. Kahlan could not afford to hesitate. His instinct to turn away tensed his muscles even though he was well aware that nothing he could do would be fast enough.

The sea of people stood wide-eyed, frozen in shock. Several Mord-Sith in red leather had already begun to leap a distance that Richard knew they could never make in time. He saw Cara's red Agiel beginning to spin up into her hand, soldiers' hands going for swords, and Zedd's hand lifting to cast magic. Richard knew that not one of them had a chance to make it in time.

At the center of it all, Richard saw the woman holding

Kahlan's forearm down out of the way as the bloody knife in her other hand arced around toward Kahlan's chest.

In that instant everyone had only begun to move.

Into that silent void in time, thunder without sound suddenly ignited.

Time crashed back in a headlong rush as the force of the concussion exploded through the confined space of the banquet hall.

The impact to the air raced outward in a circle.

People near the front cried out in pain as they tumbled backward to the ground. Those farther away in the rear were knocked back a few steps. In shock and fear they too late protectively covered their faces with an arm.

Food flew off tables and carts; glasses and plates shattered against the walls; wine bottles, cutlery, containers, small serving bowls, napkins, and fragments of glass were blown back by the shock wave sweeping across the room at lightning speed. When it hit the far end of the room the glass in all the windows blew out. The bottoms of curtains flapped out through the shattered windows. Knives, forks, food, drink, plates, and pieces of broken glass clattered across the floor.

Richard was by far the one closest to Kahlan as she had unleashed her Confessor power. Too close. Proximity to such power being loosed was dangerous. The pain of it seared through every joint in his body, dropping him to a knee. Zedd fell back, knocked from his feet. Nathan, a little farther away, staggered back, catching Cara's arm to steady her.

When pieces of shattered glass finally stopped skipping across the floor, the tablecloths and curtains finally settled and stilled, and people sat up in stunned silence, the woman in bloody blue robes was kneeling at the Mother Confessor's feet.

Kahlan stood tall at the center of the settling chaos.

People stared in shock. None of them had ever seen a Confessor unleash her power before. It was not something done before spectators. Richard doubted that any of them would ever forget it as long as they lived.

"Bags, that hurts," Zedd muttered as he sat up rubbing his elbows and rolling his shoulders.

As Richard's vision and mind cleared from the needle-sharp stab of pain that had instantly stitched its way through every joint in his body, he saw that the woman had left a bloody handprint on the sleeve of Kahlan's white dress.

Kneeling there before the Mother Confessor, the woman didn't look at all like an assassin. She was of average build with small features. Limp ringlets of dark hair just touched her shoulders. Richard knew that a person touched by a Confessor's power didn't feel the same pain as those nearby, but, more than that, things such as pain would be merely distant considerations to her. Once touched by a Confessor, the Confessor was all.

Whoever the woman had been, she was no more.

"Mistress," the woman whispered, "command me."

Kahlan's voice came as cold as ice. "Tell me again what you have done, what you said to me before."

"I've killed my children," the woman said in a dispassionate voice. "I thought you should know."

The words cut through the somber silence, running a shiver up many a spine, Richard was sure. Some people gasped.

"That's why you came to me?"

The woman nodded. "Partly. I had to tell you what I had done." A tear ran down her cheek. "And what I had to do."

With her mind and who she had been now gone, Richard knew that her tears were not for killing her children, but for having intended to kill Kahlan. The Confessor who had touched her was now the only thing that mattered to her. The guilt of her intent now crushed her soul.

Richard bent and carefully took hold of the woman's right wrist as he pulled the bloody knife from her grip. Disarming her was no longer necessary, but it still made him feel better. She didn't seem to notice.

"Why would you do such a thing?" Kahlan asked in a commanding tone that stilled everyone's breath for a moment.

The woman's face turned up to Kahlan. "I had to. I didn't want them to face the terror of it."

"The terror of what?"

"Of being eaten alive, Mistress," the woman said, as if it was obvious.

All around guards eased in closer. Several Mord-Sith who had tried to stop the woman, but hadn't been able to make it in time, now slipped up behind the woman. Each of them had her Agiel in her fist.

Kahlan had no need of guards or Mord-Sith and had no fear of a mere knife from a single attacker. Once touched by her power, a person was helplessly devoted to the Confessor and incapable of disobeying her, much less harming her. Their only concern was to please her. That included confessing any crime they were guilty of if Kahlan asked.

"What are you talking about?"

The woman blinked. "I couldn't let them suffer what's to come. I did them a mercy, Mistress, and killed them swiftly."

Nathan leaned close to Richard and whispered, "This is the woman I told you about, the one who works in the kitchens. She has a small amount of talent to see the future."

Kahlan leaned down toward the woman, causing her to shrink back. "How could you know what they would suffer?"

"I had a vision, Mistress. I have visions sometimes. I had a vision and I saw what was going to happen if they lived. Don't you see? I couldn't let such a gruesome thing happen to my babies."

"Are you telling me that you had a vision that told you to kill your own children?"

"No," the woman said, shaking her head. "I had a vision of them being eaten alive, of fangs ripping and tearing at them as they screamed in terror and pain. The vision didn't tell me to kill them, but after what I saw I knew what I had to do lest they suffer such a horrific fate. I was doing them a mercy, Mistress, I swear."

"What are you talking about, eaten alive? Eaten alive by what?"

"Dark things, Mistress. Dark things come for my babies. Dark things, feral things, coming in the night."

"So you had a vision and because of that you decided to kill them yourself."

It was a charge, not a question. Nonetheless, the woman thought it was and nodded, eager to please her mistress.

"Yes. I slit their throats. They bled out and lost consciousness quickly as they faded gently into death. They did not have to suffer what fate would have had them suffer."

"Faded gently?" Kahlan asked through gritted teeth and barely contained fury. "Are you trying to tell me that they didn't suffer, didn't struggle?"

Richard had seen people's throats cut, and so had Kahlan. They did not go gently into death by any means. They fought for their lives in terrifying, mortal pain, and as they fought for the breath of life they choked and drowned on their own blood. It was a horrifically violent death.

The woman frowned a little as she tried to recall. "Yes, some, I guess. But not for long, Mistress. It was a brief struggle. Not as long as they would have struggled if they lived and the things in the night had come and gorged on their innards."

When Kahlan's eyes turned up at the sound of worried whispers being exchanged, the crowd fell silent.

"This is what happens when you think you can see into the future." She clenched her jaw as she glared at the people watching. "This is the result—lives cut short."

Kahlan turned that glare back down to the woman at her feet. "You intended to use your knife on me, didn't you? You intended to kill me."

"Yes, Mistress." Tears sprang forth anew. "That's why I had to tell you what I had done."

"What do you mean?"

"I had to tell you why I had killed my children so that you would understand why I must kill you. I meant to spare you, Mistress."

"Spare me? Spare me from what?"

"The same fate, Mistress." Tears began to run down her cheeks. "Please, Mistress. I cannot bear the thought of such a death as I saw awaiting you. I can't bear the thought of your body being ripped open as you scream, all alone, no one to help you. That's why I have to kill you—to spare you that fate like I spared my children."

Richard's knees felt like they might again give out.

"And what is it that is supposed to be eating me in this illusion of yours?"

"The same thing as would have eaten my children, Mistress. Dark things. Dark things stalking you, running you down. You won't be able to escape them."

The woman extended pleading hands. "May I have my knife back? Please? I must spare you that fate. Please, Mistress, allow me to suffer the pain of such a murder to spare you the agony and horror you will otherwise face. Please, Mistress, allow me to kill you swiftly."

Kahlan regarded her would-be murderer with a look devoid of all emotion.

"No."

The woman's bloody hands went to her chest, clutching her bloody blue robes. She gasped for breath that wouldn't come. Her eyes opened wide as her face reddened. Her lips turned as blue as her robes. She slumped to her side where she convulsed once in death. What air she had left finally wheezed from her lungs.

Kahlan's gaze rose to the stunned onlookers, a silent indictment of anyone thinking prophecy could help them.

Her green eyes, beginning to brim with tears, finally turned to Richard. It was a look that nearly broke his heart.

He slipped an arm around her waist. "Come on. You need to rest for a while."

Kahlan nodded as she leaned into him just a little, welcoming his solace. Already Cara, Zedd, Nathan, and Benjamin were moving in protectively around her. Mord-Sith and men of the First File screened them from the gathered throng.

Kahlan gave Cara's arm a squeeze. "I'm so sorry. I wanted this celebration to be perfect for you."

"But it was, Mother Confessor. The woman failed to harm you, you're alive and well, and a would-be assassin is dead. What could be more perfect than that? On top of that, I now get to lecture you on letting people get that close to you."

Kahlan smiled as she started away with Richard helping to hold her up.

CHAPTER

11

"How is she?" Zedd asked when Richard closed the door behind himself.

"She's fine." Richard flicked a hand to dismiss his grandfather's concern. "She just needs to rest."

Zedd nodded. As a wizard who'd once worked with Confessors, he probably understood better than anyone that a Confessor needed time to recover after unleashing her power, but none of them could recover as quickly as Kahlan. In the past, when the situation called for it, she had sometimes forgone resting at all.

Kahlan was stronger than the others had been in a number of ways. For those reasons her sister Confessors had chosen her as their leader, the Mother Confessor. Now all those others were dead.

Still, using her power was exhausting, not only physically but emotionally. It was near to the equivalent of carrying out an execution.

Yet that wasn't really the worst of it. The real core of her weariness this time was the knowledge that something sinister was going on and it had taken innocent lives. Kahlan didn't believe, any more than Richard did, that this was one lone

THE OMEN MACHINE

individual acting on a delusional vision she'd had. There was something more to all of it. That, on top of using her power, and it coming during such a joyful celebration in front of guests, was what had really left Kahlan drained.

Zedd looked up at Richard with one of those looks Richard knew all too well. "It's rather peculiar that the woman dropped dead."

Richard nodded. "That's been bothering me, too."

"A person touched by a Confessor's power is concerned with nothing other than pleasing the Confessor who touched them." Zedd arched an eyebrow. "They can't very well please her if they're dead. Unless, of course, she tells them that they can please her by dying, and Kahlan didn't do that."

Apparently, his grandfather had been thinking along the same lines as Richard. "It doesn't make any sense," he agreed. "People don't just drop dead from a Confessor's touch. Something else is going on."

Zedd rubbed a bony finger back and forth along his jaw. "Could be that the woman understood how utterly repulsed Kahlan was by her killing her children and so she thought that Kahlan would want her dead."

"I don't know, Zedd. That doesn't make a lot of sense to me. The whole purpose of a Confessor is to obtain confessions from killers, to find out the truth of what happened, of what terrible things they've done. They aren't repulsed by confessing their crimes. On the contrary, they're usually overjoyed that they can please a Confessor by telling her the truth when she asks for it. They want to live so that they can please her."

Cara folded her arms. "Well, I'm not moving from this spot until the Mother Confessor is recovered and on her feet again."

Richard laid a hand gently on Cara's shoulder. "Thanks, Cara."

Richard's mind was already on to other things, on to putting the pieces together. When the woman with the knife had tried to kill Kahlan, as frightening as it must have looked to the people there, she'd actually had no real chance of success. No knife attack was fast enough to beat a Confessor releasing her power. Cara standing in the way could not have stopped the woman as effectively as Kahlan was capable of doing herself. No single attacker had a chance against a Confessor.

But she couldn't use her power again until she recovered. Richard was more than happy to have Cara watch over Kahlan in the meantime.

He turned to Benjamin. "General, would you please post men at either end of the hall?"

Benjamin gestured up the corridor. "Already done, Lord Rahl."

Richard saw then the contingent of the First File off in the distance. It was enough men to fight a war. "Why don't you stay here with Cara. Keep her company. Kahlan needs to rest for a couple hours."

"Of course, Lord Rahl." Benjamin cleared his throat. "While you were in there with the Mother Confessor, we found the woman's two children. Their throats had been cut, just as she said."

Richard nodded. He hadn't doubted the woman. Someone touched by a Confessor couldn't lie. Still, the news left him feeling sick at heart.

"Please do something else for me, General. Send someone to find Nicci. I haven't seen her since yesterday at your wedding. Tell her I need to see her."

Benjamin lightly tapped his right fist to his heart in salute. "I'll send someone right away, Lord Rahl."

Richard turned to the prophet. "Nathan, I'd like you to take me to see the woman you spoke about. The one you said could see things. The one who claims to have a message for me."

Nathan nodded. "Lauretta."

Zedd and Richard both followed behind Nathan. A group of guards stayed with them but at a distance. Rikka, in her red leather, took the lead in front of them.

Nathan took a slightly longer route through the private corridors, rather than the public passageways, to get to the area where staff and other workers lived. Richard was glad to avoid the public areas. People would undoubtedly want to stop him to talk with him. He didn't feel like talking about trade issues or petty matters of squabbles over authority to set rules. Or prophecy. Richard had more important things on his mind.

At the top of the list was what the dead woman had said about her vision. She had called the threat "dark things." She had said that those dark things were stalking Kahlan.

The boy down in the market earlier that morning had said that there was darkness in the palace.

Richard wondered if he was putting things together too easily, things that didn't really belong together and only sounded like they did because they shared the word "dark." He wondered if he was letting his imagination get the best of him.

As he marched along beside Zedd, with Nathan leading the way, he glanced down at the book Nathan was holding and remembered the lines in the book that matched what he'd heard that day about there being darkness in the palace, and decided that he wasn't overreacting.

The corridor they passed through was paneled with mahogany that had mellowed with age to a dark, rich tone. Small paintings of country scenes hung in each of the raised panels along the hall. The limestone floor was covered with carpet runners of deep blue and gold.

Before long they made their way into the connecting service passageways that provided workers with access to the Lord Rahl's private areas within the palace. The halls were simpler, with plastered, whitewashed walls. In places the hall ran along the outside wall of the palace to their left. Those outside walls were made of tightly fit granite blocks. At regular intervals deep-set windows in the stone wall provided light. They also let in a little of the frigid air each time a gust rattled the panes.

Out those windows Richard saw heavy, dark clouds scudding across the sky, brushing towers in the distance. The greenish gray clouds told him that he was right about the coming storm.

Snowflakes danced and darted in the gusty wind. He was sure that it wouldn't be long before the Azrith Plain was in the grip of a spring blizzard. They were going to have guests at the palace for a while.

"Down this way," Nathan said as he gestured through a double set of doors to the right. They led out of the private areas and into the service passageways used by workers and those who lived at the palace.

People in the halls, workers of every sort, moved to the side as they encountered the procession. Everyone, it seemed, gave Richard and the two wizards with him worried looks. No doubt the word of the trouble had already been to every corner of the vast palace and back three times over. Everyone would know about it.

By the looks on the somber faces he saw, people were no longer in a celebratory mood. Someone had tried to kill the Mother Confessor, Lord Rahl's wife. Everyone loved Kahlan.

Well, he thought, not everyone.

But most people sincerely cared about her. They would be horrified by what had happened.

Now that peace had returned, people had come to feel an expectant joy about what the future might hold. There was a growing sense of optimism. It seemed like everything was possible and that better days were ahead.

This new fixation on prophecy threatened to destroy all that. It had already ended the lives of two children.

Richard recalled Zedd's words that there was nothing as dangerous as peacetime. He hoped his grandfather was wrong.

CHAPTER

12

R ichard and Zedd followed Nathan into a narrow hallway lit by a window at the end. It led them through a section of quarters where many of the palace staff lived. With its whitewashed, plastered walls and a wood plank floor that had been worn down from a millennium of traffic, the passageway was simpler than even the service hallways. Most doors, though, were decorated with painted flowers, or country scenes, or colorful designs, giving each place an individual, homey feel.

"Here," Nathan said as he touched a door with a stylized sun painted on it. When Richard nodded, Nathan knocked.

No answer came in response. Nathan knocked harder. When that, too, received no answer he banged the side of his fist against the door.

"Lauretta, it's Nathan. Please open the door?" He banged his fist on the door again. "I told Lord Rahl what you said, that you have a message for him. I brought him along. He wants to see you."

The door opened a crack, just wide enough for one eye to peer out into the hallway. When she saw the three of them waiting she immediately opened the door all the way.

"Lord Rahl! You came!" She grinned as she licked her tongue out between missing front teeth.

Layers of clothes covered her short, heavyset form. From what Richard could see, she was wearing at least three sweaters over her dark blue dress. The buttons on the dingy, off-white sweater on the bottom strained to cover her girth. Over that sweater she had on a faded red sweater and a checkered flannel shirt with sleeves that were too long for her.

She pulled up a sleeve and then pushed stringy strands of sandy-colored hair back off her face. "Please, won't you all come in?"

She waddled back into the dark depths of her home, grinning—giddy, apparently—to have company come to visit.

As strange as Lauretta was, it was her home that was strangest of all. In order to enter, since he was taller than she was, Richard had to hold aside yarn objects hanging just inside the door. Each of the dozens of yarn contraptions was different, but all of them had been constructed in roughly the same manner. Yarn of various colors had been wound around crossed sticks into designs that resembled spiderwebs. He couldn't imagine what they were for. By no stretch of the imagination could they be considered attractive, so he didn't think they were intended to be decorative.

When Zedd saw him frowning at them he leaned close to speak confidentially. "Meant to keep evil spirits from her door."

Richard didn't comment on the likelihood of evil spirits who had managed to make it this far on a journey from the dark depths of the underworld being stopped cold by sticks and yarn.

To each side of the entrance, papers, books, and boxes were stacked nearly to the ceiling. There was a tunnel of sorts going back through the mess into the interior of her home. Lauretta just fit down the narrow aisle. It reminded him of a mole trundling down into its burrow. The rest of them followed in single file to reach a hollowed-out area in the main room where there was space for a small table and two chairs. A window not far away, visible through a narrow gap in the teetering piles, provided gloomy light.

A counter behind the table was stacked high with papers. The whole place looked like nothing so much as a lair carved into a midden heap. It smelled nearly as bad.

"Tea?" Lauretta asked back over her shoulder.

"No thank you," Richard said. "I heard that you wanted to speak with me about something."

Zedd held up a hand. "I wouldn't mind some tea."

"And some sweet crackers to go with it?" she asked, hopefully.

Zedd returned the grin in kind. "That would be nice."

Nathan rolled his eyes. Richard shot his grandfather a look. Lauretta rooted behind a sloppy pile of papers.

While Zedd sat at the table, waiting to be served, Lauretta retrieved a pot from an iron stand on a counter to the side. The pot was kept warm by a candle beneath the iron stand. The stand was surrounded by disorderly stacks of papers. Richard was alarmed to see fire being used.

"Lauretta," he said, trying to sound helpful. "It's dangerous to have fire in here."

She looked up from pouring Zedd's tea. "Yes, I know. I'm very careful."

"I'm sure you are, but it's still very—"

"I have to be careful with my predictions."

Richard looked around at the mountains of paper. Much of it was piled in loose stacks, but there were also wooden crates full of papers, and bindings overstuffed with yet more in among the paper towers.

Zedd waggled a finger at the rugged paper cliff to the side of him. "These are all your predictions, then? All of them?"

"Oh yes," she said, sounding eager to tell them all about it. "You see, I've had foretellings come to me my whole life. My mother told me that one of the first things I said was a prediction. I said the word 'fire.' And don't you know, that very day a flaming log rolled out of the hearth and set her skirt on fire. No great harm done, but it scared her something awful. From then on she would write down the things I said."

Richard glanced around. "I suppose you still have all the things she wrote down."

"Oh yes, of course." Lauretta replaced the tea on the stand after she finished pouring herself some. She set a chipped white plate with sweet crackers on the table. "When I was old enough I started writing down my predictions myself."

"Mmmm," Zedd moaned in ecstasy, waving a sweet cracker, "cinnamon, my favorite. These are quite good."

Lauretta flashed him a toothless grin. "Made them myself."

Richard wondered where and how. "So," he said, "why do you keep all of the things you write down?"

She turned a puzzled look on him. "Well, they're my predictions."

"Yes, you told us that," Richard said, "but what is the purpose of keeping them?"

"To record them. I have so many predictions that I can't remember them if I don't write them down. But more importantly, they need to be kept, to be documented."

Richard frowned, trying not to look exasperated. "What for?"

"Well," she said, confounded by the question, as if it was almost too obvious to need an answer, "all prophets write down their prophecy."

"Ah, well, yes, I suppose that—"

"And aren't those prophecies kept? The ones prophets write down?"

Richard straightened. "You mean, like the books of prophecy?"

"That's right," she said patiently. "Those are prophecy written down, just like I write mine down, are they not? Then, because prophecy is important, they are all kept, aren't they? Of course those are kept in libraries all over the palace. But I have no other place to store all of mine, so I must keep them all in here." She swept an arm around. "This is my library."

Zedd glanced around at Lauretta's library as he munched on his sweet cracker.

"So you see, I'm very careful with fire because these are prophecy written down, and prophecy is important. I must protect them from harm."

Richard was seeing prophecy in a new light—a less flattering light.

"That all makes sense," Zedd said, seemingly disinterested in continuing the line of conversation. "And your sweet crackers really are some of the best I've ever had."

She gave him another toothless grin. "Come back any time for more."

"I may do that, kind lady." Zedd picked up another and gestured with it. "Now, what of the prophecy you say you have for Lord Rahl?"

"Oh yes." She put a finger to her lower lip as she looked around. "Now, where did I put them?"

"Them?" Richard asked. "You have more than one?"

"Oh yes. Several actually."

Lauretta went to a wall of papers and randomly pulled out one of them. She peered at it briefly. "No, this isn't it." She stuck the paper back where she'd found it. She reached to the side, pulling out others, only to end up replacing them as well. She kept plucking papers from different places among the thousands and then replaced each after reading it.

Richard shared a look with Nathan.

"Maybe you could just tell Lord Rahl what your prediction was," Zedd offered.

"Oh dear me no, I'm afraid that I couldn't do that. I have too many predictions to remember them all. That's why I have to write them down. If I write them down, then I always have them and they can't be forgotten. Isn't that the purpose of writing down prophecy? So that we will always have them? Prophecy is important, so it must be written down and kept."

"Very true," Nathan said, apparently eager not to upset her. "Maybe we could help you look? Where would you have put your recent prophecies?"

She blinked at him. "Why, where they belong."

Nathan looked around. "How do you know where they belong?"

"By what they say."

Nathan stared a moment. "Then, how do you find them? I mean, if you don't remember what they say, then how do you know where they would have belonged in the first place and where you would have put them? How do you know where to look?"

She squinted as she gave serious consideration to the question. "You know, that very thing has always been the problem." She took a deep breath. The buttons on her sweaters looked like they might burst before she let it out. "I can't seem to come up with an answer to that quandary."

From the confusion they had always had with the location of books in the libraries, seemingly placed there in no order, Richard thought that it appeared to be a common problem with written prophecy on whatever scale.

Zedd pulled a piece of paper from a stack and peered at it. He waved it in the air.

"This one only says 'rain.'"

Lauretta looked up from the papers she had in her hand. "Yes, I wrote that down one day when I had a premonition that it was going to rain."

"This is a waste of time," Richard said in a confidential voice to Nathan.

"I cautioned you that it was likely nothing worthwhile."

Richard sighed. "So you did."

He turned to Lauretta. She had moved, pulling out another paper in another place near the bottom of a mountain of papers, boxes, and binders. Before he could say that they were leaving, she gasped.

"Here it is. I've found it. Right where it belonged."

"So what does it say, then?" Richard asked.

She shuffled over to him, paper in hand. She tapped it with a finger as she gazed up at him. "It says, 'People will die.'"

Richard studied her eager face a moment. "That happens all the time, Lauretta. Everyone dies, eventually."

"Yes, so true," she said with a chuckle as she returned to a teetering mound of paper to start her search anew.

Richard didn't see any more use for her prophecy than he saw in most prophecy. "Well, thank you for—"

"Here's another," she said as she read a paper hanging out

from a stack. She pulled it free. "It says, 'The sky is going to fall in.'"

Richard frowned. "The sky?"

"Yes, that's right, the sky."

"Are you sure you didn't mean that the roof was going to fall in?"

Lauretta consulted the paper in her hands. "No, it quite clearly says 'sky.' I have very neat handwriting."

"And what could that mean?" Richard asked. "How can the sky fall in?"

"Oh dear me, I have no idea," she said, snorting a chuckle. "I am only the channel. The prophecy comes to me and I write it down. Then I save it, the way you're supposed to save prophecy."

Nathan gestured at the papers all around. "You have no visions about these things, these prophecies that come to you?"

"No. They come, I write them down."

"So then you don't necessarily know what they mean."

She considered a moment. "Well, if the prophecy is for rain, I admit I have no vision to go with that, but it seems pretty clear, don't you think?" When Nathan nodded, she went on. "But when it says the sky is going to fall, I can't begin to imagine what that could mean. The sky can't very well fall in, now can it?"

"No, it can't," Nathan agreed.

"So," she said, holding up a finger thoughtfully, "it has to have some hidden meaning."

"So it would seem," Nathan agreed. "And how does a prediction like that one come to you, if not in a vision?"

She frowned as she looked up while she tried to recollect. "Well, it comes to me as words, I guess. I don't see a picture in my mind of a sky falling in or anything. It just comes to me that way, that the sky is going to fall in, like a voice in my head saying it, so I write it down just the way it comes."

"And then you store it in here?"

Lauretta glanced around at all of her precious predictions. "I suppose that future generations of prophets will have to study all of this in order to make sense of it."

Richard could hardly contain himself. He struggled to keep his mouth shut. The woman was harmless enough. She wasn't trying to drive them crazy. She was the way she was and he wasn't going to argue her out of her nature, or her lifelong obsession. It would be pointless and cruel to say something that would only end up making her feel bad.

"Oh," she said, turning suddenly to shuffle to the back of the room, "I almost forgot. I have another that came to me just yesterday. Came to me quite unexpectedly. It was the last of the prophecies that came to me for you, Lord Rahl."

Lauretta pulled at papers, reading them quickly and then shoving them back where she'd found them. Finally, she came across what she was looking for. Richard found the fact that she could find a single piece of paper she was looking for among all the thousands and thousands stacked everywhere to be more remarkable than anything she was writing down.

She hurried back, holding the paper out for Richard. He took it and read it aloud.

" 'Queen takes pawn.' " He looked up with a frown. "What does that mean?"

Lauretta shrugged. "I have no idea. My calling is to hear them and to write them down, not to interpret them. As I said, future prophets will have to do that work."

Richard glanced over at Nathan and his grandfather. "Any clue what this means?"

Zedd made a face. "Sorry, it doesn't mean anything to me."

Nathan shook his head. "Me neither."

Richard took yet another deep breath. "Thank you for passing these along, Lauretta. 'People are going to die,' 'The sky is going to fall in,' and"—he glanced down at the paper again to read the words—"'Queen takes pawn.' That's it, then? Do you have any others you want me to see?"

"No, Lord Rahl, that's all of them. When they came to me I didn't know their meaning, but I did know for certain that they were meant for you."

"Do you usually know who the prophecy is meant for?"

Her brow creased as she considered the question. "No, as a matter of fact, I don't recall ever knowing who my prophecies are meant for, or about." She looked up at him. "But you are said to be a very unusual man, a wizard of great power, so I suppose that had something to do with it."

Richard glanced at the teapot with the candle under it. "You know, Lauretta, in appreciation for bringing your prophecy to my attention, maybe I can do something for you in return."

She cocked her head. "For me?"

"Yes. I think that all of these prophecies should be in their proper place."

Her brow creased. "Proper place?"

"That's right. They don't belong here, hidden away. They belong in a library with other prophecy. They should take their rightful place in a library."

"A library . . ." Lauretta gasped. "Really, Lord Rahl?"

"Of course. These are prophecies. That's what the libraries are for. We have a number of such libraries here at the palace. What would you say to us sending men by to collect all of these prophecies and placing them in a proper library?"

TERRY GOODKIND

She looked around, hesitating. "I don't know . . ."

"There is a large library not far from here. There's plenty of room there. We could put your predictions there all together on shelves where someday prophets can study them. You could come visit them anytime you wished. And whenever you have new prophecies and write them down, they can be added to your special section in the library."

Her eyes widened. "Special section? For my prophecies?"

"That's right, a special section," Zedd said, joining in, apparently catching on to Richard's purpose. "There they could be properly looked after and protected."

She put a finger to her lip, thinking.

"And I could go there anytime?"

"Anytime you wish," Richard assured her. "And you can go there to add new ones when they come to you. You can even use the library tables to write down your new predictions."

She brightened and then took Richard's hand, holding it as if a king had just granted her part of his kingdom. "Lord Rahl, you are the kindest Lord Rahl we have ever had. Thank you. I accept your generous offer to protect my prophecies."

Richard felt a twinge of guilt over his ruse, but the place was a fire waiting to happen. He didn't want her to be hurt or die just because of prophecy. There was ample room in the library, along with all the other prophecy, to keep hers. Besides, he didn't know that her prophecies were any less valuable than all the others.

"Thank you again Lord Rahl," she said as she let them out.

Once they were on their way down the hall, Zedd said, "That was very kind of you, Richard."

"Not as kind as it may seem. I was trying to prevent a needless fire."

"You could have simply told her that you were sending

98

people to take all that paper away so she wouldn't start a fire."

Richard frowned over at his grandfather. "She's spent her whole life devoted to those pieces of paper. It would be cruel to confiscate them when there's plenty of room in the library. I thought it made more sense to make her feel good about giving them up—make her part of the solution."

"That's what I mean, the trick worked like magic and it was a kind way to do it."

Richard smiled. "Like you always said, sometimes a trick is magic."

Nathan caught Richard's sleeve.

"Yes, yes, very nice indeed. But you know the last prophecy she gave you, the one about a queen?"

Richard glanced back at the prophet. "Yes, 'Queen takes pawn.' I don't know what it means, though."

"Neither do I," Nathan said as he waggled the book he still had with him, "but it's in here. Just like she wrote it, word for word. 'Queen takes pawn.'"

CHAPTER

13

Kahlan sat up with a start.

Somewhere in the dead-still room someone was watching her.

She had been lying down with her eyes closed, but she had only been resting. She hadn't been asleep. At least, she was pretty sure she hadn't been asleep.

She had been trying to put everything from her mind. She hadn't wanted to think about the woman who had killed her children. She hadn't wanted to think about the children and how they had died. All for fear of a prophecy.

She didn't want to think about the woman's deluded visions.

She had tried very hard to put it all from her mind.

The heavy drapes were drawn. There was only one lamp lit in the room and it was turned down low. Sitting on the table before the mirror on the dressing table, the lamp was too weak to chase the darkness from the farthest reaches of the room. Darkness occluded those far corners where the faint shadowy shapes of hulking wardrobes lurked.

It couldn't be Richard she sensed. He would have let her know it was him when she sat up. Cara would have as well.

THE OMEN MACHINE

Whoever she sensed in the room wasn't saying anything, wasn't moving.

But she felt them watching her.

At least she thought she did. She knew how easy it was for anyone's imagination, even hers, to get out of hand. Trying to be honest and coldly logical, she couldn't say for sure that it wasn't her imagination, especially after Cara had planted the notion in her mind earlier in the day.

But her heart raced as she stared into the dark recesses of the room, watching for any movement.

She realized that her fist had tightened around her knife.

She pulled the bed throw off and pushed it aside. She was lying on top of the bedspread. Her bare thighs prickled at the touch of chilly air.

Carefully, quietly, she slipped her legs over the side of the bed. Without making a sound she stood. She waited, listening, her whole body tense and ready.

Kahlan stared so hard into the dark corner at the far end of the room that it made her eyes hurt.

It felt like someone was staring back.

She tried to tell where it felt like they could be hiding, but she couldn't come up with a direction. If she could sense someone watching, but wasn't able to sense where they were, then it had to be her imagination.

"Enough of this," she said under her breath.

With deliberate strides she walked to the dressing table. The heel-strikes of the laced boots she hadn't felt like taking off echoed softly back from the dark end of the room.

Standing at the dressing table, watching, she turned up the wick on the lamp. It threw mellow light into the darkness. There was no one there. In the mirror she saw only herself standing half naked with a knife gripped in her fist.

Just to be sure, she walked resolutely to the end of the room. She found no one there. She looked to the far side of the drapes and glanced behind the big pieces of furniture. There was no one there, either. How could there be? Richard had checked the room before he had taken her in. She had watched as he had looked everywhere while trying not to look like he was looking. Cara and soldiers stood guard as Kahlan had rested. No one could have entered.

She turned to the tall, elaborately carved wardrobe and pulled open the heavy doors. Without hesitation she lifted out a clean dress and pulled it on.

She didn't know if the other one, the one she had taken off, would ever be clean again. It was hard to get the blood of children off a white dress. At the Confessors' Palace, back in Aydindril, there were people on the staff who knew how to care for the white dresses of the Mother Confessor. She supposed that there would be people at the ancestral home of the Lord Rahl who knew all about cleaning up blood.

The thought of where that blood had come from made her angry, made her glad the woman was dead.

Kahlan paused to consider again why the woman would have died so abruptly. Kahlan hadn't commanded it. She had intended to have the woman locked up. There were a lot more questions Kahlan had wanted to ask, but not in public. If there was one thing Kahlan was good at, it was questioning those she had touched with her power.

The thought occurred to her that it was awfully convenient that the woman confessed what she had done, revealed what her prophecy said would happen to Kahlan, and then managed to die before she could be questioned.

When all else was said and done, that was the single thing that convinced Kahlan that Richard was right, that there was something more going on. And if he was right, then the woman had likely only been a puppet being moved by a hidden hand.

At the thought of Richard, she smiled. Thinking of him always lifted her heart.

When she pulled open the bedroom door, Cara, with her arms folded, was leaning back against the doorframe. Nyda, one of the other Mord-Sith, was with her. Cara looked back over her shoulder at Kahlan.

"How do you feel?"

Kahlan forced a smile. "I'm fine."

Cara's arms came unfolded as she turned. "Lord Rahl wanted me to bring you to him after you were rested. He's going to see that abbot."

Kahlan let out a weary breath. She didn't feel like seeing people, but she wanted to be with Richard and she, too, wanted to hear what the man might know.

Cara's eyes narrowed. "Why is your face so pale?"

"Just still a bit tired, I guess." Kahlan studied Cara's blue eyes for a moment. "Would you do something for me, please, Cara?"

Cara leaned in and gently took hold of Kahlan's arm. "Of course, Mother Confessor. What is it?"

"Would you please see to having our things moved?"

Cara's squint was back. "Moved?"

Kahlan nodded. "To another room. I don't want to sleep here tonight."

Cara studied her face for a moment. "Why?"

"Because you planted strange thoughts in my head."

"You mean you think someone was watching you in there?"

"I don't know. I was tired and probably imagined it."

Cara marched past Kahlan and went into the room, Agiel

in hand. Nyda, a statuesque blonde with the same single braid as all the Mord-Sith, was right on her heels. Cara pulled the drapes aside and looked behind furniture while Nyda looked in the wardrobes and under the bed. Neither of them found anything. Kahlan had known they wouldn't, but she also knew that it was a waste of effort trying to convince a Mord-Sith that she didn't need to be suspicious.

"Did you find anyone in your room?" Kahlan asked when Cara planted her fists on her hips and glared around at the room.

"I guess not," Cara admitted.

"I'll see to moving your things, Mother Confessor," Nyda said. "Cara can go with you."

"All right."

"Any particular bedchamber you prefer?" Nyda asked.

"No. Just don't tell me which one it is until you take us there tonight."

"So someone was watching you," Cara said.

Kahlan took Cara's elbow and turned her toward the door. "Let's go see Richard."

CHAPTER

14

Richard stood when the door opened. Out of the corner of his eye he saw Kahlan rise beside him when she saw that Benjamin had the abbot with him. She had only arrived with Cara a moment before. Richard had barely had the chance to ask how she felt. Kahlan had smiled and said she was fine.

He saw a distracted aspect in her eyes that told him otherwise. He supposed that she had reason enough to look anything but cheerful.

Richard saw, too, the way Cara stayed a half step closer than usual to Kahlan.

Kahlan had on a pristine white Mother Confessor's dress. Cara was wearing red leather.

General Meiffert led the man wearing the straight black coat into the comfortable meeting room. Benjamin noticed his wife's change of outfit, but made no comment.

The abbot removed his black, rimless hat to reveal tousled blond hair that was cut short at the sides. He put on a warm smile. Richard thought it looked forced.

"Lord Rahl," Benjamin said, holding out a hand in introduction, "this is Abbot Ludwig Dreier, from Fajin Province."

Rather than extending a hand, Richard nodded his greeting. "Welcome, Abbot Dreier."

The man's hesitant gaze took in those before him. "Thank you for taking the time to see me, Lord Rahl."

Richard thought that was an odd way to put it. The man hadn't asked for an audience. He had been summoned.

Zedd, wearing simple robes, stood to the far side of Kahlan. A wall of windows beyond Zedd, to Richard's right, cast the walnut-paneled walls and niches lined with bookcases framed by fluted walnut columns in fading, cold light. A few lamps were taking over with their warm illumination.

Nathan had gone back to see how Berdine was doing in the library. Richard had asked the men of the First File to stand guard out in the corridor, rather than in the room. He hadn't wanted the abbot to feel uncomfortable. This was, after all, a representative from one of the areas Richard ruled, not a hostile land. Still, a Mord-Sith in red leather standing at arm's length to his side couldn't put anyone at ease.

More than that, though, the man had been insistent about prophecy earlier in the day. When the woman had tried to kill Kahlan she had given her vision of the future as her excuse for murder. Richard and Kahlan were not exactly indulgent of people who let prophecy direct their lives, or who used it as license for the harm they caused. From the events at the reception, the abbot would be aware of their feelings, and that he was at the wrong end of them.

Richard gestured to one of the comfortable chairs on the other side of a low, square table covered with a slab of black marble cut through with whorls of white quartz. "Won't you have a seat, Abbot?"

The man sat on the forward edge of the chair, his back

straight, his hands folded on his knees, his hat hooked on his thumbs. "Please, Lord Rahl, call me Ludwig. Most everyone does."

"All right, Ludwig. I'm embarrassed to admit that I know far too little about your homeland. When the war was raging it was all any of us could do to stay alive another day. There was no time to learn more about those who fought so valiantly with us. With the threat of tyranny ended, the Mother Confessor and I hope to soon visit all the lands of the D'Haran Empire.

"So, since we know so little about Fajin Province, we would appreciate it if you could tell us a bit about the land you rule."

Abbot Dreier's face went red. "Lord Rahl, you have been misinformed. I am not the authority in my homeland."

"You aren't the ruler of Fajin Province?"

"Dear Creator, no."

Fajin Province, in the Dark Lands, was one of the small, outlying districts of D'Hara. Richard wondered why whoever was in charge hadn't come. It would have been a chance for them to take a place beside those who ruled much larger lands and have a say in the future of the D'Haran Empire.

Leaders of the lands near and far had come to the grand wedding. Although Cara and Benjamin's wedding was the central event, that highlight served as a chance for representatives from all the lands to come together and meet. None wanted to miss such a remarkable and unprecedented event. Richard had spent time with a number of the representatives. Only a few leaders had not been in good enough health to make the journey and had been forced to send emissaries. A number of the rulers had large escorts of ambassadors, officials, and advisors.

"You serve in some capacity of authority, though?" Richard asked.

"I am but a humble man who has the good fortune to have been called upon to work with people more gifted than I."

"More gifted? In what way?"

"Why, prophecy, Lord Rahl."

Richard shared a surreptitious look with Kahlan.

He leaned forward. "Are you saying that you have prophets, real prophets—wizards with the gift of prophecy—in your homeland?"

The man cleared his throat. "Not exactly, Lord Rahl, at least not like the tall prophet you have here that I've heard so much about. We are not anywhere near that fortunate. I apologize for giving such a misleading impression. We are but a small and insignificant land. Compared to the prophet you have with you here at the palace, those we have are of minor ability. Still, we do what we can with what we have."

"Then who governs in Fajin Province?"

"Bishop Hannis Arc is the ruler of our people."

"Hannis Arc." Richard leaned back in his plush chair and crossed his legs. "And why didn't he come?"

Ludwig blinked. "I wouldn't know, Lord Rahl. I rarely meet with the bishop. He rules from the city of Saavedra, while I live and work in a small abbey in the mountains some distance away. With my helpers at the abbey we collect information from those who are talented enough to be visited by forewarnings. We regularly provide those bits of prophecy to the bishop in order to help him in the decisions he must make in his capacity as the ruler of our land. Of course, if we uncover especially significant omens we immediately inform the bishop. Those are the only times I actually see him."

Zedd rolled his hand, impatient to get to the heart of the matter. "So this bishop . . ."

"Hannis Arc."

"Yes, Hannis Arc. He is a religious man, then? He rules as a leader of a theological sect?"

Ludwig shook his head as if fearing he had yet again given the wrong impression. "The title 'bishop' is purely ceremonial."

"So then this is not a religious rule devoted to the Creator?" Zedd asked.

Ludwig looked from face to face. "We do not worship the Creator. It is not possible to worship the Creator directly. We respect the Creator, appreciate the life He has given us, but we do not worship Him. That would be rather presumptuous on our part. He is everything, we are nothing. He does not communicate with the world of life in so simplistic a fashion as to speak directly to us, or to hear our pleas.

"Hannis Arc is the inspirational leader of Fajin Province. He is our guiding light, you might say, not a religious leader. His word is law in Saavedra and other cities as well as the rest of our province."

"If his word is law," Kahlan asked, "then what need has he of predictions from your abbey? I mean, if he depends on the utterances of people who are possessed by a vision, then he doesn't really rule, now does he?"

"Mother Confessor?"

"If he looks to people who provide visions, then he is not really the leader of Fajin Province; those who provide the visions are the ones whose word is really law. They direct him with the visions." Kahlan arched an eyebrow. "Isn't that right?"

Ludwig twiddled with the hat on his thumbs. "Well, I don't—"

"That would make you the ruler of Fajin Province," she said.

Ludwig vigorously shook his head. "No, Mother Confessor, that is not the way it works."

"Then how does it work?" she asked.

"The Creator does not speak to us in the world of life directly. We are not worthy of such common communication. The only people who hear the voice of the Creator are those who are deluded.

"But from time to time He does give us guidance through prophecy. The Creator is all-knowing. He knows everything that has ever happened; He knows everything that will ever happen. Prophecy is how He speaks to us, how He helps us. Since He already knows everything that will happen, He reveals some of those future events through omens."

Kahlan's expression had gone blank, a Confessor's face, a visage Richard knew well.

"So," she said, "the Creator gives people these visions so that they will cut their children's throats?"

Ludwig looked from Kahlan, to Richard, and back to Kahlan. "Perhaps He wanted to spare them a worse end. Perhaps He was doing them a kindness."

"If He is everything, and we are nothing, then why didn't He simply intervene and prevent that grisly end from visiting the children?"

"Because we are nothing. We are beneath Him. We cannot expect Him to intervene on our behalf."

"But He intervenes to give prophecy."

"That's right."

"Then He is intervening on our behalf."

Ludwig nodded reluctantly. "But it is in a more general sense. That is why we all must heed prophecy."

"Ah, I see." Kahlan said. She leaned in, tapping a finger on the marble table. "So you would have been pleased had that woman today murdered me, because of prophecy that you believe is the divine revelation of the Creator. You are therefore sorry that I am alive."

The man's face lost its color. "I am simply a humble servant, Mother Confessor, gathering what I can for the bishop."

"So that he can use what you provide to intervene on behalf of the Creator?" Kahlan asked. "Much like that woman today used prophecy as an excuse to slit the throats of her children."

Ludwig's eyes darted between Richard, Kahlan, and the floor. "He only uses the omens we give him to guide him. They are only a tool. For example, we had people who predicted that this joyous gathering would be marred by tragedy. I believe Hannis Arc did not want to see the palace, after such a victory as we all had, visited by a tragedy, so he chose not to come. We only provided him with our best information. He is the one who chooses what he will do with that information."

"So he sent you," Richard said.

Ludwig swallowed before answering. "I hoped that if I came to the palace I would learn from those experts here more about prophecy, about what our future holds. The bishop thought it would be valuable for me to come for this reason, to learn what prophecy reveals for us all."

Kahlan had the man fixed in a green-eyed glare. "Maybe while you're here you can visit the graves of those two children who were not allowed the chance to live life, to see what the future actually held for them. Their lives were cut short by a woman who relied on visions of the future to make her decisions for her."

Ludwig broke her gaze and looked down. "Yes, Mother Confessor."

The man clearly didn't agree, but he was not going to argue. He had been full of bluster at the reception when he thought that others were with him in his belief about the overriding importance of prophecy, and that the palace itself supported that belief, but now, in the presence of those who would question his beliefs, his courage was failing him.

"What can you tell me about a woman named Jit?" Richard asked.

Ludwig looked up at the change in subject. "Jit?"

Richard could see in the man's eyes that he knew the name. "Yes, Jit. The Hedge Maid."

Ludwig stared at Richard for a moment without blinking. "Well, not much I'm afraid," he finally said in a weak voice.

"Where does she live?"

"I can't recall." Ludwig ran his fingers over his upturned collar. "I'm not sure."

"I was told that she lives in Kharga Trace. Kharga Trace is in Fajin Province, isn't it?"

"Kharga Trace? Yes, yes it is." His tongue darted out to wet his lips. "Now that you mention it, I believe that I do recall that she lives in Kharga Trace."

Richard watched Ludwig's gaze wander off. "Tell me about her. About this woman, Jit."

The abbot looked back at Richard. "I don't know much about her, Lord Rahl."

"Does she provide predictions for you?"

Ludwig shook his head, eager to discourage the notion. "No, no she doesn't do that sort of thing."

"Then what sort of things does she do?"

The man gestured with his hat. "Well, she lives in a very inhospitable place. She provides cures to some of the people in the more remote areas. Simple things, I believe. Potions and concoctions, I think. But not many people live in Kharga Trace. Like I said, it's a harsh and forbidding place."

"But people travel there from other places in the Dark Lands to see her for these cures?" Richard asked.

Ludwig worked his hat around and around in his fingers. "I wouldn't really know, Lord Rahl. I don't have any dealings with her. I can't say for certain. But people are superstitious. I guess that some believe in the things she offers."

"But she doesn't offer prophecy."

"No, not prophecy. At least, not that I know of, anyway. Like I say, I don't know much about her." He gestured to the windows. "Not like you, Lord Rahl. Your prediction proved true. That's quite a blizzard coming up on us. As you predicted, I don't think anyone will be venturing out across the Azrith Plain for a few days at least."

Richard glanced to the windows. They shook as gales of wind rattled snow and sleet against the glass. It was going to be a cold, black night.

He looked back at the abbot. "You leave prophecy to those of us here at the palace. Do you understand?"

The man paused a moment to consider his words. "Lord Rahl, I am not visited by predictions of the future. I have no ability. I only report what I hear from those who do. I suppose that you could silence me if you wished to do so, but that will not silence visions of the future. The future will be upon us whether we are willing or not.

"There will always be omens of future events. Those who have visions of it will reveal those visions whether we want to hear them or not."

Richard let out a deep breath. "I guess you're right about that, Abbot Dreier."

O ut in the corridor, as Ludwig was leaving, Richard spotted Nicci coming their way. With her black dress and long blond hair flowing out behind her she looked like nothing so much as a vengeful spirit come among them to vent her wrath. She glanced at the abbot as he hurried past her. Ludwig deliberately didn't look at the sorceress on his way by, as if fearing that if he did she might bring lightning down on him. Such a thing wasn't entirely out of the realm of possibility.

Richard thought that there were few things as dangerous-looking as a stunningly beautiful woman who was angry, and Nicci looked very angry. He wondered why.

"What's the matter?" he asked as she came to a halt.

She clenched her jaw a moment before she spoke.

"I've been dealing with fools."

"What do you mean?" Kahlan asked.

Nicci aimed a thumb back the way she had come. "All they want to hear about is prophecy. They want know what the future holds, what prophecy says. They think we're privy to the secrets of the future and we're withholding those secrets from them."

Kahlan glanced over at Richard as she asked, "Who, exactly, are you talking about?"

Nicci pulled thick locks of blond hair back over her shoulder. "Those people." She flicked a hand back the way she'd come. "You know, the representatives from the different lands. After the reception nearly all of them sought me out wanting to know what I knew about prophecy and what it had to say about their future. They wanted to know about the omen that caused the woman to kill her children.

"They think we know all about the prophecy behind the vision the woman had and that we're keeping that information from them. They want to know what other dire omens we're withholding from them."

Kahlan nodded. "I know what you mean. They were all of a mind to hear prophecy from us as well."

Richard raked his fingers back through his hair. "As much as I don't like it, and as angry as it makes me, I guess that it's to be expected from people who have just heard that a woman killed her children to spare them what she says she saw in a vision."

Zedd pushed his hands up the opposite sleeves of his robes. "People can't help fearing such grim warnings. They fear to believe that they're true, fear what it will mean in their lives, and so, in the grip of that fear, they believe such things. We can try to reason with people—Richard and Kahlan both did so—but overcoming fear is hard to do, especially after hearing of a vision so fearsome that it would cause a woman to murder her children because of it."

"I suppose," Nicci said. Her blue eyes flashed anger again. "But that doesn't mean I have to like it. All because of what a crazy woman says."

"I didn't see you at the reception," Richard said. "Where did you hear about her killing her children?"

Nicci frowned up at him. "Hear about it? I was there."

"There? What do you mean you were there?"

Nicci folded her arms and stared at him as if he were the one who was crazy. "I was there. I was down in the market helping to get people organized and hurrying them along to move into the passages in the plateau and out of what is shaping up to be a monstrous storm. They need to move into shelter. Those tents aren't going to protect them."

"That's true enough."

Nicci sighed as she shook her head. "So, I was down there in the market when the first one hit."

The creases in Richard's brow deepened. "What do you mean, when the first one hit? First what?"

"Richard, aren't you listening? I was there when the first child hit the ground."

Richard's jaw dropped. "What?"

"It was a girl, not ten years old. She came down on a log wagon, on one of the upright stake poles. That pole was bigger than my leg. She came down face-first, shrieking all the way. It went right through her chest. People were screaming and running around in confusion and panic."

Richard blinked, trying to makes sense of what he was hearing. "What girl are you talking about?"

Nicci looked at all the faces watching her. "The girl that the woman threw off the palace wall, over the edge of the plateau, after she had her vision."

Richard turned to Benjamin. "I thought you said you found the children."

"I did. We found both of them."

"Both?" Nicci's brow drew tight. "There were four of them. All four of her children hit within seconds of one another. The first, the girl, was the oldest. When the woman threw them off the top of the plateau they all landed right there near me. Like I said, I was there. It was a horrifying scene."

Kahlan seized a fistful of Nicci's dress at her shoulder. "She killed four more?"

Nicci didn't try to remove Kahlan's hand. "Four more? What are you talking about? She killed her four children."

Kahlan pulled Nicci closer. "She had two children."

"Kahlan, she had four."

Kahlan's hand slipped from Nicci's dress. "Are you sure?"

Nicci shrugged. "Yes. She told me so herself when I questioned her. She even told me their names. If you don't believe me you can ask her yourself. I have her locked up in a cell down in the dungeon."

Zedd leaned in closer. "Locked up . . . ?"

"Wait a minute," Richard said. "You're telling me that this woman killed her four children by throwing them off the side of the plateau? And you locked her up?"

"Of course. Haven't you been listening to anything I've said?" Nicci frowned around at everyone. "I thought you said that you knew all about it. Her husband found out what had happened and was going to kill her. He was screaming for her blood. I was afraid that the guards who grabbed the woman were going to let him have her. I sympathize with his feelings, but I couldn't allow it for now. I had her locked up, instead, because I thought you or Kahlan would want to question her."

Richard was incredulous. "Why did she do it? What did she say?"

Nicci appraised them all as if they had collectively gone

mad. "She said that she had a vision and couldn't stand the thought of her children having to face the terror to come, so she killed them swiftly instead. You said that you knew about it."

"We knew about the other one," Richard said.

"Other one?" Nicci looked from face to face, finally settling on Richard. "What other one?"

"The one who cut her two children's throats and then came to the reception and tried to kill Kahlan."

Nicci's concerned gaze darted to Kahlan. "Are you all right?"

"I'm fine. I took her with my power and had her confess. She told us what she had done and what she intended to do."

Nicci pressed her fingers to her forehead. "Wait, you're saying that there was a second woman who also had a vision and killed her children?"

Kahlan and Richard both nodded.

"That would help explain why people are so unnerved and want to know what prophecy has to say about it," Richard said.

"What's going on?" Nicci asked.

"I don't know, yet." Richard rested the palm of his left hand on his sword. "We saw a sick boy down in the market this morning who said that there is darkness in the palace, and then a blind woman who said that the roof is going to fall in."

Nicci reflexively glanced up. "The roof?"

Richard nodded. "Yes, and some other things that make just as little sense."

Nicci's troubled blue eyes turned to Richard. "When I asked the woman what her vision had been, she said that she couldn't let her children live to face what will happen after the roof falls in."

"That makes three people who have said that very thing."

"Three?"

"Yes." Richard tapped the hilt of his sword with a thumb as his mind raced down all the various dark paths, trying to think of where they could be leading. "Besides the blind woman, a fortune-teller told me the same thing. That makes three people who said it. Plus the book."

With a finger on the side of his chin, Nicci turned his face back toward her. "Book?"

"Nathan found a book, *End Notes*, that says those very words—that the roof is going to fall in—and a number of the other strange things I've heard today."

"I know the book, *End Notes*." Nicci folded her arms as she appraised Kahlan's eyes and then looked back at Richard. "Strange things. Like what?"

"Nathan took me to see another woman a while ago about her predictions. She said that the sky is going to fall in. 'Sky' is not the same as 'roof,' but it does have a certain similar ring to it. Then she told me another prediction, and that one, word for word, is in the same book. But it makes no sense."

"What did this woman say that's also in the book?"

"Actually, she wrote it down a day or two back. She writes down all her predictions. She fancies herself a prophet. It said 'Queen takes pawn.' Like I said, it makes no sense."

Nicci didn't look at all mystified. "It's a move in chess."

Richard couldn't help frowning again. "Chess? What's that?"

"It's an obscure, little-known game."

"Never heard of it." He looked around at the others. None of them had ever heard the word, either. "What is it? Something played with a ball, like Ja'La?"

Nicci waved off the notion. "No, nothing like that. Chess is a board game. It has a variety of pieces, like a queen, king, bishop, pawn—things like that. Queen takes pawn is a move in the game. It means what it sounds like. The queen captures a pawn, removing it from play, killing it, I guess you could say."

Zedd let out a frustrated sigh. "I've never heard of such a game."

"Like I said, it's pretty obscure. As far as I know it's only played in a few remote places."

"What places?" Richard asked.

"Well, for one, Fajin Province." Nicci gestured back down the hall yet again. "In the Dark Lands, where the abbot is from."

Richard looked off down the hall, almost as if he thought he might see the abbot.

"By the way," Nicci said, "what were you doing with the little weasel?"

"I was asking him about a Hedge Maid."

Nicci rammed the heel of her hand into his chest, driving Richard up against the wall. Fury flashed in her blue eyes.

She gritted her teeth. "What did you say?"

Richard took hold of her wrist and removed her hand from his chest. The angry glare remained firmly in place.

"I wanted to know about a Hedge Maid named Jit. She lives in a place called Kharga Trace in Fajin Province. Why?"

Nicci held a finger up right in front of his face. "You listen to me, Richard Rahl. You stay away from Hedge Maids. Do you understand me? Stay away. You have no defense against a Hedge Maid. None of us do. You stay away from her. Their magic is different than any of ours. Not even your sword would protect you from them."

"You mean she might try to do us harm?"

"Hedge Maids are vipers. If you leave them lie under their

rock they're not likely to bother you, but if you go poking at them in their hidey-hole they'll come out and kill you in a heartbeat. Hedge Maids deal in occult powers. Stay away from her. Do you hear me?"

"Well I don't know that—"

"It would be best if you never breathed her name again." Nicci shoved him against the wall again to make her point. "Do you understand me!"

Richard rubbed the back of his head where it had smacked the wall. "No, not really. What's a Hedge Maid?"

Nicci let her hand drop. Her eyes went out of focus as she stared off.

"A Hedge Maid is an evil, nasty, dirty, wicked, foul, vile being, an oracle who trades in the darkest kinds of suffering and depravity. Everything they do revolves around death."

"How do you know this Jit?"

"I don't. But I know all too well what a Hedge Maid is."

"And how do you know what they are?"

Her blue eyes cooled as they turned up to focus on his face. Her deadly words came in little more than a whisper. "Do you forget so easily that I was once a Sister of the Dark? Do you forget that I was once committed to the Keeper of the underworld? Do you forget that I was once Death's Mistress?"

CHAPTER
16

"H ow's your hand?" Richard asked.

Kahlan turned from peeking out around the edge of the drapes where she had been watching the storm rage. It was so black outside that she could see only small patches near the light coming from some of the windows that looked out on the vast palace complex. The windows higher up on walls and in towers looked like dots of lights floating in midair, assailed by sideways slashes of snow.

She could see that the blizzard had piled up huge drifts of the wet, heavy snow. At times the snow turned to sleet, only to once more shift the world back to white chaos.

She lifted her hand out to Richard, holding it under the light of the lamp on the bedside table. The scratches left by the boy had turned to an angry red. It hurt a little but she didn't want to say so. Where she was concerned, Richard was a dedicated worrier; she didn't need to stoke those fires.

He took her hand and inspected it in the lamplight. He let out a grumbling noise. "It looks swollen."

"It's a little red," she said, taking the hand back, "but I don't think it's doing too badly. It's normal for scratches to get this way as they heal. How about yours?"

He lifted his hand to show her. "Mine looks about the same. I don't think they look any worse than can be expected."

"Not the worst problem of the day."

"Not by a long shot," Richard agreed.

He went to one of the cabinets to look for something. He finally pulled out his pack.

Kahlan smiled. "I haven't seen that for a while."

"It has been a while since we traveled anywhere. Maybe we should. Zedd wants us to visit him when he returns to the Keep."

"I would like to see Aydindril and spend some time at the Confessors' Palace again. It would be good to see the city doing well after all it's been through."

But she knew that they would not be going to Aydindril to see the Wizard's Keep or the Confessors' Palace anytime soon. Innocent people were dying. Whatever the cause, Kahlan could feel in the pit of her stomach that it was going to overshadow everything else. She wanted to scream against the unseen darkness that was descending on them, but that would do no good.

Richard closed the cabinet door. "With all that's going on I don't know that Zedd is going to want to be returning to the Keep before we figure out what's happening and get it resolved. I'm glad we have him here to help us."

Kahlan watched as Richard lifted the baldric over his head and then propped his sword against the bedside table. He set his pack on the bed and started rooting around inside. She couldn't imagine what he was looking for. With a smile he at last brought up a small tin. It made her smile, too, seeing it again.

He gestured to the edge of the bed. "Come and sit."

As she did, Richard dabbed his finger in the tin and then

lifted her hand. He gently smoothed some of the herb salve along the scratches. It felt cool and immediately started to quell the ache.

"Better?"

"Better," she said with a smile.

It had been years since she had seen that tin of healing cream that Richard had made from aum, among other things. Having grown up in the woods, he knew about plants and how to make cures from them. After he spread some of the ointment on his own red scratches, he replaced the tin in his pack.

So much had happened since she had first met him in his woodland home. Both their lives had completely changed. The world had been turned upside down as it went through a nightmare war. She couldn't count the times she had thought that she would never see him again, or feared he was going to die, or worse, thought that he had been killed. The terror had seemed as if it would never end.

It finally had. They had not just survived but after years of struggle they had won the war and brought peace to the world.

But now the world felt like it was again slipping into darkness.

Sitting on the edge of the bed, Kahlan took up his good hand and held it to the side of her face. She hid her silent tears against his hand.

Richard gently ran his hand through her hair as he pulled her head against him.

"I know," he said softly. "I know."

Kahlan put her arms around his waist. "Promise me that you won't let whatever is coming take you from me?"

Richard bent and kissed the top of her head. "I promise."

"A wizard always keeps his promises," she reminded him.

"I know," he said with a smile.

Everything was going so well. They had fought for so long, suffered so much. It wasn't fair that something was coming for them again, but she knew it was. And she knew that Richard knew the same thing. He held her to him as she gave in to weakness and wept. She never let anyone but Richard see that weakness.

"What are we doing in this room?" he finally asked.

"Just trying to keep us away from prying eyes."

"So you sensed someone watching you, earlier?"

She shrugged, still holding him. "I don't know, Richard. It seemed like I did, but I couldn't be sure. It sounded so creepy when Cara told us about it. Maybe I was just imagining it."

She looked up at him and laughed through her tears. "But if you think I'm taking off my clothes tonight, Lord Rahl, you have another think coming."

Richard lay back on the bed. Kahlan crawled up and snuggled up to him, putting her head on his shoulder.

"Just hold me," she whispered. "Please?"

He circled his arm around her and kissed the top of her head.

She wiped at her tears. "I can't remember the last time I cried."

After a long moment, he said, "I can."

She pressed herself into him. She couldn't believe that she really had him, that he was really hers, that he really and truly loved her.

She couldn't believe that she was going to lose him to darkness seeking darkness.

17

Kahlan woke to the distinctive sound of Richard's sword coming out of the scabbard. The clear ring of the Sword of Truth's steel brought her wide awake and brought her heart rate up.

She lifted her head from his shoulder. "What is it?"

Richard had the sword gripped in a fist above her. He shushed her as he gently, carefully slipped out from under her loose embrace. It was a bewitchingly fluid movement that ended with him standing silent and still beside the bed looking into the darkness.

Kahlan expected that at any moment something might fly at him out of that darkness. Nothing did.

"What is it?" she whispered.

"Do you feel like someone is watching us?" he asked back over his shoulder.

"I don't know. I was sound asleep."

"You're awake now."

Kahlan sat up. "I don't know, Richard. I could convince myself that I do, but I don't know if it's real or just my imagination."

Richard stared off at the darkness at the end of the room. "It's real."

That made Kahlan's heart beat even faster. She inched closer to him, making sure to stay out of the way of his sword in case he needed to use it.

"Can you tell what it is?"

His muscles relaxed. "It's gone."

Kahlan squinted, trying to see better in the dimly lit bedroom. "You mean it's gone like maybe you were imagining it and now you realized as much?"

Richard turned to her. "No, I mean that when I deliberately looked back at it, it left. It was there. I have no doubt of it."

The tension might have gone out of his muscles, but she recognized all too well the rage that still lit his eyes. It was the magic of the Sword of Truth he was gripping tightly in his fist. It was the righteous rage of the Seeker.

Kahlan could hear distant thunder. She rubbed her arms against the chill. "Who, or what, could do such a thing? I mean, who could look in at us that way?"

"I haven't any idea. Zedd didn't know either."

Richard slid the sword back into the gold and silver scabbard he was holding in his other hand. As the sword slipped back into its lair, the anger faded from his gray eyes.

Richard lifted the sword's baldric over his head and let it rest on his right shoulder while Kahlan went to the window and drew the drapes aside enough to peek outside. "It's light out."

"What about the storm?"

"Looks like it's worse. You're quite the prophet."

"Great," Richard muttered. "Now all the representatives get to stay around and badger us about prophecy some more."

"They're just worried, Richard. You have to admit, something is going on. They're not stupid. They know it too. You are the Lord Rahl. They look to you to protect them from things they don't understand and fear."

"I suppose," he said as he turned to a knock on the door.

After pulling on his boots he went to the door and looked out. Kahlan could seen Nathan down the hall talking to Benjamin. Cara had been the one who knocked. She was wearing her red leather and a grim expression. When Nathan and Benjamin saw Richard and Kahlan they hurried over.

"You look like you slept in that dress," Cara said as Kahlan joined Richard at the door.

"I'm afraid that I did."

"Ah," Cara said with knowing nod. "So it was in your room, watching you again."

"I don't like the idea of taking off my clothes in front of prying eyes."

"Did you and Benjamin sense anyone watching you in your room again last night?" Richard asked Cara.

"No, and I was waiting for them. They never showed up so I guess it was looking for you, as you suspected, and not us. It was quiet all night—until this morning, anyway."

"Why, what happened this morning?" Kahlan asked.

Nathan leaned forward, impatient to get down to business. "Do you remember the stocky regent in the red tunic, the one at the reception yesterday who wanted to know if there is some prophetic event lying ahead for us?"

Richard yawned. "The regent who said that our future is rooted in the past and part of that past is prophecy? All that roundabout nonsense?"

"That's the one."

Richard wiped a weary hand across his face. "He was pretty insistent about how everyone is eager to hear my insight on prophecy and what the future holds for us. I suppose he can't wait for me to meet with him and the others so that I can reveal the future to them."

"Not exactly," Nathan said. "He had a vision of his own early this morning."

Richard straightened with a suspicious look. "I didn't know that any of the representatives were gifted with even a little talent for such things."

Nathan leaned closer. "He's not. That's the strange thing. His aides said that the regent had never before given any kind of prophecy. They said that he was always fascinated by it, and sought out people who claimed to be able to foretell the future, but he had never shown any ability for it himself."

"So what was this important prophecy of his?"

"He said only that he'd had a vision."

"But he didn't reveal this vision, didn't say what he saw?" Kahlan asked.

"No. He only told his aides that he'd seen what the future holds. They say that he was a talkative man, but after saying he'd had a vision he was unusually quiet and seemed distracted."

"If he didn't reveal the nature of his prophecy, then what's so meaningful about it?" Richard wiped a hand across his face. "For that matter, how do we even know that he's telling the truth?"

"We don't, I suppose, but after he told his aides that he'd had this vision, he walked outside into the teeth of the storm, still dressed in his bedclothes, and jumped off the side of the plateau."

"He killed himself?" Richard gaped at the prophet. "With no word on the nature of his vision?"

"No word at all," Nathan confirmed.

Richard drew a deep breath as he considered the regent's sad end. "Well, I guess Cara was right, it was an eventful morning."

"I'm afraid that's not all, Lord Rahl," Benjamin said. "After the regent's inexplicable behavior, and considering the two women yesterday who killed their children after having a vision, I suggested to Nathan that we ought to go check on anyone else he knew of who showed any history of visions, even if it was only a minor ability."

Richard looked back at Nathan. "There are others?"

Nathan shrugged. "I hardly know everyone living at the palace. There's no telling how many people might have had small premonitions. I do know of a man, though, who from time to time claims to foresee future events. I've never tested him so I have no idea if he really can, if he's telling the truth. But considering recent events I thought we'd best pay him a visit."

Richard nodded as he considered. "That makes sense."

"When we got to his quarters," Benjamin said, taking up the story, "we heard screams coming from inside. We broke in the door and saw that the man had his wife down on the floor. He was straddling her. She was struggling mightily trying to fight him off. The man had a knife in his fist, trying to kill her. Three young children were huddled in the corner, crying in terror, waiting their turn to be murdered, I believe."

Nathan gestured to head off making more drama of the story than he apparently thought it warranted. "Nothing had happened, yet. As the man held his knife up in the air to strike, I used a quick bit of magic, that's all, throwing him off the woman so that he would be unable to carry out his intentions. The general and some of his men rushed in and disarmed him."

"So then no one was hurt?" Kahlan asked.

"No," Nathan said. "We got there in time to prevent another tragedy."

Kahlan let out her breath. "That's a relief."

"So this man had also had a vision?"

Nathan nodded. "He's a jewelry maker. He told us that he had a vision that men are going to come to his house to rob him but he won't be there. In this vision, the thieves torture his wife and children, trying to get them to reveal where the gold he uses to make jewelry is hidden. They don't know. The men don't believe them and over a period of hours torture his family to death, one at a time, trying to make them talk. The man insisted that he could not bear to allow such a horrific thing to happen to his family, that it was better to kill them quickly than let them endure the agony they would otherwise suffer."

Richard looked puzzled. "That's not at all like the other prophecies."

"We have him locked up, if you want to question him," Benjamin said.

Richard nodded, lost in thought.

The general hooked a thumb behind his weapons belt. "There is something else, Lord Rahl."

Richard looked up. "What else?"

Benjamin took a deep breath. "Well, my men managed to get all the people and their animals down on the plain into the plateau before the worst of the storm descended on us last night. While the last of them were being ushered inside, the men conducted a wide sweep, wanting to make sure that they didn't miss anyone, that no one was left behind or got lost in the storm to freeze to death in one of those flimsy market tents.

"While they were scouting they found a boy who had been dragged off and killed. He was maybe ten, no older."

"Killed?" Richard asked. "What do you mean he was dragged off? How was he killed?"

The general didn't shrink from the question. "He'd been partially eaten, Lord Rahl."

Richard blinked in surprise. "Eaten?"

"Yes, Lord Rahl. His insides had all been eaten out. His face had been chewed off. The skull had long gouge marks from teeth. One arm and the other hand were missing. Animals had feasted on him, tore him open, and mostly ate out his innards."

Richard sagged a little at the news. "A small boy, out in the storm, lost, away from people, would be easy prey for wolves, or even a pack of coyotes. It was probably Henrik, the sick boy I talked to, the one who ran off."

"My men took account of everyone we herded inside. We were still trying to find the boy you had talked to. We talked to his mother. She told us that her boy hadn't come back. She was worried sick."

"That must have been him, then—the dead boy you found."

Benjamin was shaking his head before Richard had finished. "That was our thought, too, but it wasn't him. We described the clothes to the mother. She said that wasn't what Henrik wore. A little later a man came to us for help. He was looking frantically for his boy. My men asked what he was wearing. The man described the dead boy's clothes perfectly."

Richard pressed his lips together in regret. "Then that means that the sick boy, Henrik, is lost out there on the Azrith Plain. In this storm he's frozen to death by now. If a pack of wolves didn't take him first."

18

It was a long journey down to the dungeons, but it was something Richard had to do. He needed to question the woman who had thrown her four children to their death. He needed to try to figure out what was happening.

Kahlan had gone instead to meet with the representatives to try to calm their concerns about prophecy while Richard was looking into the source of those concerns. Richard's flip tongue had more than once gotten him into trouble. Kahlan would be less likely to get frustrated with them than he would. She had been schooled in diplomacy.

He wished that Verna, the Prelate of the Sisters of the Light, could have gone with Kahlan to help explain the dangers of a layperson inferring anything from prophecy. Prophecy was not at all as clear as it sounded. That was because it was not intended for those who weren't gifted. It was actually a kind of private message passed down from prophets in the past. Only a prophet could have the visions a true prophecy engendered and in that way understand its true meaning.

Verna knew a great deal about those dangers. After all, the Sisters of the Light had imprisoned Nathan in the Palace of the Prophets for nearly a thousand years out of fear that he would reveal prophecy to ordinary people.

Verna could have helped dissuade people from thinking they could properly understand prophecy. Unfortunately, along with Chase and his family, she had left for the Wizard's Keep immediately after Cara's wedding. There were gifted boys there who needed supervision and training. Zedd was supposed to return as well, but he had wanted to stay for the reception, and now the storm and troubling events had further delayed him.

As Richard stepped off the rusty iron rungs of the ladder, the captain of the dungeon guards straightened and clapped a fist to his heart in salute. Richard dipped his head in response. He glanced around in the flickering torchlight as he brushed grit off his hands. At least the smell of burning pitch helped cover the stench.

The captain looked worried to see the Lord Rahl himself down in his dungeon. His level of concern eased a bit when he saw Nyda come down the ladder. The tall Mord-Sith's red leather outfit and blond hair stood out in stark contrast to the dank, drab stone room. The captain flashed a polite smile at Nyda as he nodded in greeting. He obviously knew her.

Richard realized that Mord-Sith were hardly strangers to dungeons, especially this one. In the past, enemies, real or imagined, would have been held in these dungeons and Mord-Sith would have come to torture information out of those with the gift.

Having once been one of those prisoners, Richard knew all about it.

He gestured to the iron door. "I want to see the woman who killed her children."

"And the man who tried to kill his family?"

"Yes, him too," Richard said.

The captain worked a big key in the door. The lock resisted for a moment, but after the latch clanged open, the man yanked the heavy iron door open enough to slip through. After hooking the keys on his belt, he took a lantern from a table and led the way into the inner dungeon. In a well-practiced sweep of her arm, Nyda took another lantern off an iron peg in the wall.

Before Richard could go through the door, she stepped in front of him and went in first. He was quite familiar with Mord-Sith's insistence on going first so they could check for danger. He had long ago learned that his life was easier if he let them have their way and didn't argue with them over such minor issues. He saved commands for times when they really mattered. Because of that, the Mord-Sith heeded his commands.

The captain led them down a series of narrow passageways that in most places had been carved out of solid rock. Even after thousands of years, the chisel marks looked as fresh as when they had first been cut through the stone.

They passed cell doors behind which criminals were held. Up ahead, in the light of the captain's lantern, Richard saw fingers sticking out, gripping the edges of tiny openings in the iron doors. He saw eyes looking out through some of the black openings. When the prisoners saw Nyda coming behind the captain, the fingers withdrew and the eyes disappeared back into the blackness. No one called out. No one wanted to draw her attention.

At the end of a particularly narrow, crooked passageway with doors spaced farther apart, the captain came to a halt at a cell on the left. There were no fingers in the opening, no eyes looking out. When the heavy door was pulled open, Richard saw the reason. The outer door opened not into a cell, but into a small inner room with another door. The second, smaller door held the prisoner in an inner room.

The man used a long sliver of fatwood to transfer a flame from his lantern to a second hanging on an iron peg. "These are the shielded cells," the captain said in answer to the question on Richard's face.

Even though the palace had been constructed in the form of a power spell that strengthened the gift of any Rahl, and weakened that of others, the shields around the cells were an extra layer of protection to contain anyone gifted, no matter how powerful they were. No chances were taken with the gifted.

The captain lifted his lantern to look in the small opening in the second door. When he was sure that the prisoner wasn't going to spring at him, he unlocked the door. He used all his weight to pull on the door. Rusty hinges squealed in protest as they gave ground. When the door had been opened enough for Richard to enter, the captain went back out in the hall to wait.

Nyda, Agiel in her fist, entered first. The woman, sitting on the floor, scrambled backward until her back was pressed against the far wall. She didn't have far to go. She shaded her eyes from the sudden intrusion of light. She didn't look at all dangerous. Except to her children.

"Tell me about your vision," Richard said.

The woman looked at Nyda and then back to him. "Which vision? I have had many."

That wasn't what Richard had been expecting to hear. "The vision you had that made you kill your children."

The woman's eyes reflected points of lamplight. She didn't answer.

"Your four children. You threw them over the edge of the cliff. You killed them. Tell me about the vision that you thought was cause enough to do such a thing."

"My children are safe now. They are in the hands of the good spirits."

Richard stuck his arm out in time to bar Nyda from stepping in to ram her Agiel into the woman. "Don't do that," he said softly to her.

"Lord Rahl—"

"I said don't do it."

He had no sympathy for the woman, but he didn't want her tortured with an Agiel, either.

Nyda briefly glared at him before pointing her Agiel at the woman. "Answer the question or I will spend some time alone with you making sure that you don't ever fail to answer any of Lord Rahl's questions again."

The woman's eyes turned toward him. "Lord Rahl?"

"That's right: Lord Rahl. Now answer his question."

"What vision did you have that made you kill your children?" Richard repeated.

"I have no children, thanks to you!" The woman held one arm out protectively, expecting the Agiel.

Richard planted a boot on the bench carved out of the solid stone of the cell wall. He rested an elbow on his knee as he leaned toward the woman. "What are you talking about?"

"You won't protect us from what is to come when the roof falls in. You instead scorn prophecy's warnings." The woman lifted her chin defiantly. "Those children, at least, no longer have to fear what is to happen."

"And what is going to happen?"

"Terrible things!"

"What terrible things?"

The woman opened her mouth to tell him. She seemed surprised to realize that she had nothing to say.

"Terrible things, that's all," she finally said.

"I want you to tell me about the terrible things that are going to happen," Richard said.

She blinked in confusion. "I, I don't . . ."

She unexpectedly clutched her throat as she slumped to the dark stone floor, where she convulsed once before going still.

Richard turned to someone behind him as his right hand went to the hilt of his sword.

There was no one there.

"What's the matter?" Nyda asked as she turned, looking for a threat.

Richard glanced around. "I thought I felt something, but I guess it's just the nature of this place."

He bent to the woman. Her lips were covered in red froth. It was all too obvious that she was dead.

"Well, isn't that something," Nyda said. "You should have let me use my Agiel. If you had, we might have gotten answers."

"I don't want you using that thing on people unless it's absolutely necessary."

She regarded him with the singular, menacing look that all Mord-Sith seemed to be able to conjure at will. Richard knew that it was an aspect born in madness. He knew because he had once been lost in their world.

"It was necessary," she said. "There is a growing threat to you. It is foolish to hesitate or to shy away from doing what is necessary to prevent that threat from harming you. If it harms you, it harms all of us. What threatens you threatens us all."

Richard didn't argue. He thought that maybe she was right. "I think that if you had used your Agiel she would have simply dropped dead right then."

"Now we'll never ever know."

Richard held his tongue. He wasn't in the mood to argue about what was done and over and couldn't be changed. He instead turned away from the dead woman and stepped over the high doorsill to the waiting captain.

"The woman is dead. Take me to see the man who was put in here this morning, the jeweler, before he too drops dead."

The captain glanced through the open door, perhaps expecting to see blood, then gestured. "It's the cell down there, Lord Rahl, across the way."

In short order he had the outer door unlocked and the key turning the lock of the second door. After looking through the small hole in the door, he pulled it open.

Nyda cut in front of Richard and went in ahead of him, lantern in one hand and Agiel at the ready in the other.

"You bastard!" the man cried as he went for Richard when he stepped inside.

Nyda's Agiel caught him across the throat. He fell back with a shriek, pressing his hands to his throat as he gasped in agony.

This time Richard didn't protest Nyda's use of her Agiel. The man had given her ample cause.

Richard was losing his patience and didn't waste any time with formalities. "You tried to kill your family today. Why?"

"Because of what's going to happen to them, that's why." His voice was hoarse and gravelly from the lingering effects of the Agiel. His eyes bulged with anger. "It's your fault!" Blood came out with his words.

"And how do you figure it's my fault?"

The man jabbed a finger toward Richard. "Because you won't listen to prophecy." He had to swallow back the pain and blood. It was lowering his voice, but not his fury. "You think you're too important to heed prophecy. You think you know better."

"I know a great deal about prophecy," Richard said. "It isn't as simple as you seem to think."

"It is. I've had visions of the future before and they're stone simple to understand. What's more, they always come true."

"What kind of visions have you had?"

The man was still comforting his throat. His anger cooled a little. He cast a wary look at Nyda before answering.

"Things such as having a feeling that a customer I hadn't seen in a long time would come to me with a commission. He soon did. One time I was making a ring for a wealthy man, and while working on it I had a premonition that the man would die before the ring was finished. The next day the man died."

"Those are different," Richard said. "Those are small things, small foretellings. Those aren't the same thing as prophecy."

"They came true. They were foreknowledge and they came true, just as I had envisioned them."

"Having a premonition that someone is going to return for more of your work is not the same as a vision that would cause you to try to murder your family."

"Not murder! Mercy!"

The man sprang up, his hands going for Richard's throat. Nyda dropped him with her Agiel. He hunched on the floor, arms folded across his chest, gasping in shuddering pain. She put a boot on his back and leaned down close.

"If you try that again I will make you sorry you were born. After I get done with you, you will curse my very existence until the day you die, but you will behave yourself. Do you understand me?"

The man, trembling in the lingering pain from the touch of the Agiel, nodded as he panted, trying desperately to catch his breath. Nyda pushed him with her boot. He toppled back. Finally he sat up with his back against the wall, glaring at Richard.

"My family is going to suffer unimaginable torture because you keep me locked in here where I can't give them a merciful end."

"I heard all about your vision. Even if it was true, you are the one who will be responsible for their pain, either that of torture or the death you would inflict on them, all because you never stopped to think that there might be another way."

The man blinked in confusion. "Another way? What do you mean?"

"Well, let's say that you really do believe that your premonition is true, that men will come and torture your wife and children to try to make them reveal where your gold is hidden."

"It is true!"

"Fine, let's say it is. Then why didn't you do something to protect your family?"

The man swallowed, still trying to recover his breath. "Protect them?"

"Yes. If you care so much about them then why wasn't your first thought to protect them? Why wouldn't you go to someone—the First File, or Nathan the prophet, or me?"

"No one would help me. No one would believe me or be able to prevent those murdering thieves from coming and grabbing my wife and children. My family will be tortured."

"Because of you." When the man frowned at Richard, he went on, "The men in your vision want to know where your gold is hidden. Your wife and children don't know, so they can't reveal the location. The thieves don't believe them and try to torture the information out of them."

"That's right!" the man said, shaking his finger at Richard again. "They will suffer that torture and die because you don't heed the vision and see that it's true."

"No, they will suffer it because you don't believe it's true."

The man paused, confused. "But I do believe it's true."

"If you truly believed your vision was true then all you had to do was to tell your wife and children where you have your gold hidden. Tell them that it's a secret, but if anyone ever threatened to harm them, they should instead let the thieves have the gold. If you had simply done that, then you could have prevented the vision from coming to pass. Unless you value your gold more than your family?"

"No! Of course not!"

"Then why didn't you just let them know where your gold is stashed? Or else why wouldn't you think to take them away from here, away from the threat?"

The man looked genuinely confused. "I don't know."

"Why was your first thought not to protect them, but to kill them?"

The man face had gone ashen. He had no answer.

"I've had similar threats against people I love," Richard

said. "My only thought was how to protect them, how to defeat the prophecy. In the end I did. I didn't murder them."

The man's gaze fell away. His certainty, his conviction, his rage, was gone.

But then he looked up again, conviction returning to his eyes in a hot rush. "Their suffering and death will be because of you! You are keeping me locked up in here when you know what will happen. My family will suffer unimaginable agony because you won't allow me to save them from my vision by giving them a merciful death. Their suffering will be your fault.

"All because you will not do your duty to your people by heeding prophecy."

Richard didn't answer. There was no answer to madness.

The man slid his back up the wall until he was standing. He glared at Richard.

"You do not deserve to be the Lord Rahl. Soon, everyone will realize that."

CHAPTER

20

Kahlan ingratiated herself with the representatives by first laying out an elaborate midday meal. Tables around the room were covered with platters of meats, fish, fowl, and sweet delights of every sort. Other tables offered a variety of wines. Musicians played soft, soothing music while servers carrying trays of colorful, honeyed nectar drinks threaded their way through the crowds. Guests plucked the heavy-bottomed glasses containing the prized drink from the trays as the servers passed.

Gazing out at all those assembled, Kahlan felt a pang of loneliness. She wished that Richard could be there with her. She missed him. But he had work to do.

So did she.

Circulating among the milling crowd as they sampled food and wine from the different tables and drinks from trays, not taking the time to eat herself, Kahlan smiled and greeted everyone personally, thanking them for attending as she saw to their every pleasure or whim. Staff were at hand to make sure the representatives had everything they wanted.

A number of people brought up prophecy, pressing their belief that it was one of their most important tools for guiding them into the future, insisting that she and Richard would do well to be more mindful of what such predictions had to say to them all. Kahlan listened patiently, occasionally gently asking for clarifications of certain assertions.

Cara, not trusting anyone, even these leaders from around the D'Haran Empire and allies in the war, was rarely more than an arm's length away. Several times as Kahlan made her way through the room, people stopped her, wondering if the kitchens had this or that. Kahlan indulged them, immediately turning to ask the ever-attentive staff trailing not far behind to see to fulfilling the special requests.

When the elaborate luncheon finally drew to a close, she led the representatives into a nearby room where she stepped up onto a broad dais so that everyone could see her. Vanilla-colored walls decorated with intricate molding and blue carpets trimmed in gold gave the room a hushed, intimate feel.

Through a wall of double doors that led out to the terrace in the back, Kahlan could see that the storm had turned the world to white. The wind from time to time rattled the glass in the doors.

Now that people were fed and relaxed, Kahlan clasped her hands as she stood before them on the elevated platform, waiting patiently for conversations to die out and everyone's attention to turn to her. Out of the corner of her eye, she saw Nicci arrive. The sorceress glided to a halt beside a table just behind Kahlan. Tall chairs, their backs carved to look like eagles with their wings spread, chairs Richard and Kahlan had used in the past as they'd greeted petitioners, many of whom now roamed the room, sat in commanding positions behind the table. Cara, in her red leather, stood behind Kahlan to her left.

Kahlan took a deep breath and began.

"I know that many of you have concerns about the direction of the future. I have heard that you are all interested in what prophecy has to say to us about that future. A number of you have expressed those concerns to me personally in a most direct fashion. Because I recognize that all of us here are interested in insuring our common, successful future, I wanted to give everyone this opportunity to speak and air their concerns."

Kahlan waited until everyone was smiling before she went on. "You all know that there has been some trouble caused by those who think they have been visited with prophecy. Several of these people have acted on their fears in the most unforgivable way possible. You even saw one of them yesterday and heard what she had done to her children as a result of what she said was a vision of the future. Her children, unfortunately, are now dead and have no future. Prophecy obviously held no value to help them, and only resulted in their untimely deaths.

"This is why Richard isn't here with us this afternoon. He is attending to these matters along with serious issues of prophecy. As a gifted wizard and the Lord Rahl it is his responsibility to see to these issues. We all know from everything that has happened in recent years that he is more than competent to handle such matters.

"But my husband didn't want to ignore your questions and concerns, either, so he asked me to be here with you today in order to address those concerns and answer any questions you might have."

Kahlan spread her hands. "So, if anyone has anything to say, please do so now, with all of us here, so that we might clear the air and resolve the issue."

Everyone looked pleased.

Queen Orneta wasted no time. "Our concern," she said as she folded her bare, slender arms and stepped to the front of the crowd, "is that prophecy is our most important guide."

"Prophecy is not our most important guide," Kahlan said. "Reason is our most important guide."

With a flick of her hand the queen dismissed Kahlan's view. "Prophecy reveals what must be done if our people are to prosper into the future."

"Prophecy, as you view it, reveals what will happen."

"That's right," the queen said.

"So if you believe it reveals what will happen, then it makes no difference if you know it or not. You can't change what will happen, or it would not be prophecy, but merely speculation."

The queen's gazed darkened. "Prophecy is given to help us, passed down through magic, to be our guide into the future it reveals."

"In any event," Kahlan said as she again smiled her assurance to the crowd, "as I told you, we are dealing with it. You needn't concern yourselves with the complexities of prophecy. Besides the Sisters of the Light, we have Nathan the prophet here with us helping Richard with matters of prophecy. We also have other gifted people as well, like First Wizard Zorander"—she lifted a hand back—"and sorceress Nicci. That's to say nothing of Richard himself. Right now he is seeing to such matters, as is his duty and responsibility to all of you. I can assure you, Lord Rahl takes his responsibility very seriously."

"Yes," Queen Orneta said in a tone of feigned indulgence, "so we have been told."

Kahlan shrugged. "What more would you like?"

The queen held one bony elbow as she casually fingered

her jeweled necklace with her other hand. "Mother Confessor, I want what all of us gathered here want. We've all heard dark warnings of the future. We want to know what prophecy has to say of such events."

"Let me assure you, Queen Orneta, we also take such concerns very seriously. After all, we are all on the same side and share a common interest in the future prosperity of the D'Haran Empire. Please understand, though, that prophecy is a very specialized area. Those who are gifted in it, and who have experience in dealing with it, are handling it. Everything that can be done is already being done."

The crowd fell silent, all eyes watching the broad-shouldered King Philippe from the western Midlands, as he stepped forward. He was a hero who had fought valiantly for their cause and had from early on been loyal to the newly formed D'Haran Empire. Though many others in the room were his equal in standing, even they looked up to him.

He wore a grand military-style coat in a deep mahogany color that fit his powerful frame with tailored precision. At his hip, on a broad, tooled, tan leather belt, he wore a gleaming, engraved, ceremonial sword lavishly adorned with gold and silver. It was no less a formidable weapon in his hands for all its embellishments. Kahlan knew that he was a reasoned leader, but she also knew that he had a volatile temper.

His wife, Catherine, his ever-present shadow, glided forward with him. She wore a beautiful dark green brocade dress embroidered with vibrant gold leaves. She looked stunning in the dress. Though she was a queen with as much authority as her husband, she had little interest in matters of rule.

She was also quite pregnant. Kahlan knew that this would be their first child, and they were eagerly looking forward to it now that the war was over.

King Philippe gestured around at the gathered dignitaries. "We are the leaders of the lands that make up the D'Haran Empire. Many of us here were loyal to you, Mother Confessor, before that, in the Midlands. All of our people have fought, bled, and died to help us stand here today, triumphant. They have a right, through us, to hear the shape of the future they have fought so hard to make possible. On their behalf, as their representatives, we should be informed of what prophecy has to say so we can make sure it is being heeded and not ignored."

A roar of voices rose as everyone agreed with King Philippe.

Queen Orneta, not keen to cede her informal leadership role in arguing their position, swept a skeletal arm back at the crowd, calling for silence. "Prophecy must be obeyed. What we want, Mother Confessor, is for you to reveal what prophecy says so that we may see for ourselves that you are heeding it."

"But I have just spent a great deal of time with all of you, listening to your concerns and explaining why prophecy is not meant for the uninitiated."

The queen smiled in that patronizing manner that for some queens seemed to be an inborn ability bordering on theatric gift.

"So you have," she said, glancing over at King Philippe as if telling him that he should let her do the talking. "Yet we have all heard the dark warnings from various diviners back in our homelands, those with a bit of prophetic talent. That is one reason we were all so eager to come here for this gathering. Something significant is happening—the signs are all there.

"We want to know what dark foretelling prophecy holds so that when this storm ends we might send word home to our people so they can prepare for looming dangers. Prophecy can be of no value if it is kept secret."

Kahlan straightened her back. She let the smile slip away as she put on her Confessor's face. The queen's talent at presenting an intimidating presence was no match for Kahlan's.

The crowd fell into an uneasy quiet.

"I'm not at all sure that you really want to hear prophecy."

Queen Orneta did not take the chance Kahlan had just given her to withdraw her challenge.

"Mother Confessor, every one of us here appreciated the fine meal you just served us. You are an adroit hostess, but what we really want, what we demand, is to be informed of what prophecy has to say so that we can make sure that you and Lord Rahl bow to what it tells us must be done."

"That's right." King Philippe lifted a fist to punctuate the point. "We must know that you and Lord Rahl follow what prophecy says must be done."

"Ah, so you think that we must bow to prophecy, regardless of what action prophecy calls for, even though I have explained that it is not nearly so easy to understand prophecy from the words alone? You still insist that it's the words themselves that define prophecy and that they must be heeded? Is that it? And you fear that we won't have the strength to do just that?"

A few people throughout the room shouted their agreement. Others nodded insistently. Many more all tried to speak up at the same time, saying that that was their whole point.

Kahlan nodded sorrowfully. "So, is this everyone's conviction?"

It was apparent from the outcry that it was.

"Prophecy must be served," the queen said when the clamor had died down. "It must be revealed and obeyed."

King Philippe, standing not far from Queen Orneta, folded his arms with finality, making clear his agreement.

Kahlan's glare moved from Queen Orneta to the pregnant Queen Catherine. "You, too, would choose prophecy for your unborn child? After you have seen what prophecy did to those other, innocent children? How it brought them only pain and a terrifying death?"

Catherine cast a concerned look at her husband before she stiffened her resolve and gave Kahlan a single nod. "The Creator has given us prophecy. It must be heeded, Mother Confessor."

Kahlan's gaze rose again to sweep across the crowd.

"Are you all quite sure of this?"

Everyone spoke up impatiently that they were. Some shook their fists again to reaffirm their conviction.

"Well," Kahlan said as she slowly, sorrowfully, shook her head, "I had hoped to convince you that prophecy and action based on it should be left to the experts in prophecy, but since you all insist, I am left no choice but to bow to your wishes."

The representatives were obviously pleased to finally have gotten their way, even if their enthusiasm was somewhat tempered by the weight of responsibility they were so willingly assuming.

"You shall have what you demand," Kahlan said. "You shall hear what prophecy holds in store for you."

CHAPTER
21

Everyone inched forward, eager to finally hear what none of them had ever heard before: real prophecy from one of the books of prophecy.

Kahlan looked back over her shoulder at the grim sorceress who had been quietly observing. All eyes went to the woman, who possessed powers most of these people had never seen unleashed and could not imagine. Nicci's unapproachable beauty, and her icy-cold confidence, only added to the air of danger about her.

"Nicci, would you please bring the book you have with you and read the prophecy we recently discovered that speaks to the issue of our immediate future and the role that all these people here today have to play in it?"

Nicci bowed her head. "Of course, Mother Confessor."

The woman's smoldering, silken voice only confirmed her displeasure with what she had heard from those gathered. While everyone was excited by the gravity of what they were witnessing, and by the prospect of hearing real prophecy that was rarely uttered outside of tightly guarded rooms, they were also cautious of the menace that Nicci represented. While Cara was intimidating enough, Nicci was a forbidding presence on a whole other level. In her revealing black dress she looked every bit of her former persona of Death's Mistress, a title everyone in the room knew even if not one of them ever mentioned it except perhaps in whispered gossip among themselves.

Their desire to hear prophecy, though, overwhelmed their concern. No one looked like they wanted to change their mind.

"Please read to these good people exactly what it says." Kahlan shot a glare out at the crowd. "Don't hold anything back. I'm afraid that they have made it quite clear that they want prophecy to be revealed to them just as it has been laid down, and they want it to be followed."

"You did your best to warn them, Mother Confessor."

Kahlan nodded. "So I did."

Nicci picked the book up off the table. She held it in the crook of her arm as she stepped up beside Kahlan. She wasn't smiling. There was something about her posture, her cool expression, that made most everyone watching unconsciously retreat a half step from the dais.

"What I have here," Nicci said, briefly lifting the book for them to see, "is a core book of prophecy, written by a renowned prophet from an age when the gift of prophecy was at its height. As all of you suspected, it contains dark prophecy of the most serious nature that has direct relevance for us all in this room."

Everyone inched closer again.

Nicci opened the book, holding it in one hand, about to read, but then looked up again. "Since this is such an ancient text, it is in High D'Haran, the language of that time. Do any of you speak High D'Haran?"

Most people shook their heads as they looked around to

see if anyone else could understand the ancient, nearly forgotten language. No one could, of course. Richard had learned it, but other than him, there were only a handful of people left alive who understood High D'Haran. Nicci was one of them.

"Well," Nicci said with a cool smile, "I am fluent in High D'Haran, so I will translate what it says here for you, rather than speak the prophecy in its original language, if that's all right with everyone."

"Well of course we want it translated," Queen Orneta snapped as she folded her arms again, sounding like she was scolding a lowly servant. "Just get on with it."

Nicci's cold blue eyes turned to the queen in a way that made the queen lose a little color.

"As you wish, Your Majesty."

Kahlan wished she had a voice as soft, as silken, as beautiful as Nicci's. The woman's voice fit her perfectly. It was as flawless and arresting as everything else about her. It also had that rare quality that, while it was usually painfully alluring, with the slightest change in pitch it darkened to deadly.

Nicci carefully, slowly, turned over a page, scanning the text until she found what she was looking for.

King Philippe circled an arm around his queen and drew her a little closer. Kahlan watched as Catherine stroked a hand over her belly, as if to soothe her restless child.

Kahlan forced herself to look away from the pregnant woman, and push her own thoughts and feelings aside.

Nicci tapped the page. "Here it is. Because it is so important, so central, it's a rather long and detailed prophecy. I apologize, but I will have to go slowly and carefully in order to translate it accurately for you."

"Yes, yes," the queen said. "Would you please just get on with it?" Others grumbled their impatient agreement.

"Very well." Nicci cleared her throat. "It says, 'In the aftermath of victory, in a raging spring storm beyond anything seen for many years, as the leaders of all the lands gather, the ill winds of change bring a storm of coming events that threatens to cast the world into suffering, terror, and devastation. Dark perils lie hidden, ready to steal the night, to hunt the innocent, and to devour them.'"

People gasped. Nicci looked up from under lowered brows and waited a moment until the whispers died out. When they did, she went on.

"'In this cusp of time, in this pivotal, stormy moment, as the leaders are all gathered, the fate of the world hangs on what is done in this moment, for this is their only chance to assure a favorable future.'"

People's mouths hung open as they waited for Nicci to reveal what prophecy would say must be done to avoid such a sinister outcome and to insure a favorable future. Nicci checked to make sure everyone was paying attention before resuming the translation of the prophecy. She needn't worry. Every eye was locked on her, waiting.

"'Just as life itself must be turned over through the passing into death of some so that it can be continually renewed with new blood, so too the leadership gathered must be renewed. For the terrible fangs of fate to be vanquished, the leaders of all the lands, while they are gathered, must be purged. The future for new life, new hope, can only be assured in this way.

"'Staying such a cleansing for fear of shedding the blood of these few would mean a dark age of agony, suffering, and death for their people. To bring forth fresh life, to insure that prosperity and safety of all the lands will follow on the spring, the blood of their leaders must here be shed.

" 'It is thus written and set down that the lives of these gathered leaders must be forfeit if the world is to be spared unspeakable suffering.' "

Nicci's cutting gaze slowly turned up to take in the audience. Her voice made the change from silken to deadly.

"There you have it: prophecy. Prophecy that reveals a dark and terrible future if not heeded. Prophecy that, as you all have insisted, must be heeded.

"Prophecy that stipulates that all of you must die."

22

The room had fallen dead silent. No one dared blink. No one dared move. Everyone was afraid to so much as exhale.

"But . . . but . . ." Queen Orneta finally stammered.

"But nothing," Kahlan said in a voice as deadly as Nicci's had been. "Prophecy is not always truly revealed by the words. Prophecy can have occulted meaning—I've told you all that. Nathan told you. Lord Rahl told you.

"Nathan and others with extensive experience in the arcane subject of the veiled meaning hidden within the words of prophecy have been urgently helping Lord Rahl with this one, trying to learn if there is a chance that in this case it has another meaning other than what it sounds like it means. That is the calling of prophets—deciphering the true meaning of prophecy. As Richard and I have repeatedly tried to tell you, prophecy is not intended for the uninitiated and it should be left to the experts."

A chancellor from a southern D'Haran province, dressed in a floor-length dark blue robe cinched at his ample waist with an ornate gold belt, lifted a finger. "Yes, of course you're right,

Mother Confessor. We can see that, now. Perhaps we had best—"

"However," Kahlan said in a clear, cutting voice that silenced him, "sometimes prophecy means precisely what it says."

"But could it be that this one has a hidden meaning?" King Philippe asked.

Kahlan regarded the king with the blank expression that she had mastered, as did all Confessors, at a young age. It was a countenance that became an immutable part of her the first time she unleashed her power on a condemned man and commanded him to confess the truth of his horrific crimes.

"You demanded to hear prophecy so that, as you said, you could make sure that Lord Rahl and I bow to what it says must be done. As Queen Orneta so succinctly put it, prophecy must be served. It must be revealed so that the stipulated action can be taken."

Queen Catherine, tears beginning to stream down her cheeks, put an arm protectively over her unborn child as she looked to her husband. He could not look her in the eye.

Queen Orneta turned from worried to indignant. "You can't be serious. We simply don't believe—"

"General," Kahlan called out.

At the side of the room General Meiffert stepped away from the wall and saluted with a clap of his fist to his armored heart. "Mother Confessor?"

"Do you have the execution teams in place and ready?"

The word "execution" rippled in worried whispers through the room.

"Yes, Mother Confessor. We're ready. The beheadings can begin at once."

The crowd went wild.

THE OMEN MACHINE

"Beheadings?" the chancellor cried out. "Are you crazy? You can't be serious. . . . You wouldn't!"

Kahlan regarded him with the blank expression of a Confessor viewing the condemned. "The prophecy calls for the blood of those of you gathered here. It is quite specific." Kahlan turned to Nicci. "Am I correct?"

"Yes, Mother Confessor. There can be no doubt of my translation." Nicci consulted the book again. "It says, quite clearly, 'To bring forth fresh life, to insure that prosperity and safety of all the lands will follow on the spring, the blood of their leaders must here be shed.'"

Kahlan looked back at the chancellor. "I assure you, beheadings are quite bloody. Prophecy will be served."

"What about you?" Queen Orneta shouted. "You're a leader, too. If it includes us then it should include you, too!"

"I choose to believe that the prophecy does not mean to include me." Kahlan lifted a hand, signaling over their heads, as she went on. "But it clearly includes all of you."

All around the room, the men of the First File, smartly dressed in leather armor and chain mail with weapons belts hung with gleaming swords, axes, knives, and maces, stepped away from around the sides and back of the room where no one had noticed them gathering. The soldiers moved in among the people to begin seizing them by their arms, insuring that there could be no escape.

"We're not going to stand for any such thing!" the queen protested.

"Actually," Kahlan said in a calm voice, "you don't have to stand for it."

"That's better," Queen Orneta huffed as men came up on either side of her.

"Standing would be too troublesome for this kind of execution." Kahlan's voice was ice. "You will each be made to kneel so that your heads can be placed on heavy wooden blocks. An axeman will then do the deed swiftly and efficiently. We have a number of teams assembled, so I can assure you the beheadings will all be over quickly. Prophecy will be served. Through your sacrifice your lands and your people will be safe. So says prophecy."

Queen Catherine stepped forward, lifting one arm while cradling the other around her belly. "But my child has not had a chance to live, yet." Tears coursed down her cheeks. "You can't condemn my unborn child to death!"

"Catherine, I have not condemned your child. You said, and please correct me if I'm wrong, 'The Creator has given us prophecy. It must be heeded.' So you see, it is not me, but prophecy that calls for this. If anything, by your insistence on adhering to prophecy, you have condemned your child."

Kahlan turned her back on the crowd and started away.

"Do you mean to say that you really intend to have us beheaded?" the frantic chancellor called out. "You're serious?"

Kahlan turned back. "Deadly serious," she said, as if surprised he would doubt her. "We tried in every way we could think of to convince all of you that prophecy was meant for those who understand its arcane nature, but none of you would have it. I had the execution teams assembled just in case my last attempt to convince you failed and everyone instead demanded to hear prophecy and have it followed. You all did—every one of you—therefore I have no choice but to carry out your will. You all made this choice yourselves."

The crowd went crazy again, protesting that they hadn't meant to usurp the rule of Lord Rahl, or the Mother Confessor.

And then the chancellor pulled away from the grip of a soldier and dropped to his knees. He placed his forehead to the ground. When other people grasped what he was doing, they jumped to join him. Soon the whole roomful of representatives and rulers, even the pregnant Queen Catherine, were on their hands and knees with their foreheads pressed to the floor. The soldiers standing among them didn't do anything to stop them.

"Master Rahl guide us. Master Rahl teach us. Master Rahl protect us. In your light we thrive. In your mercy we are sheltered. In your wisdom we are humbled. We live only to serve. Our lives are yours."

It was the devotion to the Lord Rahl that until a few days before had been recited twice each and every day in the Palace of the Prophets for hundreds, if not thousands, of years. At Cara's wedding Richard had told everyone that their lives were their own, not his, and that they should no longer bow to him or to anyone else. They all had, after all, just defeated tyranny.

Even if that devotion was no longer required, they apparently thought that this was an appropriate time to remind themselves, and Kahlan, of their loyalty.

Kahlan let the chanting go on for a while before she said, "Rise, my children," the traditional phrase used by the Mother Confessor when people went to a knee to bow before her. She rarely cared about the old tradition.

Today, she cared.

On her command the crowd began coming to their feet. They were much quieter and looked considerably more respectful.

"Mother Confessor," a woman dressed in a rose and cream silk dress said, "we demanded when we should have listened. I can't speak for the others, but I, for one, am sorry. I'm not sure what came over us, but we were wrong. You and Lord Rahl have done things for us that no one, much less any leader we've ever had, has ever done. You both brought us out of the wilderness of despair. We should have trusted you and realized that you have never had anything but our best interest at heart."

Kahlan smiled. "Apology accepted." She glanced around at the crowd. "Does anyone else share this sentiment?"

The throng rushed the dais, clamoring that they did.

Kahlan didn't prolong their distress. "Well, then, it seems that we've assembled the execution teams for nothing. If you are satisfied to leave prophecy to us, we promise to work to understand its true meaning and to heed it where we believe it is necessary to do so in order to protect all of you to the best of our ability. With our last breath if need be."

A number of people wept with relief, including Queen Catherine. A few people went to a knee to kiss the hem of Kahlan's dress as she stood on the dais before them. It wasn't something she approved of.

"Enough of that," she gently chided. "Please, rise now."

The terrible weight of fear lifted from the crowd. Everyone, even Queen Orneta, was openly grateful that the ordeal had ended as it had. It was obvious that most of them were also shamed by their behavior.

Kahlan, too, was relieved that the ordeal was over.

Streams of people came to the dais to be heard, to personally thank her for changing her mind, and to assure her that they would let her and Richard handle prophecy as they saw fit. They each apologized for their attitude and promised they would not again be so disagreeable or unreasonable.

Kahlan graciously accepted the apologies and their promises of cooperation and let them know that she would not hold it against them in the future.

As the people at last all filed out of the room, Benjamin joined Kahlan, Cara, and Nicci before the table on the dais.

"You are quite the actress, Mother Confessor." Benjamin smiled. "You even had me sweating for a moment, and I knew the truth of what you were doing."

Kahlan let out a sigh. "Thank you for your help, Benjamin. You and your men played your parts well. You helped save us a real problem, even if it wasn't the way I would have preferred to have gained their cooperation."

"But you did. At least it's over." He gave her a puzzled look. "Where did you ever come up with something as devious as that?"

"It was a trick I learned from Zedd not long after I met Richard." Kahlan shook her head, distracted by troubling thoughts. "But I'm afraid that it's not over. We have only averted the problem for the moment. There is something going on that has nothing to do with the true attitudes of those people.

"I know many of these representatives. They're good people. They all stood by us in the darkest hours of the war and fought with everything they had. Many lost their family. They all lost people they knew and cared about.

"This simply wasn't like these people. Someone, or something, is manipulating them. We may have stopped the trouble for the moment, but it didn't originate with these people, so it will undoubtedly resurface."

"Kahlan is right," Nicci said. "But even a good person can be swept up with the sentiments of a crowd and come to hold perverse beliefs."

Cara frowned. "And as a result, run a knife between your ribs."

"That's what we need to prevent," Nicci said. "Until we can get to the source of what's really happening, I'm afraid that we're only reacting to the situation, not controlling it."

Cara sighed in agreement. "Let's hope that Lord Rahl gets to the bottom of it pretty soon."

Kahlan gestured to the book Nicci was holding. "By the way, what book is that?"

Nicci held it up. "This? When you sent word that you needed my help, and what you needed, I wasn't near a library, so I ducked into the kitchen and grabbed this. It's a cook-book."

"Well, you cooked up a pretty good prophecy," Kahlan said.

Nicci smiled distantly. "I wish we could have stopped those two women as easily before they killed their children."

"At least we stopped the man, that jeweler," Benjamin said.

Kahlan nodded. "I hope Richard was able to learn something down in the dungeon that can help us."

CHAPTER

23

Richard closed the double doors behind him as he stepped into the small entry. He had been told that Kahlan was waiting for him. He was eager to see her, to be away from everyone else and alone with her.

As he rounded the corner into the bedroom she looked up at him in the mirror. She was sitting on a padded bench at the dressing table brushing her long hair.

"So, how did it go with the representatives?" he asked.

"In the end they saw the wisdom of leaving prophecy to us."

Despite how tired he was, and how concerned he was about what had happened down in the dungeon, Richard couldn't help but smile at the sight of her, at the sparkle of life in her beautiful green eyes as she set down the brush and stood to face him.

"That's a relief, but I knew you could do it." Richard put one arm around her waist as he used a finger of his other hand to lift a strand of hair back from her face. "I'm glad you were there to handle it. I'm afraid that I would only have gotten angry and scared the wits out of them. I don't have your patience for diplomacy. So, what did you say to convince them to back off?"

"I threatened to chop off their heads if they didn't."

Richard laughed at her joke, then kissed her forehead. "I imagine you charmed them into submission and had them eating out of your hand by the time you were through."

Kahlan rested her forearms on his shoulders and clasped her hands behind his head. "Richard, I may have dissuaded them for the moment, but something more is going on than we're seeing."

"You'll get no argument from me."

"What did the woman who killed her four children have to say?"

Richard sighed as he let his arms slip from her waist. "She said that terrible things are going to happen so she killed her children to spare them."

"What terrible things?"

"I asked her that. She couldn't seem to come up with anything. Then she dropped dead, just like the woman who tried to kill you yesterday."

"She died? The same way, simply dropped dead?"

"I'm afraid so. She convulsed and died like the woman you touched. That would seem to confirm that it had nothing to do with you using your power on her."

As Kahlan turned away to stare off in thought, Richard looked around at the spacious room. The sunken, white panels of the coffered ceiling were each decorated with gilded moldings in geometric patterns. The wall behind the bed was covered in soft, padded, dark brown fabric. The bed had a canopy with enough sheer fabric to make the tall corner posts, carved into stylized figures of women, look like nothing so much as good spirits spreading gossamer wings. Ornate chairs set opposite a couch were upholstered in striped, dusty green satin.

"I haven't seen this room before."

"Neither had I," Kahlan said. "I had a trying day with all the representatives, so I lay down and rested for a while. I didn't sense that I was being watched, like I did the last time. Maybe this room is far enough away from the other two rooms that prying eyes won't find us here and we can get a good night's sleep."

"I could use that," Richard said, absently, as he scanned the room for any hint that someone, or something, was watching them. He didn't sense anything out of the ordinary.

The room was a great deal larger than the other two they had used. Tall wardrobes with a white crackled finish stood facing each other in a wing off to the side of the bed. Opposite the chairs there was a comfortable-looking couch with a low table set with a platter piled high with dried fruit. Richard took a couple of slices of dried apple and chewed one as he strolled around the room, looking for any hint of anything out of place, any hint of trouble.

They had trouble enough.

He was pretty sure that all the representatives would have wanted to know why he hadn't been there. He was sure, too, that Kahlan had told them that he was seeing to the matters having to do with their concerns. They probably thought they were being snubbed, that he was ignoring their concerns. He couldn't keep them informed of every little thing he was doing, or he would never have time to do any of it.

"Why do you think this is happening all of a sudden?" Kahlan asked. "And why now?"

"Well," Richard said as he glanced behind a dressing screen, "that woman who tried to kill you yesterday at the reception didn't make a lot of sense."

"Since when have murderers made sense?"

"It was a pretty clumsy assassination attempt, don't you think? I mean, it may have seemed to the people at the reception that it was a close brush with death for you, but you and I both know that it wouldn't be that easy to kill you like that. If her true purpose was to kill you she could have chosen any number of other ways that would have had a far better chance."

"You and I know may know that, but she probably didn't."

"That's possible."

"She was determined and committed. After all, she'd just proven that by murdering her children. She probably thought that surprise would work, that she could walk up and stab me."

"Or maybe she didn't."

"What do you mean?"

Richard pulled the drapes aside to peer out through the wavy glass in the double doors. Snowdrifts lay in sinuous, curving forms to cover most of the railings and all but a few edges of the big round stone pots. The snow had turned wet and heavy. It was coming down in mad swirls that continually shaped and added to the drifts. When a gust of wind rattled the doors, Richard checked that they were bolted securely.

"Maybe the real purpose," he said, "was to make people fear prophecy, fear the vision she had, fear the visions others are having, fear the future. She had quite an audience. Covered in blood like she was after killing her children because of her vision made a lasting impression on all the people there. Maybe that was the real purpose behind what she did."

"That seems to be quite a stretch, Richard. After all, her

attack and my taking her with my power had been predicted by both that woman you went to see, Lauretta, and the book *End Notes*. Both prophecies said the same exact thing, 'Queen takes pawn.' That doesn't sound like my would-be assassin was trying to make people believe anything. It seems to confirm that there are relevant prophecies that are coming true. That one did, anyway."

Richard turned to her as he let the draperies fall back across the glassed doors. He arched an eyebrow.

"At least, it seemed to. If prophecy says that a statue will topple, and someone deliberately topples it to make sure that the prophecy is fulfilled, is that actually fulfilling prophecy? Or is it merely someone wanting to make it look like the prophecy was true?"

"How could you distinguish the difference?"

"That's always the problem with prophecy, now isn't it? But there seems to be something more to this."

Kahlan extinguished the lamp on the dressing table, then went to the nightstand and turned down the wick on the one there until it was barely glowing. It cast the room into cozy near-darkness.

"You mean, you think that someone is deliberately meddling to make it look like prophecy was being fulfilled?"

"Actually, I'm worried that there's more to it than we're seeing, and that's what the prophecy is really predicting. I think that the prophecy was actually predicting that a woman who would be taken by you was being used by others. I think that's what the prophecy is really warning us about."

Kahlan rubbed her arms against the chill. "So you don't think that it's actually a prophecy about what I would do—queen takes pawn—but instead that it's a warning that someone unseen is manipulating events? Using her as a pawn?"

Richard nodded. "Exactly. I think that someone is up to something. I think the prophecy is actually warning as much. Lauretta had written down another prediction. It said 'People will die.'"

Kahlan's gaze searched his. "People die all the time."

"Yes, but in the last couple of days a number of people have died under very mysterious circumstances. The two soldiers down in the market who were looking for the sick boy were found dead, six children were murdered, both their mothers died, a representative jumped to his death, and then there was that boy down in the storm who was attacked by animals and eaten."

"When you put it all together like that the prediction does seem to cast a shadow over so many mysterious deaths." Kahlan laid a comforting hand on his arm. "But the boy was different. He was most likely caught alone and attacked by wolves. It's horrifying, but not mysterious, like the others."

Richard arched an eyebrow. "I don't like coincidences."

Kahlan sighed. "Let's not get carried away about that death, making it a part of something bigger, just because of our concern about what could be behind the others."

Richard nodded his agreement even though he didn't agree. He was getting a headache thinking about it all. "We should get some sleep."

She looked around the room. "I haven't felt anyone watching, and I've been here quite a while. Why don't we get undressed and go to bed like normal?"

Richard could see that she was tired. For that matter, so was he. They hadn't gotten much rest the night before.

"Sure. Sounds good to me."

Kahlan turned her back to him and held her hair up out of the way so he could undo her dress. Richard unhooked it and eased the dress off her shoulders enough to give each a kiss. He was glad for the chance to be so pleasantly diverted from all the dark thoughts swirling in the back of his mind.

Kahlan slipped out of her dress and laid it over a bench against the wall. Richard watched the inviting curves of her liberated form as she quickly crossed the room, climbed onto the bed, and slipped under the covers. He didn't think that there was anything in the world as graceful as the way Kahlan moved.

She tented the blankets with her knees and hooked her arms around them. "Richard, stop thinking about a prophecy that's been in a book for thousands of years. You need some sleep."

He smiled at her. "You're right."

"Then why are you just standing there?" Kahlan crooked a finger at him. "Hurry up and get in here with me, would you, please, Lord Rahl. I'm freezing."

Richard didn't have to be asked twice.

24

Richard was lost in kissing the soft, sensual curve of Kahlan's neck when the slightest noise, something alien to the quiet bedroom, made him look up.

Kahlan propped herself up on her elbows under him, catching her breath as she peered across the room to where he was looking.

"What is it?" she whispered so softly that he barely heard her.

Richard put two fingers across her lips to keep her from saying anything more as he stared into the small side wing where the wardrobes stood.

He felt something there, something in that dark alcove. It was watching him.

The heavy drapes were drawn, but if they hadn't been, it wouldn't have helped; the night was in the black depths of the raging storm. With only one lamp lit in the room and its wick turned down low there was only enough light to make out the vague, bulky shapes of the wardrobes. There wasn't enough light to really make out any details in the room and not anywhere near enough to make out whatever it was that seemed to be in their room, watching them.

Richard squinted, trying as hard as he could to see better in the dim light, trying to make out what he thought seemed just a little darker than the rest of the near-darkness. He thought that he could see a shadowy hint of something.

As he stared, he could feel it looking back at him. He was sure that, unlike the last time, this time he not only felt it watching, he could sense its presence in the room.

That presence was icy cold and evil.

He couldn't begin to imagine what it could be. After all, men of the First File were stationed all up and down the corridors. These were not the kind of men who fell asleep on watch, or got bored and didn't pay attention. These were battle-hardened men who were always ready for any threat. These were the elite of the D'Haran forces. Not one of those men wanted to be the one who let any threat get so much as a glimpse of Richard and Kahlan.

Whatever it was, it had not skulked in past the guards to get into the bedroom.

Whatever it was that Richard saw crouched in the alcove was dark and indistinct and not very large. It waited, still and silent, perfectly centered between the two dark forms of the tall wardrobes.

Richard wondered what it was waiting for.

From outside he could hear the wind howl and moan and occasionally rattle the doors, only to die out and let the room fall silent again. The only sound inside the room that Richard could hear was Kahlan's breathing and the faint hiss of the burning wick of the lamp.

Richard couldn't tell if whatever it was he was staring at was nothing more than a murky dark area, or if it only looked that way because it was so dark in the room that it blurred the edges of a shadowed form.

Whatever it was, it was as dark as pitch.

Whatever it was, its gaze was unwavering.

Whatever it was, it was heartless.

Richard thought that maybe it looked something like a dog poised there watching them.

As he stared, trying to make it out, he realized that, oddly enough, it looked more like a small child, maybe a girl, hunched forward, long hair fallen down around the lowered head as it crouched on the floor.

He also knew that it couldn't be real. There was no way that anything could have gotten into the room. At least, he didn't think it could be real.

Real or not, Richard knew that Kahlan was seeing the same thing he was seeing. He could feel her heart hammering against his chest.

His sword stood leaned up against the nightstand. He was in the middle of the bed, tangled up with Kahlan. The weapon was just beyond an arm's length away, just out of reach.

Something, some inner sense, told him not to move.

He thought then that maybe it wasn't some inner sense, but rather simply the feeling of alarm at something dark crouched not far away, watching them.

Either way, he was afraid to move.

The thing, if it was a thing and not simply some trick of the dim light, or even his imagination, remained stone-still.

He told himself that if it turned out to be nothing more than a shadow he was going to feel pretty foolish.

But shadows didn't watch.

This thing was watching.

Unable to endure the silent tension any longer, Richard slowly, ever so slowly, started to shift himself off Kahlan in order to reach toward his sword.

When he began to move, the thing started to uncurl, to slowly rise as if in response to his movement. A soft sound accompanied the movement, a brittle sound like sticks, muffled in cloth, snapping. Or maybe it sounded more like bones cracking.

Richard froze.

The thing didn't.

As it rose, the head began to turn up. Richard could hear soft riffling pops as if the thing was dead and stiff, and every bone in the spine cracked under the effort of the forced movement.

The head continued to lift until Richard finally saw the eyes glaring out at him from under a lowered brow.

"Dear spirits," Kahlan whispered, "what is that?"

Richard couldn't even venture a guess.

From across the room, lightning quick, the thing suddenly bounded toward the bed.

Richard dove for his sword.

O ut of the corner of her eye Kahlan saw the dark thing charge toward them as Richard dove off her and across the bed.

As he slid toward the edge of the bed, his hand snatched the hilt of the sword. He rolled off the bed, yanking the sword free of the scabbard in one fluid movement as he landed on his feet. The ringing sound of the Sword of Truth's steel cut the silence like a scream of rage that sent a shiver rippling across her flesh.

As the dark shape vaulted toward them Richard spun to face the threat. Kahlan ducked back out of the way.

With lightning speed, the weapon swung around in an arc. The blade whistled as it swept through the air to meet the streak of a shadow.

Razor-sharp steel cut through the center of the inky form.

But even as the blade was cleaving it, the dark form evaporated like dust losing its shape, a shadow decomposing into eddies and swirls as it vanished.

Richard stood beside the bed, sword in hand, panting with rage. As far as Kahlan could tell, the source of his awakened anger was no longer there. She heard the soft, distant rumble of thunder, and the faint hiss of the lantern on the table between the chairs and the couch.

Kahlan scooted across the bed toward him. She peered around at the dark room, trying to see if the form had reappeared somewhere else. She wondered if she would be able to see it if it did.

"I don't feel anything watching us," she said, still scanning the darkness for the silent threat.

"I don't either. It's gone."

Kahlan wondered for how long. She wondered if it would suddenly appear again somewhere else in the room.

"What in the world do you think that could have been?" She stood up beside him, her fingers trailing along his muscular arm momentarily on her way to the lamp to turn up the wick.

Richard, still in the heat of rage from having the sword in his hand, scanned every corner of the room as the lamp finally helped illuminate what had been only dark shapes before.

"I wish I knew," he said as he finally slid the sword back into its scabbard. "It's starting to have me watching every shadow, listening to every sound, worrying if something is really there or wondering if it's just my imagination."

"Reminds me of when I was little and thought there were monsters under my bed."

"There's only one problem with that."

"What's that?" she asked.

"This wasn't our imagination. We both felt it. We both saw it. It was here."

"Do you think this thing tonight was what we felt watching us before?"

Richard glanced over at her. "Do you mean, do I think that this imaginary monster in our room is the same imaginary monster that was in our room last night?"

Despite her level of concern, that made Kahlan smile. "I guess it sounds silly when you put it that way."

"Whatever it is, I think it has to be the same thing that's been watching us."

"But we could never see it before. Why did it show itself tonight?"

He had no answer. All he could do was sigh in frustration.

Kahlan hugged herself with bare arms as she nestled in close to him. "Richard, if we don't know what's going on, or who, or what is looking into our room watching us, how can we hope to stop it? How are we ever going to get any sleep?"

Richard put an arm protectively around her. "I don't know," he said in a tone of regret. "I wish I did."

Kahlan had an idea. She looked up at him.

"Zedd's power is weakened in the palace, but Nathan is a Rahl. His power is amplified in here. Maybe we can have him hide nearby, or stay in a room beside ours and see if he can sense where it's coming from, where that person is hiding as they watch us. If he could sense where they are, then while they're busy watching us he could send men to grab them."

"I don't think that will work."

"Why not?"

"Because I suspect that it's not originating here in the palace. As you said, the palace reduces the power of anyone but a Rahl. I think that for them to do something like this they would have to be someplace else. I think they have to be projecting this, this power, or observation, or whatever it is, into our room from outside the palace."

"So there is no way to stop them? You mean that we're going to have to endure someone watching us in our bedroom every night?"

Kahlan watched the muscles in his jaw flex as he clenched his teeth in frustration.

"The Garden of Life was constructed as a containment field," he finally said, half to himself. "I wonder if that would shield us from prying eyes."

Kahlan was taken with the idea. "Containment fields were created to prevent errant magic, no matter how powerful, from getting out, or getting in."

"Then maybe . . ." he said as he considered.

Kahlan folded her arms. "I'd rather sleep in a bedroll on the grass in there if we could be all by ourselves than on a big soft bed in here with someone watching me."

"I know what you mean," Richard said. "If fact, maybe we should."

"I'm game," Kahlan said, stepping into her underclothes.

He sat on a bench at the foot of the bed and stuffed a leg into his pants. "Me too. But what I can't figure out is why someone, or something—or prophecy—is playing this game of riddles with us."

Kahlan opened a drawer and pulled out some of her old traveling clothes. "Maybe prophecy is trying to help you."

Richard frowned as he buttoned his pants.

"The thing that bothers me," he finally said as he leaned over and snatched up his shirt, "is that the prophecies that seem like they may be saying the same thing use different words. Some say that the roof is going to fall in, but another said that the sky is going to fall in. The roof and the sky aren't the same thing. Yet those two warnings have something in common: they say that both are going to fall in. And, there's also a certain commonality to roof and sky."

"Maybe they were meant to be the same thing, but the exact right word was lost in a translation, so the language used was imprecise. Or maybe it was meant to be oblique."

Richard pulled on a boot. "Or maybe the warnings of the roof falling in and the sky falling in are metaphors."

"Metaphors?" Kahlan asked as she drew a pair of pants up her long legs.

"Yes, like the one about queen takes pawn. That was obviously predicting that you would take that woman with your power. Calling her a pawn was telling us that she was being used. She was a puppet. I think the hidden hand directing that puppet wanted all the representatives gathered here at the palace to see the show."

"You mean you think that roof is a metaphor for the sky, or the other way round?"

"Could be," Richard said. "You know, like calling the night sky a roof of stars."

"So what do you think prophecy about the roof or sky falling in really means, then?"

"Maybe that it's life, the world, that is going to be falling in around us."

Kahlan didn't like the sound of that.

They both froze at the sound of a loud howling shriek outside in the hall.

Something heavy thudded into the double bedroom doors. For a moment, Kahlan thought they might be knocked off their hinges, but they remained firmly in place.

Richard and Kahlan both stood stock-still, staring at the door.

"What could that have been?" she whispered.

"I can't imagine." Richard's fingers found the hilt of his sword. "Let's find out."

Richard cracked open the door just enough for them to peer outside into the hallway. Reflector lamps mounted on the walls lit the corridor and a nearby intersection of halls. Through the narrow slit Kahlan saw heavily armed men racing in from every direction.

Splashes and smears of blood stained the marble floor in the hall.

Lying against the door at their feet was a big black dog with two pikes sticking from its side. Blood still flowed from several other gaping wounds.

Richard opened the door the rest of the way. The dead dog's head flopped over across the threshold. One of the officers, seeing Richard and Kahlan at the door, rushed up.

The powerfully built man swallowed as he caught his breath. "I'm sorry, Lord Rahl."

"What in the world is going on?" Richard asked.

"Well, this dog here was racing up the halls, growling and snapping at people. We were finally forced to kill him."

"Where did he come from?" Kahlan asked as she moved into the doorway beside Richard.

"We think he must belong to one of the people down in the market. When everyone was brought inside because of the storm, people had to bring their animals in as well. The horses and mules were put up in the stables, but dogs stayed with their owners. I think that in all the confusion down there some of them must have run loose. This one apparently got away from its owner and made it all the way up into the palace."

Richard squatted down beside the dead dog and stroked a hand along the wiry fur. Even in death, its teeth were still bared in a snarl. He patted the dog's shoulder, sorry that he had to die.

"So this fellow probably ran away from his owners?"

"That's what I suspect, Lord Rahl. We spotted him racing up through the halls, headed this way. We tried to catch him, but in the end he was too vicious and we had to take him down. I'm sorry to have disturbed you both."

Richard waved off the concern. "It's all right. We were just about to head up to the Garden of Life anyway." He again ran his hand over the black fur. "Too bad this poor fellow had to die."

While the officer's explanation sounded plausible enough, Kahlan couldn't help thinking of the prediction from the woman who had tried to kill her, couldn't help remembering her words.

"Dark things. Dark things stalking you, running you down. You won't be able to escape them."

High up in the People's Palace, Richard and Kahlan, with a contingent of soldiers of the First File accompanying them, made their way through a series of intersections that formed the arms of the central part of the spell-form that was the palace complex. Those arms, tracing the template of a complex formula, drew power in toward the Garden of Life.

The footsteps of the soldiers whispered off the polished granite floors and echoed off the great slabs of stone standing between black granite columns that lined the broad passageways. Each polished slab between those columns, laced with multicolored crystalline veins, was like a work of art.

Besides the men following behind Richard and Kahlan, there was a sizable force already stationed throughout the passageways. This part of the palace was always heavily guarded and strictly off-limits to the public.

Richard paused at the great doors, momentarily taking in the carvings of rolling hills and forests. The elaborate scene on the doors was sheathed in gold.

The Garden of Life had been created as a containment field for any dangerous magic that might need to be unleashed. It also protected those handling such power from any nefarious intervention. Beyond the gold-clad doors some of the most dangerous conjuring ever conceived by the mind of man had been unleashed. The magnificent doors were, like many other things in the palace, meant to be a reminder, when dealing with such potentially deadly things, of the beauty and importance of life itself.

The garden was also a touchstone of great events in Richard's life. He had been brought to the garden at the lowest point in his life. It had also been the scene of his greatest triumphs.

By the way Kahlan put a hand gently on his back, he knew that she must have realized what he was thinking.

Finally, he pulled one of the massive doors open. The guards took up posts up and down the hallway as Richard and Kahlan went into the Garden of Life alone.

Once inside, they were enveloped with the heady fragrance of flowers that grew in great swaths beside the walkway that wandered toward the heart of the room. Beyond the flowers small trees created a intimate forest gathered before a vine-covered stone wall. Beyond the wall, the center of the expansive room contained an area of lawn that swept around almost into a circle. The grass ring was broken by a wedge of white stone, upon which sat a slab of granite held up by two short, fluted pedestals.

High overhead, a ceiling of leaded windows let light flood the room during the day. At night they offered a view of the stars that always made Richard feel rather small and lonely.

This night there was no view out the windowed ceiling. Richard could see that a thick blanket of snow covered the glass. When lightning flashed, he could see that in some places the windblown snow had been reduced to a thin layer that let the lightning show through, but in other areas, on the lee side of the peak, the snow was so thick that not even the flashes of lightning could penetrate the dense covering. Intermittent thunder rumbled through the room, making the ground tremble underfoot.

After putting flame to a few torches around the edge of the grassy area, Richard sat with Kahlan on the short stone wall at the edge of the small indoor forest. Together they gazed out across the open area, as if looking out on a meadow.

When he took hold of her hand Kahlan flinched.

"What's wrong?"

She lifted her hand to glance at it briefly. "Just a little tender, that's all."

He could see that the scratches on the back of her hand were swollen and had turned to an angry red. The scratches on his own hand were red, too, but not as bad as Kahlan's.

Holding her fingers, he turned her hand to inspect it in the torchlight. "It looks worse."

She took her hand back. "It will be better soon." She rubbed her arms against the chill and changed the subject. "I don't feel anyone watching us. You?"

Richard listened to the torches hissing softly for a time as he looked around the vast room. "No, I don't either."

He could see that she was so sleepy she could hardly keep her eyes open. The stress of someone watching them not only kept them awake, but made what sleep they did get fitful. He put his arm around her and drew her close. Kahlan snuggled tight against him and laid her head on his shoulder.

Richard thought they ought to lay out their bedrolls and get some sleep. He liked being under the trees. It reminded him of all the times he'd slept under the stars. It reminded him of his Hartland woods, of when he first met Kahlan there.

"Back in the woods," she said in a dreamy voice.

Richard smiled. "So we are."

"Kind of nice for a change."

He thought so, too. Beyond the glass above them the storm howled in fury, but under the occluding layer of snow they could see none of it. Lit from underneath, Richard could see runnels of water snaking down the glass, so he knew that the snowstorm must be changing to sleet, or maybe even rain. When snow changed to rain it usually signaled the end of a spring storm. Sometimes, that was the most violent part of such storms, when they brought destructive winds and lightning.

"Do you think it's safe?" Kahlan asked.

He glanced over and saw her gazing up at the glass roof. In places the drifts were quite deep. The rain was packing the snow tighter, and making it a great deal heavier.

"I don't know. I don't know how much weight the glass can hold."

"That's what I was thinking . . ." she said softly, half to herself. "I wonder if it has ever broken in the past. It could be pretty dangerous being underneath it if it were to break in."

If the roof fell in.

The leaded glass was the roof in this room.

If the sky fell in.

In this room, the glass roof was the sky.

Richard stood. He understood the two different prophecies. They really were the same.

"I think we should get out of here."

"I think you may be right. I don't like the idea of all that glass coming down on us."

Just then, a lightning strike lit the room with a flash and a deafening blast. As Richard shielded Kahlan, turning her away from the blinding illumination, he saw the lacework of lightning arcing and crackling through the heavy metal framework that held the glass over the center of the room.

Glass shattered, sending shards flying everywhere. One sliver hit the back of his shoulder; another shard stuck in his thigh. A piece nicked Kahlan's arm.

Once the glass ceiling was cracked by the the lightning hitting the metal framework, the tremendous weight of wet snow brought the center of it cascading down. Lightning lanced a route through the opening toward the floor of the room.

At the same time that the tremendous weight of it all came crashing down, hitting the floor hard enough to make the whole room shudder with a resounding thud, another bolt of lightning lashed in through the breach in the ceiling and made it to ground.

The impact of all the wet snow and the jarring jolt of lightning sent a shock wave through the room that blew the torches out.

In the sudden darkness, Richard could hear a great rending groan as stone cracked and began breaking apart.

27

As they ducked, trying to avoid being hit by the debris flying in every direction, Richard and Kahlan both covered their ears against the deafening sound of thunder crashing and stone breaking. In the staccato flashes of lightning, Richard glanced back over his shoulder and saw the floor in the center of the room caving in.

Great granite blocks under the floor groaned as they twisted apart from one another and fell inward. Grass, dirt, and a thick bed of sand poured into the expanding hole, like the sands of an hourglass falling inward.

When the broken sections of glass finally stopped falling, Richard looked up to see in the flashes of lightning a jagged breach in the ceiling surrounded by twisted pieces of the heavy metal framework. Fortunately, most of the ceiling all around the room held in place. By the looks of the framework that Richard could see, the builders had overbuilt it for all but the rarest of events. It had, after all, stood for thousands of years. But the nearly inconceivable combination of snow made dangerously heavy by a cold rain, along with being struck by lightning, had been too much for the glass roof to withstand.

Wind whipped in through the opening, swirling sleet and snow down through the room and into the gaping hole in the center of the floor.

Keeping a wary eye skyward for any hanging pieces of glass that might come down on him, Richard pulled the shard of glass out of his leg and tossed it aside. He quickly retrieved a steel and flint from his pack and used them to light a torch in an iron stand not far away. Worried that people below the collapsed floor had been hurt or killed, he rushed toward the opening even as dirt and sand was still sliding down into the dark maw.

Kahlan clutched at his sleeve. "Richard! Stay back. The rest of the floor could fall in and you could go with it."

He held the torch out, trying to see into the hole. The flame flapped in the gusts of wind that lashed down into the room from the break in the ceiling. He leaned down, peering under the edge on the opposite side of the opening in the floor. It looked like the floor of the Garden of Life was actually held up by a series of radiating arches of a vaulted ceiling underneath it.

"It seems to have stopped," he said. "I think the lightning must have damaged the structure below that supports the room enough that the weight of all that falling snow broke open the weakened spot, but it looks like the rest of it is stable. See there? The lightning hit the thinnest place in the vault, between two heavy arches."

Kahlan inched up close behind him. "Are you sure?"

"Pretty sure." Richard crouched down and held the torch out, trying to see what was down below. It wasn't a room of the palace, as he expected.

"Look there," he said, pointing inside the hole to the left. "There are stairs over there."

Kahlan frowned as she leaned over a little more. "There wasn't any opening for stairs up here."

"You're right. It looks like there used to be a stairway up to the Garden of Life, but it was covered over."

"That doesn't make any sense," Kahlan said. "This room was constructed very deliberately as a containment field. It doesn't make any sense that it would have later been closed off from below. For that matter, being a containment field, it doesn't make sense that there were ever stairs. The opening for them would have weakened the field."

"May not make sense, but that's what it looks like."

"Unless what's below is within the containment field," she said, thinking out loud, "or used to be."

Richard inched in closer. The rest of the floor, supported by the beams of an arch system under them, seemed stable. "The stairs may have once led up into the Garden of Life, but they end at a landing. See it, there? It no longer comes all the way up. I want to get down there."

Kahlan shook her head. "The landing is too far down to jump."

Richard stood, holding the torch out, looking. He pointed. "There's the shed where the people who tend to the garden keep tools. These trees have to be kept trimmed to keep them from overgrowing and getting too big, so there must be a ladder."

When he pulled open the shed door, Richard saw that there was indeed a wooden ladder inside. He handed Kahlan the torch. The ladder was heavy, but he was able to handle it by himself.

When he reached the hole he slid the ladder down the side until it rested on the landing. Enough of the ladder stuck up out of the hole for a good handhold.

Richard looked up through the jagged opening in the glass roof. Snowflakes drifted down, but the wind was slowing. He could see breaks in the clouds, and through the breaks, stars. The storm was ending.

"Why don't you wait here," he said as he started down.

"Right," she said, "like that's going to happen."

"Well at least wait until I get down onto the landing and see if the steps are safe."

Kahlan agreed to that much of it. She stood at the edge of the hole, foot braced on a freshly exposed stone block, torch in hand, peering down to watch him descend the ladder. When he looked up at her, the dislodged granite blocks at the edge of the hole reminded him of a line of crooked teeth, as if he were being swallowed down the gullet of a stone monster.

As he stepped off the ladder the area around him brightened with an eerie greenish light coming from a proximity sphere sitting in an iron bracket. Richard had seen the ancient devices before. They were used to illuminate various areas of the People's Palace and the depths of the Wizard's Keep, among other places. They looked like nothing more than a solid piece of glass, but they had been invested with ancient magic so that when someone gifted came near them they began to glow.

As he lifted the hefty glass sphere out of the bracket, the light it gave off warmed in color.

Kahlan stepped off the ladder beside him. "At least we don't have to carry the torch."

"Guess not," Richard said as he squinted down into the darkness. "This doesn't make any sense."

"What do you mean?"

He brushed cobwebs out of the way. "I would have thought there would have been a room or some area of the palace under here, but this looks like no one has been down here in a thousand years. Maybe longer."

Kahlan glanced around at the thick gray layers of dust clinging to the walls. "A lot longer."

As Richard started down the steps he carefully stepped around chunks of fallen stone and areas of sand and dirt that covered large parts of the stairs. Kahlan, a hand on his shoulder, followed him down, careful to also step around rubble.

At the bottom of the long flight of stairs they reached a walkway at the outer edge of a room. The walls were made up of granite blocks, and soaring arches created a vaulted ceiling, all supporting the center portion of the Garden of Life. The dark stone, its surface dirty and decayed, looked ancient. Richard didn't think the place had seen the light of day for millennia.

Rather than being flat, the center portion of the floor rose up in a dome formed by fat stone ribs filled in between with simple stone blocks. The dome forced them to use the walkway around the outer edges of the room. A lot of debris from above covered the dome, but much of it had slid down to build up in the well against the wall that was the only walkway. Richard started around the room, climbing over the rubble. Kahlan clambered over huge stone pieces fallen from above, going around in the opposite direction.

The room appeared to serve no purpose except possibly as an inspection area for the structure. There were other places in the palace that were intended only as inspection ports for the foundation, or hidden parts of the support columns, connections, and beams, so he didn't find that much of it surprising.

Richard wondered why, though, if that was true, it had been closed off from the Garden of Life. The stairway above the landing where the ladder rested appeared to have been dismantled. Since that part of the garden's floor had collapsed, there was no longer any way to know if there had ever been access up into the garden. He supposed that it could have been nothing more than a construction access that had been sealed over.

"Over here," Kahlan called out. "There's a spiral staircase over here in the corner that goes down to what's below."

28

Richard held the glowing sphere out ahead of him as he wound his way down the spiral of wedge-shaped stairs. There was no railing, making the descent into the darkness treacherous, especially since a lot of the sand and dirt from the floor of the Garden of Life that had fallen into the room above them had in turn poured down the spiral stairs. Richard had to pause in places to use the side of his boot to move dirt and debris aside so that they would have a safe place to step.

As they went ever lower into the blackness, the confining shaft for the spiral stairs opened up into a dark, dead still room. The light of the sphere Richard was holding cast only enough illumination into the distance to see that the simple, unadorned room was made of stone blocks. There were no doors or other openings that Richard could see. The room was empty except for what appeared to be a block of stone sitting in the middle.

"What in the world could this place be?" Kahlan asked.

Richard shook his head as he looked around. "I don't know. Doesn't look like much of anything. Maybe it's just an old storage room."

"It doesn't make any sense that they would seal off a storage room the way this place has been sealed up."

"I suppose not," Richard conceded.

Kahlan was right. It didn't appear that there had ever been any convenient access to the place.

As he moved into the gloomy room, proximity spheres set in wall brackets began to glow. By the time he made it around the perimeter of the room the four spheres, one on each wall, had all come to life, if weakly. Each sphere brightened as he came close and dimmed as he moved away. Even so, they cast sufficient light to banish enough of the blackness for them to see.

Looking around the room for any sign of what the place might have been used for, Richard only distantly noted the nondescript monolithic block sitting in the center of the room. He thought it might be a leftover block of stone used in the construction of the palace walls. The only thing that Richard thought was odd about it was that it sat square with the room, as if it had been carefully placed. It served no structural purpose as far as he could see.

Snowflakes drifted down from the stairwell and into the room to mix with the dust they had stirred up. Up above, the storm raged across the land, but the remnants of gusty wind could not make it this far down. Snowflakes floating by, catching the light of the proximity spheres, sparkled in the murky light.

A quick search around the perimeter confirmed that the room had no doors. There were no other stairs, or openings of any kind. There was no way out but the spiral stairs that had brought them down into the still grave of a room.

Richard wasn't sure why, but the place was making the hair on the back of his neck stand out.

The still, silent room had the feel of a place deliberately built to be sealed over and forgotten. But why would anyone seal off and bury an empty room?

Kahlan inched in close to him. "Something about this place is creepy."

"Maybe it's because it's a dead end. There's no way out but the way we came in."

"Maybe," she said. "I sure wouldn't like to get trapped down in here. No one would ever find you. Why would this place be sealed up like a tomb?"

Richard shook his head. He had no answer.

He half expected to see bones on the floor, but there were none. There were burial vaults in the lower reaches of the palace, but the Garden of Life was at the top of the palace, and besides, the tombs were grand places meant to revere the dead. None had the forsaken feel of this room.

As he looked around more carefully, Richard spotted something low against the far wall. He thought it might be a narrow ledge in the stone, maybe a stone block sticking out a little more than the rest. He held the sphere out to see better as he leaned in. He brushed away a layer of dust and crumbled granite flakes from the surface and saw that it was individual, small strips of metal, piled in tight, neat, orderly stacks.

He picked a strip of metal off one of the stacks and turned it in the light, trying to figure out what it was, or its purpose. Each was only a little longer than his longest finger, and soft enough that he could easily bend it. All the strips looked to be identical. Stacked tightly and evenly as they were, and covered in dust and dirt, the mass of them looked like part of the wall, like a ledge in the stone.

Kahlan bent close, trying to see it better. "What do you think they are?"

Richard straightened the strip of metal and set it back in its resting place atop one of the stacks. "They don't have any markings on them. They seem to be nothing more than simple strips of metal."

Kahlan's gaze swept along the wall. "They're stacked all around the edge of the room. There must be tens of thousands of them, maybe hundreds of thousands. What could they be for, and why are they buried in here?"

"It seems like they were left and forgotten. Or it could be they were hidden away."

Kahlan's nose wrinkled. "Why hide plain strips of metal?"

Richard could only shrug as he looked around, trying to see if the room held any other clues to its purpose. The place didn't seem to make any sense. He scuffed the side of his boot across the floor. It was stone, covered with what was probably thousands of years of dust and crumbled, decayed granite from the surface of the walls. Even though he knew from being above the room that it had a vaulted ceiling above, the ceiling down inside the room was flat, a false ceiling, probably plastered over but now the same dark, dingy color as the walls.

All in all, other than the stacks of metal and the odd block of stone in the center, it was an unremarkable room. Except, perhaps, that it led to nowhere. Had the floor of the Garden of Life not collapsed, there would have been no way into the buried room. If not for the roof falling in, the room could easily have remained undiscovered for a few thousand more years.

As Kahlan trailed her fingers along the wall, looking for any hint of writing carved into the stone, or possibly a hidden passageway, Richard turned his attention to the square block that sat in the center of the dingy room. Oddly enough, the stone floor stopped short of the block, leaving a narrow gutter of dirt all the way around it. The block was slightly more than waist high. If he and Kahlan would have reached across from opposite sides, they wouldn't have been able to touch their fingers.

He couldn't imagine what it could be, or what it was doing there.

With snowflakes drifting past, he squatted down, holding out the glowing sphere to see better, and brushed the flat of his hand along the surface of the side.

He was surprised to realize that the surface was not stone, as he had thought, but thick, heavy metal.

He rubbed away at the dust and grime of ages, trying to see it better. The surface of the metal was corroded and dirty, making it look like the stone in the room, but there could be no doubt, it was metal. Beneath the filth where he wiped his hand across the surface, metal glinted in the light of the sphere.

"Look at this," Richard said.

Kahlan glanced back over her shoulder. "What is it?"

Richard thumped his fist against it. Even though it seemed to be extraordinarily heavy, he could just barely tell from the sound that it was hollow.

"This thing is made of metal. And look at this, here."

He held the sphere out so she could see better as she came up next to him. There was a small slot, starting in the top and cut down into one side of the thing. Some of the curious strips of metal were stacked in the slot.

Kahlan removed one of the metal strips, inspecting it. As far as Richard could tell it was devoid of any markings, the same as all the others stacked against the wall.

He rubbed more of the dirt and debris off the side. "There's some kind of emblem or something on the side. Kind of hard to tell what it is."

With a heavy thud that shook the ground and made both of them flinch, light shot up from the center of the top. Dirt in the space between the metal monolith and the stone floor, disturbed by the thump, lifted into the still air.

As one, Richard and Kahlan took a step back.

"What did you do?"

"I don't know," Richard said. "I was brushing it with my hand to clean away the dirt to see what's on the side."

A deep mechanical groan started within the thing. Metal moved against metal, giving off grating sounds. The sound, like heavy gears turning, grew louder as if the whole thing came to life. Richard and Kahlan backed away a little more, not knowing what to do.

Abruptly, the light that had shot up from the center of the top changed to an amber color.

Richard leaned in and saw that there was a small hole in the center of the top where the light was coming out.

That was when he saw a hint of more light coming from a small opening on the other side of the thing. He rushed around and brushed dirt from the top surface of the metal box. A slit, two hand-widths wide but narrow, was filled with a piece of heavy glass, making a small window that was flush with the surface of the top.

The glass was thick and wavy, but with the aid of the light coming from somewhere down inside he was able to look in through the window, down into the interior of the metal box. He could see that the entire box was filled with gears, wheels, levers, and moving parts all fit together into a complex machine that was all in motion at once.

Some of the trip levers and shafts holding the smaller parts were small, only as thick as his little finger. But some of the fat mounting blocks holding the bigger shafts had to weigh thousands of pounds, with the larger gears they held probably weighing a great deal more. The diameter of some of the gears exceeded his height, with teeth more than a hand-width wide. The heavy framework holding it all together was enormous not only in size but in complexity.

The surfaces of all the massive pieces of machinery down inside were rusted and pitted. As the gears turned and the interlocking teeth engaged against each other, the surface of those teeth was abraded so that the metal, where it slid together, was polished to a high luster. Reddish dust from countless centuries of inaction was being grated and worn away so that it began to float through the interior of the metal box, making it look like a rusty fog down inside.

As Richard tried to see down through the floating dust inside, he couldn't see a bottom. It was hard to see past all the intricate, complex workings, bulky levers, wrist-thick shafts, and massive geared wheels, but he was able to see glimpses of yet more mechanical parts down lower, down to a great depth inside, until the layers of inner workings obscured the view of the lower reaches. The haze of stirred-up dirt and rust made the inside of the machine look as if it were filled with smoke.

Richard moved over so Kahlan could take a look through the narrow window. As he moved aside, he discovered another opening in the side of the machine not far to the left below the window. He bent down, holding the glowing sphere close. The opening was nothing more than a narrow channel. A few pieces of the same metal strips lay stacked in the channel.

Kahlan pointed at the ceiling. "Richard, look."

The light coming from the tiny hole in the center of the top of the machine was projecting a symbol onto the ceiling.

The design drawn in lines of light slowly rotated as the gears within turned.

Looking through the window, Richard could see wheels and gears line up holes in metal plates over the beam of light in order to project a collection of emblematic elements into the single unified symbol appearing on the ceiling above, while yet other gears turned the whole assembly, rotating the projected image.

"That's the same emblem that's on the side."

"What's making the light?" Kahlan asked.

"It looks to be something like the light coming from the proximity spheres."

Richard moved around the machine, brushing away the crust of its long sleep. Each side had the same emblem—the same symbol that was projected onto the ceiling, rotating above their heads.

Richard stared up at the projection as recognition washed over him.

"Dear spirits," he whispered under his breath.

29

K ahlan looked from Richard's troubled face to the
glowing symbol made of lines of amber light slowly
turning on the ceiling.

"You recognize it, don't you?"

Richard nodded as he watched the complex emblem of
light rotate on the ceiling above the box.

"Regula."

Kahlan didn't like the sound of the word. She thought she
remembered it. She squinted in thought as she tried to recall
where she'd heard the word. It finally came to her.

"You mean *Regula* as in the book in the library that we
were looking at the other day?"

"That's the one," Richard said. "That symbol was on the
spine."

"That's right," Kahlan said in wonder. "I remember now."

As he was focused on studying the symbol made up of
light above them, Kahlan cradled her throbbing hand against
her stomach. It was getting worse just since earlier in the night,
since they saw that thing watching them in their room. It
stung so badly that it nearly made her eyes water. The stitch

of pain finally eased up. She let out the breath she had been holding.

She'd had much worse injuries, and suffered far greater pain, so she wasn't overly concerned. It was more of an annoyance than anything. She knew, though, that even such simple injuries could develop into serious infections, so she knew she should probably ask Zedd to take a look at it before it got any worse. He would be able to heal it.

Richard had in the past used his gift to heal, but it wasn't something he could do at will, like other wizards. Not for minor things, anyway. His gift was not only more powerful than Zedd's, or Nathan's, or Nicci's, but it was unique in the way it worked. Possibly because he was a war wizard, his power required great need, or anger, as a component in order to come to life within him. Healing a scratch, as painful as it was becoming, was not enough. It would be better to let Zedd look at it.

But with the representatives causing trouble over the strange prophecies, the thing that had been watching them in their room suddenly attacking them, and now the collapse of the floor of the Garden of Life and the discovery of what was beneath it, there were more important immediate concerns. She would have Zedd look at her hand when she had time.

"Do you know what Regula means?" Kahlan asked.

Still looking up at the symbol projected onto the ceiling, Richard nodded. "Yes, but it's kind of difficult to translate accurately. In High D'Haran '*regula*' means to regulate."

"That sounds simple enough."

His gray eyes finally turned down to look at her. "It may seem that way but it's not. Its full meaning is a great deal more significant than that simple translation sounds."

Kahlan studied his eyes for a moment. "Well, can you give me some kind of sense of what it means?"

Richard raked his fingers back through his hair, apparently considering how to explain it. "I guess the best way to put it is that Regula represents, well, a kind of autonomous control, but as in . . ." He made a face as he tried to come up with the right word. Finally he did. "As in to regulate with a sovereign authority."

"Sovereign authority?"

"Yes. Something like the way the laws of nature regulate the world of life."

Kahlan didn't like that sound of that. "So if that symbol up there is also on the book, then maybe the book can help us figure out what this thing is. Maybe even what it's doing down here."

"Could be," Richard said as he studied the lines of light once again. "There's a problem, though."

"And what would that be?"

"This symbol may be the same, but it's backward from the one on the spine."

Kahlan shook her head. It was nearly indecipherable to her. It looked like little more than a collection of little circles and hen scratchings within circles with a triangle tying parts of it together along with a collection of other strange designs she'd never seen before.

"How in the world can you remember that it's the same symbol? As complex as it is, how can you be sure it really is the same, much less that it's backward?"

His gaze returned to her. "Because I understand some of the language of symbols. A lot of spell-forms are really ideas expressed through symbols or emblems rather than words. Symbols, even ones I've never seen before, stick in my head.

That's how I solved a number of things in the past. This one is largely new to me. But elements of it seem oddly familiar."

Kahlan sighed as she idly picked one of the metal strips out of the opening near the glass window. Something about it caught her eye. She was surprised to see that there were markings on it. She held it closer.

She was stunned by what she saw.

"Richard, look." As he bent close she held it out in the light for him to see. "This one in here isn't blank."

Richard took it from her when she held it out and carefully looked over the line of symbols seemingly burned into the metal.

"They're all different," he said, half to himself.

Kahlan looked in the slot where she had found it. "There are two more strips in here." She pulled them out, took a quick look, and then handed them to him.

He looked them over, one at a time, studying each for a moment. "More symbols. But they're different. Each strip has distinctive emblems on it. Look, this one has a whole string of markings, but the one that was on the bottom only has a few."

When the machine began to make more noise, as if a whole bank of additional gears had been engaged, Richard bent to look into the slit of a window. Kahlan could see the light from inside reflecting in lines that moved parts of symbolic elements over the contours of his face.

"I can see a strip of metal being pulled out from the bottom of the stack on the other side. It's being pulled into the machine and going way down inside."

Kahlan put her head close to his, trying to see what he was talking about. Then she saw it, way down among the gears, shafts, and levers, being pulled through by a small pincer mechanism holding the front of the metal strip. The pincer was attached to a large wheel that carried the strip of metal up and around with it to place it in a track where a series of levers moved it along different junctions of track until another geared pincer finally picked it up.

Kahlan and Richard both turned aside a little as a flash of intense orangish white light ignited deep within. Out of the corner of her eye she could see a bright pinpoint of light dance across the metal strip. The focused beam of light from far below moved with lightning speed but in a tightly controlled manner. The light was so intense that she could see a moving, glowing white-hot spot of light shining through the top of the metal where the beam hit it from underneath.

As the strip came around with the wheel, another mechanism took it in turn and rotated it around so that the symbol that had been burned into the underside of the metal was now facing up. At exactly the correct point in the arc of the gear, the pincers opened and a lever on a geared mechanism swung in from the side to push the metal strip through a slot in the side of the machine.

She heard it drop into the tray.

Richard and Kahlan straightened from the little window and looked at each other.

"Did you see that?" he asked.

Kahlan nodded. "Pretty hard to miss."

Richard pulled the strip of metal out of the tray. He immediately tossed it on top of the machine and shook his hand, then blew on his fingers. He pushed the hot metal strip around with a finger for a moment until it cooled, then gingerly picked it up and studied the single symbol etched into it.

"What about that one? Do you recognize it?" Kahlan asked.

Richard stared at it with a troubled expression. "I'm not entirely certain. It's not exactly the same, but it's pretty close."

"Pretty close to what? What is it?"

Richard looked up at her again.

"It's the emblematic representation for fire."

CHAPTER

30

O utside of the Garden of Life hundreds of heavily armed guards filled the corridor in both directions. They all looked a great deal more than edgy. Kahlan realized that they would have had to have heard the lightning hit the Garden of Life. They probably heard the glass roof breaking and falling as well. They undoubtedly wondered what in the world had been going on beyond the doors.

They might even have feared that it was an attack of magic of some sort, and so they were standing ready in case they were called upon to defend the palace.

She knew, though, that despite their worry, none of them, not even a Mord-Sith, would dare to enter the Garden of Life while the Lord Rahl was inside unless he invited them in.

The grim look on Richard's face and the set of his jaw as he came marching out probably only confirmed to all the men watching him approach that they had made the right decision to remain outside.

The only people who regularly went into the garden were the staff assigned to tend the grass, flowers, shrubs, and trees. Only the most highly trusted people on the palace staff were allowed to work in the garden. Even then, when they went in to do their work officers of the First File watched them at all times.

During the war, when they were under constant threat and there were dangerous objects of magic containing tremendous power locked away in the Garden of Life for safekeeping, not even the people who tended the garden had been allowed to go in to take care of the plants and trees. As a result it became for a time a wild, overgrown place that had taken on an eerie look that in a way matched the gloomy mood of everyone in the palace.

After the war had ended, it had taken a lot of work to return the garden to the state of splendor it was now in.

Kahlan had a feeling, though, that even such occasional tending was at an end and the Garden of Life was about to again become strictly off-limits to everyone except on Lord Rahl's instructions.

Throughout history the Garden of Life had been a place where the Lord Rahl, from time to time, had unleashed some of the most powerful magic in existence.

It had been a place that on occasion had been a gateway to the underworld itself.

Magic was a mystery to most people and therefore greatly feared. Kahlan knew that magic could be glorious, wondrous, a magnificent affirmation of life. But Kahlan knew magic's other side, its dark and dangerous side. Most people only knew magic as a dark, mysterious danger. For the D'Haran people, the Lord Rahl was their protection against those dark dangers of magic. For their part, these soldiers were meant to be the steel against steel. They would lay down their lives in that service.

But it was Richard's responsibility as the Lord Rahl to deal with any matters involving magic.

It seemed that the Garden of Life had once again become the stage for dangerous magic.

Nyda stood before the ranks of soldiers, her arms folded, watching Richard and Kahlan come. The Mord-Sith was in her red leather. She looked to be in a foul mood, but for a Mord-Sith that wasn't necessarily at all unusual.

"What's going on?" Nyda asked.

As Richard stormed past, he took her by the arm and turned her around to walk with him, but he spoke to the commander of the soldiers on his way by.

"No one is to go in there. No one. Do you understand?"

The commander clapped a fist to his heart in salute. "Of course, Lord Rahl."

The commander immediately assigned men to guard the doors and then issued orders to the rest of them to take up stations along the hallways and intersections. The hall came alive with movement and the echoing jangle of metal as men rushed to take up their posts.

Richard leaned close to Nyda. "Go get Berdine. Bring her to the library."

Nyda, still being carried along with him by her arm, pointed downward. "You mean the library down there, below us, where she has been working?"

"That's right. Get her and send her there. Then get my grandfather and bring him there, too. You had better bring Nicci, Nathan, and Cara as well."

"All of them? Now, in the middle of the night?"

"In the middle of the night," Richard confirmed.

Nyda leaned out past Richard to look over at Kahlan. "What's going on?"

"The roof fell in."

CHAPTER
31

Kahlan's throbbing hand lay in her lap as she sat in a wooden library chair, not far from Richard's side, as she worked on translating a few passages in a book written in an obscure language she happened to know. She was having trouble making her eyes focus. Richard needed her help to cross-reference a few descriptions in the book that he and Berdine were studying.

Kahlan yawned and looked up when she heard a commotion and saw Zedd storming in through the doors at the far end of the room. His robes looked like they were having a difficult time keeping pace with the rawboned wizard. Richard only glanced up momentarily from the book he was absorbed in reading.

Kahlan went back to her work but from time to time checked out of the corner of her eye as Zedd made his way resolutely across the gold and blue carpets. His face, set with grim creases, fell into shadow between each of the reflector lamps hung on columns at the end of the rows of shelves.

"Bags, Richard, what's going on?"

"No need for that kind of language. I need to see you, that's all."

Zedd came to a halt on the other side of the heavy mahogany table. Finally having a chance to catch up, his simple robes swirled in around his legs. He took in Kahlan's face, searching her expression for any hint of the nature of the problem, before returning his attention to Richard.

"I have good reason for my language. Do you have any idea what it's like to be awakened in the middle of the night by a Mord-Sith?"

Kahlan glanced up at the windows on the balcony. She could see only darkness. Morning was still a long way off. She knew they weren't going to have a chance to get any sleep. At least the storm seemed to have broken.

Richard didn't look up from the book. "As as matter of fact, I do. Did she use her Agiel to wake you?"

"No, of course not."

"Then believe me, you have nothing to complain about."

Zedd planted his fists on his hips. After again assessing the look on Kahlan's face, he seemed to think better of what he had been about to say. His tone softened.

"What's going on, my boy?"

"There's been an incident."

Zedd scowled at his grandson a moment. "An incident. What do you mean, there's been an incident? You mean, like the cook burned the gravy? That kind of incident?"

"Not exactly." Richard sighed as he leaned back in his chair to look up at his grandfather. Kahlan could see the weary frustration in Richard's gray eyes. "We found something buried under the Garden of Life."

Zedd cocked his head. "What do you mean, you found it? How did you find it?"

"The roof fell in."

"The roof . . ." He glanced again at Kahlan. She didn't have so much as a smile in her.

Zedd looked back over his shoulder when Nathan charged into the library leading Nicci, Cara, Benjamin, and Nyda.

"What's going on?" Nathan demanded in a booming voice from halfway across the room.

"Seems the roof over the Garden of Life fell in," Zedd announced. "I don't know yet what the boy did to cause it to collapse."

"Me? I didn't do—"

"So then the fragment prophecy is confirmed," Nathan said. "Doesn't sound all that important, though. Not important enough to wake us all in the middle of the night."

Richard folded his arms and waited until both wizards fell silent. When they looked at him innocently, waiting for him to explain, and he was sure they would remain silent, he finally went on.

"There's more to it. The glass roof was covered in heavy, wet snowdrifts. When it all fell in it landed in the center portion of the floor in the Garden of Life. The weight and shock of the impact, along with a lightning strike, in turn caused the floor to give way." Richard wiped a weary hand back across his face. "There's a room buried under there that looks not to have had a visitor in thousands of years."

Zedd placed his hands on the table and leaned in with a scowl. "Obviously there must be something in that room that would cause you to send Nyda to wake us in the middle of the night."

"Obviously."

Nathan turned to Zedd. "What do you think is in there?"

"Well how should I know?"

Nicci shot them each a hot glare. "Would you two give him a chance to tell us?"

Zedd's mouth twisted irritably. "All right, so what did you find?"

Berdine leaned forward and tapped the book she and Richard had been sharing. "Lord Rahl says it speaks in this language."

Both Zedd and Nathan blinked in astonishment.

" 'It'?" Nicci asked. "What are you talking about? What do you mean?"

"Yes, what do you mean?" Nathan added.

"Berdine is being dramatic." Richard tossed a metal strip across the table to his grandfather. It spun on the mahogany tabletop, reflecting flashes of lamplight for a moment before it slowed to a halt. "In a second room down under the Garden of Life there is a machine that inscribes these strips of metal with symbols."

Zedd stared in astonishment. "A machine?"

Nathan cocked his head to eye the metal strip on the table. "A machine that inscribes symbols?"

"Yes. I believe that the inscriptions are a form of language. That's what Berdine was talking about when she said it speaks."

Zedd smoothed back his unruly shock of wavy white hair. "A machine . . ." With great care he picked up the metal strip. His bushy brows drew down as he studied the series of designs. Nathan looked over one shoulder, Nicci the other. Cara, Benjamin, and Nyda peered around from the side.

"What kind of symbols are these?" Zedd asked. "I've never seen anything like most of these before."

Richard lifted the book, letting them see the spine. He didn't look any happier than his grandfather. "Symbols out of this book, *Regula*."

Zedd eyed the book as if it were a treacherous agent of the Keeper himself. "It would have to be that one."

"I'm afraid so," Richard said.

Zedd gestured at the book. "I know a few words of High D'Haran here and there, but I don't know that one, '*regula.*' What does it mean?"

"It means to regulate with sovereign authority."

"Sovereign authority," Zedd scoffed.

Nathan arched an eyebrow. "Richard is being restrained in his translation."

"Quite restrained," Nicci added under her breath.

Kahlan sat in silent worry about just what it was that the Regula machine was supposed to regulate. Everything about it—the size, the complexity, the way it burned messages in an ancient form of language onto the metal strips with focused beams of light, and especially the way it had been hidden and sealed away for ages yet still seemed to function—had her stomach tightened into a knot.

As Nathan took the strip of metal from Zedd to have a closer look, Zedd again waggled a hand at the book. "So what does the book have to do with these strips of metal?"

"I believe that the book is what Berdine thought it was from the first, a wordbook, a manual of sorts. I think that the book is the means to decipher the symbols in order to be able to understand what the strips say."

"Then it's a good thing we have the book," Nathan said in a cautious tone that suggested he didn't think it could be that simple. "So what have you been able to figure out about the symbols?"

Richard stared off a moment before speaking, apparently reluctant to have to admit it aloud.

"Nothing, I'm afraid."

Nathan's scowl grew. "I thought you said the book was intended as a means to decode the strips?"

"I believe it is. But it doesn't work."

His grandfather's brow drew down even tighter. "What do you mean, it doesn't work? If it is what you say it is then it has to work."

"I know," Richard said in a quiet voice. "But it doesn't."

32

Zedd peered again at the metal strip when Nathan handed it back, squinting at it as he turned it in the light. He finally surrendered with an unhappy sigh.

"You say that this machine you found inscribed these symbols? What kind of machine could do such a thing?"

"It's a big square metal box." Richard flicked his hand. "About as big as from here to the end of the table, there. It has a small slit fitted with a glass window so that you can see down inside. The box is filled with all kinds of gears and levers and mechanical mechanisms all linked together. From looking down in, you can see that it goes much deeper than it looks like from the outside. It's not sitting on the ground, it's coming up out of the ground."

Zedd glanced at the book lying open on the table. "Can you tell anything at all from the book about these designs that the machine inscribes on the strips?"

"Well, since symbols are a language of sorts, much like an innkeeper might have a drawing of a mug of ale on his sign, or a farrier might have a horseshoe nailed to his gate, that means that these strings of symbols are saying something, but it's something complex. Some of the symbols on the strips are familiar, but a lot of what's inscribed on them are unlike any designs I've ever seen before. Since these same symbols appear in the book, I believe that the book must be a means to decipher the metal strips."

"That's what Berdine means when she says it talks?" Nicci asked.

Richard nodded. He tapped the book as he fixed the three standing before him with a meaningful look. "This book, *Regula*, calls these symbols the language of Creation."

"That's a bit of a leap at this point," Nathan said. "Especially since the book doesn't work to decode the symbols the way you thought it would."

"I realize it may look that way at the moment, but I believe that's the true purpose of the book. Just because I haven't been able to figure out how to make it work, yet, doesn't mean that it isn't the true purpose of the book. I'm missing some kind of key to turn the lock keeping its secrets hidden, that's all."

Zedd broke Richard's gaze to look down once more at the metal strip he was holding. He finally spoke in a quiet, troubled tone.

"I recognize a few fragments of those symbols."

"From the Wizard's Keep," Richard confirmed with a nod.

"So these are emblems like those inscribed on the walls at the Keep, in that they represent specific things?"

"Something like that, but not exactly. It's more than that."

"How can it be more than that?" Nathan wanted to know. "If a symbol represents something, like a skull with crossed bones under it represents mortal danger, then that's what it represents. How can it be more?"

"I believe that what really matters is how the symbols are used in combination," Richard said. "From what I can gather from this book, these pictorial devices are not simple emblematic representations in and of themselves, like a mug, or a horseshoe, or your example of a skull and crossed bones.

"It's true that parts of them are recognizable as independent symbolic entities, but I believe that falls short of the full intent of their use here. By studying this book I can see by the way simple elements are assembled into more complex images that they are in fact parts of a complex language, rather than single concepts. I think that the symbols actually have somewhat different meanings depending on how they're combined.

"This one"—Richard tapped a metal strip lying on the table—"is the simplest of them. It's different. It's a symbol that represents one thing, from what I can make out of it, anyway. It isn't combined with anything else, so in this case I don't believe that its meaning is intended to be modified by any other element. Its meaning is therefore singular. This singular concept is all the machine wanted to say."

Zedd shot Richard an incredulous look. "What the machine wanted to say? And what would that meaning be? What did the machine want to say, as you put it?"

"Fire."

Zedd's brow drew down again. "Fire?"

"Yes, that's the symbol for fire. For some reason I can't seem to work the translation in the book, but I know because I've seen it before in the verification web for the Chainfire spell—remember?"

Nicci folded her arms. "I certainly remember that one."

Zedd grunted that he also remembered it all too well. "Why would this machine inscribe 'fire'—if that's what it really means in this case—on a strip of metal?"

"I don't know," Richard admitted with a sigh. "I was hoping

that you three could go down there and take a look at the machine and see if you can figure out what we're dealing with. It might be nothing more than a curiosity from an age long past, but if it's anything more, I'd like to know about it. It must be powered by magic of some sort. Maybe one of you has encountered that kind of power before and you will recognize it."

"How do you know that it's powered by magic?" Nathan asked.

Richard shrugged. "What else? It's certainly not run by a water wheel. The light coming from inside looks like the kind of light given off by the proximity spheres. I'm hoping that one of you knows something about the magic the machine uses, maybe even what its purpose was, or is. I'm worried about its location—right in the heart of the palace, under the Garden of Life, the heart of the elaborate spell that is the palace structure."

Zedd turned the metal strip around and around, studying it with a leery eye. "All right," he finally said. "We'll take a look. Have you been able to learn anything at all from the book about what any of the other symbols on the other strips mean?"

"So far all I know is that the elements of the various symbols are actually intended to be combined—that the string of them is more than the sum of their parts. At least, that's what the High D'Haran explanations say, that the string of component parts when put together form a language."

"The language of Creation," Zedd said in a sour tone.

"Yes. Because of that, I think it's a mistake to try to interpret the symbols individually. If you try, then you lose sight of the true meaning expressed by the combination. Those strings of symbolic inscriptions are the language of Creation. I just can't figure out how to decode it."

Zedd gestured with the strip of metal. "So you're saying that these strings of symbols are actually meant to be combined, like the words in a sentence, in order to communicate some kind of information, or to tell a story?"

Berdine lifted an eyebrow at Richard. "Dear spirits, isn't that a wonder? I think he's finally paying attention."

Zedd ignored her. "So if you haven't figured out anything at all of this language from the book, then you can't even guess at what these longer emblematic statements might mean."

Richard tapped the end of his pen on the table for a moment. "I'm afraid not."

33

Looking more concerned than either Zedd or Nathan, Nicci didn't appear nearly so skeptical, or dismissive. Kahlan knew that Nicci had come to trust Richard, and believe in him, in a deeply personal way that was ironclad. Kahlan, of course, felt an even deeper sense of trust in Richard that only unconditional love could bring. Zedd had for the most part raised Richard, so he knew him well enough to know better than Nicci how much trust Richard's word warranted, but having raised Richard, he found it hard to admit it out loud, or to keep from interrogating him to be doubly certain.

Nicci did not take anything Richard said lightly, and so she wanted to press. "Why doesn't the book work the way it should? What do you need to make it work? What's missing?"

Richard succumbed to a sigh. "I don't know."

Nicci wasn't satisfied. "You must have learned something."

He ran a hand over the open book. "From everything I can tell it should work, but it simply doesn't. Berdine and I have been going around in circles and getting nowhere. In essence, the book says 'When combined with these elements in this way, this design means this.' But when you apply the rules the string of symbols only ends up as meaningless nonsense. I can't for the life of me figure out why it won't work the way it's supposed to."

Zedd gestured dismissively toward the book. "Perhaps this book, *Regula*, doesn't really have anything to do with the machine, like you thought it did, or at least not as much as you assumed it must. After all, with a machine hidden away for untold ages, and a book of unknown origin with half of it missing, how can you know for certain that there really is a direct connection between the two?"

Richard shrugged. "Simple." He turned the pages back to the beginning and spun the book around to his grandfather. "This emblem, here, taking up this whole beginning page, is the same symbol that's on the spine. It defines what this book is, what it's about. It's the same symbol that's on all four sides of the machine."

"That same symbol is on both—the book and the machine?"

Richard confirmed it with a nod.

Zedd thought it over for a moment. "Do you have any clue as to what the emblem means?"

"I'm afraid not."

Zedd paced in agitation for a moment. "This is on the machine? This same drawing? The whole thing, exactly like this, every detail the same?"

"Exactly the same," Richard said. "The whole emblem, every line, every motif, every detail. I tried to decipher it from the translations in the book, but I can't make sense of it, either. It seems like it should work out, but it doesn't." Richard tapped the center of the design. "This symbol, this here in the center, looks like it might be a stylized figure nine."

Zedd eyed it unhappily. "It certainly appears that way."

"Why would there be a nine in the center of this?" Kahlan asked. It seemed to her an odd thing to have in the center of so many occult elements. She especially didn't like the way the top part of the nine looked to be made from a serpent's head. She hated snakes.

Zedd glanced momentarily at the complex symbol. "Nine is an important trigger element. It links a number of laws of magic that have powerful influence over events. Threes are elemental in magic. Among other things, they are used in proofing magic. Threes construct nines—three threes make nine. They give nines power, help make them a Creative element." Zedd stirred a finger over the drawing. "That's likely the purpose behind the triangle, here, around it. It has three sides. I have to tell you, Richard, multiples of three are often trouble."

"You mean, like the three children of trouble? Bad news coming in threes? Things like that?"

Zedd nodded. "I believe that's the origin of the sayings. These three symbols at the points of the triangle are supporting elements in the construction of the web. They help tie it to the nine to strengthen the bond, make it more powerful."

"So do you have any guess at what it could mean, then?" Richard asked as he studied the emblem.

Zedd scratched his cheek. "I haven't the faintest idea."

Nicci leaned in, using a finger to trace the figure without touching it. "See the way this nine in the center ends with a hook?"

With that quiet question it was as if Nicci had slipped on the robes of the teacher she had once been to Richard, his instructor in the use of his gift. It had turned out to be a futile effort, but not for any failing on Nicci's part. It was simply that Richard's gift was unlike anyone else's. Since no one understood it or how it functioned they couldn't teach him anything about using it.

By the slight shift in Nicci's bearing Kahlan suspected that the sorceress knew something about the device in the center of the emblem.

It was clear to Kahlan that Richard suspected the same thing. "What of it?"

"Well, what does that hook tell you? What does it suggest? Why would it end with a hook?"

"A hooked nine makes this more than a web using the simple figure nine," Richard said, thinking out loud. "So, it's intended to hook something together, or to hook it to something."

"It's there for a reason," Nicci prompted.

"It's hooking all of this, this"—Zedd gestured irritably around the edge of the emblem—"whatever it is, together."

"Or it is hooking it to a host," Nicci said with demure authority.

Richard looked up from the emblem. "A host?"

Nicci had been waiting for his gaze. "Whoever, or whatever, this is intended for. A host. It's meant to hook it fast to them. So what is the nature of the hook?"

"The nature of the hook?" Richard was intently focused on the lesson being laid out before him even though he couldn't yet grasp its meaning.

"What did Zedd say about this figure?"

Richard glanced at his grandfather momentarily before returning his attention to Nicci. "He said it was Creative."

"And what does that tell you?"

Richard rested his chin on the tips of his fingers as he gazed down at the curl of the backward nine in the book. "That makes sense," he said, half to himself. "It has to do with Creation. The curled figure nine almost looks embryonic. . . ."

"And the hook?" Nicci asked so quietly that Kahlan knew the words were meant for him alone.

"The nine is Creation, life," Richard said under his breath. "Life is a cycle. Birth, life, death. Life and death together. Creation needs death to enable life to continue to exist, to continue to come about. Death must eventually follow Creation."

Richard looked up suddenly. "The hook is death."

The room was dead silent.

Richard's gaze stayed locked on Nicci. "The hook is the symbolic representation of death, of the Keeper of the underworld, always waiting to eventually reap the living."

Kahlan felt goose bumps tingle up her arms.

Nicci's blue eyes revealed her inner satisfaction at his sudden insight. "Very good, Richard."

In that instant, as she and Richard, the sorceress and the wizard, looked into each other's eyes, it was as if no one else was in the room, as if no one else existed. Kahlan wondered if even Zedd had known the shades of meaning Nicci had just taught Richard about that figure.

Nicci's smile ghosted away. "I don't like this, Richard. I don't like it one bit. People don't go to this much trouble and effort with such things, only to bury them . . . unless it had turned out to be great trouble. To see such elements dealing in such dark powers at the center of it all confirms it."

Richard puzzled at the symbol for a moment. "Why is the nine backward?"

Everyone leaned in, gazing down at it, as if seeing it for

the first time. Nathan frowned at the book, unable to offer a reason. Nicci shook her head, not even able to venture a guess.

"Backward?" Zedd asked as he peered down at the symbol.

"Yes. The whole emblem is backward. You can tell because the nine is backward as well."

"Good question," Zedd said. "I just assumed it was intended to be that way. But now that you mention it, it does seem backward."

Richard stared at the drawing for a long moment. He suddenly looked up at his grandfather.

"Backward . . . that's it!" He shot to his feet. "Zedd, you're a genius!"

"Yes, I'm well aware of that." He cocked his head. "But . . . how exactly have I outdone myself this time?"

"You've just helped me figure out how the book works. You've given me the key to get past the locks." He looked down at Berdine. "It's backward. Everything in this book is backward."

Berdine made a face. "Backward?"

Richard nodded, then turned back to his grandfather. "The rules we've been applying don't work, and as a consequence the translations don't work. It should be a relatively straight-forward process to translate the elements so we can begin to understand the language on the strips, but the translations aren't working properly. You just helped me figure out the reason."

Zedd looked more than a little suspicious. "And what would the reason be?"

"It's a trick meant to protect the information." Richard

dropped into his chair. "It's all backward from the way the machine sees the emblem."

"What do you mean, the way the machine sees the emblem?" Nicci asked in a careful tone.

Zedd waved a hand, insisting on being the first one to ask the questions. "What do you mean it's backward? What's backward?"

"The symbols in the book," Richard said. He lifted the book to show Kahlan the emblem on the spine. "This symbol is the same one that's inscribed on the machine we found. Remember?"

"I remember." Kahlan couldn't understand what he was getting at. "They're all the same—the ones on the sides of the machine, the one on the first page of the book, and that one on the spine. If they're all the same then they must have been deliberately drawn that way because they're part of the language of Creation. So what makes you think they're backward?"

"That's right," Zedd put in. "You said yourself you can't make the book work at decoding anything, so for all you know the nine in all of these emblems is supposed to be backward. It's stylized, after all, not necessarily intended to be literal.

"Symbolic elements are often stylized. They don't always look exactly like the thing they represent. The serpent head making the top of the nine is stylized, not an exact representation. The symbol for fire on that other strip doesn't actually look like fire, it's stylized. It very well could be as Kahlan suggested, that it's meant to be that way because it's part of the language."

"They're not right," Richard insisted. "They're all flipped around backward from the way they're supposed to be. All of them are wrong."

Zedd threw his hands up. "If every one of them, in every place, is the same, then how can they all be wrong?"

Nicci hushed the apoplectic wizard, then turned toward Richard, intent on hearing him out. "How do you know they're wrong? How do you know they're backward?"

"Because," Richard said, "this is what we see when we're looking inward. But it's not what the machine sees."

Nicci's brow lowered in a way that would have halted most people's breath and maybe made their heart skip a beat. Her intent gaze remained locked on Richard's. "You said that before, that it's backward from the way the machine sees the emblem. What are you talking about, the machine seeing?"

Richard pressed the heels of his hands together, pointing all his fingers up and out to demonstrate. "The machine used light to project the symbol upward, like this, the same symbol as on the spine of this book. It projects it out from down inside its metal box, up onto the ceiling."

Nicci straightened with the disquiet of comprehension.

Zedd, still not understanding, planted his fists on his hips. "So?"

"Well, all the other symbols—on the sides of the machine and in the book—are the same, but the one projected by light from within the machine up onto the ceiling was reversed. Up on the ceiling, the nine wasn't backward. That emblem, projected from inside the machine up onto the ceiling, is what the symbol looks like from inside the machine, looking out. It's what the machine would see on the ceiling. That's how it sees its own emblem."

"How it sees its own emblem?" Zedd repeated in frustration. "You can't be serious."

Richard pulled a piece of paper close and dipped his pen in an ink bottle and drew a large, boldly dark figure nine on it. He held it up for Zedd to see.

"This is what the machine is drawing with light, what it sees: a nine."

Zedd rolled his hand. "Go on."

Richard turned the paper around and held it in front of a lamp so Zedd could see the nine through the back of the paper. "When you look down into the machine at the light, at what the machine sees as a nine, what it is drawing with light, you see the nine like this—backward.

"The emblem, as we see it marked down everywhere, the impressions, the imprints, are what we would see looking down into the machine, at the designs in light it would be creating and projecting outward. But that's backward from the machine's view out onto the world"—Richard flipped the paper around so Zedd could see the front with the nine the way he had drawn it—"of the way it sees the emblem it projects onto the ceiling."

Kahlan rose from her chair as the simplicity of it dawned on her. "Of course. Richard is right, these are all backward."

Zedd eyed them both as if the insanity had become infectious. "You're making this machine sound alive. It's gears and levers, you said. A machine."

"Of course."

With one hand on a hip, Zedd paced as he considered it. "I

hate to say it," he finally admitted, "but as crazy as it sounds that actually does make sense. Dangerous books involving magic usually have safeguards to keep just anyone from using them. It may sound crazy when you hear it at first, but it certainly would make a powerful safeguard."

"It seems like a pretty easy safeguard to crack," Berdine said. "Sure, it took Lord Rahl a little while, but he figured it out. Seems like a safeguard would have to be more difficult to solve if it really is going to protect a dangerous book."

"You really think so?" Zedd slowly shook his head as his gaze left Berdine to meet Richard's. "The only reason he figured it out was because he activated the magic that showed him the projected symbol.

"I have a feeling that only the right person could have done that. Many forms of magic are keyed to specific users. Someone else might have found that machine, but I have a feeling that only Richard could have activated it. In so doing it gave him the solution he needed to make the book work for him so that he could use that clue to understand what the machine wants to tell him. I doubt anyone else would have had access to that clue. That makes the safeguard doubly safe."

Zedd tossed a metal strip on the table.

Richard stared at the old wizard for a moment. "Now you're the one making it sound alive."

Zedd only smiled.

Richard finally sat and scooted his chair up to the table. "Berdine, we have to invert all those rules we had listed out and then link them to the High D'Haran translations."

Berdine dipped her pen in an ink bottle and pulled a piece of paper close. "Here, let me see one of those other strips."

Richard picked one of the strips up off the table. He turned it over in his fingers a moment before looking at the symbols

THE OMEN MACHINE

inscribed on it. He laid it at the top of Berdine's paper so she could use it as reference.

"This is going to take a while," Richard told Zedd as he pulled the book back. "But we've already established all the links, so hopefully it will be a little easier this time through."

CHAPTER

35

Richard turned his attention to Benjamin, standing back out of the way with Cara and Nyda, watching. "I need you to do something, General."

Benjamin stepped forward. "Yes, Lord Rahl?"

With the back end of his pen, Richard pointed toward the ceiling. "I need you to take a work crew up there, to the Garden of Life, and have them fix the glass roof. It needs to be done as soon as possible."

Benjamin tapped a fist to his heart. "I'll take care of it, Lord Rahl."

"Zedd, Nathan, Nicci, while Berdine and I are working on this, why don't you go down there and see what you can find out about the machine."

Zedd nodded. "I would like to get a look for myself."

"And Benjamin, I need you to do something else." Richard gestured back over his shoulder. "You see that odd notch in the wall? It really makes no sense for this room to have that corner intruding into it like that. We're somewhere under the Garden of Life. I want you to see if you can't figure out a floor plan of this area of the palace."

Benjamin glanced to the notched corner. "A floor plan?"

"Yes. I want to know what's under the Garden of Life, besides the machine. I want to know how far that machine goes down through the palace. I want to know what we're dealing with. I want to know where the bottom of the machine is. We're not that far under the garden level, so I suspect that you will find that the machine is behind that odd corner sticking into this room."

Berdine was frowning back at the odd jog in the wall. "Lord Rahl, that shelf back there, against that wall . . ."

"I know," Richard said, quietly. "That's where we found this book. That's another reason I suspect that the machine is on the other side of that wall. I want to know how deep it goes down through the palace."

Benjamin hooked a thumb behind his belt. "While you're working on translating the symbols, I'll find out, Lord Rahl."

"Nyda and I will help," Cara said. "The Mord-Sith are familiar with all the corridors—public and private. We have to be able to move quickly through the palace in case there is ever an attack, so we know all the halls, pass-through rooms, and secret passageways."

"Good," Richard said. "Hopefully, we'll have these strips decoded before you finish mapping the machine's resting place."

Nathan waggled a finger over the book. "And it's complete enough? There is enough information in the book to decipher all the symbols?"

"Yes, I believe so," Richard said.

Nathan didn't look satisfied. "If that's true, if the book is a means to translate the symbols, and all the information you need is there so that you can do just that, then what part of the book is missing? What part was taken to the Temple of the Winds?"

Richard stared up at the prophet a moment before finally speaking. "According to what little it says on that topic, the part they took to the temple for safekeeping is the explanation of the purpose of the machine."

"That's not very comforting," Zedd said.

Kahlan found that thought more than a little troubling as well. Without knowing the purpose of the machine, they didn't really know what they were dealing with. The fact that the machine had been sealed away and hidden seemed to her to be a bad omen.

Richard gently slipped a hand around Kahlan's waist and changed the subject. "Why don't you go with them."

Kahlan twitched a frown at him. "Why?"

"The translations you already did were what I needed. Berdine and I are likely going to be here the rest of the night. There's nothing more you can do for now. Why don't you get some rest? I think you'll be safe from snooping eyes in the Garden of Life. Maybe you can get some sleep while Berdine and I work on decoding the symbols and Zedd and the others investigate the machine."

"We'll watch over her, Richard," Nicci said. "No hidden eyes will be looking in at her while she sleeps."

"Thanks, Nicci. Zedd, maybe when you get up to the garden you could heal Kahlan's hand. It's getting worse."

Zedd's expression reflected his concern. "Of course."

Kahlan realized that she wasn't surprised that Richard knew how much her hand was hurting. It was next to impossible for her to hide anything from Richard.

When she heard the distant howl, her gaze was drawn to the high windows. She realized that it wasn't coming from the high windows. It had to have come from somewhere else, but she couldn't tell where, exactly.

Kahlan remembered the prophecy the woman gave before she died, that dark things, feral things, would come for Kahlan in the night. The memory of the woman's words, *"Dark things stalking you, running you down. You won't be able to escape them,"* gave her a chill.

When she noticed that no one else seemed to have heard it, she thought that she must have only heard some other errant sound and mistook it for the howl of a wolf. Richard was right, she was tired. She was letting her imagination run away with her.

Kahlan kissed Richard's cheek and then trailed her hand along the back of his shoulders on her way by. He caught her hand. She wished more than anything that he could come lie with her, keep her company, keep her safe. Her hand finally slipped from his gentle grasp as she followed the others on their way to the Garden of Life.

CHAPTER

36

Hannis Arc, working on the tapestry of lines linking constellations of elements that constituted the language of Creation recorded on the ancient Cerulean scroll spread out among the clutter on his desk, was not surprised to see the seven ethereal forms billow into the room like acrid smoke driven on a breath of bitter breeze. Like an otherworldly collection of spectral shapes seemingly carried on random eddies of air, they wandered in a loose clutch among the still and silent mounted bears and beasts rising up on their stands, the small forest of stone pedestals holding massive books of recorded prophecy, and the evenly spaced display cases of oddities, their glass reflecting the firelight from the massive hearth at the side of the room.

Since the seven rarely used doors, the shutters on the windows down on the ground level several stories below stood open in a fearless show of invitation. Though they frequently chose to use windows, they didn't actually need the windows any more than they needed the doors. They could seep through any opening, any crack, like vapor rising in the early morning from the stretches of stagnant water that lay in dark swaths through the peat barrens.

The open shutters were meant to be a declaration for all to see, including the seven, that Hannis Arc feared nothing.

Many people in Saavedra, the ruling city of Fajin Province down in the broad valley below the citadel, shuttered themselves in at night.

Everyone out in the Dark Lands did.

Shutting in at night for fear of what might be outside was only wise, after all. While that was true for those down in the city, it was doubly true for those who lived out in the more remote areas. There were corporeal dangers in the night, creatures that hunted with fang and claw, worthy of fear. There were other things to fear as well, things one rarely saw coming, if at all, until it was too late.

Hannis Arc, though, did not fear the things that came out at night. He bent those elements to his own ends, mastered them, making him the source of fear, not its victim. He banked the hot coals of those fears in the hearts of others so that they would always be ready to roar to life in order to serve him.

Hannis Arc wanted people to fear him. If they feared him, they respected him, they obeyed him, they bowed down to him. He made sure that people were never without cause to fear him.

No, unlike most people who inhabited the Dark Lands, Hannis Arc was not himself burdened by fears. Instead, he was driven by a ceaseless, smoldering rage, a rage that was like a thing alive within him. That rage left no room for fear to find a foothold.

That ever-present rage dwelling within him was a brightly burning star that always guided his way. It was always there to compel him, counsel him, even to chide him, as it drove him to set great wrongs right. Anger was not only his constant companion, it was his trusted friend, his only friend.

The glow of the dozens of candles in the stand at the far end of the room wavered as the seven familiars swirled around them on their way by, as if lingering to ride the eddies of heat rising from the flames.

Mohler, the old scribe hunched over a massive book laid open on a stand not far away, straightened as if he thought he might have heard something. One of the seven glowing forms glided around him, trailing a tendril hand along his jaw. The man glanced around, seeming to feel the touch, but he couldn't find its source.

He couldn't see the familiars.

The woman standing guard back near the doors could.

With gnarled, arthritic fingers, Mohler touched his cheek, but when he could find no cause for the sensation his hand dropped to his side and he returned his attention to recording the latest prophecies from the abbey while the seven spiraled up toward the vaulted ceiling to glide along the hulking stone arches and skim just beneath the heavy beams, surveying the gloomy, candlelit room.

"It's your move," Hannis Arc reminded the hunched scribe.

Mohler glanced back momentarily to see his master watching him. "Ah yes, so it is," he said as he laid down his quill and turned from his work at the massive book to shuffle over to the stone pedestal that held the board laid out with carved alabaster and obsidian pieces.

He'd had more than enough time to consider his next move. He'd had most of the night, in fact. Hannis Arc hadn't pressed. He had already worked out the array of moves available to the man. None seemed to be good choices, although some were not as swiftly fatal as others.

Hesitantly, Mohler reached out and moved an alabaster piece to another square, taking an inky black piece that occupied it off the board and setting it aside. It was a move that he had probably pondered for hours, a move that captured a valuable piece and put him into a position to threaten to win.

Hannis Arc rose and, hands clasped behind his back, strode to the board. He stroked the knuckle of his first finger along his gaunt cheek to make it look as if the loss of his piece might have taken him by surprise and his next move required consideration. It did not.

He advanced a black pawn toward the white side. Mohler had hoped for just that move and he was ready. Without thinking it through he immediately took the pawn, placing his alabaster rook in its place on a square that now placed his opponent in peril.

Hannis Arc had been expecting such impatience from the old scribe. Unlike most people, Hannis Arc was not plagued by the flaw of impatience. He had been practicing restraint and patience all day for this very moment, just as he had practiced it for decades for other things. He finally reached out and with a slender finger and thumb slid an obsidian queen to the square where the man had placed his rook, pushing it aside. He hooked the pale rook with his little finger and removed it from play. With measured care he set the captured piece to the side.

"Checkmate."

In unexpected alarm, Mohler's gaze darted about the board, looking for salvation. His bushy brow finally lifted and he sighed in resignation. "So it is. I'm afraid that I've proven yet again to be a poor foil for your skill, Bishop."

"Leave me."

The man looked. "Bishop?" He lifted a hand back toward the book. "I have not finished recording the reports."

"The hour grows late. I will retire soon. You can enter the rest of the reports from the abbey in the morning."

Mohler bowed. "Of course, Bishop. As you wish." He started away but then stopped and turned back. "Do you need anything before I leave you? Anything to eat or drink?"

One of the familiars spiraled her form around the man, teasing at him. Mohler glanced around, almost feeling it, almost aware of her. In the end he gave up, probably ascribing the sensation to his old bones, and returned his gaze to the bishop, awaiting his master's wishes.

"No. I will want to look over the latest words from the abbey first thing in the morning."

"Of course, Bishop," the man said as he dipped another bow. He paused, hand on the door handle, and turned back, as if reading his master's dark thoughts. "You will have your revenge, Bishop. You will be pleased to see from the latest prophecies that your patience will be rewarded. You will have your rightful place as ruler of D'Hara, I know you will. Prophecy seems to say as much."

Hannis Arc glared at the man, assessing whether he was being obsequious or genuinely meant it. He saw the glint of hope in the man's eyes and knew then that it was the latter. Some men needed an iron fist to rule them. Mohler was one of those, one who found great comfort in the shadow of a great man.

More than that, though, Mohler had been there. He knew the rage that burned in his master, and he knew the reason for it.

At that thought, Hannis Arc was visited by a flash of memory he'd had times beyond counting, the jarring, jagged, fragmented impression of his father being dragged out into the courtyard in the night, fighting every inch of the way, proclaiming his loyalty to the House of Rahl even as the power-fully built soldiers began clubbing him; of clinging to his mother before she hurriedly pulled his slender arms off her and stuffed him into an entryway bench, closing the lid before the men charged back in to drag her out as well; of the terrible, singular sound made by a single violent blow of a heavy mace studded with spikes caving in his older sister's skull as she stood in the entryway, frozen in panicked fear; of the cries and grunts from his mother as she was being beaten to death; of all the blood in the entry, on the courtyard cobble-stones; of the still form of his sister lying in the entry; of the corpses of his parents on the cobblestones; of the screams of servants who had witnessed the murders; of the fading cries as they ran off into the night in fear for their own lives.

Of peeking out again from under the lid of the bench to see the heavily armed soldiers swing up into their saddles and charge away into the night, their assignment of assassination completed.

Of hiding in the darkness all night, trembling in fear that they would come back and find him.

Of hours later, just after dawn, when Mohler, a new young servant come up from the city to work at the citadel, found him hiding in the bench and lifted him out.

All because Panis Rahl believed in striking down any potential challenge to the House of Rahl before it had a chance to develop. He had his soldiers slaughter anyone, real or imagined, who could be a potential threat to his rule. Even the minor ruler of Fajin Province in the distant Dark Lands, who had harbored no particular ill will toward the ruling House of Rahl and had always been loyal, was guilty of possessing the potential to one day be a threat, and so he and his family had to die for the crime of existing.

But the cunning folk, as they were called, were not to be trifled with. Even the gifted rightly feared their occult powers. Panis Rahl knew that such powers and abilities as dwelled in the Dark Lands could be a threat, but in striking against the ruler of Fajin Province, he had made a mistake. He had struck a generation too soon.

As the fires of rage roared within him, Hannis Arc knew that the threat to the rule of the House of Rahl this time was all too real. He would see to it. He would never again tremble in fear of a Rahl. He would see the wrongs righted.

He would have revenge.

That this new Rahl ruler, Richard Rahl, was said to be different from Panis Rahl and nothing like Darken Rahl, who had managed to outdo his father in every murderous way, made no difference at all to Hannis Arc.

As vicious as Darken Rahl had been, he had also been a man distracted by an obsession. Since Hannis Arc had not yet been ready to strike, he had turned Darken Rahl's attention away with a gift to feed his obsession—he had given Darken Rahl what he wanted more than anything else. He had given him one of the boxes of Orden that had long been hidden away in the Dark Lands. Hannis Arc had no use for a box of Orden, but Darken Rahl had coveted it, and thus the gift had bought Hannis Arc autonomy as well as certain useful favors.

As Hannis Arc had heard it, Darken Rahl's obsession had ultimately been his undoing and he had ended up being killed by his son, Richard Rahl. A Rahl killing his father hardly surprised Hannis Arc.

It made no difference to Hannis Arc that Richard Rahl had not interfered with the rule of the Dark Lands or made demands for tribute. Being the ruler of D'Hara, he could at any time choose to do so, as had his ancestors.

Besides, he was a Rahl, and that alone sealed his fate.

This new Lord Rahl had led the D'Haran Empire to a great victory, defeating a tyrannical threat to their very existence. In so doing, he had unwittingly saved Hannis Arc, the man who would now bring him down.

The new Lord Rahl, like his father before him, had no idea of the abilities Hannis Arc possessed, or the powers he could command. Hannis Arc could have struck earlier, as Richard Rahl was forging the D'Haran Empire and fighting the war for their survival, but then he would have had a war on his hands. It would have been difficult to survive against the incredible might of the Imperial Order.

Instead, he had lain back, saving himself for the right time, working on his abilities, and let Richard Rahl fight the long and difficult war. Hannis Arc had even sent troops to support the effort, as would anyone loyal to the D'Haran Empire. He had saved himself and worked on his plans. Now that war was ended, the time to extract his revenge on the House of Rahl had at long last arrived.

The new Lord Rahl was said to be widely respected, admired, and even loved by many. He was a man at the height of power, a conquering hero.

Hannis Arc was pleased that the man was as powerful as he was. That would make his fall all the farther, all the harder, and therefore, Hannis Arc's rise all the more momentous, all the more satisfying.

Still, Hannis Arc knew that simply killing a man like that would accomplish nothing except to make him a martyr. Making Richard Rahl a martyr would not bring Hannis Arc the rule of the D'Haran Empire.

He knew that he couldn't merely kill a popular Lord Rahl and expect to move into the People's Palace and rule the

D'Haran Empire. It would not be that simple. After all, as a ruler of a distant province Hannis Arc was unknown to most people.

No one would respect his rule. Not yet, anyway.

Hannis Arc first needed people to stop believing in Lord Rahl, in the man, in his ability to protect them from their rightful fears. Once his people lost their respect and rejected him, Richard Rahl's fall from power would be swift.

Only then, in that moment of chaos and panic, would D'Hara be ready to cast off the shackles of the House of Rahl and at last embrace someone who would speak to their fears about the future.

While Darken Rahl had been preoccupied with his obsession for the boxes of Orden, and Richard Rahl had fought the long war for the D'Haran Empire, Hannis Arc had been working on the means to accomplish his lifelong goal of removing the House of Rahl from power and taking its place himself. His patience had at last been rewarded.

Now that goal was within his grasp. The means were at hand.

"Rest assured, Mohler, I will rule D'Hara," he said softly. "That day will come sooner than we have ever before dared hope. The great gears of change have been set in motion. The pieces are finally moving into place, all to my advantage. There will be no stopping me, now. It will soon be checkmate for the House of Rahl."

"Prophecy is on your side," Mohler said. "Surely, Bishop, the Creator is no less on your side. I have always believed that He has protected you since that awful day when your parents were murdered because He has great things planned for you. He has helped you rise up and overcome all the obstacles in your path. The Creator will see this, too, finally come to pass."

"He reveals to us through prophecy that it is so."

"I look forward, then, to a new awakening out of darkness, as prophecy itself has foretold."

Little did the man know that there had already been an awakening out of darkness.

Little did the man know that the seven familiars huddled together in the peak of the ceiling, watching, listening. Hannis Arc knew that they would report every word back to the Hedge Maid.

"Soon, Bishop, you will rule D'Hara. You will rule the empire."

37

Mohler did not look up to meet the steady gaze of the blue-eyed woman watching him as he pulled open the door. Few people had the courage to meet her gaze. Hannis Arc returned to his desk as the old scribe pulled the heavy iron-bound oak door closed on his way out.

As he scooped his dark robes under his legs to sit at the desk in his massive leather chair, he watched from the corner of his eye as the seven glided in closer.

Their flowing robes radiated a supple, bluish blush with a soft, ethereal glimmer to it. They moved with fluid grace, their robes never still, giving him the impression that he was actually looking in at them in another place, seeing them in an ethereal world of continual gentle breezes.

From a distance, each seemed as elegant a creature as ever existed. To all appearances they seemed to be made of air and light as much as flesh and bone. As they glided closer, he fancied that they looked like nothing so much as good spirits.

He knew, though, that they were anything but good spirits.

Six of them drifted idly together, like corks in a pond, watching from not far away as the seventh floated in close on the other side of the desk.

As she leaned in he could finally see beyond the edge of the cowl covering her head, see the wrinkled flesh of her pitted and pockmarked face, the knotted blue veins, the warts and ulcers that ravaged her distorted features, the hanging tags of skin, the eyes the color of rancid egg yolks. She smiled a wicked smile that promised overwhelming pain and suffering should she wish it.

Hannis Arc was not in the least bit intimidated. Rather, he was indignant to be shown such little respect. He did not try to keep the displeasure from his voice.

"Has Jit completed the tasks I gave her?"

The familiar laid a gnarled hand on the desk as she leaned over toward him. With long, curved nails, bunched, callused skin, and knobby joints, her hand looked more like a claw.

She was close enough to have rattled most people down to their very soul, close enough to paralyze a victim with fear. Hannis Arc was no more unnerved by her appearance than she appeared to be of his.

Her voice came like a hiss across silk. "You dare to demand of us, to demand of our mistress?"

Hannis Arc whipped his arm around and slammed his knife down with all the force he could muster, pinning the familiar's disfigured hand to the desktop. She let out a squealing screech that seemed as if it might break the glass in all the display cases and crack the stone walls besides. It was a shriek that he thought must be something like what would come from those dragged down to the darkest depths of the underworld. It was the stuff of nightmares brought to life.

The arms of the other six waved in rage, like pennants in a gale. They swooped in around their trapped companion, incredulous to see her stuck fast, clicking their bewilderment to one another in a tongue that sounded like nothing so much as small little bird bones snapping.

"Surprised?" He arched an eyebrow. "Surprised that a knife wielded by a mere man could harm you?"

She let out another squealing screech that was loud enough to raise the dead as she again tugged and twisted wildly at her hand pinned to the desktop by the knife. Her bluish black lips curled back in a snarl, showing her fangs as she leaned toward him. It did her no good.

The heavy desk rattled and wobbled, the feet lifting clear of the floor every time she yanked on her arm, trying without success to free it. The other six snaked through the air around her in sympathetic outrage. When they grabbed at her to try to pull her free they received a lightning jolt from the knife that shot though them, forcing them to release their grip.

"What have you done?" the one stuck fast demanded in a screech.

"Why, I have pinned you to the desk. Isn't it obvious?"

"But how!"

"Right now that is really not what should concern you. What should matter most to you now is recognizing that I am no mere man and that it would be in your best interest to show me a great deal of respect. As you have discovered, I have abilities to handle the likes of you seven arrogant little lizard-eaters. That goes for your mistress as well."

Her eyes betrayed confusion behind the hot glare of hate.

Hannis Arc smiled without humor. "Didn't the Hedge Maid tell you that much of it when she called you forth from beneath the ground to serve her? Well"—his smile widened— "perhaps she had her reasons. Perhaps you seven weren't really important enough for it to matter to her."

"You will be made to suffer for this," she said in a hiss.

"I just told you that you need to show me a great deal of respect, and instead you threaten me?" He leaned toward the familiar, glaring into her wild eyes as he seized the handle of the crescent-bladed axe propped against the desk beside his right leg. "For this offense, you lose the hand. Threaten me again and you lose your existence."

He brought the axe around with one swift, powerful swing. It thunked into the desk, sticking fast, chopping the familiar's hand off at the wrist. Freed, she wheeled in frantic pain and shot away, crashing blindly off the stone walls, knocking over a stand holding a book and breaking the glass in one of the cases.

The wriggling hand remained pinned by the knife, the wrist terminating against the axe blade stuck deep in the desktop.

"Oh, look there, you've lost some of your precious blood," he said with mock sincerity. "Well, that really is a shame."

The other six retreated to a safe distance, or at least what they believed to be a safe distance, suddenly cautious, fearing to be too hasty in their response.

As the familiar, cradling the stub at the end of her arm, slowed to glare at him, Hannis Arc crooked a finger at her, compelling her to return. Hesitantly, she approached the desk, rage and fear twisting her already twisted features. He noted that despite her rage, despite her hesitancy, she had nonetheless obeyed him.

He was pleased to see that she was beginning to respect him.

"Don't you ever threaten me again," he told her in a deadly tone. "Do you understand?"

She glanced down at her severed hand pinned to the desk. "Yesss," she hissed.

"Now, answer my question. Has your mistress completed her tasks?"

"She watches the one you want watched. She still waits for the one she has summoned. The hounds drive him and will deliver him to her." She lifted her remaining hand, pointing at him. "Once she has him, then her task is completed and she will be through with you."

"She lives in my land and will do exactly as I say, when I say it, or she will lose my protection."

"Jit does not need you to protect her."

"Without my protection, Kharga Trace would not be a safe haven from the half people. She would be meat for their stew. You all would."

The familiar paused for a moment, scrutinizing his eyes. "The half people? The half people do not exist. They are merely a dusty rumor from ages long past."

"Oh, the half people exist. In fact, did you know that they make extraordinary weapons? Weapons that can be used against the dead?"

"Bah. Whispered gossip, nothing more."

He arched an eyebrow. "And just who do you suppose made the knife pinning your hand to the desk?"

The familiar's dark gaze descended to the knife impaling her dismembered hand before finally regarding him again with a murderous look. She seemed to think better of what she was going to say and instead took a defiant tone.

"The half people are no threat to us or our mistress. Even if they do exist, they remain locked away beyond the north wall as they have for thousands of years."

Hannis Arc showed her a hint of a smile. "Not any longer."

The familiar's upper lip curled back in a snarl. "Another lie. The half people cannot breach the north wall."

"They didn't need to. I went beyond the wall and walked among them, talked with them. They listened, and in the end they chose to bow to me as their sovereign lord. So, I opened the gates for them. Now, they hunt the Dark Lands . . . but only where I tell them they may hunt, and who I tell them they may hunt."

She studied his face for a moment. "You make a mistake thinking you can control the half people."

"Jit is the one who had better worry about making mistakes."

"Jit can protect herself," the familiar hissed. "She does not need you to protect her, and neither do we. The half people would not come into the Trace. They would fear Jit as they feared the wall. They would fear to tread the Trace."

The other six floated in close around her to reinforce the point.

"Have you been beyond the north wall?" He knew they hadn't. The wall worked both ways—it had for thousands of years. "You know nothing of what they fear, and what they don't fear. Don't make the mistake of thinking that you do."

Hannis Arc yanked the axe free from the desk and gestured with it.

"They don't hunt the Trace only because I told them to stay out. They would eagerly enter Kharga Trace if I were to allow them in . . . especially if I give them the disembodied limbs of you seven for their stewpots."

The seven backed away as one and wisely remained silent.

"All of you, the Hedge Maid included, like the people of the Dark Lands, like the half people from beyond the north wall, are my subjects. You all live under my rule. You all owe your loyalty to me if you want to continue to enjoy the privileges you receive in return."

The curiosity of one of them overcame her caution. "What privileges?"

Hannis Arc cocked his head to the side. "Why, the privilege of being allowed to live, of course."

None of the seven questioned what he meant.

"You tell Jit that she had better do as she's told. You tell her my words. You tell her that she also had better make sure that her familiars show proper respect to her ruler or none of you will have any hands left with which to feed her."

They all retreated a bit more, fright clearly registering on their faces.

Abruptly, they swirled around to leave. "It will be as you have commanded, Bishop," the handless one said. "We will tell our mistress your words."

"See that you do."

Hannis Arc watched as they swirled like smoke and slipped out through the cracks around the heavy door. On their way out, as Mohler before them, they were careful not to meet the gaze of the woman standing guard there.

Hannis Arc's rage still burned out of control. He would set the wrongs right. The spirit of his father would watch from his hallowed place in the underworld as his son finally visited vengeance upon the House of Rahl.

This was the awakening of a new day in D'Hara, in more ways than one. The ages of darkness under the House of Rahl were about to be over.

Richard Rahl was about to lose his grip on power. He was about to lose everything. Hannis Arc would see to it. And when he did, a fearful people would clamor for a new leader.

Justice would finally be done.

Hannis Arc yanked the knife from the desk, the now slack hand still impaled on the blade. As he held it out toward the woman by the door, she stepped to the desk.

"Dispose of this, would you?"

As she reached for the knife, he abruptly drew it back. "No, I have a better idea." He gestured with it. "Place it in that display case, there, for visitors to see."

The woman in red leather flashed a grim smile. "Of course, Lord Arc."

CHAPTER

38

Richard yawned. He looked up from the complexities of translating the symbolic elements he was working on to see Zedd coming back into the library. Through the high windows above, the first blush of dawn revealed a clear sky.

The strange spring storm had broken, but it seemed that it had merely been the harbinger of bigger problems. It was clear to Richard that there was trouble about, but whatever the core of the trouble might be, it was hidden from him. He was getting that familiar, uneasy feeling that he was in the dark about what was really going on.

All of it, from the boy down in the market to the storm, to the strange deaths, to the variety of strange prophecies, to the machine buried for so long that had suddenly come to life, was too much to be a coincidence. Things that seemed to be a coincidence always made him edgy. He was worried the most about the machine they had discovered, worried that it was somehow at the heart of it all.

The translations of the metal strips were only confirming his suspicions.

Since he had discovered that everything in the book was backward, those translations, while tedious, had been working smoothly. The more he learned from those translations, the more his concern grew.

As his grandfather crossed the library, Richard noticed that Zedd didn't have the usual spring in his step. He thought at that moment that Zedd looked like nothing so much as an old man, a tired old man. Richard could read the creases in Zedd's face and tell that he, too, was concerned about what kind of trouble they might have on their hands. Zedd's typical exuberant, sometimes childlike way of looking at the world was nowhere in evidence. That, more than any words, framed for Richard the seriousness of the situation.

That, and the translations from the strips.

Richard stuck his hand in the book to stop the pages from turning over when out of the corner of his eye he spotted the part he was looking for.

"There's the first one," he told Berdine. He tapped an element on the page. "That's the one. What's the inversion of it?"

Berdine leaned in, looking, reading the High D'Haran explanation silently. "It has to do with falling."

Richard had already begun to grasp the language of Creation and he knew what many of the symbols meant. He had only been looking to confirm his worst fears. Berdine just had.

"That's the last symbol, so it—"

"So it ends the action of the subject," Berdine finished in a mumble. She hadn't yet figured out what Richard already had. She stuck her tongue out the side of her mouth as she wrote it down, then started turning pages in the book. "I need the subject."

Richard tapped the metal strip, showing her. "Here. If it's inverted, then this part of the device is the subject."

Zedd, coming to an abrupt halt across the table, leaned in, squinting, trying to read the paper she was working on.

"What's that, there, that you've written down?"

"It's the translation of the language of Creation inscribed on this strip," Richard said. "How's Kahlan? Were you able to heal her hand?"

"I'm a wizard, aren't I?" He gestured to the paper where Berdine was writing. "So, you've figured out how the book works? How these symbols work?"

"Yes," Richard said. "It's quite remarkable, actually. The symbols are an incredibly efficient and compact form of language. What might take sentences, or even paragraphs for us to say, the language of Creation can express in a brief line of symbolic elements. With just a few devices combined in the right way it can tell you a whole story or convey a tremendous amount of information. It's extraordinarily precise in conveying meaning in a compact fashion."

Richard had long ago learned to understand emblematic devices. He understood their language, how they represented things, and how they functioned in spell-forms. It turned out that those emblems he had already learned were rooted in the language of Creation. Without knowing it, he had already long ago begun learning to use the language of Creation.

Once he started using the book, and started translating the symbols, at some point in the night it had all clicked into place for him and he saw how what he already understood related to this new language, and how to use that knowledge to interpret the symbols the machine used. It was like opening a door he had never known was there. In a flash of comprehension, everything he already knew fell into place in helping him to understand this new language.

He came to realize that it was more like learning a new dialect than a new language. As a result he had been able to rapidly grasp how it worked. Now he no longer needed the book *Regula* to understand the symbols.

Zedd picked up the strip to look at it again, as if he suddenly, magically, might understand it. He didn't. "So if it worked, what's the translation? What does this strip say?"

Richard pointed with the back end of his pen. "That one you're holding says 'The roof is going to fall in.'"

Zedd's frown grew. "You mean, like that prophecy you mentioned? From that blind woman? The fortune-teller, Sabella, that you met out in the halls?"

"That's the one."

"After the warning about darkness from the boy down in the market the other day? The one with the fever who was delirious?"

Richard nodded. "That's right."

"The boy you thought was speaking gibberish."

"We thought it was gibberish at the time, but maybe it wasn't. After the boy's warning, I got the fortune from the blind woman that turned out to be the same prophecy we then got from Lauretta and from the machine. The boy said something else that, at the time, we thought was the fever speaking. He said, 'He will find me, I know he will.'"

"Certainly sounds like a fevered delirium."

Richard picked up another strip. "This one was at the bottom of the stack in the machine. That means it was the first one the machine made since it seems to have awakened down there in the darkness. I could hardly believe it when we translated it. It says 'He will find me.'"

Zedd gestured to the strip Richard was holding. "You mean to say that the machine predicted that you would find it?"

Richard shrugged. "You tell me."

"Are you sure that you've translated it properly?"

Richard glanced toward the door to see Nathan marching into the library. He, too, looked grim.

"Now that I have the key I needed, yes," Richard told Zedd. "There can be no doubt. It all works out perfectly." Richard reached over and picked up the third strip. "This one here, the one I thought has only the symbol for fire on it, turns out to translate perfectly in the High D'Haran key. It's exactly as I thought. It says only 'fire.'"

"What's that about fire?" Nathan called out as he rushed up.

Zedd took the strip from Richard's hand and showed Nathan. "The translation worked out just like Richard thought. It does mean fire, and nothing else."

At the far end of the library, Richard saw Lauretta trundle in carrying a load of her predictions. Two guards followed behind, lugging big stacks in their arms. It was going to be a lot of work for them to help carry all her predictions down from her room to their new home in the library. Richard was relieved to see that she was moving all that paper out of her place.

Nathan scowled. "Fire."

"That's right," Richard said. "One of the others says 'He will find me.' That's what the sick boy down in the market told Kahlan and me. The other says that the roof will fall in, like Lauretta and the blind woman, Sabella, told me."

Nathan planted a fist on his hip. "So happens that I'm here about Sabella."

"Really? What about her?"

"She's been causing trouble. A few of the representatives went to her to hear her prophesy. They are insisting that they need to learn what the future holds."

Richard sighed. "Oh great. What did she tell them?"

Nathan leaned in. " 'Fire.' "

"What?"

"That's all she said: 'Fire.' The representatives went back and told the others. They're all worked up, fearing that there will be a fire in the palace. Several of the representatives woke up a short time ago, and came running out of their rooms in their night clothes, all upset because they had dreams of fire."

"That is curious," Zedd mumbled as he rubbed his chin.

Richard caught sight of Lauretta hurrying toward them from across the library. "Lord Rahl! Lord Rahl!" She was waving a piece of paper. "There you are. I'm so glad I found you here."

Richard stood as she came to a breathless halt. "What is it?"

She put a hand to her chest as she panted a moment, catching her breath. She thrust out a folded piece of paper.

"I had another prophecy for you. I wrote it down like always. I was going to put it with the others for safekeeping until I saw you again, but here you are."

Richard unfolded the piece of paper. It had only one word on it.

FIRE.

"What is it?" Zedd asked.

Richard handed him the paper. Zedd's brow drew down as he read the single word on the paper.

"And do you have any inkling as to what this means?" he asked the woman as he handed the paper to Nathan.

She shook her head.

The tall prophet read the single word silently and then looked up. "Just like Sabella."

Zedd peered down at Richard. "Any idea what it could mean?"

Richard sighed. "I'm afraid—"

He stopped as icy realization washed over him.

He tossed his pen on the table and raced for the door.

"Come on!" he called back over his shoulder. "I know what it means! I know where the fire is!"

Zedd, Nathan, and Berdine ran to follow after him. Even Lauretta raced to catch up.

CHAPTER
39

As he ran down the service hallway, Richard could smell the smoke. Such a familiar smell when it came from campfires had always offered warmth and protection, but in the palace such an acrid smell carried terrifying implications. When he slid around the last corner he saw it billowing up thick and dark from under a door down the hall.

Berdine clutched his sleeve in one hand to prevent him from getting ahead of her. Whenever there was even a hint of trouble, all of the Mord-Sith did whatever they could to stay as close as possible to him. Berdine had lost her bubbly demeanor, turning as implacable as any of the Mord-Sith when there was a threat. From time to time as she ran, she spun her Agiel up into her fist, as if to reassure herself that it was there at the ready.

Down the hallway beyond the smoke, Richard spotted men of the First File running in from the other direction. Several of them had buckets. Water slopped out as they ran, splashing across the wood floor. Several women, awakened at the early hour by the commotion, had come out of their rooms to stand in their doorways, clutching nightgowns at their throats in fright as they watched soldiers racing past.

"What is it?" Nathan asked as he rounded the corner and caught up. Zedd was right on his heels.

Richard pointed. "It's Lauretta's place. It's on fire."

Lauretta stumbled to a halt, gasping for breath. Her short, rapid gait had left her face bright red and her hair in disarray.

"My room!" She swallowed, trying to get enough air. She pressed her hands to the sides of her head. "My prophecies!"

The soldiers with the buckets kicked open the door. Black smoke laced with crackling sparks and burning pieces of paper rolled out into the hall and along the ceiling. Flags of flame unfurled out along the ceiling of the hallway. The soldiers heaved water in through the open doorway. From the amount of smoke and the heat from the flames, Richard didn't think their buckets of water were going to be anywhere near enough.

Lauretta screamed when she saw the soldiers throwing water into her room. She pushed past Zedd and Nathan. "No! You'll ruin my prophecies!"

Richard knew that it was too late to worry about that. Besides, water was not the real threat to her prophecies. He caught Lauretta's arm and dragged her to a halt. He knew that if left to her own devices she would run into the burning room to try to save her precious prophecies. As thick as the smoke was, and as heavily as she was breathing, she would have been overcome in mere seconds.

The heat, even at a distance, was withering. Richard was relieved that the palace was made mostly of stone. Still, parts of it, like the floors under them and beams above, were wood. They needed to put out the fire as quickly as possible.

More soldiers raced up with yet more buckets of water. They ran in toward the door, turned their faces away from the heat, and heaved the water in. Angry, hot flames licked out through the open door in defiance of the water. As Richard had suspected, such an effort was hopelessly ineffective.

Zedd knew it, too. He rushed past Richard and down the hall, ducking under the lowering black smoke hugging the ceiling to make his way toward the doorway into the inferno.

Urging soldiers back out of the way with one arm, he cast the other out toward the open door as yet more smoke and flames poured out. Richard could see the air waver before Zedd's hand, forcing the smoke back into the room, but more flames boiled out of the doorway, as if to chase the wizard away. The heat drove Zedd back.

"Bags! My gift is too weak in this place."

Nathan caught up with Zedd and lifted his palms out toward the smoke-filled doorway, adding his gift to the effort. He, too, caused the air to waver, but it also slowed the amount of smoke as the flames withdrew back into the room. At last the smoke coming out the doorway was choked off entirely, confining it to the room inside, leaving the hallway in a dark and pungent haze.

Nathan was a Rahl. His gift wasn't hampered by the palace's spell. He stepped in closer, holding the flats of his hands out toward the doorway again. As Richard restrained Lauretta, he watched Nathan gradually circle his palms, sealing off the room, suffocating the fire at its source. After a few tense moments, the fire died out and the prophet spun a web that cooled the remains of Lauretta's home.

As Nathan entered the room, checking that it was safe, Richard let go of Lauretta, allowing her to follow. Weeping in misery, she rushed into the room behind Nathan.

She lifted her arms in distress. "My prophecies! Dear Creator! My prophecies are ruined!"

Richard could see that she was right. There looked to be

some stacks in the farthest reaches that might not have been totally destroyed, but the blackened, wet mess covering the floor was all that was left of most of them.

Lauretta fell to her knees, scooping up handfuls of the useless, wet ash.

"They're ruined," she wept.

Richard laid a hand on her shoulder. "You can write more, Lauretta. You can use the library as a place to write more."

She nodded absently. He wondered if she even heard him.

Out in the hall, people had gathered to see what was happening. Many of them covered their noses against the stench left from the fire.

Richard saw a number of representatives he recognized at the back of the crowd. They looked grim. The fire was obviously confirmation of the prophecy they had all heard that morning.

Murmuring warnings to one another, the crowd parted. Cara marched through as if the people were not there, expecting everyone to get out of her way. There was never any problem with that. People were only too eager to get out of the way of a Mord-Sith, especially when she looked as angry as Cara looked. The last thing in the world that most people wanted was to cause a Mord-Sith to take notice of them.

"Are you all right?" Cara asked as Richard nodded. "I heard that there was trouble."

"Lauretta's prophecies caught fire," he told her.

Among the crowd, Richard spotted Ludwig Dreier, the abbot from Fajin Province. His face was set in a stony expression as he took in all the activity. He finally moved through the onlookers to come in closer.

"Was anyone hurt?" he asked.

"No," Richard said. "Lauretta's place was full of papers. It was a fire waiting to happen."

Ludwig glanced through the doorway. "Especially since it was foretold in prophecy."

"Says who?"

The abbot shrugged. "The blind woman for one. Several others had the premonition as well."

Richard glanced past the abbot to the faces in the crowd and saw a number of representatives watching and listening.

"The woman used open flames in her room," Richard said. "There were papers everywhere. I told her myself that she had to move all the papers or there was going to be a fire."

"Nonetheless, it was predicted by prophecy."

"The man is right," Lauretta said as she stepped out into the hall, looking heartbroken. "I had the prophecy myself. I wrote it down and gave it to Lord Rahl," she told the abbot as she wiped tears from her cheeks. "I guess that now we all know what it meant."

The abbot turned his frown to Richard. "You had a dangerous prophecy about fire in the palace brought directly to you and you told none of us? You kept the prophecy to yourself?"

"I had only just told him about it and he raced right here," Lauretta said before Richard could answer, unwittingly saving him from having to explain himself. "There was no time to warn anyone, or to do anything to stop the fire in time."

The abbot let out a troubled breath. "Still, Lord Rahl, you would be well advised to take prophecy more seriously. Especially when the prophecy could have bearing on the lives and safety of others. Your duty, after all, is to protect the subjects of the D'Haran Empire. You are the magic against magic that we all depend on for our safety. Prophecy is magic that the Creator has given us and you need to take it seriously."

"I think that Lord Rahl takes prophecy quite seriously," Nathan said, glaring down at the man.

"Good," Ludwig said. "Good. He needs to take it seriously." Others back in the crowd added nods of agreement.

Cara spun her Agiel up into her fist. She pointed the red weapon at the abbot's face. "Lord Rahl does not need you to tell him his responsibility or how to carry it out. Lord Rahl protects us all."

Cara's deadly tone was a clear warning that the man was overstepping his place.

His gaze finally left Cara and returned to Richard. "Your sword can't protect you from prophecy, Lord Rahl. It can't protect any of us from the future. Prophecy is what protects us. That is why the Creator gave mankind the gift of prophecy."

Richard's glare caused the abbot's gaze to falter and drift to the ground. "That's enough."

Ludwig took a hesitant step back as he dipped his head in a deferential bow. "As you command, Lord Rahl."

Once safely withdrawn, he turned and left, several of the other representatives falling in with him and following behind.

"Let me kill him," Cara said as she scowled at the man's back.

"Let me do it," Berdine said. "I could use the practice."

Richard watched the departing abbot. "If only it were that simple."

"Oh, I think it would be pretty simple," Berdine said.

Richard shook his head as he saw the knot of people disappear down the hall. "Killing people isn't the way to have peace."

Cara looked like she agreed with Berdine, but she dropped the subject and went on to other business. "Benjamin would like to see you. I told him that I'd find you and bring you to the Garden of Life."

As Richard passed between phalanxes of guards and through the doors into the Garden of Life, with Zedd, Nathan, and Cara close behind, he noticed that scaffolding had already been erected. A number of men clambered along lengths of plank at the top. Some of the men were cutting off twisted metal, while others were beginning the work of laying in new framework so they could replace the glass and close in the roof.

The sun was up, filling the room with light. Soldiers of the First File patrolled the room, keeping an eye on the men up above near the source of light and also watching the opening into the darkness below.

Richard found it unsettling to have people in the Garden of Life. He had come to feel of it as a private refuge. He supposed that his ancestors had for thousands of years felt much the same way about the garden sanctuary, a place where the occasional release of some of the most dangerous magic in existence made the garden a frightening place to be, yet a place that most of the time offered the peace of quiet seclusion.

Benjamin, talking with an officer of the guard, spotted

Richard and rushed his way. The workers on the scaffolding kept working, but they couldn't help watching out of the corner of an eye.

"Lord Rahl, are you all right?" Benjamin asked. "I heard there was a fire. The Mother Confessor is worried, too."

"I'm fine." Richard aimed a thumb over his shoulder toward his grandfather and the prophet. "Zedd and Nathan were there, thankfully. They were able to put it out."

"That's a relief."

Richard glanced around. "Where is Kahlan?"

Benjamin flicked a hand toward the ragged hole in the floor. "She and Nicci are down there, with the machine."

As Richard started toward the ladder, Cara joined Benjamin. "I told Lord Rahl that you wanted to see him."

Benjamin fell in beside Richard. "Yes, that's right. I have the information you wanted, Lord Rahl."

Richard paused at the ladder leading down into the gaping hole. "You mean about how far the machine goes down in the ground?"

Benjamin nodded. "First of all, you were right. That funny kink in the library several floors below us is because of that thing down in the hole. The library wall has to have that odd notch in order to go around the machine. It's behind the wall."

Behind the wall where the book *Regula* had sat on a shelf. It made him wonder all the more about the placement of books in the libraries. Their locations had never made any sense. Maybe that was only because he knew far too little about them.

Richard held the ladder and let Zedd and Nathan go down first. Richard went next, with Cara and then her husband following. At the bottom of the ladder they had to climb over some of the larger rubble as they went around the walkway to the spiral stairs. In single file they all descended into the tomb of the machine.

The hushed room below was lit by the eerie light of the proximity spheres. Kahlan smiled when she saw him, looking relieved to see that he was all right. Nicci, her arms folded, deep in thought as she studied the silent metal box, only glanced up briefly. Richard was glad to see that she was there, watching out for Kahlan.

"It looks quiet," Richard said.

"Dead quiet," Kahlan said.

"It hasn't made a sound or given off that strange light you spoke of," Nicci said, emerging from her thoughts. "It appears to be as still and silent as it probably was for thousands of years."

Zedd skimmed his bony fingers along the top of the machine, almost as if fearing any greater contact, but unable to resist touching it. "That's what Nathan and I found as well. Not a peep out of it."

Richard wasn't actually all that unhappy to hear it. He would not be unhappy if the thing went back to sleep for another few thousand years.

"How's your hand?" he asked Kahlan.

She lifted it, turning it to show him. There was only a faint red mark left where it had been swollen and inflamed.

Kahlan flashed a smile at Richard's grandfather. "Despite the difficulty of using his gift in the palace, Zedd was able to heal it. Quite the accomplishment, I'd say."

Zedd waved off the flattery. "Not all that difficult, healing a scratch. Just don't ask me to reattach your head or anything demanding."

Richard was relieved that it was taken care of. It was one less thing to worry about. He turned his attention once more to the general.

"Were you able to map where this thing goes down through the palace?"

"With my help," Cara said as she dragged a finger along the top of the machine in imitation of Zedd, as if tempting the sleeping menace.

"So how many floors down does it go?"

General Meiffert shifted his weight to his other foot. "I'm afraid I can't answer that, Lord Rahl. We haven't been able to find the bottom, yet."

"I thought you said that you had the palace under here mapped out."

"We do. We were able to determine that the machine goes all the way down through the palace."

Richard was more than a little surprised. The Garden of Life was one of the highest places in the palace. There were a lot of floors below them down in the palace.

"All the way? It's that big?"

"It's worse than that, Richard," Kahlan said in a troubled voice.

"I'm afraid that the Mother Confessor is right. Once we had a diagram of the palace below here drawn out and we could see how it went down through the core of the palace, we went down into the foundation inspection tunnels below the lowest floor. We opened up a small hole in a foundation wall and behind it we found solid metal"—with his knuckles Benjamin rapped the side of the metal box—"just like the sides of this machine, here, and just like behind the wall in the library."

Richard stared at the silent machine lit in the glow of the proximity spheres. It didn't seem all that tall. He had to lean over to look in the little window. But he had been able to tell from looking down into it that it went much deeper than it appeared, much deeper than the floor where they stood.

"If it goes down through the palace foundation and into the plateau, then there's no telling how deep it goes."

No one spoke into the uneasy silence. Richard looked from one grim expression to another.

"Tell him," Nicci finally prompted.

"Well," Benjamin said with an uneasy sigh, "we actually did find more of the machine down lower."

"Down lower? You mean in the passageways up through the plateau?"

"Not exactly," Cara said, apparently unhappy with the slow pace of the explanation. "We kept mapping downward, since we had the pattern of how the machine went through the palace and the way the rooms and stairways were placed around it. Nathan and Zedd helped with that pattern. It creates such a complex layout in the palace that we've been unaware all this time that there was something that big hidden away behind the walls of various rooms and stairwells."

"We've always known that the palace is laid out in the shape of a spell-form." Nathan gestured toward what was above them. "The Garden of Life is the central node of the spell-form, giving it power as a containment field."

Richard frowned at the prophet. "You mean, you think that because the Garden of Life is a containment field, that hid the machine within the central node?"

"In a way, but not exactly," Nathan said. "The central node made it hard to know the machine was there simply because of its location within that central part of the spell-form. For the spell-form to work, the central node can't be breached from the sides, or from beneath, so the stairwells and passageways below are laid out in the same shape that the spell-form dictates. That's why the rooms and passageways go around the machine. They are actually avoiding breaching the node, not avoiding the machine or trying to hide it."

Richard was lost in thought, contemplating the design of the spell-form. Spell-forms were emblematic. He understood those designs. He understood how this one worked—in theory, anyway.

"Of course," he said, thinking out loud. "You can't breach the axis of the form. A spell's web isn't two-dimensional, it's three-dimensional. Something below would breach the axial confluence the same way that a hallway running right through the center of the Garden of Life would ruin the containment field." He looked up at the gifted people watching him. "The central part of the spell-form is walled off by the rooms and passageways below in order to protect the node."

"That's right," Nicci said. "And beyond those walls just happens to lie this machine."

The staggering implications were beginning to dawn on him. "Such an axial convergence in the spell-form is fed from below." He was taken aback by the realization. "That's why the passageways and stairs coming up to the palace, to this central node, through the plateau below, all spiral upward."

"That's what they do," Cara confirmed. "The stairs and passageways twist in a spiral upward, just like the rooms in the palace below us. That actually made it easy to diagram the plateau. It may be a great height, but the basic design, spiraling up with rooms and stairs along the way, is simple once you understand how it works."

Richard couldn't imagine a Mord-Sith thinking magic was simple or understanding how it worked. He looked from one face to another.

"Do you mean to say that the machine goes all the way down somewhere into the center of that spiral up through the plateau?"

"Worse." Cara leaned in. "Once we had started mapping it out, with Nathan and Zedd showing us how the spell-form would be drawn, we were able to go down through the palace and find the central shaft that is this node thing. That central area contains the machine. That also allowed us to map it downward through the plateau."

"But you didn't tunnel into the walls down in the plateau to see if the machine was at the core? So you aren't sure it goes that far down."

"We didn't have to," Benjamin said.

Cara folded her arms. "I sent Nyda with some of the other Mord-Sith, armed with the map we had made, to escort Benjamin down into the catacombs. Sure enough, the same pattern is laid out in those tunnels, too. They have the same protected core that the palace above has."

Richard nodded. "They would have to because they feed the axis of the spell-form—the containment field that is the Garden of Life. The spell-form has to go to ground intact. You can't breach it from below or the whole thing wouldn't work."

"Well, down there, in the lowest reaches of the catacombs, in the hub of those tunnels, that's where Nyda and I dug an inspection hole." Benjamin tapped a finger on the silent machine. "We hit the metal wall of this thing."

Richard's head spun with the dizzying implication. The machine that rose up through the palace to just under the Garden of Life came all the way up through the plateau from the Azrith Plain far below.

R ichard couldn't begin to imagine what it could all mean—what the machine really was, who had made it, and why it had so long ago been sealed away.

And worse, why it had suddenly awakened from its long slumber.

He supposed that whatever the machine's purpose had been at one time, it might have fallen into disuse and, being so massive, might have been more trouble than it was worth to dismantle, so it had simply been walled away and forgotten.

Yet, for all he knew, it could just as well be that the machine had been sealed away because it had been a source of trouble. It wouldn't be the first time that prophecy had caused trouble, and perhaps the machine was no less troublesome for that reason.

But none of that explained why it had come back to life now.

Unable to answer any of those questions for the time being, Richard turned to his grandfather. "So, what have you been able to learn about the nature of this thing?"

Zedd looked somewhat exasperated, maybe even a little sheepish. He glanced at Nathan and Nicci before he answered.

"Nothing, I'm afraid."

That wasn't what Richard had been expecting to hear, least of all from Zedd.

"Nothing? Nothing at all? You had to have been able to learn something."

"I'm afraid not."

Richard spread his hands in frustration. "But it uses magic. Can't you at least tell something about the magic it uses?"

"So you say." Zedd laid a hand on the machine. "We can detect no magic. The machine has been as silent as this grave where it rests. As far as we can tell it's just an inert collection of gears and levers and wheels and ratchets and shafts. We looked down inside, as best we could, but that told us nothing useful. All the inner workings seem to be made of ordinary metal, even if on a grand scale."

Richard raked his fingers back through his hair. "Then what made the gears turn when we were down here before?"

Zedd shrugged. "We've done everything we can think of to get it to start up, or to react, or to do something to reveal its nature, but it remains silent. We've fed in threads of magic, used analysis spells on it, and sent in conjured probes, but they reveal nothing."

"Maybe that's just because the palace weakens your power," Richard suggested.

"Being a Rahl, my power works just fine here within the palace," Nathan said as he swept his hand out over the machine, "yet my power was of no more use on this thing than Zedd's was."

Richard turned to Nicci. She had different abilities than either Zedd or Nathan did. She could wield Subtractive Magic. He hoped that maybe with her unique gift she could sense a hint of magic that Zedd and Nathan couldn't.

"You must be able to tell something about it."

THE OMEN MACHINE

She was shaking her head even before he had finished. "It's as Zedd says. None of us can detect any magic—that includes me. Kahlan told me all about what it did when you first found it. The slot where you found the strips of metal with the symbols on them is empty. It hasn't made any more since the ones you found."

Richard heaved a sigh of frustration. "But how does it do all the things it does?"

Nicci unfolded her arms to hold a hand out to the machine. "Does what? It has not turned one gear, or let out one bit of light, since you were down here last. It's as still and silent as it has been for probably thousands of years."

"But all those parts down inside were all moving and turning, all lit with some kind of strange orangish light."

"I saw it too," Kahlan said. "We're not both imagining it."

"We're not saying you imagined it," Zedd said as he withdrew his hand from the top of the machine and sighed, "only that we haven't seen it do any of those things. Unless it comes to life again, we can get no sense of it."

Richard was actually relieved that the machine had gone silent. It meant that they had one less problem to deal with. They still had the nettlesome issue of prophecy without the machine adding its own.

Richard laid a hand on the flat, iron top.

The instant he touched the machine the ground rumbled with the thunder of the sudden power of all the heavy pieces of machinery inside abruptly thrown into motion.

With a dull thud that shook the ground more sharply, light shot up from the center of the machine, like lightning in the darkness, projecting the symbol up onto the ceiling, the same symbol they had seen the last time, the same symbol that was on the side of the machine and in the book *Regula*. As massive gears inside turned, so did the emblem written in lines of light on the ceiling.

Zedd and Nathan raced to the machine and bent to look down through the window.

Zedd pointed, speaking over the roar and clatter of all the huge gears turning against one another. "Look down there. It's moving a strip of metal through the mechanism, just as Richard described it."

Nicci placed the flats of her hands on the machine, apparently trying to sense its power.

She immediately jumped back with a gasp of pain.

"It's shielded," she said, comforting the ache in her elbows and shoulders.

Zedd gingerly touched one hand to the machine, to test it, but more lightly than Nicci had done. He, too, had to yank his hand back. He shook it as if he had touched fire.

"Bags, she's right."

"There," Nathan said, pointing down at the window, careful not to touch the machine. "The strip of metal is moving through that bright beam of light."

Everyone waited silently as Nathan and Zedd peered down through the window. Richard could see lines of light, parts of emblems, play across their features.

The metal strip dropped into the slot.

Richard grabbed Zedd's wrist. "Careful, it will be hot."

Zedd licked his fingers and then plucked the metal strip from the slot and quickly tossed it on top of the machine.

Richard could clearly see the fresh emblems that had been burned into the metal. Wisps of smoke still rose from them. With a finger he pushed the strip around to better see the designs.

"Any idea what it says?" Nathan asked.

Richard nodded as he took in the collection of symbols. "Yes, it says 'Pawn takes queen.'"

"Like before," Kahlan said.

"I'm afraid—"

"Look," Nicci said, pointing down into the window. "It's making another."

As soon as it dropped into the slot, Richard snatched it up and quickly flipped the hot metal onto the flat iron top of the machine.

He blinked at what he saw.

As he stared, Kahlan put a hand on his arm. "Richard, what's wrong?"

"What's the matter?" Zedd asked. "What does it say?"

Richard finally looked up from the strip to his grandfather, and then the others.

"What it says doesn't leave this room. Understand?"

CHAPTER

42

The door carefully opened a crack in response to his soft knock.

"Abbot." She pulled the heavy, ornately carved door open the rest of the way. "I'm so glad you could come."

Ludwig removed his rimless hat and bowed his head respectfully. "How could I resist an invitation from the most beautiful queen in the palace?"

Her demure smile took the edge off her air of authority. It was exaggerated flattery and she recognized it as such. Nonetheless, she couldn't help appreciating it.

She turned her back to him as she led to him into her lavish apartment, glancing back over her shoulder to make sure he was following behind. Couches upholstered in silvery material were strewn with colorful pillows. Low tables and a desk in a small sitting area to the side were veneered in matching burl walnut. Double doors at the far end of the room led to a terrace that overlooked some of the outer rim of the plateau and the now dark Azrith Plain out beyond.

The accommodations, softly lit by candles, were fit for a queen, yet as luxurious as her quarters were, they were no better than his. He chose not to say so.

"Come, sit, Abbot," she said as she glided across an expanse of ornate carpeting on her way to one of the couches.

"Please, call me Ludwig."

She glanced back over her shoulder again, again giving him the demure smile.

"Ludwig, then."

Her auburn hair was done up on top of her head, held in place with a jeweled comb. Ringlets hung down in front of each ear. It left her flawlessly smooth, graceful neck bare.

She sat on the front edge of the cushions. The slit up the front of her long dress came up just high enough that he could see her bare knees pressed together as she leaned forward to lift a wine decanter.

"What was it you wished to see me about, Queen Orneta?"

She patted the couch beside her in invitation for him to sit. "If I'm to call you Ludwig, then you must call me Orneta."

He sat, making sure there was a respectful space between them. "As you wish, Orneta."

She poured two glasses of the red wine and handed him one.

"A queen who serves wine?"

She returned the smile. "The servants have been dismissed and sent home for the night. I'm afraid we're all alone."

She clinked her glass against his.

"To the future, and our knowledge of it," she said.

He sipped when she did. He had an appreciation for quality wine and was not disappointed.

"An interesting choice for a toast, I must say."

"You asked why I wished to see you. The toast is the reason. I wanted to see you about prophecy."

Ludwig took a longer sip of wine. "What about it?" he finally asked, trying to sound innocently puzzled.

She gestured offhandedly. "I think prophecy is important."

He dipped his head. "So I gathered from the luncheon a few days back when the Mother Confessor threatened to behead us for wanting to know more about it. You were quite impressive, standing up to her the way you did. You can't be faulted for relenting at last under such a mortal threat."

She smiled, but this time it showed less modesty and a little more cunning. "A ruse, I believe."

"Really?" Ludwig leaned in. "You think it was an act?"

Orneta shrugged. "At the time I certainly didn't think so. I guess I was caught up in the moment, the emotion, along with everyone else."

"It was a frightful moment, there's no doubt about that." He took another sip. "But now, you think differently?"

The queen took her time before answering. "I've known the Mother Confessor a long time. Not so much personally, mind you, but I'm from the Midlands. Before the war, before the D'Haran Empire came to be, the Midlands was ruled by a Central Council, and the Central Council was ruled by the Mother Confessor, so I've had dealings with her in the past. I've never once known her to be temperamental or cruel. Tough, yes. Vindictive, no."

"So you believe it was out of character for her?"

"Of course it was. We've been fighting the war a long time. I've known her to be absolutely ruthless with the enemy. Every night, she would send the head of the special forces, Captain Zimmer, out to cut the throats of the enemy as they slept. In the morning she would always ask to see the strings of ears he had collected."

Ludwig lifted his eyebrows, trying to act at least a little scandalized as she went on.

"But I've never known her to be cruel to her own people, to

innocent people, good people. I have seen her risk her life to save a child she doesn't even know. I think cutting off the heads of everyone in the room would have been a pretty brutal way to teach a lesson to the people she rules. Such a thing simply is not in her character unless she had a powerful reason."

Ludwig let out a long sigh. "You know her better than I do. I will take your word for it."

"What I want to know is why she would go to such extremes."

"What do you mean?"

"That was a pretty extreme performance, and quite convincing, at least until I thought it through. I think she did it because she and Lord Rahl are hiding something from us."

Ludwig frowned. "Hiding something? Like what?"

"Prophecy."

He decided to take a drink rather than say anything in order to let her go on to reveal her theories.

"I asked to see you because I've heard that you have something to do with prophecy."

He smiled. "Yes, I guess you could say that."

"Then prophecy is something that is respected in your land?"

"Fajin Province. That's where I come from. The bishop—"

"The bishop?"

"Hannis Arc. Bishop Hannis Arc is the ruler of Fajin Province."

"And he believes that prophecy is important?"

Ludwig inched a little closer along the couch and leaned in, confidentially. "Of course. We all do. I collect prophecy for him so that it might guide him in ruling our land."

"As Lord Rahl and the Mother Confessor should do."

He shrugged one shoulder. "That is what I believe."

She poured him some more wine. "As do I."

"You are a wise ruler, Orneta."

This time she was the one who sighed. "Wise enough to know that prophecy is important." She laid a hand on his forearm. "It is a great responsibility to lead a people. And prophecy can be a lonely belief, at times."

"I'm sorry to hear that—being lonely in your beliefs about prophecy, I mean. So, there is no king for you?"

She shook her head. "No. Duty has been my companion since I ascended to the throne in my late twenties after long years of grooming for the position. That makes it hard to, well, hard to find the time for myself, for the companionship of one who shares beliefs with me."

"That's a shame. I think the Creator gave us the capacity for passion for a reason, just as He gave us prophecy for a reason."

Her brow twitched. "Yes, I've heard some talk of what you've mentioned to others, talk about your beliefs that prophecy has a connection to the Creator, yet you do not worship the Creator. That seems a curious contradiction."

Ludwig took a drink to give himself time to gather his thoughts.

"Well, have you ever spoken with the Creator?"

She let out a laugh, putting fingertips to her chest. "Me? No, He has never deemed it worth His time to speak to me."

"Exactly."

The laughter evaporated. "Exactly?"

"Yes. The Creator created everything. All the mountains, the seas, the stars in the sky. He creates life itself. He creates all living things."

She turned more serious and leaned in a little. "Go on."

"Can you imagine a being that could do such things? I mean, really, can you imagine a being such as the Creator? A being that created everything, and continues to create new life in uncountable numbers every day? Every new blade of grass, every new fish in the sea, every new soul born into the world. How could we, mere men, even imagine such a being? None of us can, really. We have no point of reference for creation out of nothing on such a cosmic scale. That's why I say the Creator has to be beyond what you or I could ever begin to imagine."

"I suppose you have a point."

He tapped his temple for emphasis. "So if our small human minds are incapable of even imagining such a being, then how can we know Him? Or presume to think that He notices us individually? If we cannot possibly know Him, then how could we have the temerity to worship Him? How can we presume to think we know that He would even desire such worship? Why would He? Do you long for the worship of ants?"

"I never looked at it that way, but I see what you mean."

"That's why He hasn't spoken to you—to any of us. The Creator is everything. We are nothing. We are specks of dust that He brings to life, and then when we die our worldly bodies return to specks of dust. Why would He talk to us? Would you stoop to talk to a speck of dust?"

"So you don't think that the Creator cares about us? We are just specks of nothing to him?"

"We believe, where I come from, that the Creator does care about us, but in a general sense—we are His creation, after all—and so He does speak to us, but not directly."

She was caught up in the story, and returned the hand to his forearm as she inched closer to him.

"So you think He really does care about us? And so He somehow speaks to us?"

"Yes, through prophecy."

Dead silence hung in the room.

"Prophecy is the Creator speaking to us?"

"In a way." His tongue darted out to wet his lips. He leaned toward her. "The Creator created all things. He created life itself. Don't you suppose that He would have an interest in what He has created?"

"Yes, but you said He doesn't speak to us."

"Not directly, not individually, but He does speak to us in a sense. He created life, and He also gave some the gift—magic—as a way for mankind to hear him. He knows all things—everything that has happened and everything that will happen. Through the gift of magic that He gave mankind, He gives us prophecy so as to help guide us."

She went back to drinking her wine as she thought it over. After a moment, her gaze turned to him again.

"Then why would Lord Rahl and the Mother Confessor not want us to know the prophecies that the Creator Himself has given us to help guide us? After all, they are both gifted."

Ludwig arched an eyebrow at her. "Why indeed?"

Her frown grew. "What are you saying?"

He studied her face a moment. She really was an attractive woman. A bit thin, but very appealing, actually.

"Orneta, who would have an interest in us not knowing the words of guidance the Creator has given mankind so as to help us avoid dangers to our lives? Guidance so that we might live?"

She stared off a moment, thinking it over. Realization bloomed on her face. She looked back, her eyes wide.

"The Keeper of the underworld . . ." she breathed.

CHAPTER

43

Orneta straightened a little, pushing back with a hand braced on her knee as she thought better of the suggestion. "You're saying that the Keeper of the underworld is, is what . . . bewitching Lord Rahl and the Mother Confessor? That they are possessed?"

He put a hand over hers, hoping to show her the seriousness of what he was telling her. "Death struggles ceaselessly to take life from the living. The Nameless One, as he is called where I come from, exists only to harvest the living, to pull them from the world of life into the eternal darkness of the underworld. He sometimes casts his seductive whispers over the living in order to use them to do his bidding."

She pulled her hand away and seemed to gather herself up. "That's preposterous. Lord Rahl and the Mother Confessor are not devoted to the Keeper of the underworld. I have never known two people who are more devoted to life."

Ludwig didn't let her withdraw. He leaned toward her again. "Do you suppose that those who are possessed by the Nameless One are always aware of it? If they were, they could not be an effective servant of his covert, dark intent, now could they?"

He had her interest again. "You mean, you think that they are being unknowingly swayed by the Keeper of the underworld? That they are unwittingly doing the Keeper's bidding? That they are possessed but unaware of it?"

He tilted his head toward her. "Don't you suppose that if the Keeper wanted to use someone, wanted to possess someone to do his bidding, that he would pick the last people anyone would suspect? Pick someone trusted, admired, followed?"

She looked away again, thinking. "I suppose. In theory, anyway."

"In our experience, the possessed may be entirely unaware what has happened to them as they still work for the good, at least to outward appearances. But whenever the Nameless One wants, he pulls the invisible strings he has hooked fast to them. In that way they are the perfect host, seeming to all the world to be good people, people who can be trusted, all the while primed and ready to do the Keeper's bidding."

She fussed with the jeweled necklace that disappeared down between her breasts. "It does seem to makes sense that the Keeper would pick someone who would not be suspected of secretly working to accomplish his purpose. But still . . ."

"Where I come from we are always suspicious of those who turn away from prophecy. Among those of us charged with protecting our people from the dark forces of the Nameless One, we know that when someone professes a disbelief in prophecy, it is often a key sign of possession. Prophecy, after all, is the Creator's words, coming to us through the gift of magic, guiding us toward life. Why would anyone turn away from it . . . unless they listen instead to dark forces?"

Orneta stared off into her thoughts for a time before finally speaking, and even then it was half to herself.

"He does always have that woman, Nicci, close at hand. People say she is also known as Death's Mistress. . . ."

"And Lord Rahl and the Mother Confessor do both seem to be opposed to prophecy against all good sense. You yourself tried to reason with them to no avail."

She looked back at him, an intensity in her eyes. "Do you really mean to say, I mean really, that you believe Lord Rahl and the Mother Confessor are agents of the Keeper?"

With a thumb, Ludwig brushed a bit of fuzz from his rimless hat. "We believe in prophecy, and so we study it exhaustively, both from people who give forth omens, and from books of prophecy. We have many ancient texts that we study for clues as to how to protect people from the Nameless One taking them before their time of life is justly over.

"In the study of those ancient texts, we have come across references to Lord Rahl."

"You have?" She frowned, interested again. "And what did they say about him."

"In those ancient volumes, he is named *fuer grissa ost drauka*."

The frown was still firmly fixed on her face. "That sounds like High D'Haran. Do you know what it means?"

"Yes, it is High D'Haran. It means 'the bringer of death.'"

She looked away, close to tears, or panic, he didn't know which.

"I'm sorry. I've spoken out of place." He started to stand. "I can see that I'm upsetting you. I should never have—"

She seized his arm and pulled him back down beside her. "Don't say such a thing, Ludwig. Not many men would be brave enough to face such a terrible truth, much less share it with a stranger, an ally of the D'Haran Empire, who holds a position of power."

"I pray it isn't so, honestly I do, but I can think of no other explanation as to why they so strongly, so obstinately, reject prophecy. If you are not of a mind to throw me out, then I would tell you more."

Her hand tightened on his forearm. "Yes, please, don't hold anything back. I must hear it all if I am to come to a true conclusion."

"From our experience in this, I'm afraid that I must tell you that agents of the Keeper serve his evil schemes by trying to hide prophecy because prophecy reveals future acts of evil, the Keeper's evil intended to take life, acts the Creator knows about and is revealing to us through prophecy as a warning."

"But still," she whispered, "it's hard to believe—"

"Did you know that Lord Rahl has discovered an ancient machine hidden within the palace?"

She set her glass down and turned to face him more directly. "A machine?" She frowned. "What sort of machine?"

"A machine that is said to give forth omens about the future."

She stared intently. "Are you sure of this?"

He set his glass down beside hers on the tray. "I have not seen it with my own eyes, but I have heard, among other things, the whispers of workers who have been in the Garden of Life."

"Does anyone else know of this omen machine?"

He hesitated. "It is not my place to talk out of turn, Orneta. Others have spoken to me in confidence."

"Ludwig, this is important. If what you say is true, this is the most grave of matters."

"Well, there are others among the leaders here who, behind closed doors, have spoken of these things."

"Are you certain of this, or is it just palace rumors?"

He licked his lips again, and again he hesitated before going on.

"King Philippe asked to speak with me about these matters, much as you did. He has heard the whispers about this machine—I didn't ask the source—and further, he has heard that it has awakened from a long darkness and begun issuing omens again, as it once did in ancient times. Lord Rahl is keeping these omens a secret, just as he is keeping the existence of the machine a secret.

"King Philippe believes as I do that there can be only one reason to conceal prophecy, and a machine that can issue it, a machine perhaps built by ancients at the direction of the Creator Himself so that He might help mankind."

She clasped her hands in her lap, her queenly calculation seeming to return to her expression.

"Philippe is no fool."

Ludwig shrugged a little to show her that he was uncomfortable, but also letting her know that he wanted to tell her more. "King Philippe, along with some of the others, thinks that we would be better served having a leader of the D'Haran Empire who studies and uses prophecy to lead us. He thinks it is our only salvation into the future through the hints of dark foreboding we have all heard from those in our homelands with at least a little ability at divination. He thinks we need a leader of the D'Haran Empire who respects prophecy for what it is: the Creator's warnings to us that must be heeded."

"You mean someone like your bishop, Hannis Arc?"

He winced a little at the suggestion, as if he thought he was being far too presumptuous. "I must admit that his name has been mentioned by King Philippe and others as being a leader well versed in the use of prophecy, a leader who would let prophecy guide his hand and thus the people of the D'Haran Empire, as he now does in Fajin Province."

She considered a moment before pressing again, still struggling with accepting it. "Why wouldn't Lord Rahl tell any of us that he has discovered an omen machine? Such a thing could do so much good."

He cocked his head in a reproachful manner. "I think you already know the answer to that, Orneta. There can be only one reason he would not want people to know of such a machine, or its omens."

Orneta rubbed her bare arms as her gaze cast about for salvation of some sort. "This all makes me feel so terribly lonely, so helpless."

Ludwig laid a hand on her shoulder, gently testing. "That is why we so desperately need prophecy to help us." Instead of removing the hand, she put her own hand gently over his.

"I've never been afraid to be here, in Lord Rahl's palace. All of a sudden, I find myself afraid."

When she looked up into his eyes he could see the aloneness, the fear of trusting him, the fear of not trusting him. He knew the moment called for something more to win her.

"You are not alone, Orneta."

He leaned in and gently kissed her lips.

She sat stiffly, unmoving, unresponsive to the kiss. He worried that he had miscalculated.

But then she began to give in to the kiss and melt easily into his arms. He told himself that he could do far worse than this woman. She was older, but not much. In fact, he was finding her more attractive, more appealing, with every heavy breath they shared.

It was clear that in this moment of vulnerability she was letting her passion take charge. He eased her back onto the couch. She went willingly, surrendering to him, to his hands exploring her, his hands drawing her dress off her shoulders.

CHAPTER
44

Kahlan woke with a start when she heard the howls.

With a gasp, she sat bolt upright in her bedroll, her heart hammering so hard she could hear the blood whooshing in her ears.

She frantically looked around, expecting fangs to rip into her at any instant. She snatched for her knife. The knife wasn't there. She scanned the trees, trying to see the source of the bloodcurdling howls. She saw no beasts, no fangs.

She realized that she wasn't out in the woods at all. She was inside. She had been catching a little sleep at the edge of the small indoor forest. There were no hounds, or wolves, or beasts of any kind about. She was safe. The commotion that had awakened her had been the guards opening the double doors into the Garden of Life to make way for someone. The howl had been the hinges on the heavy doors.

She pushed her hair back out of her face as she let out a deep sigh. She had to have been dreaming. It had seemed so real, but it was just a dream and its heart-pounding grasp on her quickly loosened.

She rubbed her arms as she looked around and sighed again, relieved that it had been only a dream and that it was swiftly evaporating. Overhead, driven by the cycle of the seasons, the barren tree branches were laden with buds. They would soon be in full foliage. After the ceiling had finally been repaired and fully glassed in, the spring sun had, over a period of a few days, gently warmed the Garden of Life, making it once again a cozy refuge and a place where she and Richard could sleep. It wasn't as comfortable as a real bed, but sleep came a lot more easily when they didn't feel unseen eyes watching them.

As she wiped the sleep from her eyes, Kahlan had to squint as she looked up at the full moon shining down from overhead. By its position in a black sky she knew that she had been asleep for only a brief time. That meant it was still the dead of night.

She was reminded that it was night, too, by the heady fragrance of jasmine that grew at the edge of the small forest and down in front of the short wall. The tiny petals of the delicate white flowers opened only in the night.

"Is Richard down there?" Nathan asked on his way past, ignoring both the moonlight and the singular fragrance, gesturing instead toward the dark, gaping hole as he marched down the path through the trees and toward the center of the Garden of Life. He was the one the guards had let in.

Kahlan nodded. "Yes, he's with Nicci, watching the machine in case it awakens again. Why? What's wrong?"

"We have trouble," he said as he headed for the ladder.

Kahlan saw that he had something in his hand. She threw the blanket aside and sprang up to follow after him.

The men of the First File, after having closed the door, took up defensive positions. There were a good two dozen of the elite of the elite standing guard inside the Garden of Life. It would have required only two or three of these of men to hold off an army. It was somewhat disconcerting to have them nearby, watching over her, but they didn't watch her the way the thing in the bedrooms had. They were watching out for her safety. She didn't know why the thing in the bedroom had been watching, but she knew that it wasn't to keep them safe.

Ever since the machine had given the first of its last two prophecies, the one that said "Pawn takes queen," Richard wasn't taking any chances with her safety. Whenever she left the Garden of Life without him, she left with a small army, Nathan, Zedd, or Nicci, and at least two Mord-Sith.

It wasn't that she didn't like having protection from whatever the dark danger was that seemed loose in the palace, it was just that it made it rather awkward when meeting with the representatives. It put people on edge, giving the impression that the palace was under siege. The representatives were aware, though, that something was going on and there had already been an attempt on her life, so there was justification for the protection. But the unknown nature of the threat made them all the more interested in what prophecy might have to say. They felt they were being excluded from vital information.

Most of the representatives had settled comfortably into their new quarters in the palace, at least for the time being. A few of the rulers had gone home, leaving ambassadors or high officials in their place.

Richard and Kahlan thought that it was important for all parts of the empire to feel a sense of unity, of common purpose, and to be governed under uniform laws. The rulers and their representatives from all areas of the far-flung empire not only were encouraged to maintain offices for official business but had their own, permanent residences in the palace. The palace was a virtual city atop the plateau and was certainly large enough to accommodate them.

Except, of course, for all the princes. At least for the time being, every prince had been sent home.

People naturally wanted an explanation. Richard wouldn't give them one. To do so, he would have had to reveal the last prophecy from the machine, and he didn't want to do that. He didn't want to lie, either, but he had to tell them something. So he had simply told them part of the truth, that word of a threat had been brought to his attention.

There had been three princes at the palace. One was an important man who had come representing his father, the king of Nicobarese. The other two princes were less important, but Richard had taken no chances. He had sent each prince home guarded by a sizable force of men led by competent officers who had been handpicked by General Meiffert.

That left no princes at the People's Palace, even if it left some of the representatives confused and curious, and a few resentful of the secrecy. It couldn't be helped. The consequences of the last omen given by the machine were not something Richard wanted to risk. The resulting questions at times tried Richard and Kahlan's patience, but they had dealt with it as best they could and everything had eventually quieted down as people moved on to other issues of more immediate concern to them.

When Kahlan reached the bottom of the ladder leading down below the Garden of Life she had to hurry to keep up with Nathan. He had long legs and he wasn't slowing to wait for her. The bright moonlight coming through the hole in the garden floor lit the dome in the room directly under it, the room over the tomb where the machine rested. Kahlan hadn't brought a torch, so she was thankful for the moonlight as she scrambled over large blocks of stone that had once been the supporting structure for the floor of the garden and had not yet been removed.

Richard, keeping watch over the machine in case it awakened again, had heard them coming and was at the bottom of the spiral stairs, waiting. Nicci joined him to see what was so urgent.

Kahlan saw Richard use two fingers of his left hand to lift the sword at his hip a few inches and then let it drop back, checking that it was clear in its scabbard. It was an old habit that had always served him well.

"What is it?" he asked when the prophet reached the bottom of the spiral stairs.

"You know that last prophecy, the omen that the machine spit out after the one saying 'Pawn takes queen'?"

Richard nodded. "The one I told everyone I didn't want to leave this room."

It had, technically, left the room. Nathan had found it in the book *End Notes*. Being in that book not only made the prophecy all the more disturbing, but, Nathan said, confirmed its validity.

"Tonight," Nathan said, "after the moon came up, Sabella, the blind woman, gave a prophecy to a group of representatives." The prophet waggled a hand at the machine sitting silently in the center of the room lit by proximity spheres. "It was the exact same prophecy that thing gave, the one I found in the book *End Notes*."

Richard wiped a hand across his face. "I'd like to send Sabella somewhere far away to ply her trade in fortunes."

"Wouldn't do any good," Nathan said. "At the same time that she was giving the prophecy, three other people, three people who have never before been visited by foretelling of any kind, fell into some kind of trance and while in a stupor gave the exact same prophecy."

Richard stared a moment. "It was the same? Are you sure?"

"Yes. Word for word the same. A number of people attending these half-conscious people heard the omen. A far greater number of people know about it by now. The whole palace would know it by now if most of them weren't asleep. By morning I'm sure it will be gossip on every tongue, especially since you sent the princes away."

Richard frowned in thought. "Why would these other people have the same prophecy, yet you don't? You're a prophet. You're the one who should be having the prophecy."

Nathan shrugged. "Maybe it's not really prophecy."

"It's almost as if the machine wants to make sure that people hear the omens it gives," Richard said, half to himself. "At least we got the princes safely away. Maybe people will think—"

"It gets worse."

Richard looked up at the prophet. "Worse?"

"When Sabella gave this prophecy, and then I heard about the others who had spoken the same words, I went to check and, sure enough, Lauretta was there, down in the library below here, frantically writing this."

Nathan handed Richard the paper he was holding. Kahlan put a hand on Richard's shoulder as she leaned in to see it in the eerie light of the proximity spheres. Richard unfolded the paper as if fearing it might bite him.

It said, *While at the palace, on the full moon, a prince from the west shall fall to fangs.*

"It's the exact same omen that the machine gave," Richard

said in a troubled voice. "Word for word." He turned to Nicci. "Could these prophecies be from that game you mentioned before. They all sound something alike."

"The first of these latest two, the one saying 'Pawn takes queen,' is the exact reverse of the prophecy from before— 'Queen takes pawn.' Both, though, are moves in the game of chess." Nicci gestured to the paper he was holding. "But this last one about fangs taking a prince, even though it sounds like it could be a move in the same game, actually has nothing at all to do with the game of chess."

Richard sighed in disappointment. Kahlan couldn't imagine if the two prophecies were connected or not.

"Lord Rahl! Lord Rahl!"

It was Cara, screaming down from above. She raced down the spiral stairs three at time until she could duck low enough to see them.

"Lord Rahl, Benjamin sent me. You need to come to the representatives' apartments at once. Hurry."

CHAPTER

45

Kahlan followed close on Richard's heels as they ran past clusters of people gathered in the halls, everyone from the night cleaning staff to representatives who were staying in the nearby apartments. Plush carpets laid over the white marble floors cushioned their footfalls and muted the jangle of armor.

Kahlan kept her eye on snatches of red leather out ahead of Richard as Cara led them through the maze of halls. She took them around corners and down the ornately paneled hallways among the luxurious guest quarters where the representatives were staying.

A number of the emissaries and officials stood among soldiers in the network of corridors along the way. They shouted questions as Richard and Kahlan ran past. Neither of them answered or slowed. They could hardly tell people what was going on when they didn't know themselves.

As they rounded an intersection, Kahlan saw guards up ahead blocking people from going any farther up the hall. When they saw Richard coming, the guards pushed people aside to make way for him. With all the men of the First File looking grim and implacable, the people appeared to be generally doing what the guards asked of them.

Kahlan saw Queen Orneta working her way to the front of the observers crowded into the corridor. The queen looked as concerned and confused as everyone else.

Beyond the guards keeping people back were hundreds of men of the First File packed into the broad corridor. All the soldiers wore armor of some sort, either leather, chain mail, or polished breastplates, depending on the unit they belonged to and their duties. All of them were heavily armed and all of them had one kind of weapon or another in hand.

Companies of men with spears tipped in razor-sharp broadpoints all stepped back against the wall, spears all vertical, as Cara, Richard, Kahlan, Nathan, and Nicci raced past. The spearmen could close ranks in a hallway and present a nearly impenetrable wall of sharpened steel if need be. Men with swords stepped aside as well but also kept a wary watch up ahead.

Kahlan wondered what could have drawn this many men.

When they finally broke through the crowds of people and the massed soldiers, they came to a relatively open section of the corridor where even most of the soldiers were kept back.

General Meiffert and a handful of men waited up ahead outside ornately carved double doors of one of the apartments. While Kahlan knew that these corridors were where high-ranking guests and representatives had their quarters, she didn't know who occupied this one.

As they all came to a stop outside the doors, Richard glanced down at the floor. Kahlan followed his gaze and saw thin trickles of blood running out from under the doors, across exposed white marble, and then finally under the rug.

Cara, Agiel in hand, moved in close beside Richard. Nicci closed in beside Kahlan, boxing her and Richard in between a Mord-Sith and a sorceress. Nathan finally caught up, bringing up the rear.

Richard gestured at the doors as he addressed the general. "What's going on?"

"We're not sure, Lord Rahl. People in a nearby apartment were awakened by howling, and then the most horrific screams."

Richard drew his sword. The unique ring of steel echoed through the hallway.

"Do you know whose room this is?"

General Meiffert nodded. "It's King Philippe's room."

"And why is everyone standing around out here?" Richard's tone carried the heat of the sword's magic. "Why didn't you go in there and see what's wrong?"

The general's jaw clenched as he ground his teeth. "We've been trying our best, Lord Rahl. But try as we might, we haven't been able to break the doors down. At least, not yet. A lot of these rooms are for important guests who feel the need for safety, so the doors are heavily reinforced and they are backed with massive bolts."

Kahlan saw that the doors were gouged and damaged from the effort.

"With as much trouble as we're having getting in, and as hard as we've been trying, it could also be some kind of shield of magic barring the doors," the general added.

"I suppose it's possible, but magic is weakened in the palace unless it's used by a Rahl," Richard said. "Who could be using magic to shield the doors?"

Kahlan could see the anger of the sword in his gray eyes, and she could see him fighting to control it.

When the general had no answer, Nathan spoke up. "Richard, even someone with weakened power could likely muster enough force to create a shield strong enough to help bar a door." He cocked his head, as if listening. "I can't detect anything, but that doesn't mean it isn't shielded."

The general turned at a sound of men rushing in from behind him. "No matter—we'll get it open now."

A group of soldiers shuffled up the hall, carrying a long iron block with a bar down each side for handholds. The battering ram was heavy enough that it took eight muscular men to carry it and they were still having trouble.

Just then, King Philippe, sword in hand, ran up behind the guards holding people back, trying to shove his way through. When General Meiffert signaled to let the man through, he rushed up behind Richard and Kahlan.

"This is my room. What's going on!" he demanded.

"We don't know, yet," the general said.

King Philippe saw the blood running out across the floor. He frantically rattled one of the the door handles, trying to open the door. "My wife is in there!" He threw a shoulder against the door repeatedly but it didn't budge.

Richard seized the man's jacket at the shoulder and pulled him back. "Let these men through. They have a ram, let them at the doors."

In a state flashing back and forth between anger and panic, King Philippe looked at Richard and then the men with the ram. He quickly moved to the side and gestured with an arm, urging them on.

The men didn't waste any time. With a grunt of effort, they rushed forward with the heavy ram. Gathering as much speed as they could in the confines of the corridor, they raced in. The ram crashed into the doors with a resounding thud. It felt to Kahlan like the entire wall shook with the impact, but the doors held tight.

They backed across the corridor and came again, driving the ram into the doors, sending small splinters flying. Where it hit, the ram left an impression embossed into the carving of vines and a ring of splintered wood, but the doors remained intact. A third time was no more fruitful.

Kahlan thought that it would be best if someone with the gift breached the doors. "Nicci, Nathan—can't one of you do something?"

Richard wasn't in the mood to wait for that.

"Move aside!" he impatiently yelled out when the men with the ram stepped back to gain room to make another attempt.

As the men backed away, without wasting another moment, Richard gripped his sword with both hands and lifted it over his head. With a mighty swing the blade whistled through the air, arcing toward the doors. The Sword of Truth had been made thousands of years before and invested with great power. There was nothing it couldn't cut through in the hands of the Seeker, except one thing: those he knew to be innocent.

With an earsplitting crash the blade smashed through the heavy doors. Sharp wooden fragments sailed through the hallway, ricocheting off the walls. Everyone nearby ducked away, covering their faces with an arm. Only the briefest pause later, a second swing shattered another ragged swath down through the doors, sending huge splinters flying through the hall and skittering across the carpets. Kahlan could see that a heavy beam inside that had barred the doors had been shattered by the sword.

Richard threw a powerful kick into the center of the two

broken doors. They both ripped from their hinges and toppled into the room.

As the heavy doors crashed to the ground and clouds of
dust and debris billowed up, Richard dove through into the
dark room.

CHAPTER

46

Kahlan tried to follow Richard into the room, but Cara, Agiel in hand and bent on protecting him, raced in ahead of her. Before Kahlan could follow, Nicci slipped in front of Kahlan and dashed in with Cara, both women worried about Richard diving headlong into trouble. Kahlan, no less concerned, cut in front of Benjamin and ran into the darkness after them.

A frantic King Philippe tried to follow, but soldiers restrained him. Benjamin urged the king to let Lord Rahl and the rest of them find out what was going on, first.

Inside, they came to a halt. The room was dead quiet.

Kahlan held her breath against the stench of blood.

Glancing back over her shoulder, she could see Benjamin silhouetted in the doorway, waiting to see if they needed reinforcements. On the opposite side of the room, to either side of double doors, sheer curtains billowed in a light breeze, looking like ghosts in the moonlight.

"I can't see a thing in here," Cara whispered.

Nicci ignited a flame that floated in midair above her palm. She quickly found a stand with a few candles still affixed to it and righted it, then sent the flame into the candles.

As the level of light rose, Kahlan could at last see more than the mere hints of shapes in the moonlight coming through the open doors on the opposite side of the room.

"Dear spirits," she whispered into the terrible quiet.

Nicci retrieved a few lamps from the rubble, lit them, and set them on a table that was still upright.

In the lamplight they were finally able to see the full extent of the devastation. Splintered furniture lay overturned. Cushions were scattered. The leather chairs were slashed by what looked to be either claws or fangs, Kahlan didn't know which.

A nearby couch had been turned red with blood. Blood splatters crisscrossed the walls in swaths, as if flung there in terrible rage. The amount of it everywhere was shocking.

At their feet Queen Catherine lay on her back. Her scalp had been partly peeled away. Gouges looking to be left by fangs raked across her exposed skull and cut through the upper part of her face. Her jaw was torn partially away. Her eyes, as if still filled with paralyzing shock, stared unseeing at the ceiling.

Since the remnants were so completely soaked in blood, it was impossible to tell what color her dress had once been.

Catherine's entire middle was ripped open. She had nearly been torn in two. Her left thigh muscle, stripped off the bone, lay flopped out to the side. Long gouges, also appearing to be left by fangs, raked down the length of the bone.

Viscera lay strewn out across the floor. It looked like a pack of wolves had been at her, their fangs ripping her open and pulling her apart. What was left hardly looked human.

Kahlan's knees felt weak. She could not help thinking about the woman who had murdered her children, the woman Kahlan had taken with her power. This was what the woman had predicted was going to happen to Kahlan.

Then, among the organs and intestines, she saw an umbilical cord snaking its way across the floor.

At the end of it were the bloody, pink remains of Catherine's unborn child. Its little toes looked perfect. The top half of the body was gone.

From what remained, Kahlan could see that it was a boy.

A prince.

With a scream of fury, King Philippe finally pulled away from soldiers reluctant to be too forceful with him. He bulled his way into the room. When he reached his wife he froze stiff.

Then he screamed, a cold cry such as could only be brought forth by such a horrific sight, a cry that would have made the good spirits weep.

Richard put an arm around the man's shoulders and tried to gently pull him back and away from the sight.

King Philippe jerked away and turned in fury toward Richard. "This is your fault!"

Nathan lifted a hand in warning. "It was no such thing."

The king ignored him. He brought his sword up, pointing it at Richard's face. "You could have prevented this!"

Richard, his own sword still in his fist, its rage still in his eyes, slowly brought his blade up and used it to turn the point of King Philippe's sword aside.

"I can only imagine how you must feel," Richard said in as calm a voice as he could muster with the sword in his hand and its rage pounding through his veins. The violent death at his feet only served to feed his own rage. "Your anger and hurt is entirely understandable," Richard told him.

"How would you know?" the king yelled. "You care nothing for your people, or you would have helped us by using prophecy to prevent this!"

"Prophecy would not have prevented this," Richard said.

"You sent those three princes away because of prophecy! You knew! You could have prevented this! You wanted this to happen!"

Nicci kept the king locked in her gaze. Any wrong move, and her power would crash into the king before he knew what had hit him. Kahlan didn't think that the king even realized the mortal danger he was in, from Nicci, from Richard, from Nathan, and no less from Kahlan.

"You don't know what you're saying," Nicci warned. "You are looking for guilt in the wrong place."

He turned the sword toward her. "I know perfectly well what I'm saying! I only just now learned of the prophecy saying that here in the palace a prince would fall to fangs on the full moon. Had Lord Rahl told us of this prophecy, we could have prevented this from happening!"

"And had you not been out chasing prophecy," Kahlan said in a deadly voice of her own, "you could have been here to save your wife and unborn son from this fate. They fell to fangs because you were off chasing prophecy, when you should have been at their side protecting them. Now, you seek to shift blame away from yourself and onto others."

Richard gently put a hand out, touching Kahlan's arm, as if to say to let the man be. She was right, of course, but it would do no good at the moment to press the issue.

Richard's sympathy did not register with the king. He again turned his sword toward Richard. Richard's eyes remained focused on the man, but he didn't move to knock the sword aside. Despite what the king might think, Kahlan knew that he would not be fast enough. When he wished it, the blade Richard held could move like lightning and strike just as hard.

"You have failed in your duty to protect your people," the king growled.

"He's been doing everything he can to protect everyone," Kahlan said, ready to reach out and take the king with her own power if necessary.

His glare turned toward her. "Really? Then why has he not told us that he found an omen machine."

Richard blinked. "What?"

King Philippe swept his sword back, indicating those outside. "We all know of it. The question is, why would you keep such a machine secret, and the warnings it has given—prophecy that could only come from the Creator Himself?"

"We don't know anything about the machine, much less if it is meant to help us or harm us," Richard said. "We can't put our trust in words coming from a source we know nothing about. That's why—"

"Just where do your loyalties lie, Lord Rahl? With life or with death itself? Who do you really serve?"

Cara lifted her Agiel, pointing it at the king's face. "You are now treading on very dangerous ground. You don't know what you're talking about. I suggest that you take greater care to make sure you don't say something you would come to greatly regret."

Richard gently lowered Cara's arm. "I would have done anything to prevent this," he said to the king.

"Anything but tell us the truth." His gaze left Cara and moved to Richard. "There have been rumors that you are afraid to sleep in your own bedchambers, now we know why. Yet you would not warn your people of the danger loose in the palace. You have failed in your duty to us!"

Richard glared back, but didn't answer. Kahlan knew that it was pointless to try to talk sense into the man at such an emotional moment, standing as they were over his murdered wife and unborn child.

King Philippe gritted his teeth. "You are not fit to lead the D'Haran Empire."

"I swear to you," Richard said, "I will find out who is responsible for this and see justice done."

"Justice? I know who is responsible." The king straightened his shoulders and sheathed his sword. "I withdraw my land from loyalty to your rule. We no longer recognize you as the legitimate leader of the D'Haran Empire."

He looked down briefly at the remains of his wife on the floor before him, then closed his eyes for a moment as if fighting back tears or maybe a cry of anguish, or maybe an urge to pull his sword again.

And then he turned and stormed away.

CHAPTER
47

His sword still gripped tightly in his hand, Richard circled his free arm around Kahlan's shoulders. She gently rested a hand on his back, silently returning the understanding. No words were needed, or at that moment would have been adequate.

Without saying anything to the others watching him, Richard led her out of the room. Kahlan had seen violent deaths beyond counting, and to an extent had gotten used to it, built a shell to protect herself from feeling it, but that protective shell had slowly softened since the war had ended. Still, violent death was not something new to her. This death, though, more than most, seemed to have rocked her to her core.

Maybe it was because Catherine had been pregnant. Maybe seeing an unborn child that had been ripped from his mother and killed was what had gotten to her. Maybe it was because it reminded her of her own unborn child that had died because she had been savagely attacked when she had been pregnant. She held back a cry of anguish, and did her best to hold back tears, though she thought that in the absence of her husband to look after her remains as a final act of devotion, Catherine deserved at least tears.

Outside the room, Richard paused. The carpet over the white marble floor, where the blood ran under it, was rumpled up a bit, probably from the boots and effort of the men with the ram as they had tried to breach the door.

For some reason, Richard stood frozen, staring at it.

Puzzled, Kahlan looked more closely, and then she, too, saw something, some kind of mark, back in the dark fold under the carpet.

With the tip of his sword, Richard flipped the carpet back.

There, under where the carpet had lain, stained with Queen Catherine's blood, with the unborn prince's blood, was a symbol that had been scratched into the polished marble. The symbol was circular. It looked to Kahlan something like the designs drawn in the book *Regula*.

"Do you know what it says?" she asked.

Some of the color had left Richard's face. "It says, 'Watch them.'"

"'Watch them'?" Nicci asked, looking down at the symbol. "Are you sure?"

Richard nodded, then turned to Benjamin. "General, please see to taking proper care of the queen. Before you have the room cleaned, inspect it carefully, inspect every splinter, look for footprints in the blood to see if this has been staged by men or if it was animals. Look for broken teeth. Animals sometimes lose teeth in a violent attack. Look for fur. See if you can learn anything that will help us to understand what happened here. I want to know if it was men or beasts that did this."

"Of course, Lord Rahl."

Richard pointed with his chin. "The doors at the back of the room are opened out onto the terrace. Whatever or whoever did this undoubtedly got in there."

General Meiffert glanced back through the broken door-way. "The room is close enough to the ground that some-thing could have gotten in there, but I've never heard of wolves being up on the plateau. Dogs, occasionally, but not wolves."

"Something was up here," Richard said. "It could have been a pack of dogs. Dogs, even domesticated dogs, will kill people like this if they pack up."

The general nodded as he glanced back through the doorway. "I'll personally see to having the room carefully checked."

"I have to go look into something," Richard said. "Tell the other representatives that for now we have reason to believe that the queen was killed by animals—most likely wolves or dogs. Have them keep their exterior doors closed and locked. You should also station men outside to watch for anything suspicious. If you see anything on four legs running loose, kill it and inspect the contents of its stomach."

When the general clapped a fist to his heart, Richard started off at a trot. Momentarily surprised, Kahlan and the others quickly followed behind as he ran off down the corri-dor. Guards backed out of the way when they saw him com-ing.

When they reached the people being kept back, the guards moved everyone out of the way so Richard and the rest of them could get through.

Representatives snatched at his sleeve, wanting to know what had happened and if there was danger about. Richard told them that there was, and that the soldiers would see to it, but he didn't slow to explain or to discuss it.

Once finally away from the guest quarters, they went through doors that were always guarded, and into the private sections of the palace, the sections where the public wasn't allowed. It was a relief to be away from people, to be away from their questions, from the accusations in their eyes. The small group took a shortcut through rooms that were lit only by a few lamps, and small libraries where the only light came from open doors at either end, or from low fires in a hearth.

"Where are we going?" Kahlan asked as she trotted along beside Richard once they were out into a wider corridor.

"To the last bedroom we stayed in."

Kahlan thought about it for a moment as she listened to their footfalls echoing back from the distance.

"You mean the bedroom where we . . . saw something?"

"That's right."

Before long they reached a familiar hallway. The walls were paneled and at intervals had pedestals with crystal vases holding cut tulips. Partway down the hall was the bedroom Kahlan had found for them, the last bedroom they had stayed in before they had moved to the Garden of Life to sleep, not long after the woman who had tried to kill Kahlan predicted that she would be taken by the same thing as would have eaten her children. Dark things, the woman had said.

"Dark things stalking you, running you down. You won't be able to escape them."

When they reached the doorway to the bedroom, Richard kicked back the carpeting.

There, hidden under the carpet, scratched into the polished marble floor, was another symbol. It looked to Kahlan like the last one, the one stained with Catherine's and her unborn child's blood.

"It says the same thing," Richard said as he stared down at the ancient design scratched into the floor. " 'Watch them.' "

"This was the last place where we felt someone watching

us," Kahlan said. "I wonder if Catherine felt someone watching her."

"What I want to know is who put this here, and how is it that they weren't seen."

48

Richard stood alone, hands clasped behind his back, staring at the machine, trying to work out what could be going on. He had lain down with Kahlan for a long time up in the Garden of Life, holding her until her tears had ended, waiting until the tension had gone out of her body and her breathing had slowed. When she had finally fallen into a fitful sleep, he had come alone down to the room where the machine had been buried and forgotten for uncounted centuries.

He still didn't know who had created the thing, or why. It would seem that it had been created to give prophecy. An omen machine, the king had called it.

Somehow, as inconceivable as that was, it still sounded too simple. The book, after all, called the machine Regula, and that meant so much more.

But the book *Regula* down in the library was merely a translation of the symbols, of the language of Creation, that the machine used to convey its predictions. The book only helped them to understand the omens that the Regula machine issued. It did not explain why it called the machine Regula. "*Regula*" meant to regulate with sovereign authority. What that had to do with omens Richard couldn't imagine.

He supposed that in a way, through its prophecies, the machine actually was controlling what was happening. Or someone else was, and making them look like prophecies coming from the machine. It also seemed that the prophecies issued by the machine were not enough. Those same prophecies also came to light through various people in the palace, as if to insure that the messages could not be kept secret.

It could be, he imagined, that the machine was very much regulating—controlling—what was going on through its recent prophecies, so in that way the name Regula fit, although that seemed a stretch.

It seemed to Richard far more likely that the answers to the machine's true purpose were in the part of the book that was missing, the part hidden away in the Temple of the Winds. Whatever was in that part of the book had to be important, or else dangerous, to warrant being hidden away in the Temple of the Winds.

Richard didn't relish the idea of again setting foot in that place. It would be far from simple and could easily create more problems than it solved.

He tried to push the troubling thoughts aside. He wanted to be up in the Garden of Life with Kahlan, to be in her arms, to have her tell him that everything would be all right . . . to tell him again that it wasn't his fault. He knew that it wasn't, but that still didn't make him feel any better. It couldn't undo what had happened.

He had to find out what was going on and put a stop to it.

He knew that the representatives would be in an uproar, not only over the murder of a queen while she was a guest of the palace, but even more so over King Philippe denouncing Richard as the ruler of the D'Haran Empire. It was a declaration driven by raw emotion, but even so, Richard knew that there were a number of people who would side with King Philippe and follow his lead. Richard wasn't sure what he could do about it, but at the moment, he had bigger worries.

While the king and others found it convenient to blame Richard—and Richard blamed himself for failing to link the prophecy to an unborn prince—that didn't get to the heart of what was going on. He needed to figure out what had really happened and why. Something, or someone, had been in that room and had killed Queen Catherine.

He was convinced that someone was behind it, that it was deliberate. After all, someone had set about watching the queen. Someone had scratched that symbol in the floor outside her room. Someone was watching and when she had been alone they had struck. At least, that was the way it seemed to him. He had to admit that as incriminating as the symbol was, the murder might not actually be connected to it. He couldn't let himself become locked into only one possibility.

He was even more puzzled as to how someone could have gotten into the Lord Rahl's quarters, past all the guards, and then, unseen, scratch that same symbol in the floor outside their bedroom door.

As much as he wanted to be with Kahlan, he needed to think things through. More than that, though, he needed to be alone.

Somehow, it seemed certain to him that the machine, a machine that could issue omens, had to be at the heart of the the darkness that had settled over the palace.

Richard remembered what the sick boy down in the market, the boy who had scratched Richard and Kahlan, had said. He'd said there was darkness in the palace. Darkness seeking darkness.

Richard no longer doubted that there was darkness in the palace. It had descended on them all.

He reached out and placed a hand on the machine.

"What are you?" he whispered, wondering out loud to himself. "Why are you doing this?"

As if in response, a low rumble came from the machine as the gears began turning against one another. It wasn't like in the past, though. In the past it had always started with a jolt that shook the ground.

This time it began softly, the shafts and gears slowly beginning to move, to gather momentum. In the past it had always been a sudden, thunderous initiation of movement. It had always started at full speed.

This time, it was very different. It was a quiet beginning that was building toward that eventual mechanical mayhem.

Richard leaned over, looking into the slit of a window. He saw the light inside gradually intensify as the slowly turning gears picked up speed with the machine's awakening. The same symbol projected up onto the ceiling as in the past, though this time instead of igniting at full intensity, it gradually grew in strength.

Before long, though, the inner workings of the machine were in full motion. The ground around it rumbled. The light burning up from deep inside steadily grew brighter. The symbol on the ceiling rotating above his head glowed.

A latch on a rotating wheel popped up beneath the stack of strips on the other side of the machine and pushed a strip partway out from under the stack. Pincers then plucked the blank metal strip from the bottom of the stack.

As the strip was pulled onward through the interior mechanism, the light from below intensified again, narrowing and closing down into a beam that burned lines and symbols into the underside of the strip. As the light inscribed the underneath side of the strip, it caused hot spots to glow through onto the top of the metal.

After passing over the beam of light, the strip moved along the same as he had seen others move through the machine in the past to finally make it all the way across and drop into the slot near the small window.

Richard licked his fingers and plucked the strip from the slot where it rested. He tossed it onto the top of the machine to cool.

He blinked in surprise when he realized that the strip had not been hot at all. He reached out and touched it, testing. It was cool to the touch.

Frowning, he pulled it close. There were symbols burned into the metal as before, but for some reason this time the process hadn't left it hot. He couldn't imagine why not.

Richard turned the strip around so he could read it. He bent closer to the light of a proximity sphere and deciphered the unique collection of elements assembled into a single emblem that made a phrase in the language of Creation.

I have had dreams.

Richard stood frozen, staring at it. He thought that he must have read it wrong. He rotated the metal strip around, looking at each element in the circle, as he worked out the translation again to make sure he had it right and then spoke it aloud.

"I have had dreams."

He took a step back from the machine.

It had always given a warning in the past, an omen, some kind of prophecy. This didn't make any sense, and it didn't sound at all like prophecy.

It sounded as if the machine had . . . said something about itself.

As he stood staring, Regula paused momentarily as shafts disengaged and gears slowed; then the gears interlocked and picked up speed again. The machine drew another strip from the stack on the other side and pulled it through the inner mechanism, in the process passing it over the focused beam of light to engrave a new message on the second strip.

When it dropped into the tray, Richard stood looking at it for a long time before he finally pulled it out. The second strip was as cool to the touch as the first had been. He held it up in the light, looking at the unique organization of symbols that made up the two emblems burned into the metal.

Hardly able to believe what he was seeing, he read it aloud.

"Why have I had dreams?"

The machine seemed to be asking him a question. If it was, he had no idea how to answer it.

Richard remembered then having heard before what was now written in the language of Creation on both strips. It had been the boy down in the market, Henrik, who had said "*I have had dreams.*" Richard and Kahlan hadn't been able to understand why he'd said it. They had thought he was sick and delirious. He had then asked "*Why have I had dreams?*"

Now the machine had just asked the very same thing.

The boy hadn't been delirious.

It had been the machine speaking through him.

The boy had also asked if the sky was still blue. And it had asked why they had all left it alone. Only it had said "me"— why had they left "me" all alone in the cold and dark. It had said it was alone, so alone.

The machine was asking why it had been buried alive.

It had also said *He will find me, I know he will.*

Richard wondered if that was a prophecy . . . an omen.

Or was the machine expressing a fear?

CHAPTER
49

Henrik lifted his head from gulping water out of the brook to look back through the trees into the deep shadows. He could hear the hounds coming. They crashed through brush, snarling and barking as they came.

With the back of his fist, Henrik wiped fresh tears of terror from his cheeks. The hounds were going to catch him, he knew they were. They wouldn't stop until they had him. Ever since that day at the People's Palace, when they had showed up outside the tent, sniffing and growling, they kept coming for him.

His only chance was to keep running.

He stuck his foot into the stirrup and hooked his wrist over the horn of the saddle to help pull himself back up onto the horse's back. He spun the reins around his wrists, locked them to his fisted hands with his thumbs, and then thumped the mare's belly with his heels, urging it into an easy gallop.

He had hoped to take an extra moment to eat something more than a biscuit and a single piece of dried meat. He was starving. He was thirsty as well, but he'd only had time to lie on his belly and gulp a few swallows of water from the brook before he had sprung up and run back to his horse.

He had desperately wanted to eat more, to drink more.

But there was no time. The hounds were too close.

He had to keep running, keep ahead of them. If they got to him they would tear him apart.

He hadn't known where he was going at first. His instinct had made him bolt from his mother's tent and had driven him onward. He knew his mother would want to protect him, but she couldn't. She would have been torn apart and then they would be on him.

So he'd had no choice but to run for all he was worth until, exhausted, he had happened upon the horses. They had been in a small corral with some others. He hadn't seen anyone around. He needed to get away, so he snatched up a saddle and took two horses. He was lucky enough to have discovered some traveling food in the saddlebags or he would probably have starved to death by now.

He never gave a thought to it being wrong to take the horses; his life was at stake. He simply ran. Who could blame him? Would people really expect him to be torn apart and eaten alive rather than take a couple of horses to get away? What choice did he have?

When it grew too dark to see, he was forced to stop for the night. A few times he had come across an abandoned building where he had been able to hole up for the night, safe for a time from the hounds. Then, in the morning, he made a run for it before the hounds knew he was up. Several times he had slept in a tree to be safe from them. The hounds, somewhere down in the darkness, eventually grew tired of barking and took off for the night. He thought that maybe they went off to sleep themselves, or to hunt for food.

Other times, when there was no place of safety, he had been able to get a fire started. He huddled close to it, ready to grab a burning branch and brandish it at the dogs if they came close. They never did. They didn't like the fire. They always watched from a distance, their heads lowered, their eyes glowing in the dark, as they paced back and forth, waiting for morning.

Sometimes when he woke they were gone and he dared hope they had finally tired of the chase. But it was never long before he would hear them baying in the distance, racing in toward him, and the chase would be on again.

He pushed the horses so hard keeping ahead of the hounds that the one he rode at first had given out. He switched the saddle to the second and left the first behind, hoping the hounds would be satisfied with the horse and he could get away.

The hounds hadn't taken the horse, though. They'd kept coming for him, instead. They had followed him through the mountains, through the forests, ever onward, ever deeper into a dark, trackless land of immense trees.

Now he was beginning to recognize the gloomy wood he was passing through. He had grown up several days' travel to the north, in a small village hard against the hills beside a branch of the Caro-Kann River.

He had been in this place, on this trail, before, with his mother. He remembered the towering pines clinging to the rocky slope, the way they closed in overhead, obscuring the heavily overcast sky, making it dark and dreary down among the brush and bramble.

The horse skidded, trying to find footing on the steep descent down the side of the grade. The woods were too thick and it was too dark in among them to see what lay down ahead. For that matter, he couldn't see far off to the sides, either.

But he didn't need to see. He knew what was ahead.

After a long descent down the ill-defined, twisting trail,

the ground flattened out into a darker place where the trees grew closer together, and the underbrush was thick. There were only rare glimpses of light through the trees. The tangle of shrubs and small trees made it nearly impossible to take any course but the thinned area that served as a trail.

When he came to a rocky rim, the horse snorted in protest and refused to go on. There was no place beyond that was safe for a horse. What trail there was made its way down between and over cascading lifts of rock and ledges.

Henrik dismounted and peered over the edge down into the misty wilderness below. He remembered that the trail down was narrow, steep, and treacherous. The horse couldn't take him any farther. He looked back over his shoulder, expecting the hounds to come bounding out of the trees at any second. By their growls and yelps, he knew they were getting close again.

He quickly unsaddled the horse so that it would at least have a chance to get away. He slipped off the horse's head gear and slapped its flanks. The horse whinnied and bolted back the way they had come.

Henrik spotted the big black dog that led the pack as it broke through the trees. It didn't go after the horse. It was coming after him. He turned and without further delay headed down over the edge of the rocks.

While the trail was too steep and jagged for the horse, with crags and splits in the sloping rock face, loose scree in some spots, and rugged outcroppings in others, he knew that the hounds would have no trouble following him down through the narrow defiles. He knew, too, that they could probably scramble and bound down the rock faster than he could. He had no time to waste.

Henrik didn't question where he was going, or why; for that

matter, he didn't even think about it—he simply started down. Since that first day when he had scratched the Lord Rahl and the Mother Confessor and then dashed away, he hadn't questioned what he was doing or the need to run. Crossing the Azrith Plain, he hadn't even questioned where he was running. He had simply run from the hounds. He had instinctively known that if he'd taken another course they would have had him. In his mind, there had been only one possible direction to run and he had taken it.

By the time he made it to the bottom his face was covered with sweat and grime. He'd looked back a few times and had seen the short-haired brown dog that was usually near the front of the pack. Both the black and the brown dogs, the two leaders, were powerfully built, with thick necks. Long frothy drool swung from their jowls as they snarled when they caught sight of him.

That quick glimpse was all Henrik needed to bound down the trail as fast as he could, slipping downward between rock outcroppings at a reckless rate. In places he had simply let himself slide down the steep funnel of dirt and scree because it was faster.

He finally stumbled off the precipitous path onto a flatter area among vines and tangles of brush. The air was oppressive. The place stank with rot.

Out under the deep shade of thick growth he could see trees with broad, flaring bottoms that seemed made to help them balance in the soft, boggy areas. Here and there cedars grew on patches of slightly higher ground, but the broad-bottomed trees were the only ones standing in the stagnant stretches of foul-smelling water. Their gnarled branches, extending outward not far above the water, held veils of moss. In places the moss dragged in the water. In other places, twisting vines hung down all the way to the water from somewhere in the canopy above, providing support for smaller vines with deep violet flowers.

Lizards darted up the wispy trailers of plants as he came close. Snakes, lounging over branches, tongues flicking the air, watched him pass. Things under the water swam lazily away, leaving a wake of quiet ripples that lapped at the soggy trail.

The deeper into the wooded bog he went, the thicker the tangle of shoots and vines grew as they closed in from the sides, making the way in a tunnel through the snarl of woody growth. Out beyond, unseen birds let out sharp calls that echoed across the still stretches of water.

Behind, the hounds sounded like they were in a rabid rage to get to him.

He paused in the dark tunnel of dense woods, uncertain if he dared go on.

Henrik knew where he was. Before him, the tangle of growth and trailers of vine marked the outer fringe of Kharga Trace. He had heard from his mother that a person had to have a powerful need to go into this place, because not many ever came out again. He and his mother had been two of the lucky ones who had made it back out, making it seem all the more foolish to tempt fate twice.

His heart pounding, his breath coming in rapid pulls, he stared ahead with wide eyes. He knew what was waiting for him.

Jit, the Hedge Maid, was waiting for him.

There was only one thing worse than facing the Hedge Maid again: the certainty of being torn apart and eaten alive by the pack of dogs chasing him.

He could hear them getting closer. He had no choice. He plunged ahead.

CHAPTER

50

After a frightening race along the trail as it tunneled in places through the dense growth, the landscape opened somewhat as he reached some of the more open stretches of water. The trail, never more than inches above the muddy water, was gradually taken over by tangled roots, sticks, vines, and branches all woven together into a mat that made a walkway of sorts. Without it, the solid ground of the trail in places would simply have vanished beneath stretches of duckweed. As it was, the pathway of sticks and vines barely cleared the surface of the dark brown water.

Henrik worried about what would happen should he slip off the trail of tangled shoots and branches. He worried about what waited in the water for the unwary, or the careless.

He was so tired, so afraid, that only raw fear kept his feet moving. He wished he could be back, safe, with his mother. But he couldn't stop or the hounds would get him.

While the stick and vine walkway was in places wide enough for several people to walk abreast, much of it was only wide enough for one person. In those narrow places where it became a bridge over stretches of open water, there were sometimes handholds or even rails made of crooked branches, lashed by thin vines to supports sticking up out of the tangle of wood underfoot. The whole thing creaked and moved as he made his way farther out onto it, as if it were a partially submerged monster displeased to have someone walking on its back.

Henrik couldn't tell for sure how far the hounds were behind him because sound carried so well across water. He wondered if the dogs would have a hard time of trying to walk on the mat of tangled vines and branches that made up the bridge through the watery world. He wondered if maybe their paws would slip down between the woven mass and get caught. He hoped so.

Mist prevented him from seeing very far into the distance among the moss-draped, fat-bottomed trees. As mist closed in behind him, he couldn't see very far back the way he had come, either. Among the snarl of roots snaking out from the nearby trees he could see eyes watching him.

He moved toward the center of the stick and vine bridge when he saw something in the water pass close by. Whatever it was dragged a torn, fleshy mass behind. There were bite marks all over the pale, decomposing meat. There was no way to tell what animal it had come from, but by the size of the splintered bone hanging from the trailing end, it looked to have once been fairly big. He wondered if it was a human thighbone.

Henrik glanced down, nervous about how low the branch bridge rode in the water. It moved and swayed in a sickening way as he raced along it. He didn't know if it was a floating bridge, or if it was supported from underneath. What he did know was that in most places it barely cleared the surface of the water. He worried that something might reach out, grab him by his ankle, and drag him into the murky water.

He didn't know if that would be worse than being caught by what pursued him from behind, or worse than what waited for him ahead. He desperately wanted to avoid any of those three fates, but he could think of nothing to do other than to plunge ahead, running from one threat, avoiding the second, and into the arms of the third.

His legs grew tired as he raced onward across the endless bridge through the gloomy swamp. Unseen animals called out, their sharp cries echoing through the mist and darkness. It seemed that he was crossing a vast, shallow lake, but since he couldn't see very far, it was hard to tell for sure. Big round leaves, something like lily pads, rode above the surface of the water in places, standing up as high as they could, hoping for a touch of sunlight that probably only penetrated the canopy on brief, rare occasions.

Several times Henrik slipped. The railing saved him. By the more distant barking, he judged that the hounds were having trouble keeping up and falling back. Still, they were back there, coming for him, so he dared not slow down.

As it grew darker, he was relieved to finally encounter lit candles along the bridge. He didn't know if someone came out to light them at nightfall, or if they were always there and kept burning. They had been lit the last time he had come this way with his mother. As dark as it was in among the looming stands of smooth-barked trees, they would be a help even in the day.

The farther he went, the wider and more substantial the bridge of tangled branches and vines became. The trees all around, standing up out of the water on snarls of roots, crowded in closer together. The vines hanging down from the darkness above, too, became thicker, some of them looping between trees and staying above the surface of the water. Many eventually became overgrown and weighted down with plants climbing up from the water or tendrils curling down from above. The growth to each side became so dense that it once again seemed that the bridge tunneled through a rat's nest of branches, vines, and bramble. The one constant was the murky water to each side. All too often he saw shadows move through the depths.

The candles become more plentiful as the stick bridge went farther in through the dark tangle of undergrowth. The candles were simply placed in crooks in the tangle of branches and sticks.

The occasional railings after a time developed into structures curving up from each side that seemed to be protecting the bridge from the encroachment of the thick undergrowth, or maybe from what lurked in the water. The walls, thick at the bottoms, thinner as they went higher, in places topped over the bridge with encircling branches that almost felt like claws closing in from overhead.

The candles grew so plentiful that at times it almost felt like passing between walls of fire. Henrik supposed that the bridge didn't catch fire and burn down because it was so wet and slimy. Slick green moss and dark mold covered most of the woven mass of roots, twigs, branches, and vines. It made the footing treacherous.

The farther Henrik went, the thicker the mat of woven branches that made up the walls became until they eventually closed in overhead and he felt like he was inside a cocoon of twisted wood. He could see out only through occasional small gaps. It was getting dark, though, so there wasn't much to see. Inside, the flickering glow of hundreds of candles lit the way.

When he realized that he didn't hear the hounds anymore, he paused, listening for them. He wondered if they feared to venture out across the twig causeway and so had finally given up the chase.

He wondered if maybe he didn't need to go on. Maybe the hounds were gone and he could go back.

But even as he thought it, an inner drive compelled him to move onward into the Hedge Maid's refuge. As soon as he took a few steps, it was hard not to take yet a few more into the candlelit tunnel.

Finally, with supreme effort, he did force himself to stop. If he was ever to escape, now was the time. He turned and looked back the way he had come. He heard no hounds.

Carefully, tentatively, he took a step back toward freedom.

Before he could take another, one of the familiars, like a creature made of smoke, drifted through the walls into the tunnel of woven sticks to block his way.

Henrik stood frozen in terror, his heart hammering even faster.

The glowing form floated closer.

"Jit waits for you," she hissed. "Get moving."

CHAPTER

51

As Henrik made his way along the causeway made of intertwined vines, sticks, and branches that led him through the gloomy expanse of trackless swamp, the structure of the bridge became more substantial, in places incorporating stringy moss and grasses laced into it to help bind it all together. The floor broadened and walls grew thicker as well. In places the walls curved inward to close completely together overhead, as if it were growing that way naturally and of its own accord.

Before long the walls that had gradually grown from their beginnings as railings of sorts became a solid, integrated part of the structure joined all the way around overhead so that what had been a path, then an elevated walkway, then a bridge, had evolved into a tunnel. That tunnel widened into a larger passageway that funneled him into a maze of chambers, all constructed the same way, of the same materials woven snugly together. The same entwined materials that made the floors and walls also made up ceilings just as thick and tightly woven. Living vines, with slender leaves and tiny yellow flowers, coiled up and through the walls, in places making the framework more green than dead brown.

Within the silent interior network of cavities created by the mass of woven branches, the outside world seemed a far distant place. Inside was a world unto itself, a strange place without anything perfectly flat or straight. It was all organic curves without any sharp corners, all natural materials, none of which looked man-made yet all of which were carefully crafted. It all formed softly rounded rooms with dished floors that were completely walled off from what was outside.

Henrik wondered if it would be possible to pull apart the branches and vines of the walls if he was forced to make a quick escape. It all seemed pretty solid, but still, it was just woven branches, twigs, and vines.

As he made his way through a bowled room, the familiar gliding along somewhere behind him, he moved closer to the wall to take a closer look. He glanced to the side and saw then that many of the branches making up the heavier parts of the matrix were studded with wickedly sharp thorns. Up close to the wall, he could see that much of it looked like it was made up of a thorn hedge.

Even if he were to decide that his life depended on making an escape, he didn't see how he could get through the thorny fabric of the structure. These were not small yet troublesome thorns like those on a rosebush that would scratch arms and legs. These were long, iron-hard, sharp spikes that would mercilessly rip a person apart and soon impale them so completely that they would be held prisoner.

With the floating form of the familiar right behind him, watching over him to make sure that he didn't try to turn and run, he passed through a series of rooms of various sizes, their way always lit by hundreds of candles. Some parts were only connecting tunnels where he had to duck to make it through. They were something like hallways in a building, with smaller side corridors going off in different directions.

One of the relatively large chambers they had to pass through contained what had to be thousands of strips of cloth, string, and thin vines all hanging down from the ceiling, all holding objects tied to their ends, everything from coins to shells to rotting lizards. They hung perfectly still in the dead air. Henrik bent low to pass under some of the dense, hanging collection of strange objects, holding his breath against the stench most of the way.

The entire structure moved and creaked as he made his way through the maze, his route lit by candles, as if to welcome visitors. It felt like he was walking into a giant, tubular spiderweb, something like those he'd seen at the base of logs that were meant to funnel prey inward to their death.

He knew, though, that it was worse than that. This was the lair of the Hedge Maid.

Candles by the hundreds if not thousands lit the place, and yet the darkness they tried to hold back felt oppressive. Sounds from out in the swamp were so muted that they could barely be heard through the thick thatch all around, but the wet, fetid smell of rot had no difficulty stealing in with the muggy air. The candles at least helped mask the smell somewhat.

As he moved deeper into the Hedge Maid's inner sanctuary, several more familiars drifted in through the walls and gathered around to escort him where he needed to go. More likely, they were making certain that he didn't turn back. Whenever he glanced up at them, they stared at him with the most sickly yellow eyes and he would immediately look away. Each of the seven, when seen up close, was as ugly as death itself.

As they made their way down a broader corridor, there

were even more candles placed all along the twig walls, from the curving edge of the floor up the rounded walls higher than he was tall. The hall they were in, lit by the golden glow of all the candles, led them abruptly into a murky room with hardly any candles.

There didn't look to be room for many candles in the shadowy room. The place was filled instead with jars and containers. Some of the containers were made of tan clay. The jars were far more plentiful and in colors from tan to green to ruby red. In hundreds of places, the woven sticks and twigs had been pulled apart enough so that jars could be stuck into the knitted stick walls.

What was in all the jars, Henrik feared to imagine. From what he could see through the colored glass, most were filled with liquid that was dark and filthy-looking, though a lot of it looked like muddy water. Things floated in the liquid among the dirt and debris. He tried not to look too closely at what those things floating in the jars might be. One jar looked to be filled with human teeth.

But the jars and containers were not what frightened him the most.

It was what was woven into the twig walls themselves, behind the jars, that had tears of terror running down his cheeks.

Woven into the walls were people.

He could also see them in the walls of the corridors going out of the room in various directions. At first, he saw dozens and dozens of people cocooned in the fabric of the stick walls.

The more he looked, though, the more people he could see entrapped farther back within the walls.

Some of the people were desiccated corpses, their mouths gaping open, their eye sockets sunken, the skin of their bare arms and legs leathery and shriveled. Other bloated bodies looked more freshly dead. The gagging stink of death left him hardly able to breathe.

But some of the people woven into the walls were not dead.

They looked to be in a numb stupor, hardly breathing, only slightly aware of anything going on around them. All were naked, but encased as they were by the weaving of thorny twigs and branches around them, it was hard to see much of them.

Henrik could see their eyes roll from time to time, as if trying to make out where they were and what was happening to them. An occasional soft moan escaped a hanging mouth.

When he turned from staring at all the dead and the half-dead people laced into the walls, he came face-to-face with the Hedge Maid.

J it sat cross-legged in the middle of the room, nested in a
thatch of branches, watching him with unblinking, big
round eyes that were so dark they looked black.

Her thin hair was only a little more than shoulder length.
She wasn't big. In fact, she was not much bigger than he was.
Her simple sack dress showed that she had a rather straight
torso. Her body looked more boylike than womanly. The skin
on her thin arms looked to have seen little sunlight. It was
hard for him to tell how old she was, but, despite her pale,
smooth skin, he was certain that she was not at all young.

Her fingernails and hands appeared to be permanently
stained, possibly from handling what was in the jars all around
her.

He imagined, too, that the dark matter staining her fingernails might be the fluid leaking from the corpses woven into
the walls around the room.

But what riveted his gaze, what had his heart pounding,
what had his knees weak, was her mouth.

Her thin lips were sewn shut with strips of leather.

The leather thong was stitched right through the flesh of
her lips, leaving holes that didn't look like they had ever

entirely healed. The stitches weren't even. They looked to have been done haphazardly, with little care. The stitched strips of leather crossed to form "X"s over her mouth. There was only enough slack in the leather to allow her to open her mouth into a narrow slit.

Through that slit behind the cross-stitched leather thong, Jit let out an undulating squealing sound that didn't sound human. It ran goose bumps up Henrik's arms.

From having been here before, he knew that it was her language, her way of talking. While he didn't have the slightest idea what the sound meant, he did know that she was directing it at him.

One of the familiars, missing a hand, he noticed, leaned toward him.

"Jit says that she is pleased to see you again, boy."

Henrik swallowed. He couldn't bring himself to say he was pleased to see her again as well.

Jit, her head bobbing, let out a low-pitched grating screech, punctuated with a few clicks of her tongue against the top of her mouth.

"Jit wants to know if you brought it," the familiar said.

Henrik's mouth felt stuck closed. He couldn't make himself speak. Fearing what she would do if he didn't somehow answer, he held out his fisted hands. He didn't think that, after all this time, he could open them if he tried.

The Hedge Maid let out a soft raspy sound—half pule, half screech.

"Come closer," the familiar said. "Jit says to come closer so that she may see for herself."

Somewhere behind, there was a sound that made all the familiars pause and turn to look. The Hedge Maid's black eyes turned up to focus into the distance behind him. Henrik looked back over his shoulder to see what had caught their attention.

In the distance, there was some kind of disturbance. Something was making its way up the hall that led into the chambers.

Candle flames wavered, their light flickering, and then they went out.

Whatever it was brought darkness with it.

As it passed, the candles nearby all around it went dark. When it was beyond them, the extinguished flames slowly returned to life until they were once more fully lit.

It made it seem as if darkness itself were stalking through the tunnel of a hall, coming for them all.

As it came closer, pulling that darkness with it, extinguishing candles all around as it passed, the familiars cowered back behind Jit. Henrik could see the one without a hand trembling slightly.

Jit let out a long, low squeal and a few clicks. Two of the familiars gathered in close about her, leaning in, whispering. They nodded to more clicks and soft, grating sounds from deep in the Hedge Maid's throat.

When the form finally swept into the room, bringing darkness with it, Henrik saw at last that it was a man.

The man paused before Jit, not far from Henrik. The candles' flames in the hall behind him and those nearby in the room slowly came back to life, showing at last the man before them.

When he finally got a good look at the man, Henrik froze stiff, unable to draw a breath.

53

The man glanced down at the warm, wet place growing on the front of Henrik's pants and smiled to himself.

"This is the boy?" he asked in a deep, iron-hard voice that made Henrik have to remind himself to blink and caused the seven familiars to drift back up ever so slightly more behind Jit, as if they weren't aware that his voice alone had bulled them back.

The Hedge Maid let out a short, grating, clicking sound.

"Yes, this is him, Bishop Arc," the handless familiar said for her mistress after watching her speak in the strange voice.

Bishop Arc glared at Jit for a moment. His gaze lowered deliberately to take in her mouth sewn closed; then he again turned his terrible eyes on Henrik.

The whites of the man's eyes were not white. Not at all.

They had been tattooed a bright blood red.

The dark iris and pupil in the field of blood red made his eyes seem as if they were looking out from some other world, a world of fire and flame—or perhaps from the underworld itself.

But even as frightening as the bishop's eyes were, that was not the most disturbing aspect of the man. The most ghastly thing about him, the thing that made Henrik unable to look away, unable to stop his heart from hammering, unable to draw more than short, shallow breaths, was the man's flesh.

Every bit of Bishop Arc was covered with tattooed symbols. Not simply covered, but layered over countless times so that the skin looked something other than human. There was no place that Henrik could see that was not tattooed with some part or element of strange circular designs, each one randomly laid over another over another and over yet another, all layer upon layer so that there was no untouched skin visible anywhere. Not one speck.

The top layers were the darkest, with those under them lighter, the ones under those lighter yet, and so on, as if they continually absorbed down into his flesh and new ones were constantly being added over the top of those already there. They had an endless, bottomless depth to them, a tangled complexity that was dizzying, as if the symbols were continually seething up from somewhere dark.

Looking down through the ever-deeper levels of designs gave the man's skin a three-dimensional appearance. Because the layers made it hard to tell just where the surface of the skin actually was in all the floating elements, it gave Bishop Arc a shadowy, somewhat hazy, somewhat ghostly appearance. Henrik felt sure that if the man wished it, he could vanish at will into the fog of floating symbols.

Because of the way the underlayers were lighter than the ones on top of them, each symbol, regardless of how many layers down it was, was distinct and recognizable. The symbols were all different sizes, and from what Henrik could tell, endlessly different designs. Almost all of them seemed to be a collection of smaller symbols assembled into larger, circular elements.

The bishop's hands and what Henrik could see of his wrists sticking out from his black coat were completely covered with the designs. Even his fingernails appeared to be tattooed beneath, with the designs visible right through the nail itself.

His neck above his tight collar was covered all around, as was his entire throat. His face—every part of his face—was covered with emblems by the hundreds, if not thousands. Even his eyelids were tattooed. Even the man's ears, every fold and as far down inside as Henrik could see, were completely covered in the same kind of strange tattoos of circular symbols on top of circular symbols on top of yet more of the symbols.

While the bishop's entire bald head was tattooed over with the designs, one dominated them all. It was larger than all the others. The bottom edge of that large circle crossed over the center of his nose and swept to each side beneath his eyes, going around just above his ears to cover the rest of the crown of the skull. Inside the circle was another, and between them a ring of runes.

A triangle sitting within the inner circle crossed horizontally just above the man's brow. Smaller, secondary circular symbols floating outside the points of the triangle that broke the circles covered each temple with the third at the point of the triangle on the back of his head. The way it was laid out made it appear as if the man was glaring out with those haunting red eyes from within the circular symbol, as if he were looking out from the underworld.

In the center of the triangle, toward the front of the man's skull, was a backward figure nine.

That large tattoo covering the top of his bald head was darker than all the others, not just because it looked to be the most recently added, but because the lines composing it were heavier. Even so, lying as it was over layers of hundreds of other random emblems, it was evident that it was merely a part of a much larger purpose.

All the tattoos, in all their many different designs, still seemed to be variations of the same basic themes. There were symbols laid out in circles of every size, even circles within circles within circles, with some of the symbols contained within those circles made up of other, smaller designs. Taken in totality, it was a profoundly unsettling sight to see a man so given over to such an occult purpose.

It all made him a very dark, living, moving, fluid illustration, with every design down through the countless layers clearly discernible. Henrik imagined that if the bishop were naked, he would still be totally hidden behind the veil of symbols.

The only place Henrik could see that was not tattooed with the symbols was the man's eyes, and they were tattooed red.

Bishop Arc saw several of the familiars glance nervously behind him, back down the hall.

He smiled. "I didn't bring her with me," he said in answer to the unspoken question haunting their eyes. "I sent her on an errand."

The familiars bowed their heads in acknowledgment and as if to apologize for being so nosy.

The wide eyes of one of the people woven into the wall behind Jit stared fixedly at Bishop Arc. Terror shaped the man's expression and left him unable to look away when the bishop glanced up at him. The man swallowed over and over, as if trying to swallow a scream fighting to make its way out. All the people in the walls seemed incapable of making a sound, though this man clearly seemed like he was about to scream.

Bishop Arc lifted a hand toward the man trapped in the

wall. It was not an overt motion to point at the man, but a casual gesture, a slack hand held out on a partially raised arm, fingers barely extended. Nonetheless, it was clearly directed at the man encased in the wall and unable to stop staring at the bishop.

"Be still," Bishop Arc said in a low voice, hardly more than a whisper, but as deadly as anything Henrik had ever heard.

The man gasped, sucking in short, sharp breaths. He pulled in one last, long breath as his eyes rolled back in his head. He shook violently but briefly, then slumped, at least as much as he could slump, woven as he was into the tangle of sticks, twigs, and vines. After a final shiver, his whole body went completely slack. The last breath of air left his lungs in a long, low wheeze.

The bishop looked around at other eyes watching him from the walls. "Anyone else?"

In the silence, every eye behind layers of twigs and branches turned away.

Bishop Arc smirked at the Hedge Maid. "There you go. Freshly dead fluids for your little helpers here to suck out and feed you."

The Hedge Maid's big, black eyes revealed nothing. She let out a low, rasping squeal broken by several clicks.

One of the familiars, watching Jit speak in the strange language, waited until she was finished and then leaned toward the bishop, showing contempt on behalf of her mistress. "Jit wishes to know why you have come here."

"Isn't it obvious?" He lifted his arm out to the side, toward Henrik, as he addressed Jit. "I have come to make sure that you complete the task I gave you."

After a long pause, Jit gave him a single nod.

The bishop's brow drew down, deforming the symbol on

his forehead, pulling the center of it lower with his eyebrows. "Now, you have wasted enough of my time. I expect you not to waste any more of it. The boy is finally here. Get on with it."

Jit watched him for a moment, then turned her attention to Henrik and motioned for him to come closer.

54

Henrik feared to take a step toward the Hedge Maid. As she made a soft cooing sound while gesturing for him to come closer, he could only stare at the leather cord stitched through her lips keeping her mouth from opening more than a mere slit. Some of the holes where the leather thong penetrated her flesh oozed a pinkish fluid, as if the effort of calling him forward reinjured the wounds.

He wondered why her lips were stitched closed.

He realized that his feet were shuffling forward, even though he'd had no intention of moving. He found himself helpless to stop himself from inching ever closer to her, closer to her outstretched hands.

His own arms lifted of their own accord. No amount of strength on his part could have prevented it. His fists led the way as he moved toward her.

Her hands, stained dark—with what he feared to imagine— at last closed tight around his wrists. Closer in to her, he noticed that there was an odd smell about her, a kind of soft but sickening odor that he couldn't identify, but it made his nose wrinkle and his throat try to close off so he couldn't breathe it in.

Though she was a small woman, she had powerfully strong fingers. He tried to back away, but he couldn't. He felt trapped in her grip. He had no control, no say in any of it.

Jit made another vibrating, clicking, squealing sound. As close as he was to her, Henrik could only stare into her intense black eyes with speechless fright, unable to think of what she wanted from him, what she was going to do to him.

She leaned toward him and made the same sound again. He didn't know what she was saying. He only knew that she wanted something.

One of the familiars bent toward him over the Hedge Maid's shoulder. "Open your fists," she hissed impatiently.

His breaths coming in short, rapid pulls, he tried with all his might to do as he had been told. Despite his best efforts, his hands would not open. He'd held them tightly closed for so long they'd become frozen into tight knots. Despite how much he tried, how much he wanted to obey, he could not will his fingers to uncurl. He stared at them, trying frantically to make them open, fearing what she would do to him if he didn't do as he'd been told.

Jit seemed unconcerned. Her strong fingers began peeling his fingers open one at a time. It hurt something fierce to have them move after all the time they been held fisted. Each one tingled with stabbing pains as it was pulled straight. Showing no sympathy for his cries of pain, she did not pause at her work.

Before long, she had all his fingers pried open. She flattened his hands out, pressing them between hers, one hand at a time, stroking them for a while as if to soothe away the stiffness and make certain they would remain open before she turned them over, palms down.

The Hedge Maid snapped a small twig from the woven

mass beside her. He could see that there was a long, wickedly sharp thorn at the end. Not knowing what she intended, he again tried to pull away, but, with his left wrist caught in her iron grip, she easily pulled his hand closer. He felt like an animal in a trap about to be skinned.

Holding his hand steady, the Hedge Maid dragged the point of the thorn along the underside of the fingernail of his first finger. She turned the thorn in the light, carefully inspecting it. He couldn't imagine what she was doing or what she was looking for.

Henrik saw one of the familiars, back at the wall, working at pulling a jar out of its snug place in the weave of branches. With effort, the jar finally came free. She brought it with her to Jit's side and waited patiently as she watched her mistress at work.

The Hedge Maid dragged the point of the thorn under the nail of the second finger. She held it up. This time there was a small bit of something stuck on the point.

A sound came from deep in her throat that told him she was pleased. She held it up to show her companions. They cooed their satisfaction. Bishop Arc only glared when she showed him.

The familiar with the jar, after pulling off the lid, held it out for her mistress. Cockroaches poured out over the sides of the jar and down over the familiar's hands. They made a rattling sound as they fell by the hundreds onto the floor, scattering in every direction before vanishing down into the weave of sticks and branches. In a moment they had all disappeared.

Jit, unconcerned, dunked the thorn in the filthy water and swished it around. She pulled it up and saw that whatever had been stuck on it had come off. Satisfied, she returned her attention to Henrik.

She repeated the careful cleaning under the nails of the last two fingers and thumb on his left hand. She found more of the tiny treasure she was searching for under the nails of his fingers, but not his thumb. Out of the corner of his eye, Henrik saw a smile come to Bishop Arc's tattooed lips both times the Hedge Maid came up with a little scrap of something on the point of the thorn. Each time, she swished the thorn in the stinking liquid in the jar, leaving whatever it was to disappear down into the murky water.

Jit dropped his left hand and moved on to his right. After dragging the thorn under his first finger she brought it up close to her face for a look. There was nothing there. She cast a brief, furtive look up at the bishop and then dragged the thorn under the nail again, but it didn't produce anything the second time, either.

She moved to the next finger and did a more careful cleaning under Henrik's nail. The thorn found nothing. She repeated the search, then when it was fruitless, moved on to his third finger. It, too, didn't have what she wanted. She focused on the little finger, as if it were her last hope.

When the thorn came up without anything but dirt, her hands dropped into her lap.

The symbols all over him seemed to churn as the man leaned down a little. "What's wrong?"

The Hedge Maid made a few short sounds from deep in her throat.

"Jit says that we have the flesh of the woman," the familiar at her side said. She hesitated before finishing the translation. "But we do not have the flesh of the man."

The bishop straightened in a way that caused all seven of the familiars to back up.

One of them was not quick enough.

He snatched her by the throat and yanked her close. It looked to be a reflex driven purely by emotion. She cried out, thrashing like a snake in a snare, but she could not escape his grip. It was clear that the bishop was in a blind rage. She clawed at his tattooed hands around her throat, but it did her no good.

"Tell your mistress that I am not pleased," he said to the others.

Several of them urgently leaned in, speaking to the Hedge Maid in her strange language.

When the bishop pulled the familiar in his fist close to his face and glared into her eyes, she cried out with a shriek of terrible agony.

"Back to the grave with you," he said through gritted teeth.

As Henrik watched in frozen shock, the familiar lost the bluish glow they all had. Wisps of smoke curled up from under the cowl over her head. The whole creature writhed and withered as if everything was being sucked out of her. The skin on her hands and arms darkened as it drew in around the bones and knuckles until they looked skeletal. The flesh of her face boiled and bubbled and burned to a dark, leathery mask. Blackened skin smoldered as it shrank tighter and tighter around the skull. The eyes sunk back into their sockets. The jaw slackened and lips shriveled back, exposing the familiar's fangs.

Bishop Arc tossed the withered remains aside.

Seething with anger, he paced back toward the tunnel where he had entered. The candles went out around him as he moved, as if he were dragging a veil of darkness with him. He growled in frustration and rage.

Abruptly, he stopped and turned back. He stared at the Hedge Maid a moment, then marched back toward her. The candles behind him came back to life as he moved away from them.

"You at least have the flesh of the woman, right?" he asked Jit.

With her dark eyes fixed on him, she nodded and then took the jar from the trembling familiar beside her. She held it up a little as if to show him.

He stroked the knuckle of his first finger along his gaunt cheek.

"Change of plans," he said in a voice like ice.

As the Hedge Maid started out toward a shadowy opening at the back of the chamber, her familiars raced around the room, urgently pulling smaller jars from where they were stuck into the weave of the walls or picked up larger ones out of the diverse collections at the edges of the floor. The eyes of those people nearby encased in the walls, the ones who were still alive, watched in desolate agony.

Henrik wished he could help them, but he couldn't. He couldn't even help himself.

Jit cradled the jar with the filthy brown water containing what had been under Henrik's fingernails in the crook of her arm as she made her way back into the dark opening. The brown water sloshed around as she walked. The lid kept most but not all of the water from spilling over. Henrik saw big brown bugs emerge up out of the weave of the twigs and branches to feed at the drops that did escape, run down the jar, and drip onto the floor.

Bishop Arc glared with bloodred eyes as the familiars went about their work of finding the correct containers out of the hundreds hoarded throughout the room. The dark symbols covering his flesh made his obvious rage seem all the more dangerous. The six remaining familiars avoided meeting his gaze as they worked at finding what they needed and pulled them out of the wall or plucked them up from the floor.

Each of the familiars collected an unwieldy stash of jars clutched in the crook of their arms. The one without a hand couldn't hold as many but she did the best she could. As soon as they had what they needed, they hurried with their cargo to catch up with their departing mistress.

For her part, Jit took a staff that was leaning against the wall as she carried the single jar in her other arm. She looked back over her shoulder at Henrik and let out a series of short commands in her strange, screeching, clicking language. The familiar without a hand circled back and shoved him into line behind the Hedge Maid and in front of the rest of the familiars.

"Jit says for you to hurry up and come along." She glanced back briefly at the bishop and then leaned closer. "When this is through," she said with venomous delight, "I am going to suck you dry and feed what's left of you to the cockroaches."

Henrik froze stiff in terror. With a soft cackle, she shoved him to get him moving again.

As he stumbled forward, he thought of how much he missed being with his mother. He wanted to be back with her in their tent making bead goods. He wished that she had never brought him to the Hedge Maid in the first place.

Ever since he had realized that he was being chased back into Kharga Trace and that the Hedge Maid was going to have him in her clutches again, he had feared that this time he might not be leaving.

The bishop took up a place at the end of the line as they followed the Hedge Maid along the dark passageway lined with hundreds of strips of leather holding everything from small dead animals to empty turtle shells, to the skulls of little creatures with sharp little teeth, all hanging from the walls in layers. Henrik saw the eyes of the people in projecting areas of buttress walls watching them as they passed. When Bishop Arc met their gazes they quickly looked away. Not a peep came from the people in the walls. Henrik imagined that if he was trapped in the walls he would have trouble not crying out for help.

But there was no one to help the poor souls trapped in this terrible place. There was no one to help him.

Making their way through the labyrinth that was the Hedge Maid's lair, Henrik began to hear insects buzzing, birds calling, and other creatures whistling and chirping. As they reached an opening and emerged out into the night, the swamp creatures abruptly went dead silent.

The low clouds gliding swiftly by overhead were lit by the moon from somewhere above them so that they cast a faint glow. The ground all around was elevated enough in the midst of the dense, swampy forest to be bone-dry. The dark shapes of hulking trees surrounding them, trailing long curtains of moss, looked to Henrik like arms of the dead trailing burial shrouds as they gathered around the living.

As they crossed the clearing, he saw that the flat rocks lying here and there were not placed randomly, but arranged in circular patterns. Each stone was also placed atop slightly mounded dirt. The mounds with stones appeared to lead to the center of the open area, where the Hedge Maid set about making marks on the ground with her decorated staff. The marks she was scratching in the ground with the point of her staff were not unlike the tattooed designs all over Bishop Arc.

Iridescent blue feathers, orange and yellow beads, and a collection of coins with holes in the center hung on buckskin thongs from the middle of the Hedge Maid's staff. Henrik wondered why the Hedge Maid would be so interested in coins that she would use them to adorn such an obviously important object. After all, what good would money do her out in Kharga Trace?

Then he realized that it actually wasn't of any value to her as money, the way it was to other people. The coins must have been taken from those poor souls encased in the walls. To the Hedge Maid, shiny coins were merely decorations, like the shiny feathers. Both were tokens of the lives she had taken.

As the familiars went about arranging the jars on the ground around the Hedge Maid, Bishop Arc stood to the side, arms folded, his bloodred eyes glaring as he watched the preparations. Every once in a while one of the six familiars glanced his way. Jit did not. She went quietly about her work of drawing designs in the dirt in the center of the ring of jars.

At intervals in her drawing and soft chanting, she would open a jar, fish around in the dark liquid with her hand, and then throw whatever limp, slimy thing she had pulled out into the center of her drawing. All the while she continued making the soft buzzing, humming sound.

The Hedge Maid lifted her staff in one outstretched arm toward the low clouds drifting by overhead. She chanted a few clipped sounds, then bent and placed the staff across elements in the design she had drawn on the ground.

The design on the ground began to glow.

To Henrik's astonishment, as the Hedge Maid continued her low, musical drone and lifted both arms skyward, the clouds overhead came to a halt.

CHAPTER

56

Henrik thought that the winds must have stilled to make the clouds drift to a halt, but then he saw the clouds again begin to move. Instead of going across the sky as before, though, the clouds started to move around in a circle overhead. They stretched into long spiral shapes as they rotated over the clearing, mirroring the glowing circular symbol on the ground. Small flickers of orange light intermittently illuminated the clouds from inside.

At the same time, the six familiars seemed to have been lulled into a trance of some sort by the murmurs from the Hedge Maid. All of them began circling the Hedge Maid along with the clouds above. Their feet weren't touching the ground as they floated around Jit in a circle, gradually picking up speed. The clouds, too, picked up speed, going faster all the time, the orange and yellow light flickering like the light flashing in the symbols on the ground.

The Hedge Maid's low, steady rhythm of sounds rose in pitch.

As the familiars and the clouds moved faster, the sound Jit made became a painful, high-pitched squeal. It kept getting louder and louder, higher and higher. Henrik had to cover his ears against the pain of the sound.

Suddenly, the six forms seemed to break apart. Henrik stared with wide eyes as hideous creatures with long bony arms and legs began to pull themselves out of the glowing forms of the familiars. Their backs were humped, their flesh blotchy and wet. They had no hair. Their knobby heads had angry, bulging eyes and snarling mouths that showed wicked fangs.

Unlike the familiars from which they had emerged, these things did not glow. Flickers of light from the clouds above and the circular designs below reflected off their glistening, mottled flesh.

Henrik saw then the same sorts of creatures erupting from the mounds where the stones were. Each struggled and strained to pull itself up out of the dirt. Yet more of them broke through the surface of the mounds, pulling themselves up out of the ground, joining into the growing mass of those that were circling the Hedge Maid, dancing around her like crazed animals.

But these were no animals.

Though they appeared animate, there were not living things.

Henrik thought they looked like the dead rising up from the ground, dancing with flailing arms and legs to the tune the Hedge Maid played.

He glanced back at the low, dark structure of woven sticks and branches. He realized that these mounds must be the graves of the people encased in the walls who died. After they had served whatever purpose the Hedge Maid needed them for, they were buried out here, and there they waited until called upon to serve her again.

Henrik imagined that the Hedge Maid must be a creature born in the underworld, the spawn of the Keeper himself.

In the center of the clearing the grotesque forms had gathered by the dozens, with more coming in out of the darkness of the surrounding swamp all the time to join with the others, circling ever faster. Henrik had to press his hands over his ears tighter as the sounds Jit was making seemed enough to tear him apart, enough to tear the very air apart.

The clouds moved in time with the circling forms. The light in them flickered faster and faster as the symbols on the ground flashed in rhythm with the sounds the Hedge Maid was making and the flickers in the clouds.

The sound, the light, the spinning, horrific creatures dancing like demons, were all making Henrik dizzy. His head throbbed with the beat of it all, with the pressure of it all. He squinted, fearing to close his eyes lest he never be able to open them again, yet hardly able to keep his eyes open against the overwhelming sights and sounds.

As all this activity whirled around her, Jit reached into various jars, pulling out handfuls of teeth, or what looked to be small finger bones, or human vertebrae, and cast them into the circle. With each addition light flared and danced.

The world seemed to be flickering. He saw little flashes of red, yellow, and orange.

And then Jit picked up the jar holding the flesh she had taken from under Henrik's fingernails. The forms were rotating so fast that he could hardly make out individuals. It was all becoming a blur of dark, glistening flesh and thrashing limbs.

The Hedge Maid abruptly threw the jar she had up into the air above glowing circles and the writhing mass of forms.

Henrik saw the glass explode apart. The liquid in the jar seemed to ignite.

The world turned so bright that it looked like he could see Jit's bones right through her body.

Everything was turned to light and fire. The trees all around burned. Hot glowing embers were drawn off the trees to swirl around the incandescence coming from the contents of the jar above the center of the flaming circle.

The Hedge Maid held her hands up, summoning forces he had never imagined. She stood alone against the light, defined by it, holding sway over a world turned to an inferno.

In the center of it all, in the heart of the blinding light, standing out like bright stars, there was something brighter yet. Small bits—the bits of flesh Jit had recovered from under his fingernails—were so incandescent that they made the rest of the burning world seem dull in comparison.

Her arms raised, Jit seemed to be commanding those bright sparks to pull everything else up with them as they rotated while climbing ever higher into the sky.

Alone in the center of the roaring conflagration, Jit lifted her arms higher, commanding it all to come together.

The masses of bone men howled as they burned, their bodies coming apart in flaming sparks and smoke that was sucked into the horrific vortex of blinding radiance.

Everything around him, all the trees, the vines, the moss, the bushes, even the ground, glowed as it burned and disintegrated into flaming embers and ash, coming off in long whorls that were pulled ever inward to spiral up toward the tiny sparks of blinding light that rose up through the center of the spiraling clouds.

The wind roared, the fire roared. Henrik had to squint against the blinding power of it all. He would have covered his eyes but he dared not take his hands away from his ears for fear that he, too, would be summoned by Jit into the inferno.

Even when he shut his eyes, he saw the same things as when he'd had his eyes open.

It was a night of burning color, of blinding light, of deafening sound . . . of madness.

Everything was being pulled into the glowing light in the center of the clearing. Branches and debris ripped from trees and the entire forest ignited as it was pulled in. Trees and plants disintegrated into a thousand sparks that swirled around and upward, following the radiant sparks of flesh. The bodies of the dead that had risen came apart in crackling, glowing embers like everything else.

The howls of terror and agony kept tears running freely down Henrik's face.

The Hedge Maid lifted her arms again. The very air in the center of the clearing ignited in a blinding furnace of light.

Just when Henrik thought he would surely be pulled into it all to die in the terrible ignition of light, it ended.

The sudden silence felt like it might make him fall over.

It felt like he had been pushing against the sound, as if he'd been trying to stand in a gale. When the sound abruptly stopped, he almost stumbled forward.

His ears throbbed. His head throbbed. His whole body throbbed.

But the sound was not the only thing that was gone.

Henrik blinked. He couldn't believe what he was seeing. The raging whirlwind of fire and light was gone as well.

He looked around and saw that the moss on the nearby trees hung limp in the still, humid air, just as it had before. Every tree was still there. The ground that had broken open as the bone men had erupted out of it looked undisturbed.

It was as if none of what Henrik had just seen had actually happened.

Except, the jar was gone and tiny bits of glass, like a thousand fallen stars, lay scattered across the bare ground.

Henrik couldn't understand what had happened, what he had seen. He couldn't understand if the fire had been real, if the creatures he had seen come up out of the ground were real, if the terrible sound and all the rest of it had been real.

Bishop Arc, still standing where he had been in the beginning, looked unharmed, and unmoved. He wore the same glare as he had in the beginning. If he was surprised by the deafening display of fire and light, he didn't show it.

In the center of the clearing, the six familiars slowly circled in around Jit, tending to her, fussing over her, touching her protectively, as if to see if she had survived the ordeal. She ignored them as she used a foot to swipe away the marks she had made in the dirt with her staff when she had first come out.

The Hedge Maid turned her dark eyes toward Bishop Arc. She let out the squealing clicks that were her way of talking. Henrik could see her straining to open her mouth more as she made the sounds, but the net of leather thongs prevented it.

One of the familiars floated a little closer toward the bishop. "Jit says that it is done."

His red eyes turned from the familiar to Jit. "See that you do the other things I have asked as well." His brow drew down tight. "Don't give me cause to return."

With that he turned and stormed away. The darkness seemed to gather in around him as he went, like a black cape, making him look like a dark shadow moving across the ground.

A familiar leaning in made Henrik jump. He hadn't seen her sneaking up behind him.

"Now," she hissed, "time for you."

CHAPTER

57

Kahlan woke with a start, panting in terror. A blur of images flashed through her mind. Dark arms and claws reached for her. Fangs came out of nowhere, snapping, trying to get at her face.

She didn't know where she was or what was happening. She fought frantically, twisting, pushing at whatever it was that was reaching for her, at the same time trying to escape the grip of pain that seared through her.

She sat up abruptly, gasping for breath, and saw then that she was in the Garden of Life, that it was night. There was nothing chasing her, nothing coming after her. It was quiet.

She had been having a nightmare.

In the dream something had been chasing her, something dark and profoundly dangerous, something terrifying. It had been relentless and had been getting closer all the time. She had been running, trying to get away. But she hadn't been able to make her legs move fast enough. It had all seemed so real.

But she was awake, at last. She wasn't dreaming anymore. She had escaped the nightmare and in so doing escaped what was after her. She told herself to let it go, to stop focusing on

the dream. It was only a dream. She was awake now. She was
safe.

But she quickly found that being awake was no salvation.
While she had awakened and escaped what had been after her
in the dream, in being awake she had not escaped the pain.
Her head hurt so much she thought she might pass out. She
pressed her fingers to her temples only to have to hug her
arms across her abdomen, pressing them against the twisting
ache in her middle.

As the spike of pain drove through her head, a hot wave of
nausea welled up through her. She fought the building urge
to throw up. The throbbing pain in her head overwhelmed
her, making her all the more dizzy and sick. With all her
might, she fought back the expanding waves of nausea. The
nausea won out.

As her insides began to convulse, Kahlan urgently struggled out of the tangled blanket and crawled on her hands and
knees into the grass and away from where she'd been sleeping.
She did her best to resist the urge to throw up, but her body
would not obey her will and she began heaving so hard that it
felt like her stomach was trying to turn inside out. Undulating waves of sickness swept through her again and again in
rhythm with the pounding pain in her head, making her vomit
each time.

Kahlan realized that there was a hand on her back and another hand holding her long hair back out of the way.

She gasped for breath between the spasms. She was sure
that she had to be throwing up blood. The excruciating pain
seemed unendurable each time her muscles convulsed. It felt
like her insides were ripping.

The waves of heaving finally began to subside. As she spit

out the bitter bile, it was a relief to at least see that there was no blood.

"Mother Confessor, are you all right?"

It was Cara. It felt good to have someone there. It was comforting not to be alone.

"I don't know," she managed.

Suddenly, Richard was there as well. "What's wrong?"

Rolling trembles racked her whole body. Between that and panting for air, "Sick" was all she could manage to get out.

"I heard you scream from all the way down in the room with the machine," Richard said as he placed a reassuring hand on her back.

She ripped off a thick fistful of grass and wiped her mouth with it, threw it down and then did it again with a clean handful. She hadn't realized that she had screamed in her sleep. The waves of nausea had quieted, allowing her to catch her breath. Her head still throbbed, though.

"I was having a nightmare and I must have screamed and scared myself awake."

He pressed his hand to her forehead. "Your skin is like ice and you're soaked in sweat."

Kahlan couldn't seem to stop herself from shivering. "I'm so cold."

Richard drew her closer. Kahlan collapsed over on her side against him. His warm, muscular arms closed protectively over her.

Rather than simply hold her, though, he took hold of her wrist and lifted her arm out. It hurt to have him touch it.

"Dear spirits," he whispered to himself.

Cara leaned in. "What's wrong?"

Richard turned Kahlan's arm out a little to show her. "Go get Zedd."

Kahlan saw Cara race away back up the path through the trees. It felt good being in Richard's arms. She didn't want to ever move out of his comforting warmth.

But her arm throbbed with every heartbeat. She looked down and was surprised to see that the scratches had reappeared. Zedd had healed them, but they were back and looked worse than ever.

"It looks like Zedd's healing didn't take care of it after all," Richard said. "We'll get him back here and see what he thinks. He knows a lot about such things, but it looks to me like it might have been infected and that's why it came back. That's probably what's making you sick, too. Maybe he just didn't get the infection completely healed the first time."

That didn't sound to her like it could be the cause of the the way she felt. She'd had wounds in the past that had become red and swollen. They never made her feel this way. In fact, the arm was the least of it. It was the sudden explosion of pain in her head that had brought her awake, made her feel sick, and had made her throw up. It was that sharp stab of pain between her temples that had overwhelmed her with nausea. She didn't really think the scratches had anything to do with her headache.

She'd had headaches a few times in her life that were so strong they had made her throw up. Richard used to have them, too. He said that he'd inherited them from his mother. She thought that this one had to be something like that. Just a bad headache. That thought actually made her feel better.

She glanced down again at the angry red scratches on her arm. It concerned her to see that the wounds that had healed had not only returned but looked to have gotten worse. The arm felt a bit stiff, too, from being swollen.

Kahlan shivered in pain again. A wave of icy cold swept

over her. The pain in her head bore down on her with crushing weight.

And then, as Richard leaned over and held her close against him, she began to feel the sweet softness of his gift seeping into her. Warm relief flooded through her cold, stiff muscles. He had used his gift to heal her in the past, so she recognized the feeling of being touched by his magic. That was what he was doing now—healing her with his magic.

Richard's gift worked in a unique way, and usually only ignited within him if there was great need. His empathy for her, his love for her, his need for her to be safe, had brought it forth now to heal her.

Time became meaningless in his warm embrace, in the flow of magic coursing into her.

She felt his comforting, reassuring, loving presence in every fiber of her being.

But as much as she wanted his help, she also didn't want to allow him to do it.

She knew that in the process of healing he would have to take on her pain. He first had to lift her agony away and take it into himself, so that his gift could then flow into her to heal what was wrong. Kahlan didn't want Richard to take in this pain. As much as she wanted to be rid of the hurt, she didn't want him to suffer it.

Fighting him, though, proved useless. The strength of his gift overwhelmed her. She had no choice but to let go of her resistance. The feeling was like letting herself fall backward into an unknown, bottomless abyss. It was frightening, and at the same time a relief, a relief in the sense of letting go, of letting someone else fight for her, fight against the pain on her behalf, of being able to stand aside as the battle raged.

She didn't know how long she had been lost in that distant

place of pain with Richard there with her, joined with her, but she did know that when she opened her eyes and the world came back in around her, she was still in his arms.

Despite what she expected, the pain was still there. It was just as strong, just as oppressive as before.

She recognized that same pain in Richard's eyes as well. He had taken it into himself, but oddly enough, it had not at the same time drawn it away from her.

The effort had not healed her.

She thought that maybe she'd done something wrong. Maybe she hadn't tried hard enough. Or, more accurately, maybe she had been too fearful of letting Richard take the pain into himself and so she hadn't done enough to let go so he could help her.

Cara leaned in over Richard. "Sorry it took me so long to find Zedd. I finally did. He's coming right behind me. I brought Nicci, too."

Richard didn't respond. He was staring off at nothing.

58

Still drifting back from that distant place that felt completely detached from the real world, which was beginning to come back into focus all around her, Kahlan knew that something wasn't right, both with her and with Richard.

She saw Nicci squat down beside him. By the worried expression that overcame the sorceress when she looked into his unblinking eyes, Kahlan knew that something about the healing hadn't worked the way it should have.

Richard stared off at nothing, completely unresponsive, even as the pain raged in his eyes, even as Nicci placed a hand on his shoulder and shook him.

Nicci's long blond hair fell forward over her left shoulder as she leaned in around Richard and pressed her first two fingers to Kahlan's forehead. Kahlan felt the familiar tingle of Additive Magic vibrate and tingle through the nerves of her neck, shoulders, and arms.

Nicci withdrew the fingers and next put them to Richard's forehead. She backed away and then shoved at his chest. "Let her go. Richard, let go of her."

When Richard didn't respond, she put her arms around

Kahlan and gently pulled her out of his wooden embrace. Kahlan didn't resist. She didn't know why Nicci wanted him to let go of her, but she had no trouble grasping the concern in the sorceress's voice, or on her face.

Nicci laid Kahlan gently back on the ground. She immediately turned her attention to Richard.

With his connection to Kahlan broken, Nicci pressed the flats of her hands to both his temples. "Let it go, Richard," she murmured to him.

Richard gasped. Life, awareness, finally flooded back into his eyes. Kahlan let out a sigh of relief that Nicci had managed to pull him back from wherever he was. Richard grimaced when Nicci took her hands off him.

"What are you doing?" he asked Nicci. "Why did you stop me?"

"That would be my question," Zedd said as he appeared behind Richard.

Nicci tapped the same two fingers she had put to Richard's and Kahlan's foreheads to her own, as if signaling Zedd to test it and see for himself. Zedd immediately hiked up his robes and knelt on the other side of Richard. He put two fingers to Kahlan's forehead, then reached up and did the same to Richard.

"What?" he asked. "What am I supposed to feel?"

Nicci stared at him briefly. "You feel nothing?"

Zedd looked befuddled. "No. Should I?"

Nicci put her fingers back on Kahlan's forehead, testing, and Kahlan again felt a brief tingle of Additive Magic before Nicci repeated the test on Richard.

She let out a sigh. "I don't feel it anymore. Now that the connection is broken you can't feel it."

"Feel what?" Zedd asked with a frown.

Nicci cast a quick, surreptitious glance at Kahlan. "I don't know. Nothing, I guess. It's not important, we can talk about it later."

Richard wiped a hand across his face as he recovered from the experience of trying to heal Kahlan. She didn't really feel any better. Richard had healed far worse than this before. She couldn't imagine why it hadn't worked this time. What had her more concerned, though, was why Nicci appeared so upset.

"Why did you stop me?" Richard asked in a heated tone. "I was healing her. You didn't let me finish."

That confirmed what Kahlan had surmised, that perhaps he simply hadn't been allowed to finish. Nicci had interrupted him before he had a chance to finish the healing. But as soon as she had the thought, she realized that couldn't be the problem, because she had come back, became aware, before Nicci had come in and interrupted. It had failed before she separated them.

It had to be something else that was wrong.

Nicci let out a deep breath. "It wasn't working. You weren't healing her, you were just allowing yourself to be opened up to its contagion."

Zedd looked as puzzled as ever. He glanced at Richard, then down at Kahlan's arm. "What are you talking about?"

"I could tell that something wasn't right. The flow of his gift into Kahlan had ceased. Something was back-feeding into him from her. It was using his lifeline, his way back, to steal into him."

That brought alarm into Zedd's expression.

Nicci's gaze moved to Richard's eyes. "Did you understand? Did you know what I mean?"

Richard, looking frustrated and impatient, shook his head.

"Not really. I don't know what I felt. I don't know what happened. All I know is that it hurt. I was trying to take that hurt away from Kahlan and it just seemed to get out of hand."

"The boy heals by instinct, through empathy," Zedd told the sorceress. "He may have grown up without knowing he had the gift, and without learning how it's supposed to be done, but I've known him to heal things I can't."

"So have I," Nicci said. "He uses his gift in a unique way, but he wasn't healing this."

"Are you sure?" the old wizard asked.

Nicci nodded. "I could gauge the flow of power when I felt her, and then when I felt him. It was out of balance. The pain was back-feeding and was gaining control of him. It should have been the other way around. His gift should have been controlling the pain while feeding healing power into her, but it wasn't. He may have been acting on instinct, or doing what he's done in the past, but this time he was dealing with something different, something dangerous, and it wasn't working." She glanced at Kahlan. "Was it?"

Kahlan had to admit that what Nicci was saying made sense. "No. I don't understand, though. He's healed me before."

"That's right," Richard said. "Why wasn't it working the same this time?"

"I don't know for certain, Richard, but for some reason the problem you were trying to heal was behaving like a contagion. I guess you could say that it's like when you care for a sick person, you sometimes only end up catching what they have and then the both of you are sick."

"But the gift is supposed to protect me from that."

"The boy is right," Zedd put in.

Nicci looked reluctant to answer. "It could simply be that

with some guidance to fill in the blanks of your inexperience in using magic you might not have had the problem. I can't say for sure."

Zedd didn't waste any time arguing or questioning. "Well, it's obvious that the scratches I healed before have relapsed. They look infected. I need to go back in and fix this before we do anything else."

"I agree," Richard said as he scooted back out of Zedd's way.

"I'm not so sure that's a good idea just yet," Nicci said, rather cryptically, under her breath to Zedd.

Zedd looked perplexed by her reluctance. "Well, what I don't think is a good idea is to let this infection go unchecked. She could end up losing the arm. Worse, if the infection gets worse and moves into other parts of her body it can be fatal."

Nicci saw the anxiety on Kahlan's face and relented with a nod and a sigh. "You're right, Zedd. But let me help you."

"I would welcome any help," Richard's grandfather said as he leaned over Kahlan and pressed a hand against her forehead. Nicci laid her own hand over his.

Kahlan immediately felt the flow of his gift sweeping through her. She felt, too, the separate tingle of Nicci's magic. While they were similar, each had a unique feel to it. Mixed together as they were, it felt warm and comforting, but in a very different way than Richard's gift had felt warm and comforting. She knew that Zedd's gift felt different, so she wasn't concerned, and she also recognized the unique feel of Nicci's power. Both of their gifts blended together was an intoxicating feeling.

But she also thought that she felt the shadow of something else, something dark, tense aggressively within her.

As swiftly as Kahlan had the thought, she was swept up in

the flow of Zedd and Nicci's power. She again felt that loss of time and place as the warm glow of magic flooded through her. She could feel Zedd lifting the pain in much the same way Richard had, but with a kind of swift, experienced precision.

Abruptly, it all stopped. In a heartbeat, the mix of Zedd and Nicci's power was gone.

Kahlan opened her eyes as she gasped in a breath. It had felt like she had been under their influence for only a fleeting moment, but she knew from experience that it could easily have been an hour or two.

Zedd rocked back on his heels. He cast a worried look up at Nicci. "It's not Richard. Something is wrong. The only difference is that I knew enough to pull back. Richard didn't." He pressed his lips tight in silent discontent before adding, "It's not Richard. I can't heal her either."

Nicci regarded him with an unreadable look. "Did you feel it, then?"

Kahlan wondered what "it" was that he was supposed to feel.

Zedd's face twisted in frustration. "I don't know. I've never felt anything quite like it. It's a new one on me. I don't have any idea why I couldn't get through, but I couldn't."

Nicci's gaze remained locked on Zedd. "What did you feel?"

The creases in Zedd's face had taken on a troubled angularity as he and Nicci shared a private look. "I don't know. Something . . . something dark."

Nicci betrayed only the slightest hint of understanding, but she didn't say anything.

Kahlan didn't know for certain what they were talking about, but she recognized that the two of them shared a silent understanding about it, and she also knew that she had felt something tense within her at the touch of their magic.

Kahlan's level of alarm rose.

"Maybe Nathan could help," Richard suggested, not noticing what Kahlan had seen pass between Zedd and Nicci. "He's a Rahl. Maybe he would be better able to do it since his gift would work better here in the palace. Maybe that's all it would take."

CHAPTER

59

hat's this about me and my gift?" Nathan asked as he came to a halt behind Richard.

Kahlan saw that the prophet was clutching a piece of paper in his hand.

"Kahlan's arm that Zedd healed before has gotten worse," Richard said back over his shoulder. "He's having a problem healing it again. I was just saying that since your power isn't hindered by the spell around the palace, you might be better able to heal her arm."

Nathan frowned down at Kahlan. She held the arm out a little for him to see in the torchlight. Her head was pounding. She just wanted to go to sleep.

"I'd be happy to give it a try," he said.

"It won't do any good," Nicci said with quiet finality. "Zedd has already healed it once before. It shouldn't have come back like this. Something more is going on here that we're not seeing or understanding. If Zedd can't get back in to correct what he already did before, then you wouldn't be able to, either."

Kahlan was greatly worried about what else Nicci knew but wasn't saying.

"I'm afraid she's right," Zedd admitted with a sigh.

Kahlan pushed herself up onto her elbows. "But if you can't heal it . . ."

Zedd patted her shoulder and smiled in a reassuring manner, the old twinkle back in his eye. "Don't worry, dear one. There are a number other effective things we can do to get this taken care of. We have access to a wide variety of herbs here at the palace. It's just a scratch and a bit of infection. I've been healing such scratches and infections with poultices and herbs my whole life. I'll make one up that will have you better in no time."

"Zedd's right," Richard told her. "He always took care of my cuts and scrapes without the aid of the gift. I even have some aum with me," he told Zedd.

Zedd's bushy eyebrows lifted. "Do you now. Well, that will be a help to ease her pain while the poultice does its work of drawing out the infection." He patted her shoulder again. "I'll make it up right away and have you feeling better in no time."

Kahlan smiled as she lay back. "Thanks, Zedd."

He glanced about at the ground where she was lying, then looked up at Richard. "We need to get her to someplace more comfortable where she can rest."

"I'm comfortable here," Kahlan protested. She didn't relish the idea of being watched again in one of the bedrooms.

"Are you really?" Zedd glanced over at the gaping hole in the center of the room. "That machine down there has been giving others prophecy as they sleep—others without even a hint of the gift. Imagine the power that thing must emanate to be able to do such a thing in the first place, not to mention that it's doing it from within a containment field. I'm suspicious that that much power might have given you that head-ache while you slept."

Richard shot a frown back at the hole in the floor. "I don't have a headache, and I've been sleeping here too."

Zedd held up a finger. "But you have the gift—both sides of it. What's more, I believe that you have some kind of unique connection to the machine, so it may not affect you in the same way. But it could be harming others who spend too much time near it, like Kahlan has been doing."

With a troubled look, Richard put a comforting hand on Kahlan's shoulder.

Pain throbbed relentlessly in her head. "You really think the machine could be the cause?"

Zedd shrugged. "We don't know much about the machine. We have no idea what it's capable of, and that worries me greatly. It could be radiating a field of power that is responsible for your pain and nausea. At the very least I do know that when I tried to heal you I could sense that you're not getting anywhere near the amount of sleep you need for your body to have time to heal. That is making you suscep-tible to any number of problems. Without the rest you need, that infection is only going to get worse. That's why I think we need to get you to a comfortable bed—and more impor-tantly, away from this machine—so you can get the proper rest you need to help us get you healed."

She had to admit, that did make sense. Still . . .

"There are certainly enough comfortable places in the pal-ace," Richard told her. "We'll find you a place where you can rest and Zedd can treat your arm."

Kahlan pushed herself up on her elbows again. "And what about the problem we had in our bedroom?"

Richard showed her a crooked smile. "I have an idea about that. Not to worry."

But she was worried. Kahlan did her best to ignore the pounding pain in her head and the throbbing ache in her arm. "I'm better," she lied. She cleared her throat, trying to make her failing voice sound normal. It didn't really help.

"You don't sound better," Nathan said.

"There are more important things to worry about other than fussing over me," she said. "It was probably just a bad dream that gave me a headache, and as for my arm, well, sometimes scratches get worse before they get better. I think you're all making too much of it."

No one looked in the least bit convinced. Maybe because Kahlan wasn't convinced herself, but more so because she knew she had a fever. It was making her hoarse. She hardly had any voice left. Whenever she spoke it only revealed how bad she felt.

"I still think I ought to give it a try," Nathan said.

"If you want, I'd be happy to be your patient," Kahlan said, trying to sound better than she felt.

As Nathan stepped around Richard, Richard gestured. "By the way, what do you have with you?"

Nathan looked at the paper in his hand as if he'd forgotten he had it. "Oh, yes." He waggled it back at Richard. "From your personal prophet down in the library."

Richard made a sour face. "What does Lauretta have to predict now?"

"I'm afraid that it sounds serious. That's why I came looking for you. It's hard to say what it's actually about, but it's possible that it's another omen about Kahlan." Nathan waved the paper briefly, then turned it around so that he could read it aloud. "It says, 'A queen's choice will cost her her life.'"

"You mean you think it could be another omen about Kahlan because it's something like the one before?" Zedd asked. "Like that first one saying 'Queen takes pawn.'"

Nathan shook his head in frustration. "I don't know. I've had no visions about it. It could mean anything."

Richard's face had gone ashen. He snatched the paper from Nathan and read it himself as if he didn't believe it.

"What's wrong?" Zedd asked.

Richard continued to stare at the paper for a moment before he finally looked up at his grandfather.

"Earlier tonight," he said in a quiet voice, "the machine spoke to me."

Zedd leaned in. "What do you mean, it spoke to you?"

Richard's hand holding the piece of paper lowered as he searched for words. "It's kind of hard to explain."

Zedd didn't look inclined to let him off that easy. "I think you need to give it a good try."

Richard pressed his lips together for a moment first as he considered how to explain it. "The machine told me that it had had dreams. Then it wanted to know why it had had dreams."

Nicci's brows lifted. "It asked you a question?"

Richard nodded. Kahlan frowned as she tried to recall through her throbbing headache where she had heard those words before. They sounded familiar. Finally, it came to her.

"Isn't that what the boy down in the market said? That he'd had dreams? Then he asked why he'd had dreams. Remember?"

"I remember," Richard said. "Henrik. And you're right. He said the exact same words."

The room was silent as everyone tried to take in the implications. Through experience, they had learned that the same prophecies the machine gave also came out through others. Kahlan wondered if this could be the same kind of thing.

Richard raked his fingers back through his hair. "It wasn't just what the machine said. It was how it said it that has me so concerned."

"What do you mean, 'how it said it'?" Nicci asked. "It burns the things it says onto those metal strips. Did it give the message this time in a different manner?"

"No, it said both things by burning the symbols on the strips of metal, same as before."

"Then what do you mean by 'how it said it'?"

"You all know what the machine sounds like when it's going to give a prophecy—the sudden crash of sound that it makes when it starts into motion all at once from a dead stop?" Richard glanced around at the nods. "Well, this time it was different. Rather than that kind of sudden beginning at full speed, this time it started slowly, softly, like it was waking up."

Zedd threw his arms up in the air. "Waking up! Waking up and telling you that it had been dreaming? Dear spirits, Richard, it's a machine!"

"I know, I know," Richard said, gesturing for his grandfather to calm down and listen. "But it started slowly, quietly, all the gears and things inside gradually building speed and moving into place slowly. After it was fully up and running, then it inscribed two strips with those two things about dreams: 'I have had dreams,' and 'Why have I had dreams?'

"Even more strange, though, is that the two strips weren't hot when they came out of the machine."

"They're always hot when they come out," Zedd declared.

Richard leaned in a little, looking to each of them in turn. "Well, this time they came out of the machine cool to the touch. Both of them."

Zedd rubbed his chin. "That is odd."

"I was down there the rest of the night," Richard went on,

"waiting to see if it would say anything else. I fell asleep for a while. Then, all of a sudden, the gears started into motion again, but the usual way, the way you've seen it happen—abruptly, all at once. The sudden crash of noise instantly woke me up."

He leaned back, reached into his pocket, and pulled out a metal strip. "After it woke me up, just before I heard Kahlan scream and came running up here to see what was wrong with her"—he held the strip up—"the machine issued the same omen. And, it came out of the machine hot, like usual."

"What same omen?" Zedd asked, suspiciously.

Richard gestured at the note Nathan was holding. "The same as that. 'A queen's choice will cost her her life.'"

With his foot, Richard flipped over the carpet. He didn't see the symbol that he had seen scratched into the floor of the corridors outside their previous bedrooms and the one he'd found outside Queen Catherine's room after she had been killed. He was encouraged by that much of it. The symbol meant "Watch them." He didn't want anyone watching them while they slept, as they had done before.

He was concerned about the omen that the machine had given, the same one that Lauretta had written down, but at the moment he was far more concerned about Kahlan. He didn't know whether the prophecy "A queen's choice will cost her her life" was about Kahlan, as the first one about "Queen takes pawn" had been, or not, but at the moment he was more worried about taking care of the infected scratches on her arm. They would have to worry about the prophecy later.

Besides, trying to figure out what prophecy meant was a fool's game.

For now, he wanted to get Kahlan in a comfortable place without the machine nearby where Zedd could put an herb poultice on her arm to draw out the infection while she got some much-needed rest.

He had hopes that this place would be safe, since it was not one of the bedchambers belonging to the Lord Rahl. In those bedrooms something had been watching them. Of course, he had later discovered that there were symbols scratched in the floors outside those rooms, but still, even without the symbols, he didn't trust the official bedrooms for the Lord Rahl. They seemed too easy a target for forces he didn't yet understand. Until he knew how those symbols got scratched on floors in well-guarded halls, as well as what their ultimate purpose was, he didn't trust that those rooms would be safe.

This room was not one of the Lord Rahl's bedrooms, but instead it was a secluded guest bedroom. The wing had no guests at the moment, so it wouldn't have anyone near, and no one would really know that they were there. It was several floors above ground level, so no one could come in from outside. It wasn't big, but Richard didn't care about that. He simply wanted a safe place to sleep.

Before he could enter the room, Cara pushed in ahead of him. Benjamin already had men of the First File stationed at every intersection of halls throughout the whole wing of the palace. Rikka stood not far down the hallway to one side, Berdine on the other. Both were in their red leather. While he welcomed the guards outside the room, he didn't really put too much faith in them stopping what really mattered to him. What had been in their room before, watching them, had without any trouble slipped past guards.

This time, Richard intended to have a little surprise if the mysterious watchers again came looking in.

With an arm around Kahlan's waist, Richard led her into the room. He set the load of their packs and other gear down to the side. Cara came back from her inspection and gave him a nod to indicate that she didn't see anything that caused her any concern in the room.

"What do you think?" he asked Kahlan.

Richard saw that her gaze took in only the bed. "Looks good to me."

He was glad that she looked longingly at the bed. He was worried about her and wanted her to be able to get some sleep. Cara's face, after surveying Kahlan's, clearly reflected her concern as well.

Zedd gave Kahlan a gentle pat on the back as he came into the room behind them. "You get settled in, dear one. I'll get a poultice prepared and be back as soon as I can to put it on your arm. Then you need to get some sleep. That will help more than anything."

Kahlan nodded. Her face was ashen. By the look in her green eyes alone Richard knew how much pain she was in. He also knew that she didn't want to worry him, so she wouldn't admit the full extent of how she really felt. But he could see it clearly enough in her eyes.

Because they had been sleeping on the ground in the Garden of Life, Kahlan was in her traveling clothes of pants, a shirt, and boots.

"How about we get you out of those things and into bed?"

She shook her head and immediately crawled onto the bed.

Before they had left the Garden of Life, Nathan had tried healing her arm. He had no better luck than any of the rest of them had had. Richard was depending, now, on Zedd's poultice to draw out the infection and some good old-fashioned sleep.

Zedd leaned toward Richard. "I'll go make up a poultice and be right back." He pointed and spoke in a low voice. "In the meantime, just to be on the safe side, get rid of those mirrors."

There were twin mirrors over a dressing table. "Don't worry," Richard said, "I have something in mind for them."

Once Zedd left, Richard did his own check of the room. Not that he didn't trust Cara's search, but he wanted to be sure. Since it was a single room and wasn't very large at that, there wasn't much to check.

The wardrobes smelled of aromatic cedar and were empty. At the back of the room there were double doors with glass panes. With the back of his hand, Richard pushed the drapes aside and looked out the glass into the darkness. There appeared to be a small terrace with a potted evergreen to the side up against the fat, waist-high stone railing. Out on the grounds far below, Richard saw a patrol of soldiers.

Once Cara left, Richard tried to get Kahlan to at least take off her boots. She fussed and said that she was cold and just wanted the blanket over her. Richard knew how when he had a headache and was throwing up and terribly sick to his stomach he didn't want anyone messing with him, either. He carefully laid the comforter over Kahlan and gently tucked it up around her neck.

When Kahlan closed her eyes, he went to the drapes at the double doors in the back of the room and took off the fabric swag holding them back. At the dressing table, he took down the only two mirrors in the room. He placed the identical mirrors on the floor, standing face-to-face, and used the swag to tie them tightly together. When he was finished, he leaned the paired mirror up against the padded seat.

He sat on the edge of the bed and leaned over, hugging Kahlan to warm her up and let her know that she wasn't alone. Her eyes were closed and she didn't say anything, but she let out a little sigh to let him know that she appreciated it.

Richard woke up when he heard a knock. It was Zedd, back with the poultice. Richard handed him the small canister of aum that he had retrieved from his pack. As Zedd used a wooden slat to mix the aum Richard gave him into the slightly yellowish concoction he had in a small bowl, Richard turned down the blanket and laid Kahlan's arm out on top of it for him.

Kahlan sleepily opened her eyes, frowning, to see what he was doing, why he was disturbing her sleep. When Zedd slathered the poultice on her red, swollen arm, she winced in pain.

"It will be better soon," he told her. Kahlan nodded as she closed her eyes.

Zedd wrapped bandaging around it as Richard held her wrist up for him. "This will not only help draw out the infection, it will draw out the pain as well. I also put in a little something that will help her to sleep."

Richard nodded. "Thanks, Zedd. I'm kind of worried about how groggy and unaware she is."

"She just doesn't feel well and needs rest," his grandfather assured him as he patted him on the shoulder. "You ought to get some sleep as well."

Richard didn't think he would be able to sleep. He just wanted to sit up and watch over Kahlan.

They both turned when they heard an odd, muted, distant cry of tortured anguish.

"Dear spirits," Zedd said. "What in the world was that?"

Richard smiled as he pointed. "I put the two mirrors face-to-face. I think that something tried to look in on the room and they got a look of something they very much didn't like seeing: their own reflection."

Zedd laughed softly, trying not to wake Kahlan. "Now that, my boy, is a nice bit of magic."

The situation calls for a choice, and I've made it," Queen Orneta said. "My decision is final."

The small gathering of representatives shared looks. Duchess Marple set her cup down on the low table and leaned in a little as she looked up at Orneta. "So, you mean to say that you really believe, then, that Lord Rahl and the Mother Confessor are agents of the Keeper? Seriously?"

Orneta noted that the woman clearly sounded more scandalized than incredulous. Her eyes, too, gleamed with the prize of such sordid gossip. Some people delighted in nothing more than bringing down the powerful with scandals of unsavory sins.

Orneta was not in the least bit interested in gossip, or throwing stones at the mighty. She was driven by more important concerns. She cared about the contemptible behavior because of what it meant for her and her people.

Others in the small group whispered their more serious worry to one another. Orneta had been having intensive talks with these people over recent days. They were among the representatives who were the most concerned about prophecy, who believed firmly in it, and who wanted it used to help guide them into the future. They were greatly troubled that the Lord Rahl and the Mother Confessor wouldn't share prophecy with them. They felt that their views were being ignored.

Orneta had never really known these people to be all that concerned with prophecy, but recently it had taken center stage in their lives. It was much the same with her. She supposed that since peace had come, so had broader concerns about the future.

As they had learned from the intimate discussions with Orneta and Ludwig, there could be only one explanation as to why Lord Rahl and the Mother Confessor refused to share prophecy.

Orneta gestured to Ludwig. "As Abbot Dreier has revealed, a number of places in prophecy have been discovered that name Lord Rahl 'the bringer of death.' I take no satisfaction in telling you this. Nor do you need to take my word for it. Though I doubt that it would be wise to ask Lord Rahl to show you the reference material, it is available. Bishop Arc, reluctantly, would show it to you if you insisted on seeing it with your own eyes."

The notion that the Keeper of the world of the dead was influencing and using their leaders for his own ends was clearly alarming. Most didn't want to believe it was true, but they could not argue the evidence.

"Who but the Creator, who has created all things, would know the future?" Ludwig asked. "Since the Creator knows all things, how would He warn us, His creation, of dangers He sees for us in the future?"

Eyes big, everyone leaned in a little. "Prophecy," Ludwig said in answer to his own question. "The Creator uses omens to warn us of danger only He can see. Clearly, the Nameless

One would want to suppress that means of salvation, would he not? Would he not want to possess the most trusted among us to conceal those prophecies from us and thus to insure that we are more easily delivered into the arms of death itself?"

The implication was clear. Lord Rahl and the Mother Confessor, in hiding prophecy from these leaders, could only be working toward the Keeper's ends.

It was a sobering conclusion, and one that these people did not take lightly, one that, even for the duchess, transcended mere gossip. Orneta thought that maybe they needed a little demonstration of proper resolve to help them make up their minds as to what to do about it.

She loosely grasped Ludwig's arm. "Would you please send word to Bishop Arc that we could use his guidance where matters of prophecy are concerned? Let him know that there are some of us who view prophecy, as does he, as vital to our future, and we would like to be kept informed of what prophecy says. Let him know, also, that in return for his help, I, for one, have decided that he will have my loyalty, and the loyalty of my people."

The whispering started in again. There were also nods of approval.

Ludwig bowed his head. "Of course, Queen Orneta. I know that Bishop Arc will be humbled by your words. I can assure you, on his behalf, that wherever the future may lead our people, Bishop Arc and I will continue to use prophecy to guide us so that we all may know the dangers along the path to our common good."

"I wish that Lord Rahl would do as much," Ambassador Grandon said. He tugged on the end of his pointed beard as he shook his head in sincere regret. "We're not picking sides in a conflict—we're all on the same side, after all—so I sin-

cerely hope that Lord Rahl won't see our desire to align ourselves with Bishop Arc as any kind of betrayal."

Urgent murmurs of agreement passed among those gathered. They wanted to side with prophecy, but they trod lightly
where treason was concerned. These people were loyal to the
D'Haran Empire, but they also wanted prophecy to guide
D'Hara.

Orneta leaned both hands on the broad marble railing and
gazed out over the vast corridors of the People's Palace below.
Sunlight streamed in from glassed sections overhead. Below,
the crowds, lit by streamers of sunlight, moved through the
halls, or gathered in groups, as did the intimate group up in
the small but comfortable sitting area of the balcony.

"Treason, you mean," Orneta said without turning back.
"That's what you really mean. You mean that you hope that
Lord Rahl won't see this choice as treason."

"Well yes," Grandon said. "That's not the way I see it, or
even remotely my intent. We are still loyal to the D'Haran
Empire, still value Lord Rahl, it's just that . . ."

Ludwig, sipping on wine as he listened, arched an eyebrow. "Just that if Bishop Arc were to be Lord Arc, he would
be better suited to managing the peace, than a Lord Rahl,
who was better at managing the war."

The ambassador lifted a finger. "That's a good way of putting it. We are loyal to the D'Haran Empire, and, as I said, we
value Lord Rahl and the Mother Confessor and all they've
done for us, but we believe that Bishop Arc—Lord Arc as
you suggest—with his broad knowledge and familiarity with
prophecy, would be better suited in a leadership role. Since he
would be guided by prophecy, he would be better able to
maintain the peace and help us all take the safest path into the
future."

Among the dozen and a half people gathered, there were nods and whispers of agreement to Ambassador Grandon's wisdom.

"I would hope as much myself," Orneta said. "Lord Rahl and the Mother Confessor have fought hard to bring us to victory. I—we—are all greatly indebted to them. I fear, though, that somewhere along the line they have succumbed to the influence of dark whispers, so now we must do what is in the best interest of our people. It is our responsibility to now embrace the guidance of Lord Arc. That is my choice, and it is final."

Ambassador Grandon dipped his head in a single but firm nod. "It must be."

The duchess took refuge in sipping her tea rather than voice such a profound and final choice. Others in the group, though, did voice their solemn agreement.

Orneta was gratified that Ludwig had such a responsible position in culling prophecy from every source possible and delivering it to Bishop Arc so that he might use it in guiding his rule of Fajin Province. It now seemed that Bishop Arc would be better suited to a position as Lord Arc in guiding all the lands, rather than just Fajin Province.

When Orneta looked up from taking a drink of wine, she saw a Mord-Sith in red leather coming around a corner in the distance. As she marched their way, the Mord-Sith's gaze was fixed on Orneta.

The group with Queen Orneta fell silent as the Mord-Sith approached. All eyes were on the tall woman in red as she marched steadily toward them. In light of the gravity of their conversation, worry overcame the small group and none of them could even manage small talk.

They were, after all, standing in Lord Rahl's palace, in the ancestral home of the House of Rahl, the seat of power in D'Hara for thousands of years. It seemed somewhat distasteful, if not disrespectful, if not treasonous, to be discussing such matters while in the People's Palace.

Yet even though this was Lord Rahl's home, the home of the House of Rahl, it was also the people's house. In that sense, it was a palace belonging to the people, and so the people had every right to discuss and decide matters of relevance to their common future.

But the approaching woman in red made all that seem rather academic. The Lord Rahl was the undisputed supreme authority in this place, and in all of D'Hara. The war would have seemed to have settled that issue and only strengthened the Lord Rahl's hold on power. Unless of course Orneta and those of like mind were able, with the help of Abbot Dreier and Bishop Arc, to do something about it.

She was adamant, as were a number of other representatives, that prophecy was the rightful guiding authority handed down by the Creator Himself and it had to be obeyed. To obey it, they had to be made aware of it. To allow the Keeper of the dead to subvert the use of prophecy was treason to life. They needed a guiding leader, like Bishop Arc, who would rule as Lord Arc in conjunction with the words of prophecy.

In the silence up on the balcony, with all the representatives watching, the Mord-Sith was the center of attention as she went to the railing and glanced down at the people strolling the halls. Soldiers looking up saw her and without pause continued on their way. Other people moving through the halls noticed her as well, but their gazes didn't linger long.

Even in the People's Palace, most people had always avoided looking a Mord-Sith in the eye. Of course, since Cara, Lord Rahl's closest bodyguard, had gotten married, that caution had softened somewhat. Somewhat.

This particular Mord-Sith's hard edge, however, gave none of them any reason to abandon long-held fears.

The Mord-Sith's blond hair was done in the traditional single braid hanging straight down between her broad shoulders to the small of her back. It was impeccably plaited. Not a single hair seemed to be out of place. The sensual mix of muscles and feminine curves filled out her red leather outfit perfectly.

A small red rod, her Agiel, hung from a fine gold chain around her right wrist, dangling just beyond the ends of her fingers so that it was always at the ready.

As she turned back from surveying the halls below and then the balcony area where the small group of people were gathered, her penetrating blue-eyed gaze finally fixed on Orneta.

"Queen Orneta, I have come to speak with you. Alone."

Orneta frowned. "About what?"

"We will discuss it in private."

Orneta wasn't at all sure she wanted to speak with one of Lord Rahl's Mord-Sith. In light of her recent decision to throw her loyalty to Hannis Arc, Orneta especially didn't want to speak with her alone.

"Well, I don't know that I wish—"

"That's odd. I wasn't aware that I had given the impression that I was offering you a choice."

Orneta could feel the fine hairs on the back of her neck stand up. She didn't think she had ever heard such a silvery voice sound so menacing.

Unable to think of a way out of it, she lifted an arm in invitation. "My quarters are down this way. They're not far. Perhaps you would—"

"That will do. Get going."

Orneta glanced to Ludwig, hoping for intervention, or salvation of some sort.

By his heated expression, he didn't look to need much encouragement. "What's this about?"

At the anger in his tone, the Mord-Sith flicked her Agiel up into her fist. "It's about the most recent prophecy."

Everyone looked surprised.

"What prophecy?" Ludwig asked.

"A number of people, including that blind fortune-teller woman, were visited by a prophecy."

"What does this prophecy say?" Ludwig demanded.

The Mord-Sith arched an eyebrow at him before taking in the rest of the people watching. "I wouldn't have any idea what it said. Prophecy is not meant for the ungifted. That includes all of you."

Anger was now clearly evident in Ludwig's eyes. He had become more than fond of Orneta, and she of him. The two of them, in fact, had been together quite a bit. She was gratified that he couldn't seem to get enough of her.

"If you don't even know what it says, then what do you mean when you say that this is about the prophecy?" he asked.

"I was given orders. It was mentioned in passing that they were based on the most recent prophecy." She leaned toward him and lifted her Agiel in a threatening manner. "Now, I've wasted enough time. We have to go."

Instead of withdrawing, Ludwig tried to step between Orneta and the Mord-Sith. "I think that we should—"

The woman rammed her Agiel into his shoulder. Ludwig cried out in pain as he was driven back by the shock of the weapon. He dropped heavily to his knees. He pressed a hand to his shoulder as he groaned in agony.

He looked up, enraged. "You bitch! How dare—"

The Mord-Sith pointed her Agiel right at his face. "I suggest that you stay down and stay quiet, or I will put you down and make you go quiet—for good. Do you understand me?"

Ludwig glared at her, but he didn't move. Orneta reached out to him, appalled at seeing him hurt. She wanted to comfort him, to know that he was all right.

The Mord-Sith stepped in Orneta's way and gestured with the Agiel. "Enough of this nonsense. Get going."

CHAPTER

63

Before the woman could prod her with the weapon, Orneta took one last, quick look at Ludwig, then turned and stalked off in the direction of her quarters. She was indignant, and she was angry at the woman for hurting Ludwig, but she thought better of showing her emotion for the moment. She would make her grievance clear enough at the proper time and to the proper people, and then this woman would pay the price for her insolence, to say nothing of her needless cruelty.

At least Orneta could get the Mord-Sith away from Ludwig before he did something foolish and got himself hurt even worse.

As she made her way down the elegant corridor, Orneta tried not to move too swiftly. Rather, she moved at a stately pace, just to remind the Mord-Sith of who she was dealing with. Orneta was also in no hurry to reach her room and be alone with the woman.

A servant going in the opposite direction, carrying an armful of fresh bed linens, moved hard against the side of the hallway when she saw the Mord-Sith coming, and stayed well out of her way. The woman kept her eyes turned toward the ground as she passed, avoiding meeting the steady gaze of the tall woman in red leather.

Orneta felt like a prisoner being led to an execution. She couldn't believe that she was being treated with such disrespect. Considering her decision, it occurred to her that it wasn't entirely undeserved. For years, she had been nothing but loyal to the cause of the D'Haran Empire. She reminded herself that what she was doing was out of loyalty to the D'Haran Empire—to the people, anyway, if not the leader.

She didn't know what the Mord-Sith could possibly want, but Orneta was becoming more worried by the moment that it had something to do with her throwing her loyalty to Hannis Arc over Richard Rahl. She told herself that it was a silly worry. No one knew of her decision but her and Ludwig. And of course the group, but she had only just told them.

It occurred to her then that there might have been a prophecy that foretold of her new-sworn allegiance. Lord Rahl wouldn't tell them what prophecy said, wouldn't help them against threats those omens revealed, but that didn't mean he wouldn't use them for his own dark ends. There was no telling what a person being used by the Keeper of the underworld might know, or what they might do.

Lord Rahl was a good man, a decent man, but even such a person could become possessed so that they were not acting of their own free will; they were instead being guided by death itself. As Ludwig had pointed out, who better for the Keeper to possess in order to carry out his dark deeds than the most trusted among them?

When Orneta glanced back over her shoulder, she saw that the Mord-Sith was right behind her, wearing a grim expression.

But past the Mord-Sith, Orneta could see that the entire

group she'd been meeting with was following them up the hall. They were keeping their distance, but they were clearly intent on seeing what this was about, seeing why one of their group was being singled out. Ludwig, holding his shoulder, looking to still be in pain from the touch of the Agiel, led a concerned Ambassador Grandon, then the duchess, then the rest of the representatives. Anger darkened Ludwig's face.

Orneta was glad, at least, to have them following along. She thought that it might temper whatever the Mord-Sith wanted to see her about. Witnesses tended to cool aggression. She also was heartened to have Ludwig stand up for her.

Orneta paused and flicked her hand at the ornate doors before her, trying to gain a moment for those following to catch up. "These are my quarters."

When the Mord-Sith glared with the kind of look that sapped the strength of even the strong, Orneta opened the door and led them both inside. She nudged the door closed, but deliberately left it ajar enough that the people, once they caught up, could easily hear everything, and even peek in.

The Mord-Sith firmly pushed the door shut.

Orneta, trying to look casual, went to a low cabinet where bottles of wine, water, and sweet drinks sat on a silver tray with a half-dozen crystal glasses.

"May I offer you something to drink?"

"I'm not here to drink."

Orneta smiled cordially. "I'm sorry, but I haven't even asked your name."

The Mord-Sith's blue eyes were enough to make Orneta weak, but she tried not to show it.

"My name is Vika."

"Vika." Orneta smiled. "Well, Vika, what can I do for you?"

The Mord-Sith began advancing. "You can scream."

Orneta blinked. "I beg your pardon?"

Vika seized a fistful of Orneta's dress at her shoulder. "I said, you can scream."

The Mord-Sith gritted her teeth as she pulled Orneta forward and rammed the Agiel into her middle.

The shock of pain was beyond anything Orneta had ever experienced or imagined was possible.

As the full shock of it hit her, it would have been impossible not to scream.

Screaming ended, Orneta crumpled to the floor, trying to get back her breath as tears of hurt streamed down her face.

"Why are you doing this?" she managed between gasps.

Vika stood over her, watching. "To help you scream."

Orneta was dumbfounded. She could not begin to imagine why the woman had done such a thing, or what she meant about wanting to hear screams.

"But why?"

"Since you are so committed to having prophecy guide mankind, you have been granted the honor of being the instrument of prophecy's fulfillment. Now, let's hear a really good scream."

As Orneta stared up in frozen, panicked confusion, Vika jammed the tip of her Agiel into the hollow at the base of Orneta's throat.

Orneta screamed so hard she thought it might rip her throat. She wouldn't have been able to stop herself if she had wanted to. The pain overwhelmed her, making the muscles of her arms and neck convulse in uncontrolled spasms.

The screams were drowned out as blood frothed up from her throat and out her mouth. It ran down her chin, hanging in long, thick strings, and soaked the front of her dress.

The room darkened in her dwindling spot of vision, but

then slowly widened back into view. She was hardly aware of where the Mord-Sith was or what she was doing until Orneta saw her walk around behind her.

Without a word, Vika jammed her Agiel into the base of Orneta's skull.

Light flashed in her vision. Sparkling colors exploded in every direction. There was a most terrible shrieking sound inside her head that made the pain beyond anything that had come before. Sharp shards of suffering drove inward through her ears.

Orneta sat on the floor, limp and helpless, as the shrieking, crashing, roaring sound and the blaze of light swirled through her head.

She heard Vika's boots on the white marble floor as the woman came around in front of her. The Mord-Sith stood over Orneta, towered over her, looking down without the slightest hint of compassion, much less remorse.

Orneta had never seen such a cold and heartless look in all her life.

"That was quite good," Vika said in a calm voice. "I'm sure everyone could hear it."

Orneta couldn't hold her head up. She couldn't make her neck muscles respond. By the terrible pain, she thought that they must be torn. Her chin rested on her blood-soaked chest.

She saw blood spreading across the white marble floor. Her blood. A lot of her blood.

The Mord-Sith's boots were the same color as the pool of blood she was standing in.

With supreme effort, through the burning pain in her throat, past the blood filling her mouth, she used all her might to lift her head to look up and speak.

"What do you want of me?"

Vika arched a brow over a cold blue eye. "Well, now that you have screamed very nicely for me, I want you to die."

Orneta blinked up at the woman. She could offer no resistance, could not fight such a savage creature.

She was not surprised, though. She had known the answer before Vika had spoken it.

Orneta saw the Agiel coming again.

She felt only the first instant of exquisite pain as her heart exploded in her chest.

And then, even that breathless, crushing agony diminished into the last conscious, dimming spark of awareness.

64

Ludwig was pouring himself a last glass of wine when he heard the door behind him open and then close. There had been no knock.

He glanced back over his shoulder just enough to catch a glimpse of red leather. The familiar odor of blood reached his nostrils. It reminded him of being back at the abbey, of his work at extracting prophecy.

He turned around and took a sip of the wine as he leaned a hip against the table. It was late and he was tired.

Vika stood tall and straight, hands clasped behind her back, feet spread, chin held high, not meeting his gaze.

"Was everything satisfactory, Abbot Dreier?"

He strolled across the room toward her. "Everyone was terrified. We all heard the screams. After you came out, and before they all scattered, they caught a glimpse of the body. I especially liked the glare you gave them as you wiped the blood off your boots on the carpeting. Nice touch."

Still, she did not meet his gaze. "Thank you, Abbot Dreier."

"Did Orneta suffer a great deal?"

"Yes, Abbot, just as you instructed, I made sure that she suffered greatly."

"Good. With a Mord-Sith doing such a thing right in front of their eyes, I'm sure that a great many of the representatives now think that Lord Rahl is a monster who cannot be trusted."

"I am confident that they will rush into Lord Arc's waiting arms," she said.

"Yes," he drawled, "I'm sure they will."

She hesitated, licked her lips, and then had to ask. "Is your shoulder all right, Abbot? I was afraid that I might have gone too far."

Ludwig pressed a hand over the center of the lingering pain and rotated his arm. "You did as needed to be done. The demonstration made the impression I wanted it to make. No one will ever think to connect us. They won't know that you are with me."

Her blue eyes finally turned, ice coming back into her gaze as it settled on him. "I am Lord Arc's Mord-Sith, not yours."

He shrugged. "A fine point that I find meaningless."

"I don't think that Lord Arc would find it meaningless."

Ludwig lifted his hand toward her, releasing a flow of power into her middle as he took another sip of wine.

Vika's eyes watered as she went to one knee. Her face turned nearly as red her leather outfit. Her arms crossed over her abdomen, over the unbearable agony he was twisting mercilessly into her. She toppled over on her side, groaning in helpless pain.

Mord-Sith were well practiced at tolerating pain. But they were not well practiced in tolerating the kind he could deliver or this much of it.

Her eyes went out of focus. He knew that she was looking beyond the world of life and into the world of the dead. He knew that she would not expect to return from the terror of that dark vision.

One did not often venture this far beyond the cusp of death and return.

It was a fine line of control. He held her there, at that place near the forever point. If she did not return from that dark place, he would not really care. Lovely as she was, there were always others.

He reminded himself that Hannis Arc would care.

Ludwig released her.

Vika gasped, trying to catch her breath, as she rolled onto her back. Her arms lay spread out wide to the sides as the world of life swirled in around her again. He could see her confusion at returning unexpectedly to life. She at last blinked, looking up at him, realizing where she was.

"Don't ever get snippy with me again. Do you understand?"

"Yes, Abbot Dreier."

"I don't appreciate your insolence."

She nodded as she struggled to her feet. "Please forgive my thoughtless disrespect."

He waited until she was able to get fully upright. A tear trailed down her cheek.

"What about the rest of it?" he asked.

With a great effort not to show the lingering pain, she stiffly clasped her hands behind her back. Her posture was not quite as straight as before.

"I've taken care of it all, Abbot Dreier." Vika swallowed, still trying to regain her composure. "I was able to get into the halls where Lord Rahl's bedchambers are located and place the symbol outside his doors. I also placed the one outside King Philippe's room when I saw him leave and his wife was alone."

Ludwig took another sip of wine. "And did anyone see you as you went about your business?"

"Yes, Abbot. A number of people saw me, but none of them really looked at me. As you directed, though, I was careful not to let any of the Mord-Sith get a look at me. To everyone else, I was simply another one of Lord Rahl's Mord-Sith. Everyone is used to seeing them in the palace. Fortunately, they have all been in red leather of late. Everyone who noticed me went to great pains to not pay any attention to me. You would have thought I was invisible."

Ludwig smiled. He knew the truth of that. He knew when he had suggested it to Hannis Arc that she would be able to walk around in broad daylight, in plain sight, and no one would pay any attention to her. Hannis Arc, as powerful as he was, as clever as he was, was too insulated, too consumed with his own narrow obsessions, to know how things in the wider world worked. He could not accomplish what he did without Ludwig's guidance.

"Good," he said as he nodded in satisfaction. "Good." He set down his glass. "Now that you've finished with what I wanted done, you need to leave. I don't want to risk one of Lord Rahl's Mord-Sith getting a look at your face. The longer you're here, the greater the risk that someone will recognize that you're not one of Lord Rahl's Mord-Sith."

"I am prepared and can leave immediately, Abbot Dreier."

Ludwig nodded. "My coach is packed and waiting for me. I will shortly be leaving as well. After I'm away from the palace and the Azrith Plain and once into the woodlands you can join me in the coach for the journey home. I'm sure that Lord Arc is eager for your return."

"Yes, Abbot Dreier, I am sure he is."

He glanced up, looking for any hint of insolence in her cold, blue eyes, but he saw none.

"Is what I heard true, Abbot Dreier?"

"I don't know. What did you hear?"

Vika hesitated a moment. "That a Mord-Sith was married. That such was the reason for the big ceremony and all the guests. I was busy carrying out my orders and didn't see for myself if it was true."

"Not that it's any of your business, but that's right. It's why we're all here, all of us representatives. We were invited to attend the grand celebration of Cara's wedding."

Vika let out a noisy breath. "I just don't understand how a Mord-Sith could do such a thing."

Ludwig shrugged. "The Mord-Sith here, under Lord Rahl's rule, have gotten soft."

She nodded as she stared off in private thoughts. "It must be."

He stepped closer, walking around her, deliberately looking her over. He stopped close in front of her, looking into her blue eyes. She didn't meet his gaze.

"Our work here is done for now. You need to be on your way. I don't want to risk you being seen by the wrong person."

Vika bowed her head. "I will leave straightaway and then join you when you reach the woodlands."

Ludwig watched her shapely form from behind as she went to the door, watched the way she swayed and her hips moved. It would be an exciting change to have such a luscious creature after Orneta. Not that Orneta was bad, it was just that she was no Vika. Few women were.

But for now, like the other Mord-Sith, she belonged to Hannis Arc. One day, though, if Ludwig had his way, Lord

Arc would not be around to make demands of her. One day, Abbot Dreier would be Lord Dreier and he would make his own demands.

It would require great care, though. Hannis Arc was a profoundly dangerous man. His occult abilities were not to be taken lightly. But he was also a man obsessed.

Ludwig pulled himself back from his pleasant contemplation. He had to be on his way. All the representatives who had lost faith in Lord Rahl and sworn allegiance to Lord Arc instead were leaving, going back to various parts of the empire. He wanted to be among them.

Richard was shocked and angry.

He could hardly believe the bloody scene with Queen Orneta lying lifeless in the middle of it.

This was the second queen murdered in the palace since Cara's wedding. Both killings had been horrific.

He was even more upset to know that a Mord-Sith had done this.

Which one had done it he didn't know. Why she had done it he could not imagine.

"Lord Rahl," Cara said, "I admit to not liking the woman, to not trusting her, but I would not have done this."

Even Cara knew better than to test his patience right then.

"I didn't say you did."

"Then say something," she said.

He looked back at her. "I want to know who did this."

She pressed her lips tightly together and nodded. She wanted to say that a Mord-Sith would not have acted on her own like this, not anymore. But she could not refute the evidence or the witnesses.

Cara herself had confirmed what Richard had already known: that the queen had died from an Agiel.

There was no doubt that a Mord-Sith had killed Queen Orneta. The only question remaining was which one.

Richard didn't want to think it of any of them. They were all absolutely ruthless in defending Kahlan's life and his, and ruthless in battle, but they were also ruthlessly loyal to him.

It just didn't make any sense.

With a hand, Richard signaled Ambassador Grandon, standing out in the hall, to come forward. The ambassador dipped his head in acknowledgment of the Lord Rahl's summons and shuffled into the room, fumbling with a button in his long coat the entire way.

He dipped his head again when he came to a stop. "Yes, Lord Rahl?"

"You say it was a Mord-Sith who did this and that you saw her?"

"Yes, Lord Rahl."

"Describe her. What did she look like?"

He thought it over a moment. "Tall, blond hair. She had blue eyes."

Richard fought to keep his reaction under control as he gestured at Cara standing next to him. "Cara is tall, she has blond hair and blue eyes. Was it her, then?"

Ambassador Grandon looked up at Cara. "Of course not, Lord Rahl."

"A good many of the Mord-Sith have blond hair and blue eyes. Many people in D'Hara do."

Ambassador Grandon dipped his head again as he continued to play with the button on his coat. "Yes, Lord Rahl."

"So tell me what was different about this woman. How can we pick her out from all the other blond-headed, blue-eyed Mord-Sith? How do we know which one was responsible?"

The man finally let go of the button to tug on his pointed beard instead. "I don't know, Lord Rahl. I didn't look at her that directly, that carefully. I saw the red leather, the blond braid, the Agiel. And she had the attitude of a Mord-Sith, if you know what I mean. She was a woman to be greatly feared. I'm not sure I could point her out as the one even if I saw her again."

Richard sighed in frustration. He knew the man was right. Few people would look a Mord-Sith in the eye or take more than a brief glance. He understood the feeling, the fear, well enough.

Richard rested the palm of his left hand on the hilt of his sword, tapping the cross guard with his thumb. "What were you and the others doing with Queen Orneta? Why were all of you gathered back there on the balcony? By the looks of all the cups and glasses setting around, you were all up there for quite a while. What were you all doing there?"

When the man paled a little, Richard knew that he had hit a soft spot. "Well, Lord Rahl, we were just talking."

"Just talking. Just talking about what?"

"About prophecy."

"Prophecy. And what were you all saying about prophecy? Considering that most of those people immediately packed up, and if they haven't already gone, they are in the process of getting ready to leave."

Ambassador Grandon licked his lips, carefully considering his answer. "Lord Rahl, I stayed behind for the moment because I felt that I at least owed you an explanation."

Richard frowned. "An explanation for what?"

"For why the others have left, or are leaving, and what was decided. You see, we have heard what you and the Mother

Confessor have had to say about prophecy. We have heard what Nathan, the prophet, has had to say, but we respectfully have our own view of it."

Richard bit back a flippant answer. He paused and took a deep breath. He was the one, after all, who had told all of these people, who formerly had gone to their knees to chant a devotion to the Lord Rahl, that their lives were their own, and that they should rise up and live them. He expected them to think for themselves, to make their own reasoned decisions, to live their own lives.

Richard laid a hand on the man's shoulder. "Ambassador Grandon, we are a free people. We all need to cooperate for our common prosperity, but I am not going to torture to death those who don't want to follow my way of doing things. That was what the war was fought over—the idea that we are all entitled to live our own lives as we see fit. When I said that your lives are your own to live, I meant it. I would hope that people would see the wisdom and experience in what we say, and choose to go along willingly with us."

The ambassador looked humbled, and regretful. "I cannot tell you how grateful I am to hear such a sentiment, Lord Rahl. I guess that's one reason it makes what I stayed to tell you all the more difficult to say."

"Just tell me the truth, Ambassador. I can't fault you for speaking truth."

The man nodded. "You see, Lord Rahl, we realized that you have your own point of view about prophecy, and we can even understand that you undoubtedly have your own good reasons for that belief, but we believe that we need to know what prophecy says so that we may use it to help our people live better lives.

"Queen Orneta made the choice to throw her loyalty

behind Hannis Arc, to follow his guidance with the aid of prophecy, if he will agree to give it. We don't know for certain how he will receive our request for him to share his knowledge of prophecy but we have reason to believe that he will be open to our entreaty. After she made this decision, we all decided the same, that we wanted to listen to a leader who revealed prophecy and uses it, rather than . . . rather than you."

Richard hooked his thumbs in his belt as he took another deep breath. "I see."

"After that, when we were gathered up there on the balcony, the abbot asked the Mord-Sith who came to take the queen away what this was about, and she said that it was about the most recent prophecy. Abbot Dreier asked what the prophecy said. The Mord-Sith said that she didn't know, but that a number of people had had the prophecy. When the abbot tried to stop the woman, she used her Agiel against him—hurt him quite badly."

He gestured at the dead woman lying in a pool of blood. "The Mord-Sith took Queen Orneta away. We followed and heard what she did. After killing the queen, when she came out, we all thought we might be next. That's why none of us really looked at her. Anyway, she left then, and we were all spared. So, some of us immediately went to the fortune-teller down in the halls."

"Sabella," Richard said. "I know her."

Ambassador Grandon nodded. "That would be her."

"So what did Sabella say?"

"She said that an omen had come to her the day before, an omen saying 'A queen's choice will cost her her life.' This, of course, was after Queen Orneta had told us that her choice was to throw her loyalty behind Hannis Arc in return for his guidance with revealing prophecy." He flicked a hand toward the dead queen. "Shortly after, Orneta lost her life.

"Prophecy had been fulfilled. Further proof to many of us that we are right to believe we need to be informed of prophecy, the need to follow a man familiar with prophecy, and one who will reveal it to us."

"I see."

The ambassador hung his head. "I'm sorry, Lord Rahl, but it is our lives and we choose to use whatever tools we can to preserve life. This is what we decided, and the reason many of the representatives are leaving. Some are already gone. Some are leaving as we speak. Some are packing now and will be leaving yet tonight."

"You among them, Ambassador?"

He nodded as he tugged on his beard again. "Yes, Lord Rahl. Please do not think of it as turning away from you, but rather as wanting to open our ears to listen to a man who will reveal the dark secrets of prophecy to us."

Dark secrets. Richard was at his wits' end with the darkness that had come into the palace since that day he found the machine that issued prophecy.

Richard stood not far from a dead queen, her death predicted by the prophecy on the metal strip in his pocket. He was filled with a swirl of emotions. He thought it best to keep them to himself, especially the one wishing he could give all this up and go back to Hartland and work as a simple woods guide.

"I understand, Ambassador. I hope that you and the others will one day come to see my reasoning, and why I believe it must be as the Mother Confessor and I have said it must. You and the others are welcome to return to the palace if you have a change of heart."

The man bowed his head again and then, after one more quick glance at the queen lying dead nearby, turned and left.

On his way out, he passed Nicci on her way in. She looked uncharacteristically gloomy. She cast a brief glance at the dead queen as she was being wrapped in a shroud before being lifted onto a litter and taken away for burial. Out in the hall a quiet group of the cleaning staff were standing solemnly by to come in and scrub the place clean of all the blood.

"I hear that she was killed by a Mord-Sith," Nicci said.

"I'm happy to have any of us admit to killing," Cara said, "but only when we have actually done it."

She was in a foul mood and Richard couldn't say he blamed her. His own mood wasn't really any better.

Nicci didn't look to want to debate the subject. She looked like she had something on her mind.

"What is it?" he asked.

Nicci briefly gazed into his eyes. "First of all, I want you to know that I just came from your room. Kahlan is sleeping peacefully. I personally checked the room for anything out of place, anything out of the ordinary, any traces of magic of any kind, any problem at all. Kahlan slept peacefully through it all. Then I checked all the men guarding the room and the area. Rikka and Berdine were in the corridors. I told them to keep their eyes open for anything that seemed even slightly odd, any sign at all of anything."

Richard frowned. "What's going on?"

Her resolute gaze met his. "I was with Zedd, down with the machine, when it started softly, slowly, the way you described. It built speed, then it inscribed a prophecy on a metal strip. The strip came out cool, like you told us it did when the machine then said that it had had dreams. It then went quiet and still again. Zedd is staying down with it in case it issues any more omens. He asked me to bring the strip it inscribed to you. On the way, when I checked on Kahlan, like I told you, I asked Berdine to translate the strip for me."

Richard was getting seriously suspicious. "So what does this one say?"

She took a breath to steel herself and then handed him the strip. "I would rather you translate it yourself. I don't wish to be the messenger in this."

Frowning, Richard took the strip and looked at the one rather simple emblem on the strip, followed by a more complex element.

He felt blood rush to his face in hot rage.

The strip said *The hounds will take her from you.*

He clenched his jaw. "That's it, I've had it with that machine. I want it destroyed!"

As he headed for the door, Nicci and Cara raced to catch up with him.

66

Kahlan woke to the feel of warm breath on her face. It made absolutely no sense.

The alarm of her inner voice warned her to keep her eyes closed and to remain perfectly still.

She frantically tried to understand what was going on, but she couldn't make sense of it. She knew that it wasn't Richard. He was worried about her and would never do something that would frighten her, especially when she was not feeling well.

Her left arm hurt. She only dimly recalled Zedd putting something on it and wrapping it in bandages. But her arm was not the immediate problem.

Her experience during the war, and even more, her training and experience as a Confessor, automatically took over. She ignored her still-throbbing headache, her nausea, the ache of her arm, and put her full focus on the problem at hand. Without opening her eyes, or moving, or changing her breathing, Kahlan began to take assessment.

Something was keeping her tightly pinned under the blanket. She tried to imagine what could be holding her down. As she put her mind to understanding it, she thought that it felt rather like someone on their hands and knees directly over her, with a hand and a knee to either side, pinning the blanket down.

She knew that the room was heavily guarded, so she was at a loss to imagine how anyone intending harm could have gotten in. She couldn't think of a single person who would do such a thing as a joke. She realized that the smell of the thing was decidedly unpleasant and not human.

The heavy breathing had an element of a low growl to it.

Ever so carefully, she slitted her eyelids open just the tiniest bit.

Near to her, to each side, she could see something slender. Something slender and hairy. She realized that it could only be the front legs of an animal like a wolf or dog, possibly a coyote. In the dim light of the single lamp on the bedside table, it was hard to tell the color.

With that bit of information, the frantic, bewildered confusion began to clear. Her thoughts of what it could possibly be, thankfully, began to coalesce.

It was not a person on all fours over her. It was some sort of animal. By the weight of it on the bed, whatever it was had to be rather big, too big, she realized, to be a coyote.

And then she heard the distinctive low growl, and felt the hot breath again. By the smell of the thing, the legs she could see, and the panting growl she was pretty sure that it had to be a big dog, possibly a wolf.

She was having a great deal of difficulty conceiving of what it could be doing in her bedroom.

She recalled, then, the dog that had crashed into their bedroom door, the wildly aggressive dog that the soldiers had been forced to kill.

She didn't know how this dog could have gotten into the

room. She set aside the effort of trying to figure it out. It didn't matter how it got in. It only mattered that it had, and that the animal was dangerous—she had no doubt of that.

With her body pinned under the blanket, there was no hope of leaping up and racing for the door. It was too close to her. She would never make it.

As she opened her eyelids just the slightest bit more, she could see the muzzle snarled back, and the long teeth. If she tried to jump up, slowed by being trapped under the blanket as she was, the beast would rip off her face before she had a chance to get her arms up to defend herself.

She realized that the animal was standing between her right side and her right arm. Her left arm was trapped close to her body, but her right arm was not; it was outside the animal's legs.

She knew that she had only one chance. She also knew that she could not delay. Dogs and wolves both had a predator instinct. They were excited by prey trying to get away, by it running. As she lay perfectly still, the prey drive was being kept in check.

But only as long as she was perfectly still, and only for the moment. She knew that the dog could decide to act first.

She could hear the low, menacing growl getting deeper, getting a little louder. She could feel the vibration of it in her chest.

The dog was deciding to flush its prey.

She had no time to waste. She knew that once it sank its teeth into her, there would be no escape.

She had to take the initiative.

67

Kahlan slowly pulled in a deep breath, preparing herself. The dog sensed something. The growl rose in power. Suddenly, with all her strength, as fast as she possibly could, she used her right arm to whip the blanket up, over, and around the dog. It began to lunge. In an instant, though, before it could fully react, before it could drive forward and before its teeth could reach her face, she had the beast rolled up in the blanket.

The rotating momentum of throwing the blanket over and around it, of enveloping and trapping the animal, rolled them both over the side of the bed. They crashed to the floor, Kahlan on top of the powerful, struggling dog. Its legs, encased in the blanket, kicked frantically to escape.

Kahlan knew there were guards right outside the door. She tried to cry out for help, but her throat was so sore that her voice was gone. She couldn't bring forth a scream.

Fortunately, she had just missed knocking the bedside lamp off onto the floor with them, so she could see what she was doing. From years of experience, Kahlan instinctively reached to the knife at her belt so that she could dispatch the wildly thrashing beast.

The knife wasn't there.

She was confused at first as to why not, wondering if she had lost it when she rolled off the bed. Almost at the same time, she realized that she didn't usually wear it in the palace. She kept it in her pack, now. As she fought the dog, she looked up in the dimly lit room to see where the door was, hoping that she could try to make an escape.

That was when she saw the glowing eyes of three more dogs near the door, heads down, ears back, teeth bared, drool hanging from their mouths. They were big, powerfully built, dark, short-haired dogs with thick, muscular necks.

She couldn't imagine how in the world they had managed to get into the room. As she frantically looked around for a way to escape, she saw that one of the double doors at the back of the room was partially opened.

It was all she could do to keep the animal wrapped in the blanket under her at bay. Its hind legs kicked as it snapped and tried to bite. She had stuffed a wad of blanket in its mouth. The confusing fight was keeping the other dogs from joining in, at least for the moment. She knew that at any second they would attack.

As she looked up again, checking on where the three were, she saw one of them take a step closer.

She also saw her backpack not far to the right, near the foot of the bed. Her knife was in her pack.

There was no way she could hope to get through a door guarded by the three snarling hounds. Her only chance was to get her knife so she would at least have a fighting chance to defend herself.

Without pausing to consider the wisdom of it, she threw a leg over the squirming dog trapped in the blanket and stretched to the right for her pack. She just managed to catch the strap with her fingers.

As the lead dog of the three bounded toward her, she swung her pack with all her might. It knocked the dog from its feet and sent it sliding across the floor.

Without missing a beat, she sprang to her feet, kicked the dog in the blanket as hard as she could in the ribs, and bolted for the open door at the back of the room.

Out of nowhere from the darkness at the sides of the room, other big dogs lunged out at her, just missing her.

Kahlan gasped in fright and dove through the open door out to the small balcony. The railing caught her in the middle, driving the wind out of her. She was lucky it did, because she could see that it was quite a drop to the ground, a drop that would have killed her.

She spun to shut the door but the dogs were already through. She saw that up against the side of the building, not far from her balcony, there was another balcony. There were several feet of space separating them, and quite a drop between them.

There was no time to consider it, and no other option. She put a foot up onto the top of the railing and used it to boost herself across the space toward the other balcony. Teeth snapped closed, just missing her ankle.

She landed on the top of the fat railing on the second balcony, but slipped and fell sprawling on the floor. Looking up, she saw that on the far side of the balcony there was a narrow stairway down to the ground. She looked back and saw the dogs stand with their front paws on the balcony of her room, looking to see where she had gone.

She looked back at the stairs. This had to be how they had gotten up to her room. They had come up the stairs, leaped across to the balcony outside her room, and gotten in that way.

She saw the dogs back up on the balcony to her room, getting the space they needed to make the leap. She had no time to stop and think. She was in full terror mode as she jumped up and raced for the stairs.

She bounded down the steps three at a time as the first dog made the leap across. She panted, out of breath, as she frantically ran down the steps, hooked a hand on the end cap of the railing to spin herself around for the next flight, and launched herself down those as well.

She looked back briefly, reasoning that she could use her backpack to fend them off if they got too close. When she saw the snapping jaws lunging for her, she realized that fending them off with her pack was not going to work. She ran all the faster down the steps, taking each turn by hooking her hand over the newel and spinning around to change directions at each switchback flight of stairs.

Having to make those turns slowed the snarling pack of dogs as they slid on the stone, scrambling to gain footing as they turned the corners. Kahlan was able to gain a lead on them. It was not a comfortable lead, but it at least gained her a bit of distance from the teeth.

Her head hurt so much that she thought she might simply collapse and then they would have her.

She remembered the prediction of the woman who had murdered her children, the woman Kahlan had taken with her power, the prediction that fangs would come for Kahlan and tear her apart.

Kahlan ran all the harder.

But even as she ran, she knew that she was near the end of her endurance. She could feel her strength waning. As she found herself racing across the ground in the dead of night, she was near to dropping from exhaustion. Behind, the hounds were coming, and they were catching up again. She had no choice but to keep running.

The hammering pain in her head was close to overwhelming her. She knew that she would not be able to go on for long, and then the hounds would have her.

She remembered the horrific sight of Catherine, killed by animals of some kind. Kahlan was pretty sure that she now knew what had killed the pregnant queen.

The same thing had killed Catherine and her unborn child that was now after Kahlan. There was no doubt that if these beasts caught her, they would rip her apart the way they had ripped apart Catherine. That image, that memory, powered her legs.

The only chance she had was to run. But even if she hadn't been near to the end of her strength, the dogs were running faster. What distance she had gained on the stairs, they were rapidly making up. Worse, the initial fright that had powered her and carried her on, that burst of fear-driven strength, was expended. She was near to dropping.

She had to do something.

Kahlan saw a wagon up ahead in the darkness moving away from her.

She changed course a little and ran toward it. She was out of breath, but she knew that even a momentary pause in her maximum effort would mean that the hounds would sink their teeth into her and bring her down once and for all—they were that close.

Kahlan nearly cried out with giddy joy when she reached the wagon, but she didn't have the voice or the breath. She timed her paces right and leaped up onto the iron rung step hanging down off the back.

As the dogs leaped, snapping, trying to get ahold of her leg, she pulled herself up to the second step and, with a final mighty effort, dove up and over into the wagon.

As she landed, she cracked her head hard on something dead solid. The pain was stunning.

Her world went black.

68

It was deep in the middle of the night by the time Richard finally stepped off the spiral stairs and into the room with Regula. It had been a long journey from the guest quarters up to the Garden of Life. The palace complex was a sprawling city and it sometimes seemed that he spent half his time crossing back and forth through it.

He gritted his teeth in anger at the sight of the machine. He was fed up with the way its predictions had been at the core of every one of the recent deaths. And now the machine was predicting that the hounds would take Kahlan from him.

He couldn't get the image out of his mind of the manner in which the hounds had taken Catherine from her husband. The thought of that happening to Kahlan had him seeing red.

On the way from the murdered Queen Orneta, despite Nicci's assurance that Kahlan was sleeping peacefully, he had stopped in to check for himself. He had slipped quietly into the room and by the light of a single lamp burning on a table by the bed he had seen her, covered by the blanket he had tucked under her chin earlier, sound asleep. Her breathing had been even and she wasn't tossing and turning, so it seemed to Richard that she was resting comfortably. He had gently kissed her forehead and left her to her rest.

He had also checked with Rikka, Berdine, and the soldiers to make sure that they understood that anything at all unusual was to be taken as dead serious. They all understood.

The whole time, the words from the machine, *The hounds will take her from you*, kept running through his mind.

Zedd looked up when he saw Richard coming. "What is it?"

Richard flicked his hand at the machine. "Remember the prediction the machine issued earlier this evening? 'A queen's choice will cost her her life.'"

"What of it?" Zedd asked. "Have you figured out what it means?"

Richard nodded. "Turns out it was about Queen Orneta. She made a decision to throw her allegiance behind Hannis Arc, of Fajin Province, because he believes in the use of prophecy, deals in it all the time, and would be only too happy to reveal it to her and anyone else who wants to be guided by it. A short time later she was killed."

"Killed? How?"

Richard took a deep breath. "Killed by a Mord-Sith. It makes no sense. I don't want to believe that one of them did it, but there is no doubt that it was done at the hands of a Mord-Sith."

"I see." With a troubled expression, Zedd turned and paced a few steps away as he considered the implications.

Richard pulled the strip of metal out of his pocket and waved it as he spoke. "The machine later issued this omen— the one you sent with Nicci."

Zedd looked back over his shoulder. "What does it say?"

"It says 'The hounds will take her from you.'"

Zedd's hazel eyes reflected how tired he was. His gaze sank. "Dear spirits," he whispered.

Richard pointed back at the machine. "Zedd, I want this thing destroyed."

"Destroyed?" Zedd, rubbing his chin with his fingertips, looked up with a frown. "I understand your feelings, Richard, but do you really think that's wise?"

"Do you know of any prophecy, any at all, that results in a joyous event? Any you've seen throughout your life?"

Zedd seemed puzzled by the question, and his frown deepened. "Yes, of course. I don't recall them exactly, offhand, but I know I've seen them before and recall the general nature of a few. They are not as plentiful as more ominous prophecies, but there are prophecies of joyous events sprinkled regularly throughout books of prophecy. Nathan, as well, has had prophecies of happy events or outcomes."

"And has this machine issued a single prophecy other than simply predictions of suffering and death?"

Zedd glanced at the machine standing silently in the center of the gloomy room lit by the strange light from the proximity spheres.

"I don't suppose it has."

"Doesn't that strike you as odd?"

"Odd? What do you mean?"

"There's no balance. Prophecy is magic. Magic has to have balance. Even the existence of prophecy itself has to be balanced by free will. But there is no balance to the prophecies this thing has been issuing, is there? It's all death and suffering."

"There is the one about it having dreams," Nicci offered.

Richard turned to her. "But is that really joyous? And even if it is, is it really a prophecy? I don't think it's either."

"Then what was it?" she asked.

Richard thought about it for a moment. "I don't think it's prophecy. To me it sounds more like the machine is asking a question about itself. I've had dreams . . . why have I had dreams? That's what it asked."

He turned back to Zedd. "But the prophecies of suffering and death that it has been issuing are all the same ominous predictions. They have no balance."

Zedd looked truly puzzled. "What's your point, my boy?"

"My point is that I'm not sure that these are really legitimate prophecies."

Nicci looked skeptical. "What else could they be, then?"

"I think it's possible that someone is planting these omens and then carrying them out to make it look like real prophecy coming true. They want us to think they're prophecy. It would be like if I said that I'd had a premonition last night that I was going to draw my sword and touch your shoulder with it, and then I did just that to give the prediction validity. That may sound like I had given prophecy and it came true, but it wasn't really prophecy."

"You think someone may be sending these prophecies, or made-up prophecies, through the machine?" Zedd poked a bony finger through his unruly thatch of white hair and scratched his scalp. "Richard, I can't begin to imagine how such a thing could be done, much less know if it's even possible."

Richard threw up his arm. "I don't care. Just because I can't figure out if someone really is doing this, or how, doesn't mean that I should keep letting them get away with it."

"But to destroy such a thing without knowing anything about it seems—"

"We do know something about it," Richard said, cutting

him off. He fisted his hands. "It has been predicting terrible things and they have come true. I want these murders to stop. I want Kahlan to be safe. I want this thing silenced."

Exasperated, Zedd looked at Nicci.

"I'm afraid that I don't have an argument against it," she said in answer to Zedd's unspoken question. "There's something about this machine that has had me worried since the first moment I saw it. It was buried for a reason. Richard may have a point. Nothing good has come from it since it was discovered."

Zedd looked from Nicci to Richard. "What of the rest of the book, *Regula*, that is hidden away in the Temple of the Winds?"

Richard gestured vaguely into the distance. "Like you said, it's in the Temple of the Winds. Even if we travel there, getting in won't be easy. Even if we get in, the place is immense. There's no telling how long it will take us to find the rest of the book, if it's still there and if it isn't hidden. There's no telling if it would even be of any use to us. We have a problem, and it's right here, right now, in this room."

Zedd took a deep breath and then sighed as he considered it.

"Well," he finally said, "you may have a point. I have to admit, I haven't liked this thing from the moment it was discovered. As Nicci says, it was buried for a reason. No one goes to this much trouble to bury and hide the existence of something unless it was causing big problems."

"Then let's stop wasting time," Richard said. "We need to put a stop to it now."

Resigned, Zedd motioned for them to step back, ushering Richard and Nicci into the protected landing of the spiral stairs where Cara stood guard.

Without further fuss, Zedd turned back to the machine and ignited wizard's fire between his outstretched palms.

The room lit with rolling ribbons of orange and yellow light that played off the stone walls. Zedd's white hair was made orange in the light coming from the sinister inferno, which he turned over and over between his hands, working it into a lethal servant. The boiling ball of fire built in intensity, hissing and popping with purpose.

Satisfied that it was compacted the way he wanted it, Zedd finally flung the glowing sphere of liquid fire toward the square metal box sitting in the center of the room. The tempestuous inferno cast flickering light across the floor, walls, and ceiling as it flew, all the while hissing with deadly menace.

Richard felt the powerful concussion in his chest as the sphere of liquid flame exploded against the unyielding machine. The liquid wizard's fire, one of the most feared substances in existence because it burned so violently, engulfed the machine, crackling as it poured down the sides, burning with white-hot intensity.

Wizard's fire unleashed in a confined space was extraordinarily intense and profoundly dangerous. Even though Richard, Nicci, and Cara turned their faces away from the inferno, they still had to put hands up to shield themselves against the brutal heat and light from the concentrated conflagration. The burning roar was thunderous.

It felt as if the entire world were being consumed.

CHAPTER

69

When the violence of the wizard's fire at last subsided, Richard was finally able to open his eyes and take his hand away from his face. As the last glowing clots of conjured conflagration dripped onto the floor and extinguished with a steamy hiss, and the smoke cleared away, Richard expected to see Regula reduced to a puddle of molten metal.

It was not.

He saw that the machine was still sitting in the center of the room, looking exactly the same as the first time he had seen it. It looked untouched.

He was certain that the outer walls of the machine would be scorching hot, but as he approached it he felt no residual heat radiating from the metal. Richard cautiously reached out, carefully testing, then tentatively touching the metal surface. It was cool to the touch.

Richard had seen some of the terrible damage done by wizard's fire, yet it had done nothing to the machine. It hadn't even scoured the patina of corrosion off the surface. The symbols on the sides, the same symbols that appeared in the book *Regula*, were still in perfect condition.

If he hadn't seen the wizard's fire engulfing it with his own eyes, he might not have believed that anything had happened, much less that it had been the target of some of the most powerful conjured magic in existence.

Nicci, standing beside Richard, tested the surface with her fingers.

"Well, Additive Magic obviously didn't work. Maybe it's time to try something a little more destructive." She motioned for the rest of them to move back.

Richard shepherded Zedd and Cara back into the protection of the stairwell. He knew what Nicci was going to do. He could see the aura of power crackling around the sorceress. It gave her a kind of glowing, otherworldly appearance, almost as if she were only there in spirit.

The sorceress lifted her hands out toward the machine. The sizzling aura around her flickered with intensity. He knew that others couldn't see it, but he had always sensed the field of power around certain people. No aura he had ever seen was as strong as Nicci's.

Black lightning—Subtractive Magic—ignited in the room with a thunderous thump. Dust lifted from the floor. The proximity spheres instantly went dark.

The black lightning twisted together with a blindingly bright sudden discharge of Additive Magic. The rope of Subtractive Magic was so dark that it was like looking through a crack in the world of life into the underworld itself.

In a way, it was.

The inky black lightning connected with the machine. The end played over the surface, flickering up and down it. The rest of it, between Nicci and the machine, whipped wildly about the room as it crackled and popped where the two flows of power, impossible darkness and blinding light, touched. The air of the room smelled like burning sulfur and vibrated with the power of the conflicting forces fighting each other. Both dark and light twisted with savage effort to dominate the other, to occupy the same place at the same time. The machine was bathed in the hot glow of the Additive Magic, only to then vanish into the void of Subtractive Magic.

It was a terrifying display of incompatible powers focused with destructive intent on the omen machine.

As abruptly as it started, it stopped.

The sudden quiet made Richard's ears throb. The proximity spheres brightened, but slowly.

"It isn't working," Nicci said as her hands dropped to her sides. The aura around her calmed and then extinguished.

Richard stepped out of the stairwell. "How could it not work? What's wrong?"

"I've never felt anything like it before." Nicci ran her hand over the top of the machine as if trying to perceive its inner secrets through that light caress. "I could sense that it simply wasn't connecting."

"What do you mean it wasn't connecting?"

Nicci shook her head in disbelief as she stared at the machine. "I create a node at the other end, at the target. The flow of power then fills the void between me and the target. The node is there to create a link for the power to seek, a route to follow. Once the connection is established, the two flows of energy are released into the node, destroying what it's attached to. It happens instinctively and almost instantaneously.

"This time, as I cast my ability outward, the node just couldn't find the target, wouldn't settle where I intended, almost as if the object wasn't there. Because of that, my power couldn't connect with the object." She turned to look up at

Richard. "I'm sorry, Richard. I tried. It should have been utterly destroyed, but I couldn't even scratch the metal of the outer shell."

Richard wasn't satisfied. "There has to be a way."

"This is something the likes of which none of us has ever seen before." Nicci shook her head. "No wonder they buried it."

Richard knew something that would cut any metal.

As he drew the Sword of Truth, the unique ring of steel filled the gloomy room.

With the floodgates to the sword's magic opened, its magic inundated him. He gave himself over to it, letting the storm of power thunder through him. He let it rage for a time, letting it seep into every fiber of his being.

The others in the room, recognizing all too well what he intended to do, backed away.

Filled with the fury of the sword's magic mixing with his own, Richard slowly lifted the gleaming blade and touched the steel to his forehead.

He let his own anger at the danger Kahlan was in surge through him, interlacing with the sword's righteous wrath.

Eyes closed, he gave himself over to the volatile fusing of magic.

"Blade," he whispered, "be true this day."

With both hands, Richard lifted the sword high over his head. Without pause and with all his might and fury, he drove the blade down toward the machine.

The sword's tip whistled as it sliced through the air.

Richard screamed with the power of the magic coursing through him, with the power of his rage. The blade arced around and down toward the machine with lightning speed.

A hairsbreadth from touching the machine, the blade stopped cold in midair.

Richard was taken by surprise. He hadn't expected the blade to stop the way it had. His muscles ached with the expected release that didn't happen.

The sword's magic worked by intent. If the one wielding the sword believed that what he was attacking was the enemy, or evil, the sword would cut through it, cut through anything. If the Seeker believed the person evil, there was no defense against the blade, not even a wall of steel.

But if the Seeker, somewhere deep inside, in the darkest corner of his mind, believed that the adversary was innocent, then the blade would not cut through even paper to harm them.

Richard stood with the sword tightly gripped in both fists, the blade motionless in midair just above the top of the machine, a trail of sweat running down his temple.

And then the machine began to wake.

Shafts slowly started turning, gears engaged, and yet more of the mechanism began to gather momentum.

W ell isn't that something," Zedd said as he stepped out of the stairwell. "Seems that none of us has it in us to destroy the machine."

Richard wondered why.

He staggered back from the machine as its internal mechanism gradually came to life, the internal parts progressively gathering momentum.

He stood silently staring at the waking machine, stunned that the sword had halted so abruptly. He hadn't expected it to.

He'd had the same experience before, when somewhere deep down inside he'd had a glimmer of doubt. This time, as well, some part of him didn't think the machine was at fault for the things that had happened. Some part of him thought that it was wrong to blame the machine for the terrible things that had happened.

If he hadn't had those doubts, he knew, the sword would have shattered the machine.

Even so, he had fully committed himself. It was disorienting to come back from that lethal brink.

The fact that doubts existed prevented the sword from

doing harm. But that didn't mean that those doubts were justified. It could very well be that the machine was the source of the deaths and they would need to destroy it.

As the gears came up to speed, and the light from within projected the machine's emblem up onto the ceiling, the room filled with the mechanical rumble of all the interior components at last in full motion.

Richard didn't have to look through the window. He knew what was happening. In a moment, a metal strip dropped into the tray. He slid his sword back into its scabbard and tested the strip briefly, finding it cool to the touch. He pulled it out and in his head started translating the message.

"So," Zedd asked impatiently, "what does it say?"

"It says 'You can destroy those who speak the truth, but you cannot destroy the truth itself.'"

Zedd cast a dark look of suspicion at Regula. "So now the machine is spouting Wizard's Rules?"

"So it would seem," Richard said. He laid his hands on the top of the machine, leaning his weight on it, recovering from the experience of using the sword and having it stop cold, as he thought about what he should do next. "I'd still like to know how to destroy it if we have to."

"The thing is obviously shielded somehow," Nicci said. "But I can't detect its presence and it doesn't work like any shield I've ever encountered. There are powers involved here that we don't understand."

Zedd was nodding as she spoke. "It would appear that sometime in the past, someone else must have tried to destroy it as well. No one would have gone to this much trouble and effort to bury this thing unless it was the only option remaining to them."

"I wish I knew that story," Nicci said.

"We may one day end up having to bury it ourselves," Richard said, "just like whoever buried it in the first place."

The machine, never entirely still since inscribing the strip with a Wizard's Rule, spun back up to speed. In a moment another strip dropped into the tray. It was as cool to the touch as the one before. Richard pulled it out and translated for the others.

" 'You would fault me for speaking truth?' "

Richard recognized the words he himself had spoken to Ambassador Grandon. It was unnerving that the machine had just repeated them back to him.

He realized, then, the reason the sword would not destroy the machine. He didn't think, deep down inside himself, that the machine was actually the cause of the problems.

"I guess I did," he whispered aloud in answer to its question. He leaned on the machine. "All of this isn't exactly your doing, is it?" he asked the machine. "You're just the messenger."

The machine hardly slowed, and in a moment it was back at full speed, inscribing another strip. Richard pulled the cool metal out as it dropped into the slot and read it aloud.

" 'When the messenger becomes the enemy, the enemy gets buried.' "

Zedd, coming up beside Richard, also laid a hand on the machine. "Isn't that interesting."

Richard wondered exactly how, and why, the machine had managed to get itself unburied.

Again the machine gradually spun up to full speed and then pulled another strip through the beam of light, burning symbols in the language of Creation onto it. When the strip dropped into the tray, Richard paused for a moment before pulling it out.

"Well, come on," Zedd said impatiently, "have a look."

Richard finally pulled the strip out and silently worked the translation. It was more complex than the previous ones, but he finally got it and read it aloud.

"'Darkness has found me. It will find you as well.'"

Nicci stepped up beside Richard. "Darkness has found it?"

"That's what I had suspected," Richard said. "I think it's telling us that someone is using it, speaking through it. That's the reason the sword wouldn't harm it.

"The morning after Cara and Ben's wedding, the boy down in the market, Henrik, said that darkness was seeking darkness. He also asked why he'd had dreams. None of it made sense at the time, so we thought the boy was sick and delusional, but it had to be that the machine was somehow speaking through him, saying that it knew someone was trying to coopt it. Maybe when it began, the only way the machine could describe it was as darkness finding it and interpreted the experience of someone speaking through it as dreams."

Nicci's brow tightened. "You mean you think that what the boy said was actually the machine? That it was a cry for help?"

Richard shrugged. "Could be."

Zedd let out a noisy breath as he shook his head. "I don't know, Richard. I think we have to be careful about letting ourselves act like this collection of gears and wheels and shafts can actually say anything as a result of conscious intellect.

We're all starting to act like this thing can think on its own, like it's alive. It's a machine. Machines can't think."

"Then how is it answering Lord Rahl's questions?" Cara asked. They all turned and looked at her. She flicked a hand out at the machine. "How is it managing to tell us what we want to know, to fill in some of the blanks as we go along?"

"We might merely be reading more into it than is warranted," Zedd told her.

Cara looked unconvinced. "It says what it says. We are not making up or imagining the things it says."

Zedd smoothed back his unruly mass of wavy white hair. "There is a children's game called Ask the Oracle. It's a small box with a round hole in the top. On the side are painted scenes of the oracle with mysterious mist curling around her as she communes with the spirit world. The box holds a number of answers already written out on small discs. A child will ask a question—like will I marry someone I love when I grow up, or does so-and-so really like me—and then reach into the box and pull out a disc with an answer printed on it. They then replace the disc and the box is shaken for the next player's turn to select an answer to their question."

"Really?" Cara looked skeptical. "And it actually works?"

"Pretty well, actually. The answers are things like 'Most assuredly,' or 'Not unless something changes,' or 'The spirits say yes,' or 'The answer is in doubt,' or 'It seems likely,' or 'It won't be,' or 'Ask again later when the spirits are willing to answer.' You see, no matter what disc the child pulls out of the box, it seems to them like the box is directly answering the question they asked.

"But it's just a trick of the human mind to think that the answers fit the question, that the oracle of the box hears their question and can answer it. We're all gullible to some extent.

The answers are general in nature, but because they often seem to be so accurate people think the oracle of the box really can reveal the answers.

"Some people believe wholeheartedly in the oracle in the box. Some people actually believe that they really do have some magical power, or some connection to the spirit world which guides their hand to select the correct disc. But there is no magic involved. It is a simple trick that the human mind plays on itself."

Cara folded her arms. "So you think that this machine is simply a big elaborate trick?"

"I don't know." Zedd clasped his hand. "I'm just saying that we need to be cautious and not jump to conclusions. It's often easy to believe in ready-made answers."

Richard didn't think the explanation was that simple. "I don't know, Zedd. There seems to be more to it."

"Like what?"

"Well, the way the machinery starts up when it's about to give terrible prophecies is distinctive. It starts abruptly, all at once. And another thing, the metal strips come out burning hot. But when it seems to be . . . I don't know, communicating I guess you could say, then it starts gradually and the strips come out cool to the touch.

"We've been assuming that the strips that come out are the responsibility of the machine. I think that maybe two very different things are going on."

"I agree," Nicci said. "It could be that someone is using it, giving it something to say, possibly even forcing it to say certain things. When they force it to speak, the strips come out hot. When it speaks on its own the strips are cool."

"You think the machine is being exploited?" Frowning, Zedd scratched his scalp. "Let's assume for the moment that it's true. Who do you think would be doing such a thing? And why?"

Richard leaned a hip on the machine. "What is our problem?"

Zedd shrugged. "Our problem?"

"Our problem," he explained, "our reason for being down in this long-buried room with this exiled device, is prophecy. What does the machine do? Give prophecy. What has been central in all the recent deaths? Prophecy. What have all the representatives decided they must have? Prophecy. What has us running around in circles, always one step behind events? Prophecy from this machine."

"We know all that." Zedd arched an eyebrow. "Is there a point?"

Richard nodded. "Look at the way everyone's interest in prophecy has escalated. The prophecies that this machine puts forth have been conveniently repeated through others all over the palace. That insures that everyone knows them, which gets everyone stirred up about the importance of prophecy. Rumor and then gossip about the existence of an 'omen machine' have been on every tongue. People think we're keeping prophecy from them, that we don't want them to be safe from harm."

Zedd was paying closer attention. "What's your theory?"

"It seems to me that someone is planting these seeds." Richard leaned in a bit toward his grandfather. "What has made people believe all the more in prophecy?" With a finger, he tapped the machine. "The prophecies that have come from the machine which shortly all come true, happening exactly as they are foretold in the prophecy. That's where it all started. It has become a ghoulish game—like that children's game you describe but with bloody consequences.

"The prophecies always come true, so people believe in their importance all the more and they're even more eager to know the next one. Because this machine fits their belief that prophecy knows their future, they demand from us to know what prophecy says. And as you told us, back in Aydindril, and I would bet everywhere else, prophecy is on everyone's mind. You said that there is a brisk trade in the prophecy business. Doesn't that strike you as rather strange?"

"It has from the first," Zedd confirmed.

"Back here, the machine's prophecies have convinced the representatives of all those people preoccupied with prophecy that we're wrong, that prophecy really is as easy to understand as it sounds. They therefore can't understand why we wouldn't want to reveal the danger to their lives that is so easy to see in the prophecies they've heard. The prophecies from this machine have helped whip everyone into a frenzy of belief."

"What would you expect? They've come true," Zedd said.

"Have they? Have you ever known prophecy to be so clear-cut and easy to understand, so plainspoken and straightforward? Or to turn out just the way it says, and soon after it says it?"

Zedd looked away as he considered the question. "Actually, I can't say that I have. Prophecy, in all my experience, is ambiguous at best. What's more, it can often take centuries to come to pass. But these all happen soon after they are given."

"That's another reason why I'm so worried about the prophecy that says 'The hounds will take her from you.' The only thing I don't understand is that the strip that said it wasn't like the other dire predictions—it came on a cool strip of metal, not a hot one."

Zedd met his gaze. "Perhaps that means it isn't like the

others. Perhaps this is a real prophecy that has a hidden meaning."

Richard cast a sidelong glance at the machine. "Or it was a warning the machine wanted me to have. On top of that, it just said that darkness had found it, and it will find me as well, like it was warning me. The machine seems to have some kind of connection with me."

Zedd nodded. "That part is certainly clear enough."

"For the prophecies that come out on the hot strips, at least, we know there is no balance. They are all dire."

Zedd frowned back at Richard. "So you're saying that you don't believe that those are legitimate prophecy?"

"You tell me. Now that everyone is caught up in this prophecy frenzy, who have they all turned to for what they want? Who have they sworn loyalty to in exchange for prophecy?"

"Hannis Arc," Cara said.

Richard nodded. "And it just happens to be Abbot Dreier, from Fajin Province, who has told us and everyone else how Hannis Arc believes in using prophecy to help guide his rule, the same as all the representatives want to do. I think Hannis Arc, not real prophecy, could somehow be at the center of this."

"Like you say, though, he's off in Fajin Province." Cara gestured at the machine. "How could he be doing all of these things?"

"I don't know," Richard admitted. "But Abbot Dreier is here. Maybe he's involved, somehow."

Cara circled a finger skyward. "I thought that this place around the machine, the Garden of Life lying protectively over us, was a containment field. The whole point of a containment field is to prevent outside tampering with the dangerous magic inside. On top of that, the whole palace is made in the shape of a spell-form that weakens the gift of all gifted people in here except a Rahl."

Zedd planted his fists on his hips and turned a look on Cara. "Now Mord-Sith have become experts in magic. What next?"

"A talking machine," Nicci said.

Richard picked up a stack of metal strips from the tens of thousands piled against the wall and loaded it into the machine.

"So let's let it talk."

72

When Richard had finished filling the bin with metal strips, he moved around to the other side, to where they came out. He didn't think that it was necessary, but placed his hands on the machine anyway, just in case. Already internal shafts were spinning up to speed, levers clicking into place, and gears engaging. The machine's emblem, rotating on the ceiling, brightened in lines of glowing orange light.

"Do you know who is responsible for the darkness that you say has come into you?" Richard said down at the machine. "Can you name the darkness?"

A strip pulled off the stack and made its way through the machine, passing over the focused beam of light that burned symbols in the language of Creation onto it. When Richard picked it out, all the symbol said was "Darkness."

"That's a big help," Zedd muttered.

Richard ignored his grandfather and turned back to the machine. "Is darkness in you at the moment?"

Again the machine pulled a strip through.

" 'Darkness is not my purpose,' " Richard read from the strip.

Cara folded her arms. "It's starting to sound like that oracle in a box giving us printed discs for answers."

Richard ignored her as well. "Why are you doing this? Why are you speaking through these strips?"

When a strip came out, Richard read it aloud. "'I am fulfilling my purpose, doing as I must.'"

"What is your purpose?" Richard asked immediately.

After the strip had passed through the machine and dropped in the bin, Richard noted that it was still cool. He looked at the symbols and then read the message aloud. "'To fulfill my purpose.'"

Cara rolled her eyes. "No doubt about it, we have printed discs on our hands. Ask it if Ben really likes me. I'd like to hear what the spirits have to say."

Richard ignored her taunt and tried a different line of questioning. "Who created you?"

The strip took a bit longer to pass under the light as the language of Creation burned a longer, more complex message into it. Finally, it dropped into the slot.

Richard held it up in the light to read it. "'I was created by others. I had no choice in it.'"

Richard put a hand on the machine and leaned in toward it. "Why did these others create you?"

When the strip came out, Richard read it silently, then sighed in frustration before translating it for the others. "'I was created to fulfill my purpose.'"

He tossed the strip on top of the machine. "Why does your purpose need to be fulfilled? Why is it important?"

The machine slowed to a stop.

In the silence, they all shared looks.

Richard thought that the conversation had ended, but then the gears started turning again, slowly at first, until it eventually built up to full speed. A tab on the wheel under the strips popped up and pushed out one from the stack of blanks, where it was grabbed by pincers on another wheel and pulled through the mechanism. Richard looked in through the window and saw the strip moving over the light to be inscribed. When it dropped into the slot he pulled the cool strip out and held it up in the light of the proximity spheres.

" 'Because prophecy cannot always be trusted.' "

"That's true enough," Zedd muttered unhappily.

Richard glanced at Zedd, then asked another question. "What do you mean, prophecy can't be trusted? Why not?"

The machine pulled another strip from the stack. When it made its way through and dropped into the slot, Richard was waiting for it. He read it to the others.

" 'Prophecy grows old and corrupted over time.' "

Richard's arm lowered. "But you are the one giving prophecy."

Another strip ran through the machine and dropped into the slot.

" 'I am fulfilling my purpose, doing as I must. You must fulfill your purpose.' " Richard frowned at the machine. "My purpose? What is my purpose in all this?"

Everyone gathered closer as they waited for the next strip. Richard snatched it up when it finally dropped in the slot.

"It says, 'To fulfill my purpose.' " Richard raked his fingers back through his hair as he walked a short distance away. "My purpose is to fulfill your purpose, which is to fulfill your purpose? That makes no sense. This is pointless. We're just going around in circles."

The machine slowly spun down.

"Tell me something I can use!" Richard yelled as he turned

back to Regula. "Tell me how to protect Kahlan from the hounds that you said will take her from me!"

The machine did not answer.

After a long, dragging silence, Nicci laid a comforting hand on the back of his shoulder. "We all need to get some rest, Richard. This is getting us nowhere. We can revisit it later. You should get back up to Kahlan. That's the best way to make sure that the prophecy doesn't come true."

Richard heaved a sigh of frustration. "You're right."

He didn't know if the machine's real purpose was to give prophecy, or if it had been created to do something else. They still had no idea who had created it, why it had been buried and forgotten, or even why it had so abruptly awakened from its dreams. He wasn't even sure if he was convinced that someone could actually direct it. As confusing as the things it said were, he was beginning to wonder if darkness had really taken it over in the first place. He was beginning to think that it was just the machine being perverse. No wonder they had buried it. It was useless.

Zedd patted Richard on the back. "You're the Seeker. I'm sure you will think of something, my boy."

Richard turned away from the machine. "We're not going to find the answers we need tonight. Like Nicci says, we all need to get some rest."

Richard wasn't through asking questions of the machine, but it was late, and he wanted to get back to Kahlan. He knew that after he'd slept on it, he would have more questions. Maybe if he could ask them in the right way he would be able to begin to understand why the machine had been created in the first place and what its real purpose was. But those questions would have to wait.

As they all headed for the stairs, the machine began to rumble into activity again. As they turned back and stared, it gradually came up to full speed. A strip was pulled off the bottom of the stack and through the inner workings.

Richard watched it drop into the slot. He was reluctant to bother to pick this one up and read it. He was tired of the game. He didn't want to play along anymore. He thought that maybe he should leave the strip sitting in the machine until morning.

Before Richard could leave, Zedd pulled the metal strip out, glanced at the symbols, and then handed it to Richard. "It's cool. What does it say?"

Richard reluctantly took the strip from Zedd and held it up in the light to read the circular symbols.

" 'Your only chance is to let the truth escape.' "

"What in the world could that mean?" Cara asked.

Richard clenched the strip in his fist. "It's some kind of riddle. I hate riddles."

73

Kahlan woke, confused at feeling herself rocking. She winced as she pressed a hand over the stunning pain at the top of her head. Her hair felt wet. She pulled her hand away to look at it, but it was too dark to see much other than wetness glistening in the moonlight.

She suspected that she knew all too well what it was. As she struggled up onto her knees she touched her tongue to her hand.

She was right; it was blood.

When she swallowed, her throat was so sore that it made her wince. She ached all over and was shivering with chills even though she was sweating profusely.

Her mind raced, trying to put the fragments of memories together, trying to recall exactly what had happened. Images and impressions flashed in sickening snatches. At the same time the whole world felt like it was moving.

When she was jolted and then bounced, she lost her balance and fell forward. She had to put a hand down to keep from falling over on her face. She felt rough wood. Looking around she realized that she was in a small open space in the back of a wagon. Both the pain throbbing inside her head and the sharp stinging pain at the top of her head made her woozy. She fought back the urge to be sick.

Suddenly, a big dog bounded up out of the darkness, slamming into the side of the wagon, startling her. It dropped back, unable to make it all the way into the wagon, but it hooked its front legs over the side and held on. The dog scrambled, stretching its neck to get its massive head inside, trying to get enough of its weight into the wagon to have the leverage to get all the way in.

Strings of frothy drool whipped from side to side as the animal, even while trying to climb into the wagon, growled and snapped at her.

Kahlan immediately kicked one of the dog's legs off the edge of the wagon. The dog struggled but couldn't hold on with one paw and fell off into the darkness.

The whole nightmare of what had happened up in the bedroom was starting to come back to her—fragments of it, anyway. She remembered, too, what had happened to Queen Catherine, what a pack of dogs had done to her. Kahlan also remembered the prophecy given by the woman Kahlan had taken with her power, the woman who had killed her own children to supposedly spare them a worse death. That woman had told Kahlan that she would suffer a grim fate. When Kahlan had asked what she was talking about, the woman had said, *"Dark things stalking you, running you down. You won't be able to escape them."*

Now dark things were stalking her, running her down. Where the hounds had come from and why they were after her was no longer part of Kahlan's thinking. She was simply frantic to escape them.

Kahlan squinted in the darkness, trying to see up toward the front of the wagon, hoping to see the driver and get some help, but the wagon was piled high with things covered in a stiff canvas tarp. The only way to get to the front, where the driver would be, was to climb either over or around the load. It looked too high to go over in a rocking, bucking wagon, especially considering how dizzy she felt. She tried to look around the load, but she wasn't able to see anyone.

Kahlan called out but her throat was so sore that she could hardly make a sound. No one answered. She thought that over the rumble of the wagon it was probably hard for a driver to hear someone in the back behind his load. More than that, though, her fever was also making her hoarse. She couldn't yell loud enough. She needed to get closer before they would hear her.

Kahlan scrambled to her feet. As she put a foot up onto the side wall of the wagon to climb up around the load, a dog came out of the darkness, lunging wildly, trying to grab her ankle. As she jumped back out of the way, she saw the pack of dogs snarling and growling as they ran alongside the wagon.

Before she could try again to climb around the load, another dog leaped up, getting its front legs over the side. It sank its teeth into the canvas to help pull itself up. Its back legs scrambled, trying to get purchase on something so that it could climb into the wagon. She kicked at the dog's head. It let go of the canvas and snapped at her, trying to catch her foot even as it tried to clamber up into the wagon, but it fell off.

Another big hound jumped up on the other side, almost making it in. A third leaped up beside it.

Kahlan kicked at the dogs, knocking one after another off the sideboards of the wagon. As soon as she kicked one off, another to the back or side bounded up and hooked its front legs over the edge. Their eyes glowed red with vicious intent.

The wagon wasn't going fast enough to get away from the

pack, but it was going fast enough to keep her off balance as it rocked and bucked. When the wagon bounced on a rock, her kick missed and she had to urgently kick again to keep a dog out.

Kahlan looked back into the distance. It was dark, but there was enough moonlight that she would have been able to see the plateau with the People's Palace atop it if it had been anywhere near. Even if it was too far in the distance to see the plateau in the moonlight, she would have been able to see the lights of the city palace atop it, but it wasn't there.

She didn't know what direction they were headed, but she knew that she was somewhere out on the vast Azrith Plain.

Even as she fought off the wild pack of dogs, Kahlan knew that she was losing the battle. As she kicked one off, two more would jump up and get their front legs hooked over the side. With some she was able to dislodge their legs. With others, when they got too far in, she had to kick at their heads to knock them off.

But she knew that she was losing. With the dogs continually making running jumps at the wagon, she knew that it was only a matter of time until they made it up and in. Once that happened, they would take her down.

Kahlan felt a sudden pang of pain for how much she missed Richard. He would't know what had happened. He wouldn't know where she was. He would never know what had happened to her.

She had a vision of her own corpse, looking like Queen Catherine after she had been ripped apart by animals. Kahlan swallowed back the grief of never being able to see Richard again. She hoped he never found her body. She didn't want him to find her like that.

She spun and kicked the ribs of a dog that had clawed itself halfway into the wagon. As it yelped and fell back, she caught sight of a horse at the end of a long rope tied to the side of the wagon. It was trailing far behind, off in the darkness, staying out to the side as far as it could to keep away from the dogs.

Kahlan had no time to consider. It was her only hope to get help or get away. She snatched up her pack and then kicked a dog off the sideboards near the rope. As she leaned over to grab hold of the rope, a dog lunged out of the darkness, snapping, trying to grab her arm. She pulled back in the nick of time and its teeth caught only air. As the dog fell and rolled after missing her, she quickly bent and seized the rope.

The horse, frightened by the savage dogs, snorted and resisted Kahlan's efforts to bring it in closer. She put a boot against the sideboard and put her weight into pulling harder. Finally, she managed to drag the skittish animal in a bit closer. It danced and darted, trying to stay away.

The dogs didn't seem to care about the horse. They were fixated on Kahlan. The horse didn't know that, though.

When she had dragged the horse in as close as she could get it, Kahlan turned and saw two dogs bound up in quick succession and make it in over the other side of the wagon. They fell, their legs splaying out to the sides.

As the dogs scrambled to get to their feet, Kahlan hoisted her pack over one shoulder, untied the rope from a wooden cleat, and, holding the rope for balance, sprang up onto the sideboard. She held on to the rope for dear life as she tried to balance on the sideboard of the bouncing wagon.

The horse tried to run. As it did, it moved ahead just close enough. Kahlan leaped for all she was worth over the snarling, snapping dogs. She landed sideways, sprawled over the horse's back.

Giddy with relief not to have fallen into the fangs of the

dogs, Kahlan grabbed the horse's mane with both fists and swung one leg up and over the frightened animal's back.

Finally mounted, she thumped the horse's ribs with her heels. She wanted to go ahead to the wagon's driver to get help, but the hounds raced in and blocked the way. Others leaped up, trying to grab her feet and legs and drag her down. The horse, terrified of the dogs, cut a course sharply away from the wagon. With no time to lose, Kahlan leaned over the withers and urged the animal into a gallop. The horse was only too happy to bolt off into the night.

The pack of hounds were in hot pursuit.

A nything at all?" Richard asked Berdine in a quiet voice. "Dead quiet out here, Lord Rahl." Berdine pointed a thumb back over her shoulder. "I looked in on the Mother Confessor earlier and she was sleeping soundly. After that I took a tour of the area just to satisfy myself that there was no one around and nothing out of the ordinary. Then I came back up to this end of the hall and I've been right here outside the door ever since. The Mother Confessor has been a perfect patient. I haven't heard a peep out of her."

Richard laid a hand gently on the Mord-Sith's red-leather-clad shoulder. "Thanks, Berdine."

"Has the machine had anything else to say, Lord Rahl?"

Richard paused and looked back at her. "It's had a lot to say, but I'm afraid that none of it is very useful."

"Maybe we need the missing part of the book *Regula* in order to understand it."

He'd had the same thought. "Maybe."

Richard left Berdine outside in the hall and the soldiers of the First File off down the corridor to either side making certain that no one could get to their room.

Alone, Richard quietly closed the door behind himself as

he stepped into the nearly dark bedroom where Kahlan was sleeping. He had turned down the wick on the lamp when he had checked on her earlier, so it was difficult to see much of anything. He didn't want to turn the lamp up and risk waking her.

He was exhausted. It was going to be morning soon. He needed to get some sleep. He wished he hadn't wasted so much time with the machine.

Not wanting to disturb Kahlan, Richard thought that maybe he would sleep in a chair. She needed a good rest in order to recover from her fever. He was thankful that his grandfather had put a poultice on her arm to help draw out the infection.

His own scratch from the boy down in the market had long ago healed. He had thought that Kahlan's had as well. It was more than a little worrisome the way it had returned so suddenly, especially after Zedd had healed it with his gift.

On his way to the chair, Richard's feet caught up a blanket lying in the middle of the floor.

He thought that Kahlan, in a fevered sleep, must have thrown off her cover. He picked it up by the edge and held it up to lay it back over her.

In the dim light from the lantern, on the way to the bed, Richard paused. Something was wrong. Even if Kahlan had thrown the blanket off in her sleep, it seemed unlikely she could have thrown it that far.

The first thing that instantaneously flashed through his mind was the machine's warning that hounds would take her from him. Almost at the same time, he remembered Queen Catherine lying dead on the floor, her middle viciously ripped open by some kind of animals with fangs.

Richard dropped the blanket and rushed to the bed. Kahlan wasn't there. He stared for a moment at the rumpled, empty bed before turning up the wick on the lamp and scanning the room. He didn't see her anywhere.

When he glanced up, Richard saw that the door to the balcony was open. His first thought was that maybe her fever had driven her out on the balcony to get some relief in the cool night air.

Before he could go to the balcony, his attention was caught by his pack on the floor. Kahlan's pack had been beside it before. He knew, because he had been the one who had put them both there. He supposed that Kahlan might have wanted to get something out of it and could have moved it somewhere, but he didn't really believe that. Something told him that it would be a waste of time searching the room for it.

Richard instead ran to the balcony doors. He was worried that, at the least, she might have gotten worse. He expected to see her passed out on the balcony floor. She wasn't there.

The bedroom, like the balcony, wasn't that big. There was no way he could have missed her back in the room. Baffled as to where she could be, he reluctantly looked over edge of the railing, fearing that she might have fallen. It was difficult to see in the darkness, but not impossible. He was relieved to see nothing on the ground far below.

As he started to turn to go back inside, Richard saw that there was another balcony. It wasn't connected or even all that close, but he went to the railing closest to it anyway for a look. He saw that it had a stairway down on the far side.

He saw, then, the scuff mark on the top of the railing where he was standing. It looked to have been made by a boot.

Richard hopped up on the railing and leaped across the daunting drop to the other balcony. The doors on the second balcony were locked and it was dark inside. It was possible that Kahlan had gone inside and then locked the doors, but he didn't really believe that. It made no sense. If she feared something, there were guards and Mord-Sith just outside their bedroom door.

Instead of breaking in the door, Richard took Kahlan's more likely route. He raced in the darkness down the flights of stairs, eventually reaching the grounds of the palace.

The moonlight coming through the thin haze of clouds wasn't bright, but it was bright enough for him to recognize Kahlan's bootprints. With a lifetime of tracking experience, he also recognized her unique gait. He could read the features of the way she walked and the tracks she made nearly as well as he could read the features of her face.

There was no doubt about it. Kahlan had come down the stairs outside the palace to the grounds at the top of the plateau.

The thing that worried him the most was that he could see by the prints that she had been running as fast as she could. He looked around for other prints, the prints of anyone who might have been chasing her, but there were no other footprints.

It didn't make any sense.

Richard stood and stared off across the top of the dark plateau. What could she have been running from?

In the distance, paths meandered through elaborate gardens, but the grounds closer to the palace, where Richard had come out at the bottom of the stairs, were an open staging and loading area where supplies arrived at the palace. While most visitors to the palace entered up stairways through the interior of the plateau, an imposing portico between the staging area and the gardens welcomed important guests arriving by horse or carriage at the top of the plateau. The entrance there took guests into the grand corridors and the guest areas. Closer to Richard, in a less well lit area, were the stables and service docks.

He could see the dark shapes of dozens of wagons and carriages that were either parked or being loaded. Horses were being brought out of the stables and either saddled or hitched to wagons. Even in the middle of the night representatives were packing up and leaving the palace. The place was alive with activity. No one was arriving. All the wagons were leaving.

Richard was concerned about all the things that had happened recently and the representatives who had decided that they would rather side with prophecy and those who promised it to them. He wanted to know what could be behind it all, but at the moment his only real focus was on finding Kahlan.

Richard followed Kahlan's tracks as they traced her route through the darkness atop the plateau. She had been running as fast as she could. He could see by certain characteristics of the tracks, such as the way a print twisted here and there, that she was looking behind at something chasing her as she ran. If she had been running after someone or something, the prints would have looked different.

It made no sense. There were no prints of anything chasing her, yet he could clearly read the indications of fear in her tracks. Whatever was after her would have had to be flying not to leave prints. He knew, too, that it might very well be fevered delusions chasing her.

But the prophecy from the machine saying that the hounds would take her from him was no delusion. At least there were no tracks of hounds.

And then, in the midst of hoofprints and wagon tracks, Kahlan's footprints simply ended.

Richard went to one knee and bent to study the tracks more closely. He saw, then, the marks where her last print pushed off on the ball of her foot. It had left a heavier impression with pronounced side ridges as she had jumped up onto something. Since her footprints ended there, he knew that it was most likely a wagon or coach that she had jumped up onto.

With an icy sense of dread, Richard realized that Kahlan was gone. He couldn't understand what had happened, or why she would have run the way she did, but he could see plainly enough that she had left the bedroom, come down the steps to the ground, run across the plateau, and then jumped into a wagon.

There were wagons leaving all the time. Wheel tracks and hoofprints were everywhere. There was no telling which wagon or coach was the one Kahlan had jumped up into. If she had stayed in one of those wagons, she could be headed off in just about any direction away from the palace.

There were a number of representatives who had left overnight. Many of them were accompanied by escorts. Some of them had entire households with them, everyone from guards to attendants, to advisors, to support staff, to wagons of baggage, so there were likely numerous wagons and coaches involved.

Kahlan could be in any one of them.

Patrols that had spotted Richard ran up to see what the problem was. Richard saw other soldiers on horseback appear in the distance.

Before the powerfully built captain of the guard could speak, Richard spoke first. "The Mother Confessor came down here sometime after dark. Her tracks are at least several hours old. Did you or any of your men see her?"

"The Mother Confessor?" The startled captain shook his head. "No, Lord Rahl. My men and I have been on patrol since long before then—since before dark. I would have heard about it if anyone had seen her."

Richard had last seen Kahlan not long after it had gotten dark. "How many wagons have left here since dark?"

The captain scratched his bull neck as he tallied them in his head for a moment. "Dozens, Lord Rahl. We have manifests and logs. I can get you an exact number."

"Good. Get enough cavalrymen together for a detachment to go after each wagon. I want mounted troops to catch every wagon that left here overnight. Every one of them. I want every wagon and coach searched."

The man was nodding to the instructions, but he looked confused. "What are we to be looking for?"

"The Mother Confessor left her room sometime in the night. It's possible she was being chased by something but she's sick with a fever so it's more likely that she may be disoriented. What I do know is that she came down here and jumped in a wagon that left here tonight. I don't know which one, so the men will need to track down every wagon and search it. If she is found, I want her protected and brought back to the palace."

"Do you know where she jumped in the wagon, Lord Rahl? That might narrow the search."

Richard pointed at her last footprint. "Right here."

The man's face sagged with disappointment. "All the wagons have to turn through this area as they're leaving."

"Then they'll all have to be caught and searched," Richard said. "Get the search parties on their way immediately—before the wagons can get too far."

The man clapped a fist to his heart. "At once, Lord Rahl."

"And I need a horse," Richard said. "Right now."

The captain turned and whistled a code into the darkness as yet more men ran in from different directions. In only a matter of moments Richard was surrounded by over a hundred men.

When a dozen men on horseback galloped up, the men let them through. The mounted soldiers gathered around wanting to know what the problem was. Instead of explaining, Richard quickly appraised all the horses. He signaled a man to dismount from a strong-looking mare. The man jumped down.

"The captain here will explain my orders," Richard said as

he put a foot in the stirrup and swung up onto the saddle. "I have to go."

"We will have every wagon checked, Lord Rahl," the captain said. "Will you be going with some of the men, then?"

Richard had to have the wagons searched, just in case, but he doubted that they would find her. There was more to this, something that he had not yet figured out.

He thought about the machine's warning that the hounds would take her from him. He thought about all the trouble that had started after they had seen the boy, Henrik, down in the market the morning after Cara's wedding.

Their recent troubles seemed bound up in prophecy. A number of representatives had decided that they wanted to follow Hannis Arc from Fajin Province because he used prophecy. That was why so many had left that night.

One of the first omens had been "Queen takes pawn." Nicci had told Richard that the prophecy was also a move in a game called chess, a game that was played in Fajin Province in the Dark Lands. Henrik, the sick boy who had given the first warning that there was darkness in the palace, had been to a place called Kharga Trace in the Dark Lands of Fajin Province.

Richard remembered the boy's mother saying that she had taken him to see the Hedge Maid in Kharga Trace. He remembered the way her eyes had darted about when she had mentioned the Hedge Maid. He also remembered how nervous Abbot Dreier had gotten at the mention of the Hedge Maid.

Nicci had warned Richard about how dangerous Hedge Maids were.

He also remembered the boy's mother saying that Henrik had been bothered by hounds coming around their tent.

The captain was still waiting for Richard to tell him where he was going.

"I'm not going with any of the men to search the wagons." Richard's horse danced around, eager to be away. "Tell General Meiffert and Zedd that I'm going to Kharga Trace and I don't have the time to wait for them. I don't have a moment to waste, and besides, they would only slow me down."

"Kharga Trace?" one of the men of the patrol asked. "In the Dark Lands?"

Richard nodded. "You know the place?"

The man stepped forward. "I know that you don't want to go there, Lord Rahl."

"Why's that?"

"I'm from Fajin Province. You don't want to go to Kharga Trace. Desperate people go there to see some kind of woman said to have dark powers. A lot of people who go there, though, don't come back. That kind of thing isn't all that unusual in the Dark Lands. I was happy to leave to join the D'Haran army. I was fortunate enough to be accepted into the First File so that I might serve here. I don't ever want to go back."

Richard wondered if the man might simply be superstitious. When he had been a woods guide, back in the Hartland woods of Westland, he never encountered any dark malevolence haunting the trackless forests, but he did encounter country people who feared such things and believed wholeheartedly in them. Such stories, though, didn't tarnish his fond memories of home.

"Now that the war is over," he said to the soldier, "you really don't want to go home?"

"Lord Rahl, I don't know much about the gift, but in the war I came to see a great deal of magic to fear. What's back in the Dark Lands is different. The cunning folk there, as they're called, use occult conjuring—dark magic—that deals in things dead. It's very different in the Dark Lands than the magic of the gift I've seen since leaving."

"Different? Different in what way?"

The man looked around, almost as if he feared that the shadows might be listening. "The dead walk the Dark Lands."

Richard rested his forearm over the pommel of the saddle and frowned down at the man. "What do you mean, the dead walk the Dark Lands?"

"Just what I said. The Dark Lands are demon ground, hunted by scavengers of the underworld. If I never go back there it will be too soon for me."

Richard thought such superstitious fears sounded even more strange coming from a strong young man, a man who had faced war and terrors no one should ever have to face.

But then he remembered Nicci telling him that a Hedge Maid's powers were different and that he had no defense against them. Nicci had not only once been known as Death's Mistress, she had been a Sister of the Dark and had served the cause of the Keeper of the underworld. She knew about such things.

The thought of Kahlan going to a place like that had his heart pounding. Richard knew that the one place he didn't want Kahlan going to was the Dark Lands, and especially to the Hedge Maid. But too many things pointed in that direction to be coincidence.

Richard nodded. "Thanks for the warning, soldier. I hope to catch up with the Mother Confessor long before then."

The man clapped a fist to his heart. "May you come home soon, Lord Rahl. Come back safe with the Mother Confessor before you ever have to set foot in the Dark Lands."

Richard tightened the reins to keep the horse still. "Captain, be sure to tell Nicci, too, where I'm going. Be sure to tell her that I said that I think the Mother Confessor may be headed to the Hedge Maid in Kharga Trace. I am going to try to catch her before she can get there."

One of the other soldiers ran up and threw saddlebags over the back of the horse. "At least take some supplies, Lord Rahl."

Richard lifted his sword from its scabbard just a bit and let it drop back, making sure that it was clear. He nodded his thanks to the men and then urged the horse toward the road that led down the side of the plateau.

As Richard gave the horse reins and leaned over its withers, it complied instantly and thundered off into the night.

K ahlan woke with a start. She squinted out at the surrounding woods in the faint, first light of dawn. She
didn't see the hounds down on the ground, at least,
not yet.

They always came back.

She knew that it was only a matter of time.

She'd gotten only a few hours of sleep, and it was neither
good nor enough. At least she hadn't fallen out of the tree.
The lap of several branches had made a somewhat safe, if uncomfortable, place to rest.

The days of terror seemed endless and had blended one into
another until she had completely lost track of time. She was
exhausted from the relentless chase. Overwhelming fatigue was
the only thing that brought on sleep.

At night, when it got dark enough, the hounds would seem
to disappear for the night. She thought that maybe they went
off at night to search for food and to rest. At first, she had
entertained the hope that they had tired of the chase and had
given up.

The first few nights after leaving the palace, when she had
still been out on the Azrith Plain and the hounds had vanished

at night, Kahlan had thought that it was her chance to escape, to put distance between her and her pursuers, but no matter how fast she ran, no matter how many hours, no matter if she rode all night without stopping, the hounds were always right there when day broke, and then they would come for her again.

Because the sun rose ahead and to the right and set behind her, she knew that she was headed roughly northeast. That told her the direction that the palace would be in. She had tried several times after the hounds had disappeared at night to circle around and head back, but doing so took her back into an ambush by the dogs. She had barely escaped with her life. As they came after her she had to turn back to the northeast, her only thought to outrun them, to put distance between her and her would-be assassins.

There were times when she had wanted to give up, to simply quit running and let it end. But the memory of Catherine's gruesome end was too horrifying to allow Kahlan to surrender. She kept telling herself that if she could stay alive, if she could stay ahead of the pack of wild dogs, she had a chance. As long as she could outrun them she would stay alive. As long as she was alive, there was hope.

The thought of Richard also kept her from giving up. The thought of him finding her torn apart by the hounds was so crushingly heartbreaking that it made her fight all the harder to stay alive.

After she had left the Azrith Plain and had gotten into mountainous terrain, it had become, for the most part, impossible for her to run the horse at night. She was afraid of the animal breaking a leg in the dark. Without the horse, the dogs would easily catch her.

The horse was her lifeline. She took good care of it. At least, she took as good care of it as was possible. She knew that if she lost the horse, she would be dead in short order. On the other hand, if she didn't push the horse hard enough, the hounds would pull her down.

Kahlan looked down from her place in the branches. The horse was tied to a nearby limb of the tree, but on a long rope so that it could graze on anything it could find close enough. If she needed the horse in a hurry she had the end of the rope at hand so that she could pull the animal in close and climb down onto it.

For some reason, the hounds ignored the horse. They wanted Kahlan, not the horse, and they never attacked it. She couldn't understand it. The horse, though, was not comforted by their disinterest. Their mere presence set the horse into a panic.

Kahlan looked down, checking where the horse was. Despite how weary she was, she knew that she would have to leave soon lest the dogs arrive and terrify the horse. In its panic, the horse could be hurt. If it broke a leg, she would be done.

If she let the hounds somehow trap her up in the tree, she would have trouble getting the horse close enough to the growling, barking, snapping animals. She didn't like the thought of being trapped and risking that the horse would break loose in the confusion and get away without her. Just as soon as there was enough light to see, she would leave.

She hadn't eaten much other than some travel biscuits, a few nuts from time to time, and bit of dried meat she had in her pack. She still felt sick to her stomach and really didn't want to eat anything at all, but she knew that she needed to keep up her strength, so she forced herself.

She had a fever, and her arm throbbed painfully. She was nauseous and constantly feared that she would have to throw up. She remembered waking back in the Garden of Life with the splitting headache and vomiting uncontrollably. While she knew that she had to eat or she would get sicker, she couldn't afford to throw up, so she ate only as much as she thought she had to.

As she searched the surrounding area for any sign of the dogs, she thought she spotted something off among the trees.

It looked human.

Kahlan was about to call out to try to get some help, when she saw the way the thing moved. It didn't walk, exactly. It was more like it glided along through the shadows.

She leaned out on the branch, trying to see better. Just then, the first rays of sunlight came through the treetops.

Kahlan saw then that what she had thought was a person was actually a dog—a big black dog. It was the leader of the pack, stalking out of the trees.

She couldn't grasp how she could have thought it was a person. With the terror of seeing the pack leader, panic welled up in her and all she could think about was getting away.

Kahlan leaned down and pulled in the rope hand over hand as fast as she could, drawing the horse close to the tree before the hounds could come in close and spook it away.

When the horse was below her, she climbed down to a lower branch of the oak tree and then dropped onto the horse's back.

Kahlan looked back and saw the pack of dogs coming through the trees. When they saw her they started in howling. Kahlan leaned forward over the horse's withers as it bolted.

The chase was back on.

78

As Kahlan guided her horse among immense pines, she frequently looked back over her shoulder to keep track of how close the dogs had gotten. The colossal trees towering above her cut off almost every bit of sky. The lower branches were far out of reach overhead. Iron gray clouds made it even darker, leaving a gloomy world in the undergrowth for the horse to try to navigate.

Drizzle collected on the pine needles until the drops grew fat enough to fall. It was distracting when those fat, random drops splashed against her face. Kahlan was cold, wet, and miserable. She had to concentrate to find the indistinct trail among the nursery of small pines carpeting the lower reaches of the dense forest.

In many places they overgrew a trail too seldom used to keep open. In other places, beds of thick ferns covered over any hint of the little-traveled route through the forest wilderness.

Having grown up in a palace, Kahlan had never known much about following obscure trails. In her duties as a Confessor, she had always traveled the roads and well-used paths between population centers of the Midlands. She had also always been escorted by a wizard. That seemed so long ago that it felt like another lifetime.

To an extent, the hounds helped guide her in the sense that they left her only one real direction she could go. She just had to find enough footing for the horse. Even though the dogs were never far behind, she dared not let the horse panic and run on its own. If they left the trail there was no telling what trouble they could get into. Holes among rocks and fallen timber off the trail could catch and break the horse's legs. They might suddenly come to a cliff, or an impassable gorge, or a place so dense as to be impenetrable. If that happened, the pack of wild dogs would have her trapped and it would be all over.

She didn't want to die out in the middle of a trackless forest, taken down by dogs, torn apart, devoured and left for scavengers to pick clean.

She needed to stay on the relative safety of the trail in order to stay ahead of her pursuers. It was Richard who had taught her about following poorly marked trails that were rarely used and difficult to make out. Besides looking for small indications close by, she continually scanned the broader area ahead, looking for telltale signs of where the trail went.

The thought of Richard gave her an agonizing stab of longing. She hadn't thought about him much in recent days. She was so desperate to get away that she was hardly able to think about anything other than running and staying away from the baying pack of dogs.

Her arm hurt. Her head throbbed. She was so exhausted that she could hardly sit upright atop the horse anymore. Worse, she was so sick with fever that she feared she might pass out.

She supposed that if she was unconscious it might be the

best way to die. It might be a blessing to lose consciousness when the pack got to her.

With the back of her hand, Kahlan wiped a tear from her cheek. She missed Richard so much. He must be frantic with worry about her being missing for so long. She felt shame for not somehow letting him know what had happened.

Several of the dogs suddenly ran in out of the brush at the side, lunging at her legs. In a panic, Kahlan urged the horse into a run. Limbs flashed by. Pine boughs slapped her as she raced headlong through the woods. One branch hit her shoulder, almost knocking her off her horse.

Abruptly, the horse skidded to a halt. The ground ahead dropped away over the rim of a rocky ledge. The horse couldn't take the steep, plunging descent. She feared that they had gotten off the trail, and now they were trapped. Kahlan looked back. The hounds were coming.

As the dogs started yelping and howling in anticipation of having her cornered, the frightened horse suddenly reared up. Without a saddle there was precious little to hold on to. Kahlan snatched for the mane as she started slipping off the horse's back. She missed.

Before she knew it, she landed with a heavy thud. Stunned from hitting the ground so hard, she groaned in pain. She had landed on her infected arm. With her good arm she cradled her sore arm to her abdomen.

Before Kahlan could grab the rope, the horse bolted away into the woods. In mere seconds she couldn't see it anymore. But she could see the dogs bounding toward her, the lead dog barking with savage hunger to get at her.

Kahlan turned and practically dove down the steep drop. In places she leaped from ledges of rocks above to rocks below in a series of jarring, barely controlled falls from ledge to ledge. She was racing downward so fast that she didn't have time to think about it before each leap. She knew how dangerous it was to descend like that, but she was possessed by the panicked drive to escape the terror coming for her.

Kahlan slipped on loose gravel and fell into a slide down a channel of debris and loose ground. Rock and small shrubs flashed by as she slid downward.

Behind her the dogs leaped across the rocks as if they were made for it. They were closing on her.

With a hard impact she hit the bottom and fell sprawling on her face. Without taking the time to feel sorry for herself she pushed herself up. The way ahead looked flatter, but it also looked wet. Mist drifted among the dense trees, so she couldn't see very far ahead in the gloom.

What she could see was a thick tangle of growth. Vines trailed down from above. Heavy vegetation blocked the way off to the sides.

But she saw that she hadn't lost the trail after all. It was right in front of her, tunneling ahead through the dense underbrush.

A short-haired brown dog crashed down from the steep trail, rolling as it landed behind her. As he scrambled to get to his feet, his jaws snapped, trying to get Kahlan's leg in his teeth.

Kahlan sprang up and started running headlong into the burrow through the brush. The passage through the undergrowth seemed endless. Vegetation flashed by as she ran. She couldn't see the end up ahead. Dogs barked as they chased her through the tangled green warren.

Abruptly, she burst out of the thick underbrush into a more open, swampy area. Trees with smooth gray bark and fat bottoms of tangled, spreading roots stood in stretches of stagnant water.

Kahlan's boots sank into mud and she fell. As she struggled to get free, she admonished herself for paying too much attention to the dogs chasing her and inadvertently leaving the trail. The only good thing was that the mud slowed the dogs as well. They circled around behind her, jumping from dry spots to clumps of grasses, looking for a way to come in from the side.

Kahlan clambered back onto the trail and raced ahead, trying to jump from root to root in order to stay out of the water and morass of mud. She didn't trust stepping in the water because she feared that she would sink in and get her foot caught in a tangle of roots hidden below. She could even break an ankle. Both thoughts terrified her.

As the trail occasionally submerged into the ever-expanding swamp, Kahlan saw places in the path where branches and vines had been placed on the ground to span impassable areas. They provided a welcome way ahead across the patches of water.

The farther she went, the more substantial and frequent the knitted-branch path became. It was much easier to run with the woven mat underfoot. As she raced ahead into the thick swamp, through vines and moss hanging in sheets along the way, the walkway became even more substantial, eventually rising up above the surface of the stagnant water.

A quick look behind revealed that the dogs were having trouble. Their paws slipped down through gaps in the weaving of the walkway, sometimes becoming caught. The farther in they went, the more difficulty they had negotiating the entwined branches, twigs, and vines. Kahlan was soon so far ahead that she lost sight of them in the swirling fog.

The walkway grew strong and solid. In places there were

railings made of thick branches. Not long after that, the railings themselves became more sturdy.

Kahlan was giddy with relief. She was reaching an inhabited place of some kind. With a walkway this well built, this painstakingly constructed, she was sure it would lead her to salvation.

CHAPTER
79

Kahlan was confounded at the construction of the enclosed, candlelit tunnel. Soggy parts of the pathway that at first had been gapped with bits of branches and vines knitted together turned into a continuous mat of woven material, which then became a causeway that rose above the surface of the water into an elevated structure that eventually circled all the way around the walkway and closed in overhead. The floor, walls, and ceiling were all constructed the same way, made entirely of woven branches, twigs, vines, and grasses. Kahlan had never seen anything like the remarkably well built and solid structure.

She didn't know who had placed all the candles to welcome visitors, but she was thankful for them. She would at last be safe from the dogs that had pursued her for so long. She would at last be able to get help and return to the palace and to Richard.

Kahlan remembered the prophecy all too well. "*Dark things. Dark things stalking you, running you down. You won't be able to escape them. . . . your body being ripped open as you scream, all alone, no one to help you.*"

Now that she had found a place where it seemed clear that

there would be people, she at last dared to think that she had beaten the prophecy. Soon, she would be somewhere safe and she could at last rest. At the thought of being safe, she could hardly keep her eyes open any longer.

As she went deeper into the structure, she shed the panic that had kept her going at maximum effort for so long. Now, as the panic faded, she could feel her strength ebbing as well.

She hadn't eaten much, and she hadn't slept much for days on end. Now, along with the fever, it was all catching up with her. She was having trouble walking, but she knew that she had to keep going. She wasn't safe, yet, until she could get help.

It became an effort to keep her eyes open, to put one foot in front of the other. Her feet felt so heavy she could hardly lift them. Before long, it was all she could do to shuffle ahead.

Kahlan passed through rooms with hundreds of strips of cloth hanging from the ceiling, each holding an object of some sort, everything from coins to the remains of small animals. She was mystified by the purpose of the place and had to hold her breath against the stench as she hurried past.

Beyond, she went through a network of passageways and rooms, her way ahead lit by candles.

Kahlan paused. She thought she had heard a whisper calling to her.

"Mother Confessor . . ."

That time she was sure she'd heard it. She looked around the room and peered down the dark corridors to the side, but she didn't see anyone.

When she heard it a third time, she was listening more carefully and was able to tell where it had come from. It seemed to have come from the wall to the side. Moving toward the sound she saw then that there was a small person inside the structure of the wall itself. He was naked.

Kahlan realized, then, that she recognized him. It was Henrik, the boy from down in the market.

"Mother Confessor . . ."

Her eyes wide, Kahlan stared at the boy. "Henrik, what are you doing in there?"

"They put me in here. Please, help me?"

Kahlan pulled her knife and started cutting away at the branches and vines all woven together over him, keeping him imprisoned. As she started pulling away the vines, thorns pricked her fingers. She drew back, putting the edge of a finger to her mouth, sucking at the painful puncture. She could see the trickles of blood where the thorns had pierced Henrik's flesh as well.

Kahlan immediately went back to cutting away the webbing holding the boy in. Tears ran down his cheeks.

"Thank you, thank you," he mumbled over and over as he wept. "I'm so sorry for what I did, Mother Confessor."

"What did you do?" she asked to keep his mind off the pain of the thorns as she worked at cutting away branches and vines.

"I scratched you. I didn't mean to, didn't want to. I couldn't stop myself. I—"

"It's all right," Kahlan said as she carefully cut away the last thorny branch holding him in. She leaned in, concentrating on finding a safe place to hold it and get it off him without doing any more damage. "It's all right. Hush." He had puncture wounds from the thorns all over his chest, arms, and legs, and while certainly painful, they didn't look life-threatening.

"Run," he said in a weak voice.

Kahlan frowned up at him. "Who did this to you? What's going on?"

"Run," he said again. "Get away before they get you, too."

She lifted his arm, put it around her shoulders, and lifted him out. He winced as the thorns drew out of the skin of his back. Some were barbed and resisted. When she finally had him out, Kahlan set him down and grabbed a spare shirt from her backpack.

"You have to run," he said as she draped the shirt around his shoulders.

"I can't run," Kahlan told him. "A pack of wild dogs chased me in here. If I run, they'll get me."

His jaw dropped. "The dogs chased you here?" When she nodded, he said, "Me too. But it's worse here. You have to run. Get away."

Before Kahlan could ask what was going on, Henrik turned and raced away back the way Kahlan had come in.

"Run!" he screamed as he ran.

Kahlan stood staring, watching him vanish back up the tunnels. She couldn't run. The dogs were back that way. Besides, she had no more energy. She didn't even know if she would be able to stand much longer.

Just then, a woman in a cowled cape reached out and put a hand under Kahlan's arm. She hadn't seen the woman come up from behind.

"This way," the woman said in a low, thin, stretched tone.

"Who are you?" Kahlan asked. It was almost too much effort.

Another figure appeared on the other side and slipped a hand under Kahlan's other arm. She was also wearing a cowled cape, like the first woman. Together, they took some of her weight as they started walking her back toward a darker room.

They both had an odd bluish, spiritlike glow about them. Kahlan had the passing thought that maybe she was dead, and she was being welcomed into the spirit world. That thought quickly faded. Strange as the place was, it was was no spirit world.

Kahlan wasn't sure what was going on, but after Henrik's frantic warning, she wanted to run, but she was at the end of her strength.

"We've been expecting you," the stooped figure on the right said as her grip tightened on Kahlan's arm.

The two glowing figures dragged Kahlan into a larger room crowded with bottles, jars, vessels, and small boxes of every kind. The jars of colored glass were stuck in the walls anywhere a place could be found. Yet others, as well as pottery jars and jugs, were crowded together all over the floor. Acrid smoke rose in wisps from a shallow bowl in the center of the room.

As Kahlan was hauled toward the center of the room, she pulled her gaze away from staring at the strange collection of containers and found herself face-to-face with a small woman just coming to her feet.

The woman wasn't very big. In the dim light it was difficult to see much more than her boyish figure and shoulder-length hair.

And then the woman leaned in and gave Kahlan a broad grin with lips sewn nearly shut.

Kahlan stiffened at the evil in that grin and in her dark eyes.

The woman with the sewn-shut mouth made low, drawn-out, screeching, clicking sounds toward another one of the glowing figures that seemed to have appeared out of the walls. Yet more of them gathered close around. Including the two holding Kahlan up, there were six of them.

The cowled figure the woman had spoken to in the strange language bowed her head.

"I will leave at once, Mistress, and let him know that we have her, and that she will soon be among the walking dead."

Kahlan ran the words through her mind again, not sure she had heard them right.

She will soon be among the walking dead.

With that, the figure vanished like smoke through the walls. As Kahlan watched her go, she saw for the first time other people back in the walls, woven in the way Henrik had been. Some were near the surface of the wall while others were so far back in she couldn't see much of them. None had clothes. A number of them were clearly dead.

The small woman with the leather thongs sewing her mouth closed turned and tossed a handful of dusty material in the shallow bowl where small sticks were smoldering. Sparkling light spiraled up. Other figures, grotesque figures only partially visible, crowded into the room.

It felt like being among an assembly of ghosts, except they didn't look like ghosts of people. They were gangly, human-like, skeletal creatures. Their long arms and legs had big, knobby joints. Their flesh, tight on their slender limbs, as if they had no muscle whatsoever, glistened with mottled, slimy rot. Their demonic heads bore only a passing resemblance to humans'. They growled at the sight of her, their thin lips drawing back to reveal large mouths crowded with pointed, needle-sharp teeth.

The woman with the sewn-shut lips reached out with a filthy, blackened hand and grasped Kahlan's wrist.

Paralyzing pain instantly crackled through her. But it was more than simply pain. Besides the jolt of pain, the touch carried the sensation of utter, disheartened hopelessness.

It was like being touched by death.

As all the glowing creatures in cowled robes closed in around her, Kahlan finally got a good look at their frightening faces. It was like looking at rotting corpses. Their gnarled hands clawed at her clothes, and Kahlan knew that she had to do something, and fast. She couldn't allow them to do whatever it was they intended.

The woman with the sewn-shut mouth was touching her.

That was all Kahlan needed. More than she needed.

The world seemed to slow almost to a stop. Time belonged to Kahlan. Exhaustion, fear, pain, sickness, misery, hopelessness were forgotten.

Mercy did not exist.

The moment was hers.

In that timeless place within, that place of power, that core of her being, where her inborn Confessor power resided, Kahlan released the constraints on her ability.

Thunder without sound jolted the air.

The power of the concussion shook the whole structure.

All around the people in the walls screamed as they shuddered violently, their arms and legs shaking as much as they could in the confinement of the thorny walls. The air was filled with their howls.

When it finally died down, the woman with the sewn-shut lips merely smiled.

Kahlan's power hadn't worked on her.

Kahlan's power worked on everyone. Everyone who was human, anyway. It didn't work on certain creatures of magic, on beings that had elements of magic, or were different.

Nicci's words that they had no defense against the Hedge Maid rang through Kahlan's thoughts. This could only be the Hedge Maid.

Knobby fingers started clawing at her clothes again.

Kahlan had nothing left with which to resist, to fight. She was sick and weak, and on top of that she had just used the last bit of strength she had left in order to unleash her power.

Gnarled hands pulled at her clothes. The bony creatures growled through open mouths filled with fangs. Kahlan was upright only because of all the hands on her, pulling at her, pressing her this way and that, tearing and yanking.

As they went about their work of pulling her clothes off, the Hedge Maid turned to her jars and bottles, opening various containers, adding things to the smoldering fire in the broad, flat bowl in the center of the room. When sparks flew up, she used a slender stick to draw symbols in trays of ash to the side.

Kahlan felt tears running down her face, dripping from her jaw, as she was dragged back by the glowing figures. The demonic, bony creatures hissed and snarled at her.

Kahlan felt as if she were being conveyed by evil spirits to the torturous depths of the underworld.

She thought that maybe she was.

With the help of the snarling creatures, hands all around pulled strands of thorny vines up around her. They wrapped them around her wrists and ankles, anchoring the ends in the wall behind her, tying them in tight.

Kahlan was only barely conscious as laughing, cavorting figures danced around with strands of vine and thorny branches, adding them to the weave of the wall.

She cried out in pain when she realized that some of the creatures around her were biting her abdomen. She could feel the needle-sharp teeth sinking into her flesh. She cried out in despair and grief, too, over the thought of never seeing Richard again.

She watched in horror as the glowing figures pressed bowls against her belly, collecting the blood as it rolled down her.

Kahlan could do nothing to stop the madness. Every movement she made only worked the thorns deeper into her flesh.

The glowing figures, and the bony creatures dancing around the room, all laughed and chattered in the strange squealing clicking sounds.

Others, who had already collected bowls with blood running from Kahlan's bite wounds, took the blood to the Hedge Maid. The woman with the leather strips sewing her lips shut drank greedily. Creatures danced around her, arms flailing in the air, feet high-stepping. The room pulsed with the drumlike sound of their bony feet slapping the woven floor.

Kahlan's blood ran down the small woman's chin, dripping off in thick strings. Cockroaches emerged from the floor where the blood dropped to feast along with the Hedge Maid.

Kahlan felt merciful darkness stealing her away from the insanity raging all around her.

R ichard stood staring through the soft haze of drizzle at the tunnel-shaped entrance of tightly woven sticks and branches. He thought that it looked just a little too welcoming. The whole, carefully maintained trail through the swamp of Kharga Trace was too easy, too simple, too enticing the way it encouraged visitors in.

He wondered where the spider was.

He knew that Kahlan had gone this way. He knew because he had tracked her there. He'd seen where she'd fallen from her horse and slid down the steep slope. He'd seen her footprints, staggering in a crooked line, wandering off the trail into boggy mud and then back again.

He could tell by the tracks that she was hardly able to stand anymore. He could see by the halting, unsteady prints she left just how sick and exhausted she was.

He would have caught up with her long before had his horse not been killed. It had happened after dark when a huge wild boar had charged out of the brush. It wasn't rutting season but wild boars could be aggressive anytime, and this one certainly had been, charging in at the horse when they surprised it. As the horse went down, the boar's razor-sharp tusks slashed the horse's belly open. Richard ran the boar through with his sword, but it was too late. After killing the boar, he had no choice but to put the horse out of its misery. There had been nothing he could do for the poor animal.

With his horse dead, much of the last part of the race to catch Kahlan had been on foot. He had contemplated leaving her trail and going off to find another horse, but without knowing the area, he feared that even if he could manage to find a horse, the search would cost him too much time, so he had pressed on.

Because she was so sick and weak she hadn't traveled as swiftly as she might have, so she didn't get out too far ahead of him. But she had been going fast enough that he couldn't catch her on foot.

As he stood at the tunnel entrance to the structure, he heard someone running toward him. By the stride and the weight of the footfalls, he thought it had to be an awfully small person.

In another moment, a boy came racing out.

He was wearing one of Kahlan's shirts.

Richard went to a knee and swept an arm around the boy's middle to catch him before he could escape. He felt hot with fever.

"Henrik?"

The boy, panicked tears running down his face, stopped fighting and blinked. "Lord Rahl?"

"What are you doing here?"

The boy's chin wrinkled as fresh tears welled up. "The Hedge Maid, Jit, had me. She put me in the walls with the others—"

"Slow down. What do you mean, she put you in the walls?"

Richard could see that the boy was bloodied from wounds

all over his arms and legs. The shirt had spots of blood as well.

"Jit's familiars used branches and vines to tie me into the walls. They're full of thorns." Henrik pointed back into the tunnel. "The Mother Confessor came and saved me. She got me out. I told her to run, but I think maybe they got her."

Richard's mind raced, trying to understand what was happening as he tried to decide what to do. He had to get in there and help Kahlan, but he also knew that the Hedge Maid would be waiting for anyone walking into her lair. He couldn't help Kahlan if he was captured as well.

Richard seized Henrik by the shoulders. "Will you do something for me?"

The boy wiped his nose with the back of his hand. "What?"

"Some other people will be coming this way. I need you to go to them and tell them—"

"But the hounds will get me!"

"The hounds?"

"The hounds that chased me here. They were after me, when I was at the palace with my mother. They came after me and I ran. I had to get away. I had to. The Mother Confessor said that they chased her here, too."

Richard was beginning to understand. He shook his head.

"No, it only seemed that way to you. They weren't real. It was some kind of magic that the Hedge Maid used to get you to come here. You scratched us, remember?"

Henrik nodded. "I'm sorry, but I couldn't help myself."

"I know. I understand. You visited the Hedge Maid before, when you were sick. Your mother brought you here. I think the Hedge Maid used some kind of magic to make you scratch us. Then you came back here afterward, right? The dogs chased you here."

Henrik nodded again. "That's right. The Hedge Maid took the skin from under my fingernails, from where I scratched you both, and used it with her magic, but she could only find some of it from the Mother Confessor. There was none from where I scratched you left by the time I got here."

Richard was getting the picture. "Listen, no dogs are chasing you. It's just a trick to get you to come back here. I don't think you will see them again, not now that you came here. The Hedge Maid has no reason to chase you here anymore."

Henrik looked skeptical. "If you say so, Lord Rahl."

"You need to believe me. I know I'm right. Now, this is very important. I need you to go back the way you came and find my friends who are coming this way. I need you to bring them here. I'm going in there to get Kahlan out. But I'm going to need the help of my friends when I come out. I need you to tell my friends where I am and get them here right away. Can you do that?"

"Yes, Lord Rahl. I'll do it. Will you forgive me then, for what I did to you and the Mother Confessor?"

"Of course. It wasn't your fault. You were being used by an evil person. Now, hurry and get going. There isn't a moment to lose."

Henrik nodded and raced away back down the woven walkway.

Richard stood and looked at the structure.

And then he started climbing up onto the top of it.

82

Crouched low, Richard made his way along the top of the complex that had been constructed entirely of woven branches and vines. Fortunately, it seemed to be strong enough to hold his weight without sagging and was solid enough that it didn't flex and creak when he moved across it. The drizzle was making it slippery, though. Worse, the drizzle made places where moss and mold grew as slick as ice. Fortunately, the rough, jagged nature of the branches provided some grip for his boots.

The woven structure was surprisingly large, in places sprawling out through the swamp in several directions, with clusters of larger sections. His problem was to try to figure out where Kahlan was inside the maze of rooms and corridors. He had to get it right the first time. He doubted that once it started he would have a second chance to get her out.

All around, smooth-barked trees stood in the murky water on fat, spreading tangles of roots. Their wide-spreading branches held veils of gray-green moss. The water around the trees was in places covered with a thick layer of floating duckweed, making it look like a carpet of lawn. Richard knew that beneath it creatures lurked in the murky depths waiting for the unwary.

In places the structure made of the branches and vines was attached to the massive trees for stability and support. So many of the thick, stiff vines hung down from the trees that in spots Richard had difficulty getting through them. In other places he had to duck under low branches. In yet other places he had to brush thick webs of moss out of his way.

He wanted to go faster, but as he made his way across the slippery top of the structure he needed to be as quiet as possible so as not to alert anyone down inside.

Out in the swamp, the sharp calls of animals echoed across the stretches of dark water. When he glanced over the sloping side of the structure and saw shadows moving beneath the muddy water, Richard reminded himself to be careful. If the fall didn't kill him, something else likely would. In other places, long-legged white egrets stood on roots waiting for unwary fish to pass by. From below the water, other things hunted the egrets. As he moved ahead, he had to carefully skirt a poisonous yellow-and-red-banded snake lying over a branch hanging down in his way.

Richard stopped still, listening. In a pause between the hoots, chirps, and calls of animals out in the swamp, he thought he heard chanting. He squatted down, putting one hand to the roof for balance as he leaned forward and listened. Even though he couldn't make out any words he recognized, he was sure that it was some kind of shouting and chanting. It was hard to tell exactly where it was coming from. The strange sounds were unlike anything he had ever heard before.

As he crouched down lower, looking under wispy curtains of moss, Richard spotted what looked like trailers of fog. He thought that it could possibly be smoke. He moved ahead past the moss to get a better look and saw that it was definitely smoke. It wasn't billowing smoke, like that from a fire, but rather thin wisps of whitish smoke, possibly the kind used in certain mystic rituals.

As Richard got closer, he could smell the acrid smoke. It was laced with the stink of something dead.

When he reached the broad area where he'd spotted it, there was no chimney. The smoke simply seeped right up through the weaving of branches. He was able to hear the crazy chanting, thumping, and carrying-on right underneath him.

Richard slowly, carefully, as quietly as he could, drew his sword. He didn't think they would be able to hear him over all the noise below, but he wasn't taking any chances. The steel hissed softly as it came out into the gloom.

He'd already decided, from everything he knew, that nothing going on below him could be anything good. He knew that Henrik had been drawn to this place after having been sent to retrieve Richard's and Kahlan's flesh, and when he escaped he was covered in blood. He knew that Kahlan, through some kind of occult conjuring surrounding the flesh that Henrik had brought back to the Hedge Maid, had also been compelled to come to this place.

He had no illusions. This was going to be a fight to the death.

The sword's rage stormed through him, mixing with his own anger at Kahlan being taken prisoner. He wasn't even sure that she was still alive. It was all he could do to control the fury pounding through his veins and focus on what he needed to do.

Richard remembered all too well Nicci's warnings about Hedge Maids. She'd said that he had no defense against their powers. That meant that his sword would not work against her. He'd had that experience before, so he took Nicci's warning seriously.

There wasn't a lot that could be done about it now, though. He had no choice and no time to get help. He had to act.

But Nicci's warning didn't mean his sword wouldn't work against others, and he could hear a lot of others below him.

His only chance was surprise, swiftness of action, and violence.

Richard drew the blade across the inside of his arm, letting it bite through his flesh to have a taste of blood. A crimson drop ran down the fuller and dripped off the tip.

Richard lifted the blade stained with blood and touched it to his forehead.

"Blade, be true this day," he whispered.

Richard knew that he had to be fast. With all his fury and strength, he lifted the sword overhead, pausing for only an instant, and then swept it down between his wide-spread legs, slicing through the web of woven branches, sticks, and vines.

The sound of it parting the thick mat of woven material ripped the heavy air of the swamp.

He drew his fists in tight to his chest, held the sword upright, put his legs together, and dropped down through the raw opening.

He landed in the heart of madness.

83

Richard dropped into a crouch as he landed. Glowing, hooded forms hovered to the side while figures from a nightmare, their gaunt limbs flailing about in the air, danced around the room, high-stepping, slapping their bony feet to the woven floor, making the whole room drum. Their heads thrown back, needle-sharp teeth bared, they all chanted strange guttural sounds in time with their thumping feet.

The sound of it lifted the fine hairs at the back of his neck. The sight of it made him grip his sword all the tighter.

A haze of acrid smoke hung in the air. The sharp smell of fresh blood overlay even the stench of death.

A small woman in the center of the room, surprised by the intruder, turned to stare up at him with big, black eyes.

Her lips were sewn closed with strips of leather.

Her blackened hands and fingernails were stained with countless layers of filth. Her face had a dark patina of grime and gray soot. Fresh, bright red blood glistened on her chin. He saw it sloshing from side to side in the bowl she was holding.

In the center of the chaos, he didn't think she could be anyone other than the Hedge Maid.

And then, across the room, where glowing figures hovered in a cluster, he spotted Kahlan. It looked like she was trapped behind the very fabric of the thorny wall. All the branches and vines netting her against the wall held her up, but by the way she slumped, she looked to be unconscious.

With the heel of his hand to the center of her chest, Richard rammed the small woman back out of his way as he raced toward Kahlan. After Nicci's warning, he didn't want to risk using his sword on the Hedge Maid.

The glowing figures turned toward him. Their putrid yellow eyes glared with unbridled hatred. Beyond the edges of their glowing bluish cowls, the wrinkled flesh of their grotesque, pitted and pockmarked faces covered with warts and open ulcers contorted with rage as they howled in fury. With knobby, deformed hands, they all reached for him.

The sword's tip whistled through the air as Richard swung at them. The glowing forms faded away as the blade swept through them, only to reappear once it was past.

Richard hardly noticed, though. His attention was riveted on Kahlan. The front of her was covered in blood. He could see ripping bite marks on her abdomen, with rows of smaller, needle-sharp punctures on her shoulders and neck. The blood running down her had at first hidden the fact that she was naked. She was also unconscious.

At the sight of what they had done to her, Richard went wild with runaway rage, swinging the sword at everything around him. The chanting bony creatures bared their fangs, snapping at him as they abruptly turned from their dancing and charged in, trying to grab him.

The sword swept around with bone-shattering force, splintering limbs and skulls of the gaunt creatures. A shower of fragments from hands and arms, heads, and sharp, pointed teeth filled the air of the room. Yet even as he swung at the fiendish figures, taking off arms, legs, and heads, more of them rushed in toward him from the other side. They reached out, their clawlike hands raking his flesh.

Richard fought all the harder, without pause. His sword cut down any near enough. Severed limbs and headless bodies lay in piles at his feet. As he stepped into their advancing lines, his sword also slashed through walls, breaking jars and jugs. Glass fragments flew through the air. Pieces of sticks and vine ripped from the walls spun across the room. But the sword didn't seem to diminish the number of bony beings running and dancing around the room, as countless more poured in like ants from the dark passageways at the sides and rear of the room.

The glowing figures raced in, tearing at his shirt. They finally snatched his arms, their numbers overpowering him. With his sword stilled, the gathering of gangly creatures scuttled in, their faces thrusting toward him, jaws wide showing their menacing, crowded, sharp little teeth. They darted in, biting him.

He reached back and tried to grab one of the glowing figures by the throat, but she cackled with laughter as she evaporated into smoke, only to materialize again inside his reach, close to him, still holding his wrist. Her jaws stretched wide to show her fangs as she abruptly flew in at him. Richard ducked to the side as her jaws snapped closed and she missed.

With frantic effort, he spun away from all the hands. Jit was suddenly right there in front of him. She threw a handful of what looked like black dust up at him.

It hit him like an iron bar across the face. He fell to the ground, the sword slipping from his grasp. With skeletal fingers, the bony creatures dragged the weapon away.

Gnarled, clawlike hands reached out, grabbing him again, pinning him down. Sharp little teeth ripped at his shirt, tearing it away in shreds. Yet more of bony creatures crowded in, biting him on the chest and stomach.

Richard was having trouble making his arms and legs move. He was dizzy and couldn't seem to make his vision focus.

Jit said something in a strange clicking squealing language. The hands all around lifted him and slammed him against the wall beside where Kahlan was encased in the thorny vines. He tried to call out to her, but he couldn't seem to make his voice work. In fact, he realized that he was having trouble breathing. The dust that Jit had thrown at him was burning his lungs.

He felt sharp, stabbing pain in his legs as the thorns of the vines the creatures were wrapping around his legs sank into him, helping to keep him from moving. They were going to encase him in the wall like Kahlan, like others he could see woven into the walls all around the room.

As one of the demonic creatures, its skin covered with a greenish black sheen of slime, sank its sharp fangs into his stomach, another shoved a bowl against him to collect the blood. When it had enough, it rushed it to Jit.

Holding it with both stained hands, the Hedge Maid drank greedily from the bowl. With the leather strips sewing her lips nearly together, keeping her from opening her mouth very far, she had trouble drinking, so blood dribbled down her face and dripped from her chin.

The bony creatures looked like they could be servants of the Keeper himself. They moved in a knees-up, high-stepping crouch as they accompanied Jit, crowding in close to her like loyal little lapdogs. Cockroaches emerged at her feet all along the way to drink his blood as it dripped from her chin.

Jit spoke in the strange, clicking squealing language.

One of the glowing figures in a cowled cloak swept up to him, pointing a finger at his face. "She says that you, too, like the Mother Confessor, will soon be the walking dead."

Richard remembered what the soldier back at the palace had told him. He had said that in the Dark Lands the dead walked. Richard knew now that it was not superstition.

Richard wondered why the Hedge Maid's mouth was sewn closed.

84

It came to him.

Richard understood Regula's last message.

He just didn't know if it could do him any good.

Though the bottom half of his torso was trapped in the thorny vines, his arms were starting to get their strength back, and they were still free, so he stretched around toward Kahlan, reaching out to touch her face, hoping that somehow she would know that he was there with her. She was unconscious and didn't respond. He had to do something, and fast.

The creatures dancing and cavorting through the room, stepping among the shattered bones and limbs of their fellows, seemed to think it was funny to see his affection for Kahlan. They mocked him, mimicking his gestures, reveling in what they knew was to become of them both.

Jit turned to her work of adding pinches of this and that from jars to the smoldering fire in the shallow bowl in the center of the room. From time to time she picked up a slender stick decorated with glossy green feathers, snake skins, and shiny coins to draw spells in ash held in flat trays.

Ghostly forms curled out from the fire as she spoke key words in low, guttural, rasping, clicking sounds. Each wisp of smoke coalesced into a deformed figure looking like it had been freed from the darkest reaches of the underworld to float above them.

As Jit worked, and the frolicking creatures taunted him, Richard surreptitiously pulled off small pieces of his shredded shirt and rolled them between his finger and thumb.

When he had two of them that he judged to be about the right size, he leaned toward Kahlan to make a show of caressing her face again. Twisting around like that pulled at the thorns sticking in his legs. He had no choice but to endure it. He could hear the grotesque cackles behind him of those watching and waiting for Jit to finish her work.

With his left hand, so that it would cover her face and hide what he was doing, Richard slipped one of the rolled-up pieces of cloth into one of Kahlan's ears. With a finger he pushed it firmly into place. Without pause, he did the same with her other ear.

A claw seized his left wrist and pulled it back. Other hands wrapped a thorny vine around the arm and pinned it back against the wall. Yet other creatures pulled a strip of thorny vine across his middle. Richard's strength did no good against so many of these undead creatures.

Working as fast as he could with his free hand, he stuffed a rolled-up piece of cloth from his shredded shirt into each of his own ears.

He remembered what the machine had told him.

Your only chance is to let the truth escape.

He needed to do something the Hedge Maid wouldn't expect. When Jit turned back toward him, he grinned at her.

All the creatures drew back, murmuring to themselves at his puzzling behavior. The unexpected was frightening to them.

He again gave the Hedge Maid a very deliberate grin to let her know that he knew something she didn't.

He, in fact, knew the truth.

The Hedge Maid, her expression darkening dangerously, glared at him.

He needed to get her closer.

"You have me," he said as he smiled broadly. "Let Kahlan go and I'll cooperate with whatever you want."

One of the glowing forms, who was missing a hand, poked him with a finger. "We do not need your cooperation," she said.

"Yes you do," Richard said with absolute conviction while he smiled at the Hedge Maid. "You need to know the truth."

The cowled figure frowned. "The truth?" She turned and spoke to Jit in her strange language.

The Hedge Maid frowned at her companion as she listened, and then stepped up to him. He towered over her, but she did not fear him.

She should have.

Jit smiled back with as evil a grin as he'd ever seen, her lips parting with the grin as much as the leather sewn through her lips would allow.

Richard used his free hand to draw his knife from the sheath at his belt. It felt good to have a blade in his hand. A blade meant salvation. This one was as razor-sharp as truth itself.

The Hedge Maid didn't fear his knife, and with good reason. After all, his sword had proven impotent against her.

Richard knew that using a blade to try to cut Jit would be not merely futile, but a deadly mistake. Her aura of powers shielded her, protected her from being cut by him. She had proven that his sword could not harm her, so she certainly didn't fear a mere knife.

She should have.

In a blink, before the Hedge Maid could have second thoughts or guess what he intended, Richard whipped the knife past her face, carefully avoiding cutting her, or even the thought of it, so as not to trigger her occult protection. If he was sincerely not trying to cut her, her defenses would not react.

With deadly precision, he instead made the tip of the razor-sharp blade sweep in just between her parted lips . . . and sever the leather strips holding her mouth closed.

The Hedge Maid's dark eyes went wide.

Her mouth also went wide, something it had never done before.

Her jaws opened wide. It looked decidedly involuntary.

And then came a scream of such power, such malevolence, such evil, that it seemed to rip through the very fabric of the world of life.

It was a scream born in the world of the dead.

Jars and bottles exploded. Their contents flew everywhere. Bony creatures covered their heads protectively with their gangly arms.

Broken glass, pottery, sticks, and pieces of vine began to move around the room in fits and starts, as if driven by gusts of wind, but then, with ever-growing speed, all the debris lifted into the air and began to circle the room. Even the bony creatures found themselves dragged into the building vortex, their arms and legs flailing as they orbited helplessly around the room among clouds of broken glass and pottery and all the things they had contained.

The deadly power of the scream went on unabated, catching all the creatures up in it, along with the mass of rubble.

The forms in the cowled cloaks covered their ears as they screamed in terror and pain. It did them no good. As Jit's unleashed scream ripped through the room, they began to be drawn up in the growing tornado of sound and wreckage storming around the room.

Blood ran from the ears of those encased in the walls as they shook violently.

The bony creatures began to disintegrate, coming apart as if they had been cast of sand, dust, and dirt. Arms and legs fell apart, dissolving in the maelstrom, mixing in with the rest of the rubble circling the room. They shrieked and howled even as they were coming apart. Their terrified cries joined the cry of the endless scream coming from the Hedge Maid.

The glowing forms in the cowled capes began to elongate and rip apart in streams of glowing vapor as they were carried helplessly along in the power of the Hedge Maid's scream.

Lightning flashed and flickered as it, too, was carried around the outside of the room. The very air roared and thundered.

In the center of it all, the Hedge Maid stood, head thrown back, jaws wide, as she screamed her life away.

The poison of who she was, of what she was, her wickedness, her corruption, her evil, her dedication to death and her contempt for life in any form, was escaping in a ripping scream that was the dead end of what she worshiped.

The scream was death itself.

Now that the truth of the dead soul within her was released, it was taking the life of its host.

She was seeing the truth of her dead inner self. Life, her life, was incompatible with the death she carried inside.

Death showed her no appreciation, and no mercy.

Her face began to melt as her own evil, the death at her core, escaped its prison. Blood veins broke, muscle ripped apart, and her skin split open until her bones were exposed. It all added power and force to her death shriek.

That scream, its power, its poison, lanced into Richard as well. The pain of it was more than he could stand. Every joint cried out in agony. Every nerve fiber vibrated with the torture of the sound escaping the Hedge Maid.

He, too, was being touched by death that had been freed.

As he began to lose consciousness, Richard realized that the plugs he had made for his ears, and for Kahlan's ears, were not sufficient to stand up against the malevolence he had unleashed.

He had failed. He had failed Kahlan.

He felt a tear of grief for Kahlan, of his love for her, run down his face as the screaming, roaring, flashing world went slowly dark and silent.

I f he lives," Cara said, "I'm going to kill him."

Nicci smiled, but the thought of Richard dying sent a renewed spike of panic through her. It was too terrifying a thought to contemplate.

She laid a hand to his chest as somber soldiers gently laid his unconscious form beside Kahlan in the back of the wagon.

Blood seeped through the blankets Richard and Kahlan were both wrapped in. But Nicci could feel his heart beating, feel the breath of life in his lungs. Kahlan, thankfully, was alive as well. For now, the two of them were alive and that was what mattered most.

"He will live," Nicci said. "Both of them will, if I have anything to say about it."

By the looks of what had happened in the room where they had found them, it was perhaps surprising that they were both alive, much less in one piece. It had been frightening to have to pull them both out of the prison of thorn branches and vines they had been encased in.

"What's this?" Zedd asked with a frown.

Nicci came out of her thoughts and took the little object from him. It looked to be a rolled-up wad of cloth.

"I don't know. Where did you find it?"

"In his ear." Zedd sounded astonished. He waved a finger, pointing. "Look, there's another in his other ear." He pulled it out and held it up to show her.

Nicci bent over the side of the wagon and checked Kahlan. She had them, too. Nicci pulled a little plug out of each of Kahlan's ears and held them up to look at them.

She smiled, then, as she closed them in her fist.

"No wonder they're alive."

"What are you talking about?" Zedd asked.

"How much do you know about Hedge Maids?"

Zedd shrugged. "I may have heard of them when I was a boy, but I didn't hear much. I also heard Richard ask the abbot about them, but I don't really know anything about them. Why?"

Cara looked like she wanted to kill someone and she wasn't all that particular about who it was going to be. "I'd like to know that myself."

Nicci gestured back down the slope to the dense swamp where the structure had been that the boy, Henrik, had told them about. They might never have found it in time to save Richard and Kahlan had it not been for the boy. He had led them to where Richard and Kahlan were imprisoned.

Zedd had used wizard's fire to destroy the place, along with all its contents, including the unidentifiable, bloody remains of the Hedge Maid. There wasn't so much as a stick left.

"It is said that the sound made by a Hedge Maid, were she allowed to open her mouth all the way, is the sound of the Keeper himself and that it will pull the person making the sound and anyone who hears it into the underworld. The full scream of a Hedge Maid is death, even to herself, so at a young age Hedge Maids have their lips sewn shut by their mothers, before they can fully develop a voice."

"And the father just lets the mother sew their child's mouth shut?" Cara asked.

Nicci glanced up. "Hedge Maids, like some spiders, subdue and then suck the blood out of the male after they've mated."

"Lovely," Cara said under her breath.

"How do you know all this?" Zedd asked.

Nicci arched an eyebrow at the wizard. "I was once a Sister of the Dark, remember? Sisters of the Dark serve the Keeper of the underworld. We know a lot about the world of the dead and those who are devoted to it."

Zedd scratched his jaw and changed the subject. "So, you think that Richard and Kahlan are alive because they stuffed those wads of cloth in their ears?"

Nicci leaned in the low wagon and touched two fingers to Kahlan's head. "Here, see for yourself."

Zedd added his first two fingers to Kahlan's forehead.

"What do you feel?" Nicci asked as she watched his eyes.

Zedd was frowning. "I don't know. Some kind of . . . darkness." He suddenly looked up at her. "It's the same thing I felt the last time I tried to heal her."

Nicci nodded. She was pleased that the wizard recognized it. It would make what they had to do easier.

"That's the touch of death that a Hedge Maid carries."

Cara looked suddenly more than alarmed. "You mean to say that they have death in them—that they're going to die?"

"Not if I have anything to do with it," Nicci said. "They were touched not only by the Hedge Maid's occult conjuring, but more importantly by her scream, touched by death itself."

"But you can heal them," Cara said.

It was not a question, but Nicci treated it as such. "I'm

pretty sure that I can, now that the Hedge Maid is dead and has no connection to them." She took a deep breath. "Richard must have cut the leather strips sewing the Hedge Maid's mouth shut. Fortunately, he was smart enough to plug his and Kahlan's ears, first. It didn't stop the sound from getting in, death from getting in, but it blunted it."

"So they were touched by death from the Hedge Maid," Zedd said. "And that's what I'm feeling in her?"

Nicci finally nodded. "I'm afraid so."

"But you can heal them," Zedd said, sounding a lot like Cara had.

"I think so," she said. "I was a Sister of the Dark. This is the kind of thing I know about. But I can't do it here. I need to do it in a containment field."

"The Garden of Life," Cara said at once. "That's a containment field."

Nicci smiled at Cara and then signaled to Benjamin. The wagon started moving with a jolt. "That's why I want to get them back there as soon as possible. Zedd and I can keep them alive for a while, and heal their wounds, but we need to get them back to the Garden of Life to fully heal them, to get the touch of death out of them." She gestured up at Henrik, on the seat by the soldier driving the wagon. "He was touched by the Hedge Maid's powers and will need to be healed as well, but it's not as serious with him. He did not hear death's call."

The line of cavalry brought their horses in protectively around the wagon as it rolled through the gloom among the towering trees. The steel gray clouds were so low they stole through the treetops, as if escorting the intruders away from the Dark Lands.

Having thought it over, Cara still didn't look satisfied. "Why can't you heal them now," she wanted to know. "Why do you have to wait until you get back to the Garden of Life?"

"They have been touched by death. We need a containment field to shield them while we do what we need to do. We need to heal them, but to do so we must also remove that touch of death that is lodged within them. If we try to do that here, that touch of death will call the Keeper of the dead to them, and they will die. So, we must wait until we can do it in a containment field, in the Garden of Life."

"Oh," Cara said. "I guess that makes sense."

"The omen machine is in that containment field as well," Zedd reminded her.

"Do you have a better idea?" Nicci asked him.

"I guess not," Zedd grumbled unhappily.

"That machine saved their lives," Nicci said. "Remember the last thing it said to Richard? 'Your only chance is to let the truth escape.' The machine told Richard how to destroy a Hedge Maid. I didn't even know to do that. Richard figured it out."

Zedd's bushy brows drew down. "You really think so?"

Nicci smiled down at the two of them lying unconscious in the wagon. "Why do you think he plugged their ears?"

A slow smile overcame the old man. "The boy got it right." His frown returned in a rush. "Why do you suppose the machine told him that—saved his life?"

"Isn't it obvious?" Nicci asked.

"Obvious?"

As they walked along on each side of the wagon, Nicci gave the wizard a sidelong glance. "The machine needs him."

"Needs him," Zedd repeated unhappily.

"To fulfill its purpose," Nicci said.

"I remember," he grumbled again. "Whatever its purpose is," he added under his breath.

Nicci laid a hand on Richard's chest as she walked along beside the wagon, releasing a comforting trickle of sustaining Additive Magic into him, letting him know that he was not alone with the whisper of death inside him. On the other side of the wagon, Zedd did the same for Kahlan.

Nicci felt Richard take a deeper breath. He knew she was there. Even if he couldn't answer, somewhere deep down inside, he knew.

Nicci dared to allow herself to let go of her panic. They were both finally safe. It had been a frightening journey. Knowing where Richard had been headed, Nicci hadn't expected to ever see him alive again. At least for now, they were in good hands, and they would recover once they were back at the palace and she and Zedd and Nathan could heal them properly.

Nicci was so relieved that she had no words to fully express it. She was also angry at Richard for going after a Hedge Maid. She had warned him. She had told him how dangerous they were. She had told him to stay away from Hedge Maids. But he had gone anyway.

Nicci supposed that he had no choice. He had to go after Kahlan. Who else but Richard would walk into a Hedge Maid's lair to save the woman he loved.

Who else but Richard.

"They look cute lying there together," Cara said as she gazed down at them over the edge of the wagon.

The Mord-Sith's face suddenly went red. "You won't tell them I said that." Again, it was not a question.

Nicci smiled; for the first time in many days, she really smiled.

"Not a word of it," she said.

"Good," Cara muttered. She looked up toward the head of the line of soldiers. "General, would you get this column moving a bit faster. We have to get them back to the palace!"

Benjamin looked back over his shoulder with a smile and gave his wife a salute of a fist to his heart; then he urged his horse to pick up the pace.

END